SOME

PARTICULAR

EVIL

VERA MORRIS

First published in Great Britain in 2016 by Accent Press

This edition published in 2021 by Headline Accent
An imprint of HEADLINE PUBLISHING GROUP

3

Cataloguing in Publication Data is available from the British Library

ISBN 978 1 7861 5061 5

Printed and bound in Great Britain by Clays Ltd, Elcograf S.p.A.

HEADLINE PUBLISHING GROUP
An Hachette UK Company
Carmelite House
50 Victoria Embankment
London
EC4Y 0DZ

www.headline.co.uk
www.hachette.co.uk

There is, I believe, in every disposition, a tendency to some particular evil, a natural defect, which not even the best education can overcome.

Jane Austen

Chapter 1

Saturday, March 1, 1969

The mortuary was as cold as a butcher's fridge and smelt of Dettol and fear. Laurel Bowman stood rigid between two policemen she'd never met before.

'Are you ready, Miss Bowman?' the detective inspector asked.

The sheet undulated over the body, showing curves of breasts, a slight swelling of the belly and the lines of legs. The police were mistaken. Laurel stared at it and inhaled deeply. 'Yes, I'm ready.'

The attendant's gloved hand gripped the edge of the material. He slowly peeled it back.

'Is this your sister, Angela Bowman?'

The face was a wax imitation, a macabre joke. The harsh strip-light played on hair that was too dark, combed back from the forehead. Angela's red hair curled round her face. These features were hard, not soft and beautiful, and the skin had a greenish glow, freckles standing out across the nose and cheeks like the first signs of decay.

Pain and loss gripped her heart and ripped into her guts. She swayed and the detective sergeant moved closer, holding her arm as though afraid she'd collapse.

'Is this your sister, Angela Bowman?' the inspector asked again.

Laurel nodded, gulping back the bile rising in her throat.

The sergeant tightened his grip as she struggled to breathe. Then, as she straightened her body and raised her head, he relaxed his hold.

1

'You must s*ay* if it is her, or not.' The inspector's voice was as cold and unfeeling as the white-tiled room.

'Yes, it's Angela.'

She turned and looked at the inspector. He wore a loose, black gabardine raincoat, too large for his frame, sweeping past his knees. Iron-grey hair was painted over his scalp and the hooded eyes showed no warmth or sympathy.

She glanced at the sergeant who'd supported her. His thickly lashed green eyes, level with hers, stared back, unblinking.

'Are you in charge of this... case?' she asked the inspector.

'I am. Sergeant Diamond is also on the team.' He gave a cursory nod towards him.

She looked at her dead sister. She'd lost her. She'd never again see her smile, never hear her laughter, and never share their memories. Her breathing deepened, her hands curling into fists. 'How did she die? Who did this?'

The inspector pushed his chin forward. 'The post-mortem will establish the cause of death and no doubt our investigation-'

The man sounded like an actor from a third-rate TV crime series. Before they could stop her she stepped forward and pulled the sheet from Angela's body. Up close she could see eyeballs pushed against the lids, lips twisted as though she was trying to tell her what had happened. Purple bruises sullied the cream flesh of her long neck and small breasts. She reached out and pressed her fingers against Angela's cheek – it was cold. Cold and clammy like Plasticine. Laurel's body shook, her nostrils widened and she raised her fists. Who'd done this to her?

The sergeant pulled her back and the mortuary attendant, his eyes inflated like a frog's, scrambled to pull the sheet from her hands and cover her sister's body.

'This is not helpful, Miss Bowman. Please try to control yourself.' The inspector spoke as though she were a naughty schoolgirl who'd had a temper tantrum. Laurel felt like socking him on the jaw.

Sergeant Diamond grasped her shoulders and moved her away from the table. 'We'll get him. Whoever murdered your sister we'll find him and bring him to justice.' His low voice was angry. With the killer or the inspector? She couldn't tell.

Justice – there could never be enough justice. Even if he died a thousand times, or rotted for a thousand years in gaol, it would never be enough.

She turned again to the inspector. 'Who found her?'

Lines of irritation creased his forehead. 'I can't reveal details at this point in the investigation, Miss Bowman. I think it would be better for you to return home to be with your parents. Sergeant Diamond, will you drive Miss Bowman?'

'My pleasure, s… i… r.'

She looked from one man to the other, recognising undeniable insolence: she'd seen and heard it often enough in her job.

The inspector's face flushed maroon. 'I shall be at your house in about an hour, Miss Bowman. I need to ask you and your parents some questions about your sister's life.'

They would be waiting for her. She would see hope die in their eyes as she broke the news. They would be devastated. 'Now? Today? I don't think my parents will be capable of talking about Angela just yet.'

Sergeant Diamond touched her arm. 'I know it'll be hard, but the sooner we know more about Angela's life the sooner we'll be able to find her killer.'

'Sergeant Diamond, you are *not* to question the family. That's an order. I will do that when I arrive. Do you understand?'

Diamond's nostrils flared. 'I understand completely.'

No love lost between these two. Whatever was between them they'd better put a lid on it if they were going to find Angela's murderer.

Sergeant Diamond was silent as they drove through the suburbs of Ipswich.

'I presume this is your car?'

He nodded.

'What is it? A Chevrolet?'

He raised an eyebrow. 'Correct. '62 Chevy Corvair. Bit of a rust bucket, but I'm getting a new one soon.'

'Another American?'

'I expect so.'

The car suited him: his slim body, long hair and leather jacket said rock star rather than policeman. No wonder he and the inspector hadn't jelled. 'Will you help me when I get home? I don't know how I'm going to tell them.'

He glanced at her. 'Of course I will. Would you like me to break it to them?'

She hesitated. Knowing he'd be there if she couldn't frame the words was a comfort. 'I need to say it. But if I need help…'

He nodded, changing down a gear before a sharp bend. 'Angela didn't look like you. I wouldn't have guessed you were sisters.'

Beautiful Angela: small, delicate, with Titian hair; whereas she was a blonde, five foot eleven, with Amazonian shoulders. It wasn't only their physical differences, they had different personalities: she'd known what she wanted to do from the moment she'd won her first race at primary school, whereas Angela had drifted from job to job, and boyfriend to boyfriend, unsure of herself.

'No, you wouldn't know we're sisters… were sisters.'

4

'How did you get on?' He looked relaxed, at home behind the steering wheel.

'I thought the inspector told you not to question us?'

The eyebrow rose again. 'We're having a friendly chat, that's all.'

'She was my little sister. I loved her. I love her.' She screwed her eyes tight, trying to stop the tears. She fumbled in her pocket for a handkerchief and blew her nose.

'That's what I like, a good trumpeting into a sheet, none of this delicately wiping the nose with a lace handkerchief.'

Laurel said nothing. He was doing his best to lighten this appalling situation.

'A fisherman found her early this morning. His boat is beached just north of Felixstowe pier. He always walks under it first thing to see if anything's been thrown up by the tide. That's where he found her. By the way, try to look surprised if the inspector tells you.'

'Thank you.' At least there was one policeman she could relate to. 'Was she in the sea?'

'No, she was above high water mark.'

She wanted to know more. Was she naked? Had she been raped? But she couldn't get the words out. Thoughts of Angela suffering, terrified and fighting for her life were too awful. Over the past few months she hadn't paid her enough attention, hadn't talked with her the way they used to – and now it was too late. She twisted her engagement ring round her finger until it hurt. She'd been so tied up in her own life – would that guilt ever leave her?

'Do you mind if I open the window?' she asked, conscious of her faltering voice.

'No, fresh air will be good for both of us – plenty of fresh air today.'

He was right. A cold wind rattled through the half-opened window, making her eyes water and lifting the sergeant's dark curls so they waved Medusa-like about his head. It was a strong east wind bringing a tang of salt from the North Sea, blowing rain clouds west to shed their load on higher parts. No sign of spring in the hedgerows: the buds tight on the oaks and hawthorn. They looked as lifeless as the dead elms. They'd never leaf again.

Angela was dead. It was finally sinking in. She'd thought the police had made a terrible mistake, but that hope had shrivelled and died.

Although it was only a few hours since the police, a man and woman, had come to the family home, it seemed like a lifetime ago.

It was seven in the morning, her mum was making tea. Angela wasn't up. 'Take Angie a cup, dear,' Mum said to Laurel. Then there were loud knocks on the front door.

They told them a woman's body had been found and the contents of a nearby handbag suggested it might be her sister. She refused to believe it could be Angela. She'd rushed upstairs to her sister's bedroom. The eiderdown was smooth, her pillow plump. Where was she?

She slowly walked down the stairs. Mum saw her face and collapsed into an armchair. Dad rushed to Mum's side. He turned and looked at Laurel. She shook her head. His face crumpled. The WPC went to the kitchen and came back with a glass of water and held it to Mum's lips.

'Someone must come to Ipswich to see if the body we found is your sister,' the PC said.

'I'll go,' Laurel said.

She turned back from the car's side window and faced the road. How was she going to break the news to them?

'What do you do for a living?' he asked as they turned onto the A45.

'I teach. I'm head of a PE department in a girls' grammar school.'

'I bet they don't mess with you.' Laughter lines crinkled the corners of his eyes.

'The pupils or the staff?'

'Both; and throw in the governors and parents for good measure.'

She couldn't help smiling, though it seemed wrong, and she blessed him for trying to take her mind off Angela. 'Am I that frightening?'

'Terrifying.'

As they came off the A45 into Felixstowe she started to give him instructions. On High Road West they passed the Conservative club and the primary school. She swallowed hard, her guts twisting into knots. From High Road East they turned into Rosemary Avenue. She wanted to grip his arm and make him turn the car round. He turned the corner into Colneis Road and pulled up in front of her house. There was someone standing behind the net curtains of the window. A shadow moved towards the front door.

He turned off the ignition and faced her. 'Ready? You can do it. I'll be there.'

She knew she'd have to be as hard as granite to get through the next few hours, days, weeks, and possibly months. She'd have to be a rock for her parents. It was hell to lose a sister, but to lose a child? She couldn't imagine it. They must stand together and do everything they could to help the police find out who'd done this. That's all she cared about. Whoever he was he must pay. She wanted to see him in the dock, convicted and sent down for life.

Chapter 2

Monday, September 7, 1970

Laurel braked when she saw the sign.

Blackfriars School
Dunwich
Suffolk
Headmaster Mr P M Nicholson BA (Hons) MEd

She turned the Ford Cortina GT into a gravelled drive which looped in front of a Georgian mansion. There were two cars in the car park: a Morris Traveller with moss growing round the wooden frames of the rear windows, and an electric-blue American car – a Ford Mustang? Surely that wasn't the headmaster's car?

She'd arrived – her new home, a new career. She peeled off her driving gloves and tossed them onto the passenger seat. Had she done the right thing? As soon as she'd accepted the post of senior mistress she'd started to have doubts. Was this the kind of school she wanted to teach in? A small, private school miles from anywhere? But she'd been desperate to get away from Felixstowe – the last eighteen months had been sheer hell.

She loved her parents but their grief was killing her She often found Mum crying in Angela's bedroom, had to prise crumpled sheets from her hands, and rock her in her arms until her sobs quietened. It was making her ill listening to her parents' stilted conversation, or even worse face their silences and blank eyes as they asked themselves the perpetual questions to which they had no answers. Why did it have to happen to Angela? How much did she suffer? Who killed her? She could give them the answer to one of these questions. But she didn't dare.

She'd had to get away from the stalled investigation and especially Sergeant Diamond. When his eyes locked with hers she was sure he knew what had happened, what she'd done. In August she went on holiday, staying with a friend in Edinburgh, taking in the British Commonwealth Games. When she got back Mum told her he'd been promoted and moved to another case. She was relieved, although in some ways she would miss him. He'd never stopped trying to find Angela's murderer. If she'd known he would move away perhaps she wouldn't have taken the job, but it was too late; she'd committed herself to Blackfriars.

She was glad to be away, but was she glad to be here?

Laurel opened her door. She couldn't see anyone. She smiled, imagining boys and girls milling round, boisterous, shouting, laughing – this place would change next week when the pupils came back. Schools without people were false, empty shells; without the sights and sounds of children they were nothing. She'd have several new challenges: teaching boys, living day and night in a school and being part of the senior management. She was sure all that would help her to regain her life.

The mizzle of rain, which started as she left Felixstowe, had stopped, leaving a sea-fret swirling round the house. Glimpses of the ruined walls of Blackfriars Priory and the Leper Hospital, nearer to the cliffs than the school, came in and out of focus.

She swung her legs from the car and paused. Distant waves were thudding against the shingle beach. How long before the ruins tumbled from the cliff's edge to join the gravestones and other shattered remains of medieval

Dunwich on the sea's bed? Autumn and winter storms would rip at the sandy cliffs, eating into the land and spewing earth, trees and masonry onto the beach forty feet below, mixing with flotsam and jetsam thrown up by the sea.

She smoothed the skirt of her suit and patted the back of her head to make sure the French pleat was still intact. She hoped she looked like a senior mistress – she didn't feel like one. Squaring her shoulders, she marched to the main entrance and pushed open the door.

It was a spacious hall, with mahogany-panelled walls and floorboards. Opposite the front door a wide, shallow staircase led to a balconied corridor; at the top of the stairs was a door signed Headmaster. Left of the stairs was a cosy group of coffee table and three easy chairs; behind them cabinets displayed silver trophies. She'd been pleased at her interview to find the school still believed in sports days and competition.

To the right of the stairs was an office. Through the glass window Miss Piff, the school secretary, was bent over a typewriter, fingers a blur. Laurel knocked on the window. Miss Piff's head shot up, grey curls bobbing, her eyes widening behind blue-framed glasses. She stood up and opened the office door.

'Miss Bowman. Good journey, I hope?' With ram-rod back she held out her hand, smiling, apple-red cheeks high in her round face. Her warm voice matched her firm handshake.

'The A12 was busy, but I made good time.'

'I do hope you'll be happy at Blackfriars. We were all impressed when you came for the interview. I'm so glad you accepted the post, I was afraid you'd find us too quiet after teaching in a large school. Come into the office.' She glanced at her wrist watch. 'It's nearly sixteen hundred hours: tea time. Would you like a cup?' She waved Laurel in.

Laurel smiled as she looked down on Miss Piff, all five

foot two of her, dressed in a tweed skirt and beige twin set. 'That would be lovely.'

Miss Piff pointed to a chair in front of her desk and busied herself with teapot and kettle. 'Make yourself comfortable, Miss Bowman.'

'Please call me Laurel.' The office was well organised: telephone books, pencils, reams of paper arranged in regimented rows.

Miss Piff smiled. 'Are you sure? Perhaps when we're by ourselves; doesn't do to let standards drop. My name's Dorothy, by the way.' The red flush of her cheeks spread to the rest of her face.

'Thank you, Dorothy. I've always found school secretaries to be helpful, and the fount of all wisdom and knowledge.' She'd learnt it paid to have the school secretary on your side.

'I'd offer you a cigarette but I make it a point not to smoke in school, even in the holidays.'

'Thank you, but I don't smoke.'

Miss Piff nodded as though she approved. 'Of course, you're quite an athlete I hear – wouldn't suit your lifestyle. I wish I could stop, but I started during the war and I haven't been able to quit.' She didn't look too sad about it. Miss Piff continued to beam. 'I do like your suit, Miss... er, Laurel. It brings out the blue of your eyes.' She paused. 'Some of the staff wondered why you hadn't been snatched up by some handsome man. I better warn you some of the male members are fancying their chances – well, at least one. I told him you probably already have a fiancé.' She waited expectantly, her eyes shining behind her spectacles.

Laurel fingered the indentation where her engagement ring used to be and inwardly sighed. 'I'm afraid my height and build puts most men off. I'm more interested in my career than being a housewife. I'm thirty, so I think I'll be

11

staying on the shelf.' Her fiancé Simon couldn't take the gossip about Angela's morals; his family were horrified at the scandal of her murder.

Miss Piff nodded her head. 'Very wise. I never married, although… I live with my sister, Emily, in Dunwich village. A good relationship with a sister or brother can be a rich experience. You must come to tea and meet her.'

'That would be lovely, Dorothy.'

'Do *you* have any brothers or sisters?'

Laurel was prepared for this question. 'No. I'm an only child.'

Miss Piff moued disappointment. 'What a shame.' She passed her a cup of tea. 'The headmaster has asked to see you as soon as you arrive but he's busy at the moment: the inspector's with him.'

A school inspector? Did private schools have inspections? 'Is there going to be an inspection soon? There wasn't any mention of it at the interview.' Laurel drank the tea.

Miss Piff laughed. 'No, no. It's the *detective* inspector who's with him. He's taken over the case.'

She wanted to spit the tea out. Nearly choking, she swallowed and licked her lips; the cup rattled on the saucer as she put it down. 'I don't understand. The case? What are you talking about?'

Miss Piff's mouth formed an O and raised eyebrows pleated her forehead. 'The governors did tell you about Mr Nicholson's wife?'

The muscles tightened in her abdomen. 'We were told before we had our interviews Mrs Nicholson had suddenly died, Mr Nicholson was on compassionate leave, and we could withdraw from the interviews if it was impossible to accept the post without first meeting the headmaster. One candidate did withdraw.'

Miss Piff nodded. 'I remember; I didn't like the cut of her

12

jib. She wore high leather boots and I imagined her with a whip in her hand. I was glad when she went.'

Laurel bit her lip, wanting to smile. But why were the police involved? 'I presumed Mrs Nicholson had an accident or a sudden illness.'

Miss Piff leant forward over her desk, the lines on her forehead deepening. 'Miss Bowman, the governors should have told you. Mrs Nicholson was murdered – raped...' her voice lowered, '... and strangled. They haven't found her killer. Surely you read about it in the papers? It was on the television.'

Laurel twisted her fingers together until the bones hurt. Not again. 'I only read the sport pages, as for television...' Since Angela's murder she'd avoided news bulletins; she didn't want to see details of lurid murder cases.

'Very wise – nothing but doom and gloom in the newspapers at the moment. Those poor passengers hijacked by Palestinian guerrillas! Four aircraft at once. What is the world coming to?' She paused. 'Miss Bowman... Laurel, are you all right?'

Laurel dug her nails into the flesh of her palms. What was she talking about? Thoughts were shooting round her brain like vapour trails in an aerial dogfight. This couldn't be happening – another murder. 'I'll be fine in a moment.' She hesitated; there was genuine concern in Miss Piff's eyes. Should she tell her about Angela? No. She wouldn't tell *anyone*. 'I'm all right now. I'd be grateful if you didn't mention my reaction to anybody.'

Miss Piff nodded, glasses slipping down her nose. 'Of course not, especially the headmaster, least of all him. A school secretary learns to be discreet.'

'Thank you.'

'Shall I ring Mr Nicholson and let him know you're here, or do you want to wait a while?' she asked, tilting her head.

Laurel smoothed her hands over her skirt, trying to gain control. 'No, please ring him. Poor man. How is he coping?'

Miss Piff looked at her, seemed satisfied and picked up the phone. 'He's doing his best. Susan, Mrs Nicholson, was a... very attractive woman... to look at. She had lovely Titian hair, but she was a small person, not like you, Laurel. She didn't stand a chance.'

Chapter 3

Detective Inspector Frank Diamond – Francis to his Irish mother and Francis Xavier if he was in trouble with her – folded one leg over the other and slouched back in the armchair Philip Nicholson had indicated he should sit in.

The headmaster had a height advantage, being about six foot three to his five eleven, and seated in an upright chair behind his desk, looked down on him. Frank wasn't worried by the power play, if that's what it was.

'Inspector Diamond, is this interview needed? You have my statements on record; there isn't anything new I can tell you.' He paused, rubbing his forehead. 'This is reopening wounds that have hardly healed,' he said in a rich baritone.

Frank imagined him on the assembly platform, mesmerising the pupils with his presence and sonorous voice.

He had to admit Mr Nicholson was a good-looking, if boringly dressed, man. He reminded Frank of one of the film stars his mother was keen on, one of a long list. What was his name? Tall, dark-haired guy with chiselled features and quizzical eyebrows: Gregory Peck? The case notes he'd studied gave Nicholson's age as forty-three. He was educated at a minor public school, followed by Durham University where he'd read history, then rapid promotion teaching in boys' public schools. He'd been appointed headmaster of Blackfriars five years ago.

'Mr Nicholson, as you know, the previous inspector is ill and I've taken over the case with Detective Sergeant Elderkin, whom I believe you've met.' He nodded his head towards a large, middle-aged man wearing a navy suit, white shirt and red tie – another snappy dresser. He was seated at the rectangular conference table on the right of the office. He looked uncomfortable, his bulk squeezed into a green leather armchair, his notebook and pencil ready. 'I've studied the case notes, but I need to talk to everyone who gave statements.'

Philip Nicholson sighed. 'Yes, of course. I understand. I'd want to do the same. Have you talked with the previous inspector... Inspector Bushell?'

Frank nodded, running his hand over his chin and deciding the electric razor his mother had given him as a promotion present, wasn't up to the job. 'I have.'

'What was his opinion? It must have been a stranger – a maniac. Let's hope you catch him soon. It's six months since...'

'The inspector's opinion matches yours.' Frank glanced round the office, taking in the uncluttered desk, the children's art work on the wall behind Elderkin, and a safe to the left of Nicholson. Sea air came in through a half-opened mullioned window, but the room smelt stale.

'I'd like to go through your movements from Tuesday 7th to Thursday 9th of April.' Nicholson stared at him.

Unusual eyes, bright blue, the irises circled in black. His alibi looked solid, but he needed to check. He could tell from Nicholson's shocked expression when they'd first met he wasn't impressed by *his* appearance. He knew his former colleagues at Ipswich called him *Danger Man* or *Donovan* behind his back, commenting on either his way of working, or his appearance, or both.

Nicholson sighed, and rubbed the back of his neck. 'On Tuesday I went to Colchester for a few days to stay with my mother –'

'Why didn't your wife go with you?'

'She wanted some time to herself. We had a busy term ahead of us; she decided she'd get the house up to scratch.'

Frank wondered how he would react to the multiple-questions and no-need-to-answer technique. 'Susan, is it OK if I call her Susan?' Nicholson nodded. 'Was Susan keen on housework? Wouldn't she have liked to have the chance of doing some shopping in Colchester? You're isolated here. How did she get on with your mother? Did your mother like Susan?'

Nicholson licked his lips and remained silent.

'Don't bother answering; we'll talk about Susan in depth some other time. I need to know what made Susan tick.' He glanced at Elderkin, who was glowering and making crossing-outs on his pad. 'What mood was Susan in when you left?'

Nicholson folded his arms across his chest. 'Mood? She was perfectly happy, said she'd do some walking. She was looking forward to a few peaceful days before the summer term started.'

'What time did you leave on Tuesday?'

'About ten, I was in time for lunch with Mother.'

'That was the last time you saw Susan?'

Nicholson unfolded his arms, his hands clenching on the edge of his desk. 'I last saw her in the mortuary.' He covered his face with his hands, his shoulders heaving.

He'd expect this kind of reaction shortly after a death – not six months later. 'Did you phone her when you were in Colchester?'

He raised his head, his face crumpled with pain. 'She phoned me on Tuesday evening.'

'What time? Where's the telephone in your mother's house?'

He looked puzzled. 'In the hall. She rang just before dinner: a quarter to seven.'

'Did your mother talk to her?'

'No. She was busy in the kitchen.'

A raucous gull wheeled past the window. Nicholson flinched. He was definitely on edge. 'Did she phone on Wednesday?'

'No, she didn't. I meant to ring her but I took Mother out for dinner and we got in about ten. I was afraid I'd wake Susan up if I rang then.'

'How was Susan when you talked to her on Tuesday? What'd she been doing that day?'

Nicholson rubbed his forehead. 'Inspector Bushell didn't ask me that. I'll have to think… nothing much.'

'Take your time, Mr Nicholson, it could be important. Had she talked to anyone that day? Had she been out?'

Nicholson took out a gold-plated cigarette case from inside his sport's jacket. He flicked it open and offered it to Frank.

'No, thank you.'

Nicholson glanced at Elderkin. 'Cigarette, Sergeant?'

Elderkin looked tempted. 'No thank you, sir. I'm a pipe man.'

That figures, thought Frank.

Nicholson tapped a cigarette on the desk blotter, used a lighter, and inhaled deeply. He blew a stream of smoke towards Frank. 'No. She didn't mention seeing anyone. She'd been sorting through her clothes, getting ready for the warmer weather. We had a chat, I asked her how she was, told her we were going out to dinner the next evening, nothing important.'

'How long had you been married, Mr Nicholson?'

His hand covered his face again. 'Nearly two years,' he muttered.

There were squeaky noises as Elderkin's considerable bottom wriggled on the leather seat of his chair. He glanced at him. Elderkin was shaking his head and frowning, as much as to say, 'Give the man a chance.' Elderkin needed training.

Could he teach an old dog new tricks? A picture of a bloodhound holding a notebook and pencil flashed across his mind. He smiled at Elderkin, who looked puzzled.

The phone rang; Nicholson picked it up, listened, and looked relieved, as though the cavalry were on the horizon and he was about to be rescued. 'I'll ring back in a minute, Miss Piff.' He put the phone down. 'My new senior mistress has arrived. I'm afraid we'll have to finish. Is there anything else, Inspector?'

Frank got up, glad to be out of the uncomfortable chair. A senior mistress? He pictured a dragon-like creature with an imposing bosom and lisle stockings. Did the headmaster have any junior mistresses? 'We'll finish this tomorrow. During the next few days I'll be interviewing all the staff who were in the school at the time of your wife's murder. I should be finished before term starts, but it'll be necessary to talk to them again as new facts emerge.'

'Yes, of course. Most of them will be arriving soon. Would you like me to arrange a schedule for you?' He smiled, but his lips didn't part.

Frank shook his head; that wasn't how he worked. 'No, thanks, but I'll need a room as a base until the case is solved. If you could arrange that by tomorrow we'd be grateful. Sergeant Elderkin needs somewhere to park his typewriter. It must be lockable and I need all the keys to the room.' He straightened his leather jacket. 'I want you to think about the telephone conversation you had with Susan, see if you can remember anything else. It might be important.'

Nicholson didn't reply. He picked up the phone and dialled. 'Miss Piff, please bring her up now, thank you.' He held out his hand, palm down. 'I hope you can solve Susan's…'

More power play. Frank deliberately went into a submissive wet-fish handshake.

There was a rap on the door. Frank turned, curious to see the new senior mistress; at least she wouldn't be a suspect.

Holy Cow. Laurel Bowman was standing in front of him: the blonde Amazon in a smart, blue suit, her eyes wide with astonishment and dismay, and her perfect mouth falling open. The last time he'd seen her was on the school playing fields wearing a fetching short skirt; she'd been teaching a group of sixth formers athletics and looked ready to skewer him with the javelin she was toting above her shoulder. What in God's name was she doing here?

Chapter 4

As Miss Piff ushered her up the stairs to Mr Nicholson's office Laurel's stomach churned at the thought of meeting not only her new boss, but a police inspector. Anything to do with the police made her nervous. Miss Piff knocked, opened the door and Laurel walked in.

She was conscious of three men in the room, but only one came into focus: Frank Diamond, the detective sergeant involved with her sister's case. It was like a blow to her solar plexus. She couldn't speak. Had he followed her here? Had he discovered something? What had he told Mr Nicholson? But he looked as shocked as she felt.

A tall, handsome man walked from behind a desk. Laurel tried to smooth her face into a smile as he held out his hand.

'Miss Bowman, welcome to Blackfriars School. I was about to introduce you to Detective Inspector Diamond, but you seem to know each other?' He looked at her questioningly.

Had Diamond told the headmaster about her sister? She shook hands first with Mr Nicholson and then Frank Diamond. 'Pleased to see you again, Inspector Diamond. Congratulations on your promotion.'

Diamond introduced her to Sergeant Elderkin: a tall, solid man, with a ruddy complexion and bulbous nose. As they shook hands she noticed how small his were – they didn't go with the rest of him.

She turned back to Philip Nicholson. 'The inspector was merely a detective sergeant when we last met.'

'I hope it wasn't to arrest you, Miss Bowman.' Nicholson smiled, eyebrows raised. He turned to Diamond as if waiting for an answer.

Gosh, he's good looking, a bit like Gregory Peck in his heyday. What on earth was she going to say? She glanced at Diamond, who was looking bemused and lost for words, not his usual expression or loquacity. She shook her head slightly and hoped he'd take the hint, and not reveal their true connection.

Frank Diamond stared at her. 'I met Miss Bowman at her school in Ipswich when I had to interview some pupils. You were teaching some sixth formers how to throw a javelin, if my memory is correct.'

Laurel nodded. Thank you, Frank Diamond; she hadn't expected him to cooperate. He may have been promoted but he still didn't look like a policeman. What a contrast between the two men; Philip Nicholson: well-built, traditionally handsome, dressed in an old sport's jacket, cavalry twills and well-polished shoes. Diamond still looked like a rock star with his long, brown, curly hair and piercing green eyes; his slim body dressed in a black leather jacket, black trousers and a white polo sweater. As for those lashes, they were so long you'd swear they were false. Laurel pigeon-holed people into sport boxes – Frank Diamond: long distance runner; Philip Nicholson: rugby player.

'Sergeant Elderkin and I will push off now. We'll be back tomorrow morning to take over the office and interview any of the staff who are on site. Then Elderkin will take me for a walk round the grounds and along the shore as far as the sluice.'

Nicholson winced, his smile fading.

Poor man, having to go through all this again. Surely Diamond didn't have to stir everything up for a second time? She shuddered. She knew what he was like on a case: a lurking crocodile, waiting for an unsuspecting animal to drink on the bank of a river; once his teeth sank into the suspect he wouldn't let go, but would drag facts from them, twisting their minds as the reptile would twist its prey under water until it drowned. Laurel held back her sigh of relief as they left the office.

'You looked shocked when you saw Inspector Diamond, Miss Bowman – unpleasantly shocked if I may say so.' Mr Nicholson indicated a chair in front of his desk.

Laurel sank into it. It was warm. Warm from Frank Diamond's bottom? She bit her lip, and then smiled up at Mr Nicholson. She decided not to say anything.

He drew up his chair to the desk. 'A rather unusual policeman, don't you think? I hope he's good at his job' He frowned and pushed back a lock of hair that had fallen over his forehead.

Laurel remembered how she'd felt when the police investigation of Angela's murder seemed to stall, how frustrated she was when the inspector didn't seem to put enough effort into the search for the murderer. Only Frank Diamond kept beavering away, regularly visiting her parents to keep them in the picture.

'I'm very sorry about your wife, Mr Nicholson. I didn't know how she died – Miss Piff's just told me.'

Mr Nicholson's hand raked through his hair. 'Didn't the governors tell you? I'm dreadfully sorry, Miss Bowman, it must have been a shock.' His face creased with concern. 'How do you feel about the post now you realise the situation? You obviously know the murderer hasn't been caught. Are you happy to continue? I'd understand if you felt you wanted to leave.' He hesitated, then smiled. 'However, I do hope you'll stay.'

He was a charming man. What a lovely voice he had – delightful to listen to. 'It was a shock, but I've got over it and I'm looking forward to the new term and to meeting the rest of the staff and the pupils.'

Mr Nicholson smiled again, flashing even, white teeth.

'Thank goodness for that, and I do apologise once more for the governors' oversight.' He rose from his chair behind the desk. 'I'm sure you must want to unpack and relax after all this turmoil. I'll take you to your quarters. Is your luggage in your car?'

Laurel nodded and they made their way to the car park. The Ford Mustang wasn't there – it must be Frank Diamond's. How did he shoe-horn Elderkin into it? Not only had he been promoted but he'd bought himself a better car; from clapped-out Chevy to a Steve McQueen auto. Flash Frank and his flash American cars.

Nicholson stopped beside her car. 'Miss Bowman, I know you were offered one of the cottages on the far side of the school grounds, but would you prefer one of the flats in the main house? I can easily arrange it. You might feel safer there.'

What a considerate man. He looked worried, as though he'd be happier if she was safely tucked away in the Georgian mansion. 'Mr Nicholson, do I look as though I can't take care of myself? If so, you'll be the first man I've met to think that.' The corners of his mouth turned up in a rueful smile. Was she fooling herself, or did he fancy her?

'Miss Bowman, how you manage to look both feminine and yet capable of putting most men in an arm lock is a miracle. I take it you'd like to see the cottage?'

Was he flirting with her? If he was, she was enjoying it. But this wasn't right; he'd lost his wife recently, and in the most horrific way. She must be imagining it. 'Please. Can we walk there? I could do with some fresh air. I'll drive the car over later.'

It was brighter than when she'd arrived: now there were scudding clouds, blown by a south-westerly wind, sunshine warming the air as they walked up a narrow tarmac road running north, parallel to the public road which was hidden by a high conifer hedge. Mr Nicholson pointed out the different buildings: on the left the deputy headmaster, Mr Shipster's modern brick house, then two residential blocks, first the boys and then the girls, each capable of housing seventy-five children. To the right the school playing fields stretched out to a line of trees protecting the site from the easterly winds off the North Sea.

The road, now a pebbled track, wide enough for one car, veered right, heading towards the cliffs. Three brick and flint cottages, with tall chimneys and carved wooden gable-ends sat snugly behind the gravel road, sheltered from the north by a thick hawthorn hedge and from the east by a belt of Holm oaks. Each cottage had its own front and back gardens; the front gardens of the two end cottages were laid to grass. Laurel stopped in front of the middle cottage. On either side of a brick path, behind a white-painted gate and picket fence, were flower beds, riots of primitive colours: yellow and mauve daisies, blue spikes of belladonna and blood-red roses.

'Who lives in this cottage, Mr Nicholson? The school gardener?'

Mr Nicholson placed a hand on the gate. 'No. The appropriately named Mrs Mabel Grill, our school cook, and her Jack Russell, Muffin, live here.' He laughed at her expression. 'I'm not making it up. Mabel's been here since the year dot, well before I arrived. I hope you like plain, old-fashioned English cooking, because that's Mabel's speciality; her tour de force being syrup pudding, which is always as light as a feather.'

Laurel realised she was hungry. The only food she'd eaten recently was one of Miss Piff's digestive biscuits. She hadn't brought any food with her, she'd assumed there would be something laid on for tonight, but the school was deserted apart from Miss Piff, who would be back in Dunwich by now, no doubt eating something her sister had cooked.

Mr Nicholson walked up the path of the third cottage, the one nearest the sea. He paused under a tiled porch, and opened the door with a Yale key. 'Here you are, Miss Bowman, your home for the foreseeable future. The cottage has been aired, a fire laid and Mabel has seen to some basic provisions for you. The bed's made, there are towels, and the immersion heater has been on for several hours if you want to bathe.'

Her shoulders relaxed and she smiled at him. How thoughtful. The door opened directly into a living room; there was a brick fireplace to the right, surrounded by a wooden mantelpiece, with a tall cupboard to its right. A central green carpet covered a red-tiled floor. Two armchairs and a settee flanked the fireplace and there was a table and four chairs in front of the window.

'Mr Nicholson, thank you. You've made me feel at home.'

He shook his head looking shy and tongue-tied; he seemed uncomfortable now they were in close proximity.

He pointed to stairs. 'Two bedrooms up there.' He opened a door. 'The kitchen and the bathroom are through here.'

A good-sized kitchen was flooded with light from a large window over the sink; there was a fridge and cooker, the rest of the walls were fitted with cupboards and shelves.

Mr Nicholson opened a door. 'Bathroom through here; only a bath, no shower, I'm afraid, but there are staff showers in the modern block behind the main house, if you feel the need.'

On a table in the centre of the kitchen was a crusty loaf of bread, half-a-dozen eggs, butter, various packages and a cake tin. Thank goodness – she wouldn't have to starve.

Mr Nicholson handed her the Yale. 'The back door key's in the lock. I'll leave you to explore the rest of the house.' He hesitated. 'What had you planned for your dinner? Did you bring some food with you?'

Laurel smiled ruefully. 'I'm afraid I didn't, but luckily for me you've saved my bacon.' She pointed to the food on the table. She turned and went back to the living room. 'I see there isn't a phone here,'

'No, sorry. You could have one installed, but I'm afraid it would be at your own expense. Mr Shipster and I have phones in our houses if there's an emergency after school hours.'

'I'll have to think about that; luckily I phoned my parents from a public phone box in Dunwich to let them know I'd arrived safely.'

'That's thoughtful.' He hesitated. 'I'd be delighted if you'd join me for dinner. It's nothing special, just a casserole Mabel's rustled up for me, and some rather nice Stilton. You're very welcome to share it with me.'

His invitation seemed half-hearted and all she wanted to do was to look round the house and sort herself out. 'Thank you, Mr Nicholson, but I'm tired and I'd like to get straight before I fall asleep on my feet. Is it all right if I keep my car in front of the house?'

He moved towards the front door. 'There's a gravelled area to the right of the cottage, you can park it there; that keeps the road clear in case of emergencies. I'll wish you good night, I hope you sleep well. Please come to my office at ten tomorrow morning and I'll give you a tour of the rest of the buildings, and we can go over your duties. Hopefully Mr Shipster, the deputy head, will arrive tonight and you can meet him. Or did you see him when you came for the interview?'

'No, I didn't. I look forward to that.' The expression on Mr Nicholson's face suggested this might not be the case. She held out her hand. 'Thank you for the warm welcome, you've been most kind.'

His hand clasped hers. He was three or four inches taller than her and his large-framed body made her feel, for once, feminine, and if not exactly small, at least not like a giant. He held her hand a few seconds longer than necessary.

'Good night, Miss Bowman. I look forward to working with you.' He turned abruptly and left.

She wondered if he was looking forward to more than work. Laurel, she told herself, you have a suspicious mind. More importantly, what was she going to do about Frank Diamond? She needed to talk to him, persuade him not to blab to Nicholson. But that would mean seeing him alone, and if she did that he might start asking questions.

Chapter 5

Tuesday, September 8, 1970

Frank was getting out of his Mustang in the school car park when a sea-green Humber Hawk, with Elderkin driving, pulled up next to him. It was a large car matching its owner.

'Morning, Sergeant Elderkin. Good day for hunting suspects,' Frank said, feeling cheerful: it was a warm day, the noise of the waves on the shingle beach a faint regular beat, and the easterly sun cast a dark shadow in front of the Georgian house. Elderkin, resting his imposing backside against the side of his car, did not look cheerful, indeed he looked positively miserable. 'Morning, sir,' was all he could say.

'Nice car,' Frank said, peering into the interior.

'Ten years old,' he said. 'Bought it new in 1960. They don't make them anymore.' He patted the bonnet.

Frank had arranged to meet Elderkin at ten in the school car park. Elderkin said he'd drive himself: he didn't appear keen on Frank's driving, his car or the music on his tape player. Elderkin lived in Leiston, a small working-class town, south of Dunwich, a town boasting an engineering works and the largest police station in this part of Suffolk. He'd dropped Elderkin off the day before in front of a modest brick bungalow on the road leading to Aldeburgh. He'd not been invited in for a drink, not even a cup of tea.

Is the prospect of working with me so bad? Frank wondered. He'd have to get Elderkin on his side or Elderkin would have to go. That would be a pity, as his notes on the case were thorough and perceptive. 'This is the plan for today. First we'll see if Nicholson has solved our office problem, then we'll talk to Shipster. What's his Christian name?' He knew but he wanted Elderkin's lips to move.

'Robert, sir.'

'Ah, yes.' He rubbed his chin: smoother today. 'I think, Elderkin, we'll cut the formality. I can't see the point when we're by ourselves. If we're to work as a team, we need to not only respect each other, but to trust each other. I'd like you to call me Frank.'

Elderkin eyed him suspiciously and crossed his arms.

Frank also noted clenched fists. That went down well.

'My name's Stuart, sir,' he said.

'Excellent, Stuart. After Shipster, we'll talk to Mabel Grill, the school cook.' Was it his imagination or did Stuart look a smidgen happier, or at least less grumpy? 'She was the last person to see Susan Nicholson alive, wasn't she?'

Stuart nodded, unfolding his arms and scratching the back of his neck. 'She was. She was taking Muffin, her dog, for its usual walk. I've warned her not to take Muffin on walks alone until the murderer's been caught, but she won't take any notice. She's a stubborn woman, is Mabel.'

A stubborn woman – perhaps Elderkin has found her stubborn in other respects. Frank knew he was a widower of five years. Did the stolid Elderkin harbour lascivious thoughts about Mrs Grill? Or was he just tired of cooking for himself? 'You know Mrs Grill well?'

Elderkin shuffled his feet in the car park's gravel. 'She's a local woman. She and her husband used to run a fish-and-chip shop in Aldeburgh, her oldest son and her daughter-in-law took over a few years after her husband died. He was a fisherman; drowned he was. They still make the best fish and chips on this coast – lovely batter.'

Gosh, that was the longest speech Elderkin had given in Frank's hearing and he almost looked animated. 'You can't beat a good bit of battered cod, can you? I must give them my custom this weekend. Where is the chippy in Aldeburgh?'

Elderkin nearly smiled. 'On the sea-front, it's the only chippy in town.'

Miss Piff was not in her office so Frank and Elderkin climbed the stairs to Nicholson's office. There was a long pause between Frank's knock on the door and Nicholson opening it.

Laurel Bowman was standing near the open window. She was casually dressed in blue cotton trousers, flared from the knee and a short-sleeved white top; her thick hair tied back in a ponytail. Delicious.

She glowered at him.

After shaking their hands, Nicholson said, 'I've decided the best room for you will be Mr Shipster's office; he can move in with me until you've finished here. He's there now, deciding what he needs to bring. I'll check he's ready to see you.' He turned to Laurel. 'Miss Bowman, would you wait until I'm back? There are still a few matters we need to discuss.' He left the room.

Elderkin wandered over to the montage of pupils' art work. Frank joined Laurel at the window.

'I need to see you – alone,' she whispered.

Their eyes were level – she must be wearing flat shoes. Frank leant towards her. 'I knew you'd weaken,' he whispered, rocking on his heels, waiting for the explosion.

She clamped her lips together.

'Free Sunday? I'll meet you in Aldeburgh, near the Moot House, twelve sharp. Or do you want me to pick you up?' This must be about Angela.

'No. I'll be there.'

Frank nodded and Laurel walked away from him and started talking to Elderkin and pointing to one of the paintings. Elderkin smiled at her, he almost looked human.

31

Nicholson came back accompanied by a smaller man. Frank's impression was one of greyness, as though sculpted in stone, hard and immovable. His thick slate-coloured hair was swept back without a parting above a high forehead. Dark brown, almost black eyes were framed by heavy black eyebrows and his face jutted forward like an axe. Frank silently chastised himself for taking an instant dislike to him. This was not rational. Shipster might be a barrel of fun for all he knew.

Shipster was carrying several box files, which he slammed onto the table.

Frank held out his hand. 'Mr Shipster, I presume. Most kind of you to give up your office.' Shipster's hand was cold and smooth, like a dead plaice.

His face was as expressionless as his handshake. 'It's most inconvenient. I hope you'll be finished by the time term starts.' He pointed to the door. 'Please follow me.'

God in heaven, fancy sitting in his maths class for a year. Rigor mortis would set in, possibly galloping rigor mortis. He winked at Elderkin and jerked his head, indicating he should come too. Elderkin's mouth turned downwards, and Frank thought he saw an eyebrow flutter. Was he winking back? He heard Nicholson ask Laurel if she'd like a break for coffee. He didn't hear the reply.

Shipster's office was two doors to the right of Nicholson's. It was also a large room, smelling of dust and carbon paper. A wooden desk with a typewriter was covered in piles of papers, and there were two grey filing cabinets. He obviously liked a matching colour scheme. On the wall to the right of the window was a board consisting of a honeycomb of holes in which were hundreds of coloured pegs.

'What's this for?' asked Frank, pointing to it.

'I use it to devise the school timetable,' Shipster said, stuffing papers into a box file. 'I'll move it later. I don't want you knocking it over and ruining my work.'

Contrary to the rest of him, his voice was pleasant, low, with a BBC accent.

'Mr Shipster, Sergeant Elderkin and I would like to have a brief chat with you before we talk to some of the other staff.' He turned to Elderkin, who was wrestling his notebook from inside his jacket. 'No need to make notes, Sergeant, this is an informal talk.'

Shipster glowered beneath his bushy eyebrows. 'I hope it'll be short as well as informal. I've a great deal of material to move. This whole episode is most inconvenient.'

Frank bounced up and down on the balls of his feet. 'Murder is inconvenient, Mr Shipster, please remember that.'

Elderkin coughed, or was it a choke?

Shipster pointed to a table and four upright chairs in the centre of the room. There was nothing on the walls apart from the timetable board and a series of hooks from which hung labelled bull-dog clips, their steel edges securing wodges of paper. No sign of any children's art work. They sat down.

'Mr Shipster, as well as devising the school timetable, a difficult job in itself, what are your other responsibilities?'

Shipster brightened up and he almost smiled.

This was something he was interested in: himself.

'I'm also in charge of the curriculum, I'm Examinations Secretary, Head of Mathematics and in charge of boys' discipline,' he said, puffing out his chest.

What does the headmaster do? 'You've not left much for Mr Nicholson, have you?' Was he a loyal deputy?

Elderkin coughed again.

Shipster didn't say anything but looked not only smug but disdainful.

Frank smiled at him. He hoped it was an admiring smile. What was the relationship between the head and his deputy? He loved it when you found the first loose thread of a case. It

33

was like watching his mother starting to unravel an old woollen jumper. If you gently pulled a loose strand, slowly and carefully so it didn't break, a suspect would reveal facts about themselves, other people and sometimes the victim.

'Mr Shipster, I'd like you to run through your movements of the evening of Wednesday, April, 8th to midday, Thursday 9th, if you wouldn't mind.' Was that Uriah Heepish enough? Frank shook his head at Elderkin as he once again fumbled with his notebook.

Shipster's eyes darted from side to side – as though he wanted to get out of the room. 'Have you read the statement I made? There isn't anything I want to change.'

'Indulge me, Mr Shipster, you never know, something new might occur to you. Susan Nicholson was last seen by Mrs Mabel Grill, at… what time was that, Sergeant?' He knew but he wanted to involve Elderkin.

'About 7.30 p.m., near the sluice, sir.'

'So, Mr Shipster, where were you at that time?'

'Here, in my office, working.'

Frank raised his eyebrows. 'So late in the day? Term didn't start until Tuesday, 14th. What were you working on?'

Shipster's black eyes stared at the centre of Frank's forehead.

The power stare. He'd used it himself occasionally, but he wasn't a fan.

'The governors decided that we needed a senior mistress. They felt we should have a woman in a senior position as a role model for the girls.' His nostrils dilated and he made a sound between a sniff of disgust and a sigh. 'I was working on the wording for the advertisement, the job description and details for the interviews.'

'Why did the *governors* want a senior mistress? Didn't the headmaster want a woman in this position?'

Shipster's chin tilted upwards. 'Neither I nor the

headmaster felt there was a need. We did have a senior mistress two years ago, but that appointment proved… unsuccessful.' He crossed his arms.

Poor Laurel, she doesn't stand much of a chance. 'What happened?'

'I can't see this is relevant to Mrs Nicholson's death.'

'Mr Shipster, all information is relevant until I decide it isn't. Please answer the question.'

Shipster tried the glare again.

Frank smiled warmly at him.

Shipster looked flummoxed. 'The last woman was unsuitable for the job. She became hysterical under pressure. She resigned after an incident.'

'An incident?' Frank cocked his head questioningly.

Shipster smirked. 'She threw a telephone at the headmaster.'

'Did she hit the target?'

Shipster's thin lips twisted into a toothless smile. 'Yes, she cut his forehead. She *also* taught games.'

Was he hoping Laurel would despatch Nicholson, this time with a more lethal weapon? A javelin through the heart? Or a neat decapitation with a discus? 'What brought that about?'

'I don't know; I wasn't there.'

'Going back to Wednesday evening, did you see anyone that evening?'

'We all ate in the refectory, Mrs Grill set out a cold supper for us-'

'When you say all, you mean the other staff? Who was in the refectory with you?'

'Henry Thornback, Head of Science, Vanessa Letts, Head of English, Warren Ringrose, Art and Drama, and Antonia Habershon, the school matron. Miss Piff had gone home and Jim McFall, the school caretaker, never eats with us.'

'They were the only staff living in at the school at that time?'

'Yes, apart from the headmaster, who was in Colchester, and Emilia Mapp, who teaches foreign languages, she was in France with the school exchange. All the other staff, teaching and support, live locally.'

Frank steepled his hands and rested the point of his chin on his fingertips. 'Mrs Nicholson didn't eat with you?'

'She rarely ate with the staff.'

'When did you last see Mrs Nicholson?'

'I think it was the Monday, the day I arrived back in school. She was coming out of the head's office, about two p.m.'

'What did you talk about?

Shipster's nostrils dilated. 'We said good day to each other, that's all.'

There was a moment's silence as Frank chewed his lip.

Elderkin leant forward. 'Didn't she ask you if you'd had a good holiday? That's what you usually get, ad nauseum, when you come back from somewhere.'

Hurrah! Elderkin was making a contribution – and it was a good one. Perhaps they could jell into a team. It also allowed him to study Shipster as he focussed his attention on Elderkin.

The man raised his eyebrows as if to say, *You must be joking!* 'No, she didn't. She hurried past me; she didn't look in a good mood.'

Excellent, he was relating to Elderkin. He'd extracted the first piece of involuntary information.

'Did you like Susan Nicholson, Mr Shipster?' Frank barked.

Shipster flinched, his face taking on a pink tinge. 'I don't know what you mean. That's a very personal question.'

'Murder is a very personal crime, Mr Shipster. I'd like an

36

answer.' He eyeballed him.

Shipster swallowed. 'We didn't have very much to do with each other. I had no strong feelings about Mrs Nicholson.' He pulled at an ear lobe.

'Why didn't you check up on her when Mr Nicholson was away? You didn't see her on the Tuesday. When you didn't see her on the Wednesday why didn't you call at their house to see if there was anything she wanted? She might have been ill.'

Shipster seemed to have regained his equilibrium. 'I was very busy, as I've explained. There's a telephone at her house. If she'd been ill she would have rung matron. Anyway she wasn't ill, was she? Mrs Grill saw her that evening.'

Frank nodded and smiled. 'Very true, Mr Shipster.'

Shipster turned to Elderkin, who shrugged.

Frank saw a twinkle in Elderkin's eyes, and as Shipster turned back to him, Elderkin winked. Excellent. 'Speaking of Mrs Grill, where can we find her?'

'In the kitchen, there are supplies coming in this morning.' He gave them directions.

Frank thanked him for his time and Shipster turned wearily back to the job of moving his belongings into Nicholson's office.

'We'll be back with more questions, Mr Shipster; however, we'll let you get on with your removals.' Shipster turned to glower at him.

Miss Piff was rattling the keys of her typewriter when they came down the stairs to the hall. Elderkin tapped on the window and waved to her. He was livening up.

'Let's go round the back way,' Frank said. They could have gone down to the kitchen by stairs inside the house, but he wanted to see the outside entrance to the kitchen and the refectory.

Half-way down the side of the house Elderkin opened an

iron gate; they went down a flight of stone steps to a sunken U-shaped passageway which led them to the back of the house, the drop protected by iron railings. Overhead was a glass canopy supported by iron struts. A delivery lorry was parked at the back of the house.

A double door led into a large refectory. There were rows of long pine tables and benches, the grain of the table tops rutted, the wood white, presumably from years of scrubbing with bleach as the smell of the chemical lingered in the air. It was a gloomy space, with cold stone flooring and giant cast-iron radiators.

Frank was surprised at the size and depth of the room. The basement seemed to stretch the full width and length of the house and was divided by thick, load-bearing walls. To the left were hatches and through a partly open door the sound of a radio drifted out.

Elderkin, a smile on his face, rapped on the door and pushed it open. 'Morning, Mabel. We've come to arrest you.'

A well-fleshed woman, in a green overall, was pointing to where a tradesman was to place a box of goods. He banged it down with a metallic thud.

'Stuart Elderkin. I wouldn't mind a rest in gaol, I can tell you. Next week will be hell on earth, especially with the new 'uns, until they get used to boarding school.' She counted the boxes. 'That's right, Bert. Thank you. Fresh deliveries next Monday?'

Bert nodded, Mrs Grill signed a form and he left whistling.

'And who's this?' She pointed to Frank and turned off the radio.

'I'm Detective Inspector Frank Diamond, Mrs Grill. I'm in charge of the case.'

Mabel Grill's bones were well covered but she wasn't fat. Hazel eyes stared at him from a round, unsmiling face. 'You

38

mean Mrs Nicholson? You'll never find her murderer now, will you? If you don't catch them quick, usually you never catch them, do you?' she said accusingly, nodding her head, brown permed curls bobbing in agreement.

She could be right. He suspected his chief constable had given him this assignment knowing he was likely to fail. 'Sergeant Elderkin and I will work hard to find out who murdered Susan Nicholson; I don't like unsolved murders, Mrs Grill.'

She eyed him up and down and turned to Elderkin. 'Will he do, Stuart? Will he be better than the last one?'

Elderkin's face turned puce. 'Mabel, he's my boss. Do you want me to get the sack?'

The previous investigation hadn't been shoddy. All the routine areas had been covered. The inspector in charge was terminally ill and had retired. Poor sod. 'Sergeant Elderkin, you should have warned me. You said Mrs Grill was stubborn, but you didn't tell me she was also a dragon.' He laughed at the expression on Stuart's face.

Mabel Grill laughed back. 'Stubborn am I, Stuart Elderkin? A dragon, am I, Inspector Diamond? Well this old stubborn dragon will make you a nice cup of tea, if you'd like one?' She looked at them inquiringly.

Elderkin collapsed onto a chair. 'Mabel, I thought you'd never ask.'

As Mabel busied herself Frank looked round the kitchen. There were stainless-steel counter tops, sinks and draining boards; monster ovens, grills and pans, all shining, ready for the new term. The stone floor and green-painted walls were spotless – a thorough woman, Mabel Grill.

There was definitely a frisson between Elderkin and Mrs Grill. He certainly looked cheerful. The tea was strong and the fruit cake, which Elderkin demolished with relish and compliments, was excellent: dark with vine fruits, juicy cherries and a good deal of hazel nuts. Frank was beginning to understand the allure of Mrs Grill.

'Mrs Grill –'

'Call me Mabel.'

'Mabel, I want you to tell me about the last time you saw Susan Nicholson; I know you've been through this before, but *I* want to hear it.'

She nodded slowly, as though she was sending herself back in time to the evening in question. 'It was Wednesday, April 8th. I was taking Muffin for his evening walk. I always take him as soon as we've finished supper. I leave the others to do the washing up and the putting away. I check everything's shipshape and Bristol fashion when I get back. They know I do that so they daren't leave a spot of grease on the pans or any crumbs on the floor. I won't stand for that.'

'Who are they?' Frank asked.

'The part-timers: women from Dunwich who come in to help me cook.'

'Go on.'

'Every evening, unless it's blowing a gale, I takes Muffin down to the beach and we walk as far as the sluice. I needs the walk as much as Muffin; I like to stretch my legs after standing so long.'

'So everyone will know you always take the same walk at this time?'

Mabel stared at him, thinking. 'Yes, I suppose they would.'

'Are you still doing that walk, Mabel?' Elderkin nagged.

She nodded emphatically. 'I am, so it's no good going on about it, Stuart.' She smiled at Frank. 'He's a right fusspot, isn't he?'

'It might be a good idea to have someone else with you, Mabel. Think about it,' Frank said. Elderkin gave him the thumbs up.

40

She tossed her head. 'I can take care of myself, and I've got Muffin; he may be a small dog, but he wouldn't let anyone harm me, he wouldn't.'

Mabel did look as though she could do just that; she was about five foot five and Frank couldn't imagine anyone volunteering to go six rounds with her. He didn't fancy it.

Elderkin glanced at Frank and shrugged. He took a pipe out of his jacket pocket. Mabel glared at him. He looked at it longingly, sighed and put it back.

'Tell us about seeing Mrs Nicholson,' Frank said.

'Do you know the sluice?'

'No. Stuart's taking me there this afternoon.'

'You walk along the beach, either on the shore or you can walk behind the sand hills at the edge of the bird reserve, it's sheltered there. That's the way we went that evening. As we got in sight of the sluice I saw Mrs Nicholson.'

'You're sure it was her? How far away was she?'

'Oh, it was her all right, she was wearing her red coat and with her red hair, well, who else could it have been? I suppose I was seventy yards or so from her.'

'Her red coat?'

'Yes. Bright red, pillar-box red. No one else round here had a coat like that, not that I'd want one that colour. It was an expensive coat, she showed me the label once, can't remember the name, but it was lovely material, flared out from the waist, single-breasted, with a tie belt.'

Elderkin nodded. 'Thrown in the sluice on top of her body,' he said.

'So what happened then, Mabel?'

'She was leaning on the sluice walls, looking towards me. Then she waved, turned round, and started to walk down The Cut towards Eastbridge.'

Frank leant forward. 'So you didn't speak to her?'

'No. Muffin ran up to her and she turned round and patted

41

him.' She frowned. 'I called him back and we went home.'

'Were you surprised to see Mrs Nicholson out for a walk at that time?'

'No, not really. She often went for walks, and I've bumped into her before.'

Frank rubbed his chin. 'Mabel, I want you to think very carefully. Was there anything about that evening that worried you, or you thought unusual? If you want to mull it over, that's fine, just don't dismiss it out of hand. Keep it in your mind and get in touch with me, or Stuart if you'd prefer.' He smiled at Elderkin. 'We'll be around. We're based in Mr Shipster's office.'

Mabel leant back in her chair. 'He'll be pleased about that. I will think about what you've said, Inspector Diamond.' She frowned and gazed upwards. 'Now you've mentioned it, there is something niggling me, but I can't put my finger on it.'

Frank's heart skipped a beat. Something wasn't right. Mabel didn't look like an imaginative woman, if something had jarred with her it could be important – or it could be nothing. 'Did you like Susan Nicholson?'

'Why do you want to know that?' She glared at Elderkin. 'Does he think I done her in?'

'Inspector Diamond wants to know what kind of woman Susan Nicholson was,' Elderkin said placatingly.

She paused. 'I didn't like her, but I felt sorry for her.'

'Why's that, Mabel?'

'I think she was an unhappy woman, a restless woman who'd never be satisfied, whatever she had. It would never be enough.'

The elusive ghost of a red-coated woman seemed to drift in front of the stainless-steel counters. Beautiful, restless and unhappy. What made her unhappy? Who made her unhappy?

Chapter 6

Laurel stared out of Philip Nicholson's office window, her jaw clenched, fists tightly balled, fuming. What should she say to him when he came back from Mr Shipster's office? Why on earth had they appointed a senior mistress if there was no responsibility to go with the job? She was sure he'd guessed how she felt by her silence. He'd rushed out saying he needed to ask Shipster something. Was he hoping she'd take the box of keys and quietly disappear?

Beyond the modern block, which housed the laboratories and the gym, the outlines of the priory ruins were clear in the bright September sun. The stone-and-flint gateway, half-covered in ivy, stood out against a delft sky; the crumbling walls, once high, protecting the buildings inside, were like the decayed teeth of a child who ate too many sweets.

She took several deep breaths trying to formulate the words she would need to let Nicholson know this was not good enough. She must be calm and precise. There was no point in having a row and being accused of being a hysterical woman. She needed to know why she was being treated derisorily, why she obviously wasn't to be a real part of the senior administration.

She moved over to the table and sat down. She wasn't going to take a seat which placed her at a disadvantage. The door opened and Philip Nicholson came in. He juddered to a halt.

'Oh, I thought we'd finished, Miss Bowman.'

She pulled out the chair next to her and patted it. 'Please sit here, Mr Nicholson, there are a few matters I'd like to discuss.' She forced herself to give him her best smile. He looked confused, not sure whether to retreat to his desk or take up the invitation.

He sat down beside her, eyeing her warily. 'Is something the matter?'

'I'm puzzled. I can't see the specific task you've asked me to do meets my job description. Although this wasn't detailed, because of your absence at the time of my appointment, I was under the impression I would be part of the school administration with you and Mr Shipster.'

He shifted uneasily in his seat. 'The job I've given you needs doing and neither Mr Shipster nor I have the time to do it. Your role is to look after the girls' discipline; that'll be your main task. Keeping tabs on all of their goings on, and er, er, all that side of it.'

She tilted her head. 'All what side of it? I'm not clear what you mean.' She had a good idea but she wanted him to articulate it.

Nicholson wriggled in his chair, his cheeks flushed. 'Women's stuff… periods… use of sanitary towels.'

'Isn't that matron's area?'

He half-rose from the chair. 'Look, perhaps we could discuss this some other time. I need to get on with some urgent work.'

'I won't keep you a few more minutes, Mr Nicholson.' She pointed to the box of keys. 'So this is my job for the moment, to sort out the locker keys and give them to the pupils?'

He marched to his desk. 'Correct.'

Laurel stood up and followed him. 'Have I my own base to work from? Have I been given an office?'

He shuffled the meagre pile of papers in front of him, head down. 'Er, no, I don't think so. You'd better go and see Mr Shipster, he may have sorted that out. Also he'll give you your timetable.'

That should be interesting. She smiled at him sweetly.

Beast. Not so much Gregory Peck today, more Boris Karloff. 'Thank you for your time, Mr Nicholson. No doubt I'll see you later.'

He muttered something as she left the room. She quietly closed the door. He didn't want to flirt with her today. Now for Shipster.

His door was half-open and she was able to watch him unobserved as he rammed papers into a box file. Laurel wasn't enamoured by his appearance; on the day of the interview she'd briefly seen him in passing but hadn't met him. His office looked a sterile place. Did it reflect his personality? Perhaps she was being unfair, influenced by her meeting with Mr Nicholson. Mr Shipster had to move out of his office for Frank Diamond; perhaps he'd taken down pictures, or moved personal objects.

She tapped on the door and walked in. 'Mr Shipster, glad to meet you at last, I'm Laurel Bowman.'

He looked up, his basilisk face expressionless. Was he horrified at her sudden appearance or entranced by her looks? She hadn't the faintest idea.

'Miss Bowman.' The skin of his hand was cold and the touch of his fingers brief, as though he'd discovered he was shaking hands with an inmate of the leper hospital.

'Mr Nicholson suggested I see you. I believe you have my timetable, I'd like to see it so I can plan my lessons.'

His upper lip curled. 'Do you need to plan *games* lessons?' His tone suggested this was not the case.

Oh dear, now she'd *two* male chauvinists to deal with. 'You certainly do have to plan, and on an individual basis, or the pupils won't make any progress.' Got you there, you old curmudgeon. She tried her smile again, but without much hope; it hadn't worked with the head this morning, perhaps she was losing her touch.

An image of Frank Diamond appeared admiration in his

eyes as she glowered at him in Nicholson's office. How was she going to manage him when they met? Three difficult men to cope with. How many more where there in this part of the world? Thinking of Frank made her realise she hadn't thought of Angela lately, or her parents. The obstacles she'd met this morning weren't that important, but she wasn't going to give in to these two men.

'Here's your timetable, Miss Bowman. Now if you'll excuse me I need to press on with this removal.'

She glanced at it. Not much free time for any other work. She'd be doing more teaching than in her last post. She decided to try another tack. 'It must be a great inconvenience for you, having to move out of your office.'

His black eyes narrowed, and his mouth turned down. In disappointment? Had he expected her to object to the timetable?

'Yes, very inconvenient, and to no avail, I expect.'

'I didn't realise Mrs Nicholson had been murdered until yesterday. It was quite a shock.'

He stroked his chin. 'Would you have taken the job if you'd known?'

Laurel slowly shook her head. 'I'm sure I wouldn't.'

A reptilian smile creased the skin of his face. 'I believe Mr Nicholson would understand if you didn't want to stay. A woman has been murdered and the killer is still at large. Why don't you talk to him? Would you like me to negotiate for you?'

He was positively bursting to help her – help her off the premises – the hypocrite. 'Why, that's kind of you, Mr Shipster.'

The smile widened, but his black eyes were cold.

'Mr Nicholson has already made me that offer and of course I refused. I couldn't possibly let the school down. Besides,' she moved closer to him and looked down into his crestfallen face, 'as you can see, I'm tall, fit and strong. I think I can take care of myself.'

He deflated like a beached jellyfish shrivelling in the sun. She almost felt a twinge of pity for him. 'You don't think the murderer will be caught, do you? Don't you think the new inspector will be able to catch him or her?'

He sneered. 'The killer must be a man: a woman isn't capable of doing such a murder. Also she was *raped*,' he said, leering at her. 'As for Inspector Diamond, he has no local knowledge and from the looks of him, not many brains either. I don't hold much hope.'

He's in for a shock. She hoped Diamond gave him the third degree.

'Miss Piff was telling me how attractive and feminine Susan Nicholson was. She'll be greatly missed by everyone I expect.'

Shipster sniffed. 'A woman's looks mean nothing to me…'

Thanks for telling me, she wouldn't waste any more charm on him.

'… and she was a meddler.' He bit his lip as though he wished he hadn't made that remark. 'Sorry, mustn't speak ill of the dead. Now if you'll excuse me.' He turned his back on her.

She gave him a long, hard look. 'Goodbye, Mr Shipster. Oh, one last thing, Mr Nicholson said you may have sorted an office out for me. Have you?'

He turned abruptly. 'No, I haven't. Why do *you* need an office?'

Laurel felt like bringing the murder count up to two, but she took a deep breath and gave him an icy smile. 'Because I am the senior mistress of this school and I'm sure the governors would like to see me treated appropriately. That includes my own office. As my responsibilities expand,

47

which they will, I'll need a base to operate from. Please see to it. Thank you.' She inclined her head royally, and majestically walked away, pressing her lips together to prevent herself laughing at the look of incredulity on his face.

She was curious at Shipster's reaction to the mention of Susan Nicholson... a meddler, what did that mean? Intriguing. She wondered what the other staff thought of her. Miss Piff said she was attractive, but she didn't say anything about her being a nice or kind woman, good with children and animals. No. She mustn't get involved. But why not? How delightful if she could prove Shipster was the murderer. Perhaps she'd try and winkle a few facts out of Frank Diamond when she saw him on Sunday. She'd enjoyed solving petty crimes at her previous school, sometimes not so petty. If you let pupils get away with something, they usually do it again, or something worse.

She stopped to chat with Miss Piff and to ask the way to the kitchens; she wanted to meet Mrs Grill, her next-door neighbour and pay and thank her for the provisions.

She pushed open the kitchen door; a woman in a green overall, standing on stepladders, was stacking huge cans into a cupboard. 'Hello. Mrs Grill?'

The woman turned. 'Yes?'

Laurel walked towards her, holding out her hand and smiling. 'I'm Laurel Bowman, your new next-door neighbour. I came to thank you for the food supplies. They were most welcome as I hadn't brought any food with me.'

Mabel Grill's face lit up, she climbed down, and after rubbing her hand on her overalls shook Laurel's hand heartily. 'Glad to meet you. Hope everything in the cottage was all right?'

'Wonderful. I feel very lucky living in such a lovely spot and it's great to be able to hear the sea as I lie in bed.'

'I heard you'd come from Felixstowe, that you were a

Suffolk girl. Didn't you hear the sea there?'

'Suffolk born and bred, but we lived in old Felixstowe, a mile or so from the sea.'

Mrs Grill nodded in recognition. 'Nice town Felixstowe, but it's not doing as well as it used to; people want to go to Spain for their holidays,' she said contemptuously.

It wasn't long before the tea was brewed and cake cut. Laurel was relieved that she'd met one person – no, two with Miss Piff – she liked. She wondered how she could bring up the subject of Susan Nicholson without sounding ghoulish.

'You just missed that new inspector and Stuart Elderkin. They came to ask me about the last time I saw Mrs Nicholson.'

'Really? When did you see her? Lovely cake, by the way.' Wow – that was lucky.

Nodding her head at the compliment and seeing Laurel's interest she told her about seeing Susan Nicholson. 'Have you met Inspector Diamond yet? Mind you he won't want to talk to you, will he? – seeing as you've only just come here.'

'Yes, I did meet him and Sergeant Elderkin yesterday, in the head's office.'

'What did you think of him? He seems sharp. I hope Stuart gets on with him. That last inspector wasn't up to much. I know he's ill, poor chap, but he was too near retirement, if you ask me. Stuart told me about this new one coming. They're a bit put out at Leiston police station; think he might be a bit of a whiz kid, as he went to university. He said policemen at Ipswich called him Donovan behind his back 'cos of his long hair.'

He was much better looking than baby-faced Donovan. Poor old Frank, you and me both: not welcomed by our fellow workers. But at least he can pull rank, she wasn't sure if she could. 'We only met briefly, so I couldn't say.'

Mabel poured herself another cup of tea, waving the pot at

Laurel who shook her head. 'I thought he was tasty; if I'd been a bit younger ...' She winked at Laurel, who laughed at the thought of Frank Diamond being pursued by Mrs Grill.

'What about your husband? Wouldn't he have something to say about that?'

Mabel put her mug on the table. 'I've been a widow for a few years – but I've got a good memory.' She winked again. 'Mind you, Stuart Elderkin seems to have taken a shine to me.' She pulled a face but her tone suggested the attention wasn't unwelcome. 'Pity he's not a bit younger.' She raised her eyebrows. 'What about you?' She glanced at Laurel's left hand. 'Is there some poor chap you've left behind in Felixstowe?'

There was a poor chap, a very poor chap, but he'd done the leaving, not her. Simon couldn't understand why she was fixated on finding Angela's killer. When she'd asked if they could postpone the wedding he'd lost his temper and said Angela was a tart who'd got what she deserved. As far as he was concerned the engagement was finished. After what he'd said, even if he apologized, she wouldn't take him back. 'No, I'm footloose and fancy free, but at the moment I think I'll concentrate on my new job.'

'Very wise. But I'd have a closer look at Inspector Diamond, if I were you; he's good looking and he's got a sense of humour. I like him. He's sharp, asked some pointed questions, made me think.' She nodded her head, eyes blank as if inwardly reflecting. 'There was something odd that evening I saw Mrs Nicholson, but...' She shook her head rapidly, as though it was a kaleidoscope and she'd be able to make a fresh picture. 'It'll come to me, I expect.'

Laurel leant forward. 'Perhaps if you took the same walk and stopped when you got to the spot you saw Mrs Nicholson and tried to visualise the scene again, you might remember what's bothering you.'

Mabel sat up straight, her eyes wide with astonishment. 'That's a brilliant idea. Thank you, Miss Bowman, or being as we're neighbours, can I call you Laurel?'

Laurel relaxed: how lovely to have such a jolly, practical woman for a neighbour, *and* she was a good cook, if the cake was anything to go by. 'Of course, and perhaps we could take that walk together and you could show me the sluice. We might jog your memory. Whatever it is that's troubling you might be important.'

She shouldn't be getting involved, but she might help Mabel Grill remember something vital which could give a lead to Susan Nicholson's killer. It was too intriguing to turn down. She'd tracked down one murderer; why not use the same skills to help find another killer?

'I'll take you up on that, Laurel. We could go this evening, after supper. I'm laying on a cold meal for the staff who're coming back today, but if you like you can come and eat with me. I've got a nice piece of fresh cod my daughter-in-law brought me, plenty enough for two. We can listen to the news before our walk and hear what's happened to those poor people who've been hijacked.'

She could do without the news but the cod sounded good. 'Thanks, Mabel. I'll look forward to that and to meeting Muffin.' Wouldn't it be exciting if Mabel remembered something important when they took the walk to the sluice? Wouldn't Frank Diamond be impressed? Or would it reinforce his suspicions of her?

Chapter 7

'You look as though you enjoyed it.' Frank pointed to a clean plate.

Elderkin smacked his lips. 'I did. I wasn't sure I would, but it's a tasty way with eggs. I'll try it myself now I've seen you do it.'

Elderkin was praising Frank's mushroom omelette, which a few hours ago he'd implied was a poor substitute for a lunch-time pint and cottage pie at The Ship in Dunwich. They were sitting in the kitchen of Frank's rented cottage, the end one of a terrace of former coastguard houses high on Minsmere cliff, two miles south of Dunwich, surrounded by heath, all National Trust land.

'Glad you liked it, Stuart. You can do all sorts of fillings: cheese, prawns, and herbs. Mushroom is my favourite.'

Elderkin wiped his plate with the last piece of bread, swallowed it and washed it down with beer.

Frank was relieved the meal had gone well; he'd wanted to talk freely with him, without Stuart being influenced by the looks and nudges of drinkers in a pub. Stuart was looking relaxed – two bottles of Adman's had worked their magic.

Elderkin frowned. 'Where did you get the mushrooms? They weren't ordinary mushrooms were they?'

Frank wondered if he should lie, he wasn't sure Stuart would like the answer. No, that wasn't the way to build trust. 'I picked them early this morning; drove out to the woods.'

Stuart's face wrinkled in horror and his hand clutched at his throat as though he was about to strangle himself.

'Don't worry, Stuart, I know my fungi, I haven't poisoned you... or myself.'

Stuart sluiced the last of his beer. 'I've never eaten wild

mushrooms before. Are you sure they're OK?'

'Would I try to kill you, Stuart? I'm not going to solve this murder by myself; I need your local knowledge.'

Stuart's hand receded slowly from his throat, but he cast a surreptitious glance to his ample stomach, as though it might explode. He waved a hand to the contents of the kitchen. 'Was all this here when you came?'

All this was several copper-bottomed pans hung on the white-washed walls, a large Kenwood Chef, a set of stainless-steel bowls and sundry egg whisks, graters and peppermills.

Frank shook his head. 'One of my hobbies: cooking. Got interested when I was a student, worked in a hotel kitchen in the holidays: poor pay but good grub. I find cooking relaxing; it helps me to get my thoughts in order.'

Stuart sighed. 'Wish I could cook. You don't need to get married then, do you?'

'Stuart, I'm shocked. Surely that wasn't the only reason you got married – to have three meals a day plonked in front of you?'

Stuart pulled a lugubrious face, twisting his mouth as though he was savouring the memories of young lust, or was it the remembered smell of roast beef, Yorkshire puddings and glistening gravy? 'I loved my wife… and I loved her more when I found out what a good cook she was. I've yet to taste apple pie better than hers.'

Frank poured more beer into Elderkin's glass. 'What's Mrs Grill's apple pie like?'

Stuart winked. 'I've never tasted her apple pie,' he said lasciviously. 'But I'm looking forward to tasting it one day… soon I hope.' He downed the last of the beer.

'Mind if I smoke my pipe?' He didn't wait for Frank's answer and pulled out a briar pipe and a leather pouch of tobacco.

Frank watched as with well-practised ritual, Elderkin

53

filled the bowl.

'I'll just have a short smoke. Two or three pinches of tobacco gives me a good whiff. Don't you smoke, Frank? I've never met a detective who didn't.'

'I used to; devoted to Embassy Filters. I gave up ten years ago.'

Elderkin carefully tamped down the tobacco in the pipe's bowl. 'Why'd you do that?'

'At university I read the results of research on lung cancer. It convinced me. I know I've got to die of something at some time, but...'

Elderkin shrugged. 'One of my few pleasures nowadays.'

'Mabel didn't seem too keen on you lighting up in her kitchen.'

'I may have to give up as well if... She's not keen on tobacco smoke.'

'If you're ready, Stuart, we'll walk to the sluice and on our way you can tell me about Benjie Whittle.'

Elderkin, puffing on his pipe, looked pleased when his offer to wash the dishes was refused and followed Frank from the cottage. 'Mind if I fetch my binoculars from the car? We might see a few migrants on the Scrape.'

Frank thought of cracking jokes about illegal immigrants but resisted the temptation. So Stuart was a twitcher he'd never have guessed. 'Do you belong to the RSPB?' he asked, as they walked towards the National Trust car park.

'We began helping on the reserve, my wife Doreen and me, about 1950, saw the first Marsh harriers nesting in 1955. We helped build some of the islands in The Scrape,' he said proudly. 'Avocets nested here first time in Britain for a hundred years.'

The heath spread out from the edges of the cliffs: yellow gorse, heather and ling, dotted with pines and shrunken oaks, a tracery of sandy paths criss-crossing it. From the car park a steep, rough road, wide enough for a car, led down to Minsmere beach fifty feet below.

'What's that?' Frank asked, pointing to a wooden hut, tucked in a sheltered nook, near the bottom.

'Sells ice cream,' Elderkin said, looking disappointed it wasn't open.

At the bottom of the hill they turned right, away from the sandy cliffs, onto the beach. The brown waters of Sole Bay stretched out between Southwold's lighthouse to the left, and Easterspring power station to the right. The tide would soon be turning and a south-east wind was whipping up the waves.

Frank decided he'd buy a pair of binoculars. He'd ask Stuart's advice. They walked south on a high grassy bank; to their right was the bird reserve, reed beds stretching into the distance.

Elderkin stopped and focussed his binoculars. 'Meadow pipit.'

So Elderkin had a soul. 'We'll make a good pair, Stuart. I was a botanist, that's how I can tell a death cap from a boletus, and you're a bird expert: both observers of detail and deduction. Tell me about the reserve.'

Elderkin lowered his binoculars and smiled. 'I hope we will, Frank. I want to find Mrs Nicholson's killer.' Stuart's enthusiasm and energy increased as he talked about the history of the reserve, punctuated by stops for twitching. The path dipped down behind sand dunes.

Stuart stopped by a concrete block, half-buried in the sand, its surface pitted with ochre patches of lichen. He peered into the bowl of his pipe, sighed and knocked it gently against the concrete. 'Why did you decide to join us lot? If you've got a science degree, why didn't you go on with that?'

Frank leant against the block. 'I was going to go back to university after National Service to do some research, that was the plan, but I did my time in the RAF. They attached me to the RAFP, the Royal Air Force Police, at RAF Marsham.'

'When was that?'

'1960.'

'Nice area of Norfolk, near King's Lynn. So you were a Snowdrop, then?'

'That's right. Can you imagine me in a white cap?'

'Not with hair that long. So the police bug bit you?'

'There were some good detectives amongst the Snowdrops. Also when I was on leave once, back in Liverpool, one of my cousins got knifed in a nightclub–'

'Serious?'

'Dead serious. I got involved in the investigation.'

'Did they nail the killer?'

'They did, and as soon as I finished National Service I joined the police. I'd liked living in East Anglia and I managed to get in the Suffolk Police Force. There you are – satisfied?'

'That sounds a good, solid reason for wanting to be a copper. Were the Valiants flying when you were at Marsham?'

'Yes. Bloody giants with nuclear bombs. I managed to get a few flights in them – fantastic.' He looked at Stuart. 'How far is it to the sluice?' They continued walking.

'It's about three quarters of a mile from the cliffs – seems longer through this sand,' Stuart puffed. 'We could have a rest here.' He pointed to a wooden public hide built into the earth walls that protected the reserve from high tides and storms.

'No. Let's keep going. Tell me about Benjie Whittle; I've read the case notes, but what do you think? Is he a serious suspect?'

Elderkin blew out his cheeks. 'Not many round here believe that. I've known Benjie all his life. He's always been lacking a bit,' Elderkin tapped his forehead, 'but he'd never been in any trouble before *she* came.'

'*She* being Susan Nicholson?'

'That's right. She used to do a deal of walking, as you know, and when she first came here she often met Benjie on the shore. She was a beautiful woman, and to begin with she chatted to Benjie. I think she liked the way he treated her, as though she was royalty, a living goddess. He used to drool on about her at the Eel's Foot…'

Frank raised his eyebrow.

'His local pub at Eastbridge: he's a cottage nearby, lived there all his life.'

'What was he doing on the beach? Fishing?'

Elderkin nodded. 'Line fishing, he's got a boat, does some pots, lobster and crab; sells to the pub and locals. If the weather's too rough he's a beachcomber, usually picks up some good amber and sells it to a jeweller in Aldeburgh. He gets by.'

Frank remembered one of the photographs of Susan Nicholson in her file, a coloured photo, obviously taken during her days on the stage: a perfect oval face, delicate high cheek bones, violet, almond-shaped eyes with thick lashes and full kissable lips. He imagined her in the flesh. Hmm. It was no wonder Benjie drooled, he might have joined him given the chance.

'So you don't believe he exposed himself to her?'

Elderkin's face darkened and he kicked at a clump of marram grass. 'It was the word of the headmaster's wife against the word of a not-too-bright, inarticulate fisherman. Benjie'd never done anything like that before.'

'There's always the first time, and she was a looker.'

'He got six months. Locals rallied round, we had a rota for visiting him and when he came out they had a party at the Eel's Foot. We can't all be wrong, can we?'

The sandy path gave way to velvet-smooth grass, neat piles of rabbit droppings the clue to the manicured turf. Lichen covered more concrete blocks poking through the sand.

Stuart pointed ahead. 'There's the sluice. There used to be cottages here, but they were destroyed at the outbreak of the war.'

'Why?'

'They flooded this area in case the Germans landed here.'

Hard to imagine, on this peaceful afternoon, the concrete blocks part of fortifications; people moved from their homes, everyone on edge, waiting for the invasion.

The land rose up to the walls of the sluice, which stood sentinel between the beach and the footpath to Eastbridge. Running parallel to the path was the New Cut, a deep, wide ditch carrying water from the Eastbridge river and the marshes to the sea. Sounds of churning water rose from the pit of the sluice. Frank leaned over the brick wall; water swirled round the iron machinery that controlled the sluice gate. The drop was about fourteen feet from the top of the hexagonal walls to the iron girders below.

'Good job she was dead when she was tossed over.'

Elderkin's mouth turned down. 'Must have happened soon after Mabel saw her.'

'What about the pathology report? Was the time of death accurate?'

Elderkin wrinkled his brow. 'He's always been close before. Mind you she'd been in there overnight and the water was cold.'

Looking down at the brown waters, heaving and frothing, he imprinted the photograph he'd seen of the nearly naked body of Susan Nicholson draped over the iron girders. She was almost submerged in the spinning water: slender legs awry, one stocking still held by a suspender from a delicate girdle, small, almost immature breasts, her arms thrown back, moving to the gyrations of the water, like a striptease artist. Her clothes whirling in the giant washing machine of the sluice: the red coat, her dress, silk underwear; all torn or ripped, by the murderer or the machinery, or both.

Could Benjie Whittle have done that to her? Perhaps he saw her near the sluice and overcome with hate and lust he'd attacked, raped and killed her. He had a motive: she'd accused him of exposing his genitals to her, here on the beach. Why would she accuse him if he hadn't done it? If it was a false accusation what kind of woman was Susan Nicholson, to do that to a vulnerable man? He needed to know more about Benjie Whittle. Stuart was on Benjie's side, and if what he said was true, and he had no reason to doubt him, so were most of the locals.

He also needed to know more about Susan; her past, before she married Philip Nicholson, when she was an actress. Why did she leave the stage? Did she fall madly in love with Philip? Or had she been glad to quit acting for a steadier, more secure life?

He imagined trying to lift a dead body over the four foot wall of the sluice. She was small, but even so the murderer needed a certain strength. She'd been raped but there were no traces of semen in her vagina. There are other ways of raping a woman without using a turgid penis. It could be a ruse used by a ruthless woman; he mustn't assume it was a man, but he hadn't met any female suspects who looked strong and nerveless enough to strangle and kill another woman. Mrs Grill was well built, but... no, he couldn't see her as the killer. He needed to meet all the staff, and keep an open mind.

He realised he was gripping the walls so tightly the rough brickwork had grazed his hands. There was one woman on the scene strong enough to strangle someone, and strong enough to throw Susan's body over the sluice wall: Laurel Bowman. He'd have to check her alibi. No, this was ridiculous. She was a resourceful and fearless woman, but a murderer? But something happened in Felixstowe. If his suspicions were confirmed, he'd have to do something about it. The omelette and beer turned sour in his stomach, which was churning in unison to the waters of the sluice.

He turned to Stuart. 'Where's Whittle's hut? Do you think he'll be there?'

Stuart glanced at his wristwatch. 'I doubt it; he'll be on his way back from the Eel's Foot. We'll check the shack out and if he's not there we can walk up The Cut to Eastbridge and meet him.'

Stuart was right. Tucked behind a high sand hill was a hut built of tarred wood with a felt roof. The door was padlocked, and an oarless rowing boat blocked the door. Plastic orange buoys, two lobster pots, and tangled netting lay in the belly of the boat.

'He's a trusting cove.'

'Benjie's a good man, and he thinks the best of everyone. He was scared when he was in prison, afraid of the warders and the other prisoners. He wasn't treated too well and it was hard on him being locked up: he's spent all his life here, in Eastbridge, in the open air. I doubt if he'd been to Ipswich before he was arrested.'

'Then he'd a strong motive for murder.'

Stuart Elderkin glared at him.

Should he widen his list of suspects? Find out which locals were incensed by Susan Nicholson's treatment of Benjie? Should that list include Stuart Elderkin? Francis Xavier Diamond, it was his mother's voice speaking to him, pull yourself together, you have too much imagination. Mother, he replied, you can never have too much imagination.

'Shall we walk down The Cut; I can't promise we'll meet him, but I'll bet you we do,' Elderkin said.

Frank decided to forget his dawning suspicions of the entire population of Eastbridge, and concentrate on Benjie Whittle. 'You're on. If we don't meet him, we can walk to Eastbridge. I'd like to get my bearings. How far is it? Pity it'll be too late for a drink at the Eel's Foot.'

Stuart's face lit up. 'It's about a mile and a half, and I'm sure the landlord will be sympathetic to two hard-working members of the law.' He frowned. 'What do you think about those firemen walking out in Harlow? Leaving the station unmanned. Doesn't seem right, does it? Do you think the police will ever go on strike?'

Frank grimaced. 'Don't mention unions and strikes to me.' He didn't want to think about the unrest in the country – it reminded him of his father.

For the first quarter of a mile the public footpath towards Eastbridge ran close to The Cut, then it veered left through fields, a narrow stream running beside it.

'What's that?' Frank pointed to a flint ruin in the middle of a field.

'It's what remains of the old Leiston Abbey. There's only the chapel left. You wouldn't believe it but there's a pill-box inside, under all that scrub.'

Another war relic. It seemed a lonely place to live, but then monks liked isolation. 'When was the priory built?'

'Twelfth century. There was an estuary here then and the monks built earth embankments to try and keep out the sea, some still keep the sea water out of the bird reserve.'

Not only a twitcher, a bit of a local historian as well. Murderer? He didn't think so.

'There he is.' Stuart pointed to an approaching figure.

Benjie Whittle was five foot eight, dressed in a navy turtle-necked jumper, dark blue serge pants and wellies.

Frank knew from the case notes Whittle was forty-six. They stood waiting for him. He slowed down as he came closer, his shoulders slumped, and he raised a hand and gave a tentative wave, obviously recognising Elderkin, but unsure of Frank.

'Go easy on him, Frank, please.' He waved back to Whittle. 'Hello, Benjie, come and meet Inspector Diamond. We were having a stroll to Eastbridge.'

Whittle stumbled towards them. His moon-shaped face and pate, from which sprouted odd patches of white fluff, were weather-beaten; large, pale blue, saucer-shaped eyes looked guilelessly at Frank. His square body, short-legged, with strong arms, looked well capable of lifting a dead weight and tossing it over the sluice walls.

Frank held out his hand. 'Hello, Mr Whittle–'

'Better to call him Benjie,' Stuart whispered, as Benjie looked round, as if searching for Mr Whittle.

Frank took a deep breath and started again. 'Hello, Benjie, I'm Inspector Diamond.'

Benjie's eyes turned watery. 'You've not come to take me back to that gaol, have you? I dustn't want to go back there.' He turned to Stuart. 'Has she come back from the grave and said more things about me? I never touched her and I never did the dirty things she said.'

The man was quivering; Stuart was right, he needed to treat him gently. 'It's all right, Benjie. I only wanted to ask you a few questions. I haven't come to take you anywhere. May we walk with you to your hut?'

A tentative smile broke on Benjie's face and he shook Frank's hand. 'Thank you, sir. Can Mr Elderkin come too? I can make a brew; I've got a little stove in my hut. Would you like that?'

'We'd love a cup of tea, wouldn't we, Sergeant Elderkin?' He flinched – Stuart looked as though he was about to kiss him.

'That's very kind of you, Benjie,' Stuart said.

'I'll buy you a pint at the Eel's Foot tonight,' Frank whispered.

Frank chatted to Benjie as they turned and walked back towards the beach, deciding to leave the questioning until Benjie was safe on home territory.

Frank leant on Benjie's boat, sipping a surprisingly good brew from a spotless mug. 'You make a good cuppa, Benjie.' Now he understood why the locals had been incensed by Susan Nicholson's accusations: the man was gentle, easily upset, like a kindly, giant child.

Stuart got his pipe going and Benjie took a packet of Woodbines from his pocket. Stuart struck a match, lit Benjie's cigarette and focussed on the bowl of his pipe.

Benjie smiled and nodded. 'Thank you, Mr Elderkin. I do make good tea; lots of people have told me. I like to make it for those I know and sometimes strangers if they seem nice. They stop and we have a chat, I likes that. Sometimes I cook my dinner here, when I've caught mackerel or a little codling. Nothing better than to sit here in the sun and look out at the waves and talk to my friends.'

'Your friends, Benjie? Who are your friends?' Frank asked.

'Why the birds, of course; they come to me when I gut the fish and throw them the innards. Make a right noise, they do, wheeling round and screeching. Then my girlfriend, she sometimes comes to see me, but I've not seen her for a long time.'

God's teeth, was he talking about Mrs Nicholson? 'Who's your girlfriend, Benjie?'

Benjie chuckled. 'She's not a real girlfriend; she might not even be a girl.' He leant backwards, his eyes disappearing as he laughed.

Stuart nudged Frank's arm. 'It's a seal, his girlfriend is a

63

seal.' He put his hand to his face and sniggered.

A seal. Bloody hell, he didn't fancy questioning a seal. His shoulders heaved as he snorted with laughter.

'I got you there, didn't I, Inspector? You thought I meant... you know who.' He seemed unable to say her name. 'My silkie come to see me and I give her some fish. I tell them at the Eel's Foot all about her but they don't believe me, do they, Mr Elderkin?'

Elderkin wiped his eyes with a large checked handkerchief. 'We've only got your word for it, Benjie; none of us have seen your girlfriend.' He turned to Frank. 'You do get the occasional seal in these parts, but not often.'

'But you believed me about *her*, didn't you? You didn't think I showed my willy to her, did you? I don't show my willy to anyone, my ma told me you shouldn't do things like that. I always do what my ma told me.'

Oh, Lord, another dominant mother. Frank was losing his grasp on this interview. 'Benjie, will you tell me how you first met Susan Nicholson? Take your time, try and remember everything you can.'

He turned a frightened face towards Stuart, 'Do I have to, Mr Elderkin?' he pleaded. 'I dusn't like to think of her anymore.'

'You'll be helping Inspector Diamond and me. Our job is to find out who killed Mrs Nicholson. When we do, all this trouble will end and you can get back to your quiet life, here on the beach, with no one to bother you.'

'You won't put me back in prison?' he asked Frank.

'No, Benjie.' Frank sincerely hoped not.

There was a deep sigh. 'I was gutting a few herring for my dinner when she first came up to me. I thought she was an angel come down from heaven, she looked so lovely – like the Virgin Mary in our church. She spoke to me real nice, asked about the fish, what my name was, where I lived. I

64

made her a cup of tea and she sat down beside me, like you are now.' His face was sorrowful and his head drooped until his chin rested on his chest.

'Did she come often to the hut?'

'Whenever she saw me she came over and I always made her tea. I started to look out for her and I brought biscuits in a tin so she could have one with her tea, and I brought a sugar bowl from home so she wouldn't have to have it from a bag.'

'Why do you think she said you'd shown her your... willy, Benjie?'

He looked at Frank, his large, blue eyes filled with tears. 'She was a bad woman, that's why she said it.'

'Tell Inspector Diamond what happened that made you think she was a bad woman, Benjie.'

'Do I have to? I dusn't like to think of it. One minute she was an angel and the next minute she was a devil. She broke my heart and I couldn't love her anymore.'

'Please tell me, Benjie, I do need to know.' He really needed to know.

Benjie twisted his hands together. 'We was sat together having tea, I was so happy, she liked the chocolate biscuits I'd bought, then this little dog came scampering up. He's a lovely little dog, Choppy he's called. He belongs to Mrs Fry, my neighbour. He's not supposed to go out by himself but sometimes he runs away, and he usually ends up with me, cos he knows he'll get a few treats.' His eyes widened. 'Choppy, he could smell the biscuits and he jumped up at her and his claws caught her stockings – she always wore lovely stockings. Before I could do anything she'd thrown the hot tea right in his face, deliberate it was, and kicked him in the side. And her face went all ugly, full of hate and spite. It was 'orrible.'

A shiver xylophoned down Frank's backbone. 'What did you do?'

'I tried to catch poor Choppy, but he ran off yelping. I turned to her and I said, 'You're a bad, cruel woman doing that to a little dog. I'm going to report you to the police.' He ran his hand over his face, breathing rapidly, his eyes moving from side to side, living the scene again.

Frank took his arm gently. 'It's all right, Benjie. Thank you for telling me. Was Choppy all right?'

Benjie nodded.

'Did you tell the police?'

'They were waiting for me when I got back home. They arrested me.'

'Benjie didn't tell anyone what she did to Choppy. He told me after he found Mrs Nicholson dead in the sluice.'

Frank didn't want to go on questioning him, he could see what an effort it had been for the man to relive the destruction of his dream – but he had to. 'Benjie,' he said gently, 'I want you to tell me about the morning you found her in the sluice, can you do that?'

Benjie nodded. 'I always get up nice an' early and I come to my hut and do a good morning's work before I come back to the Eel's Foot for my dinner, unless I cook something here. If I've been potting I don't eat them lobsters and crabs 'cos I can get a good price for them. But if I've caught a nice mackerel I eat that. If it's a sea bass I don't eat that, not that I don't want to, 'cos they're bootiful…'

Frank sighed. He wanted a big steak for his supper: thick and bloody. He nodded his head encouragingly.

'That morning I come to the sluice and I was thinking it'll soon be time for them swallows to come back to me – they make their nests under the sluice, they do. I goes to the wall and look down, as I do every morning, and there she was.' His eyes were even rounder as he pointed to the ground and the three of them stared at the spot as though he would bring her back to them.

66

'What did you think had happened?'

Benjie lifted his head and stared into Frank's eyes. 'She was naked. I should have looked away, but I didn't. I could see she was dead, her eyes were open staring at me, but I knew she couldn't see me. I thought the Black Dog may have got her and flung her in the sluice.'

'The black dog?' Surely he didn't mean Choppy?

'It's a legend round here, sir,' Elderkin whispered. 'Goes back to the sixteenth century, a huge black dog burst into the Dunwich church service and caused havoc. It left great scorch marks with its claws on the church door, they're still there. Ever since, when a calf's found dead or a pet dog ends up with its throat torn out, someone says they've seen the Black Dog.'

Benjie was swaying slowly from right to left and back again, almost in a trance. 'I heard the bells from the sea the night before she died. I told them in Eel's Foot and said there was going to be trouble.'

'It's another legend, sir – the bells of the churches lost to the sea ring out when there's going to be a disaster.'

All this mumbo-jumbo was too much for Frank; it was bad enough dealing with flesh-and-blood suspects, he couldn't cope with bells from the sea and phantom animals. 'Did you see anyone else on the beach or on your way to your hut that morning?'

'No, there was no-one; it was early, too early for the birdwatchers.'

'What about the evening before? Were you on the beach then?'

Benjie screwed up his face. 'What did I say, Mr Elderkin? I've forgotten, you see.'

'You said you left the beach early, about five.'

'That's right, I remember now. I'd had a good find, a nice big piece of amber.'

'He was in the Eel's Foot at six, sir. He stayed until they closed and he was in no state to do anything more than weave home and go to bed, according to the locals.'

'What did you do when you realised she was dead?'

'I wanted to hide in my hut and hope she'd go away. I was feared. But I knew what my ma would want me to do so I ran as fast as I could to the Eel's Foot and landlord rang the police.'

So Benjie was in the clear. Or was he? He looked at Benjie's strong arms and remembered the tone of his voice as he'd said, 'A bad, cruel woman.' The case was becoming clearer in his mind and a few more brush strokes had been painted on the increasingly unpleasant picture of Susan Nicholson.

Chapter 8

Wednesday, September 9, 1970

Laurel swallowed the last of the bacon; it was salty, crisp, with a full, meaty taste. 'Good bacon from a Suffolk pig,' Mabel had said. Good old Mabel.

After their walk the previous evening, they'd spent a companionable few hours in Mabel's cottage, mainly ministering to Muffin. He'd eaten most of a young rabbit he'd caught, and was suffering. They'd had to go on their walk to the sluice without him.

Laurel frowned. She'd been disappointed Mabel hadn't remembered what worried her when she saw Susan Nicholson near the sluice on the night she died. They'd paused at the spot Mabel had stopped that evening; Mabel's face wrinkled in concentration, but she couldn't remember what was worrying her.

Laurel's morning was free, but this afternoon was the staff meeting. She hoped the other members of the staff would be more welcoming than Shipster and Philip Nicholson. The headmaster had been friendly when they'd first met, but Shipster seemed to have turned him against her. She needed Nicholson on her side, and somehow she had to assert her authority at the staff meeting, without embarrassing or usurping him. Men.

She decided she'd explore the site, and go down to the beach, but first she'd introduce herself to Antonia Habershon, the school matron, who lived in the cottage on the other side of Mabel's. Mabel didn't seem too keen on Antonia, or Toni, as she was known. She didn't elaborate and Laurel hadn't probed.

She pulled on a sweater over a white shirt, and slipped on old loafers. As she opened the front door a stiff south-westerly wind filled her lungs. There was a silver Mini Cooper parked to the left of Toni's house and the curtains were drawn back. She knocked and the door opened immediately, as though she'd been expecting her... or someone else.

A woman with strawberry-blonde hair and a round, un-smiling face looked up at her. 'Yes?'

Laurel held out her hand. 'Hello, I'm Laurel Bowman. I thought I'd introduce myself as we're neighbours.' Not another surly member of staff? A smell of coffee wafted from the kitchen, competing with the perfume Toni Habershon was wearing. The perfume won.

Toni Habershon's handshake was firm, strong. Her arms, revealed by the short sleeves of her pink cotton blouse, were well-fleshed, smooth, and almost hairless. 'Pleased to meet you, Miss Bowman.' She hesitated. 'Please come in. Would you like a coffee, or are you busy? I expect you've a lot to do.'

Although the invitation was lukewarm Laurel decided she'd accept. Perhaps over a cup of coffee she might discover a friendlier side to Toni Habershon. As she walked in she saw the cottage had the same layout as hers.

The coffee was weak and the conversation stilted.

'How has the, er,' Laurel tried to phrase the question delicately, 'Susan Nicholson's murder affected staff relationships? It must be difficult, everyone suspecting each other.'

Toni flushed, her full lips thinning. 'Why do you want to know? It's nothing to do with you.'

Wrong topic. 'I'm part of the staff now, a senior member of staff. I'm interested in how people reacted. I want to make a positive contribution to the school, and it would help me to know if anyone is still upset. I'm sorry if I've embarrassed you.'

Toni scowled. The biscuit in her hand snapped in half, falling to the floor. She bent down and scrabbled on the stone tiles. 'Why should we be suspicious of each other? The police were sure the murderer was a passing stranger, a maniac.' She slammed the pieces of biscuit in the waste bin.

'The new inspector doesn't think that's the answer to the crime.'

'The new inspector?' Toni retorted, her plucked eyebrows rising with her voice.

She looks worried. Why? Interesting. 'Yes, Detective Inspector Diamond. I met him on Monday. He seems very efficient. He's moved into Mr Shipster's office with Sergeant Elderkin, and he's re-interviewing all the staff. Mabel likes him, thinks he's a clever man.' So did she, but she wasn't going to reveal her relationship with Frank, unless she had to. Hopefully their meeting on Sunday would put that one to bed. Putting Frank to bed? There was a cheering thought.

'Mabel!' Toni snorted. 'So she's transferred her affections from Stuart Elderkin to this new guy?'

Bitch. 'I don't think it's like that. Frank Diamond seems an astute man.'

Toni's eyes narrowed. 'You're a quick judge of character making up your mind on such a brief acquaintance.'

Laurel bit her lip. 'I'm going on what Mabel said.' Time to leave. 'Thanks for the coffee; er ... is it OK if I call you Toni?'

'We'd better stick to Miss Habershon and Miss Bowman for the time being. I don't think we'll be bosom pals, do you?'

In other words, she didn't want Laurel paying her visits. Was everyone in this school arses? 'As you like, Miss

Habershon. Goodbye.' She smiled, shrugged and hoped Toni Habershon felt a heel; somehow she didn't think so.

The air was fresh after the rancid atmosphere in Toni's cottage. Mabel, although dressed for work in a green overall with a carrier bag by her side, was searching for weeds amongst the well-tended plants in her front garden. She looked up at the sound of Laurel's footsteps on the gravel.

'Been visiting?'

Laurel nodded, not wanting to talk about the unpleasant half-hour she'd spent with Toni.

'Get on well, did you?' She wrinkled her nose.

Laurel shrugged her shoulders and spread her hands wide in a gesture which she hoped told Mabel all she wanted to know.

'Muffin likes Toni, can't think why.' She looked at her wrist watch. 'I better get to my kitchen.'

'How is he?'

Mabel frowned. 'Still dodgy. Hope he doesn't disgrace himself while I'm at work. He's a clean little dog but… you don't want to know about that.'

'I'm going for a walk round the grounds and I want to go down to the beach. Would you like me to take him with me? Is he up to a walk?'

'Would you? You're a love. I'll get Muffin and give you a key to the house. You can let him in when you get back; I'll pop back after doing breakfast. Keep him on the lead, would you? In case he decides to look for another rabbit.'

Mabel came back dragging a reluctant Muffin behind her, his ears down and a stubborn expression on his face.

'Did you hear the news?'

Laurel shook her head.

'Palestinians have got over one hundred and seventy hostages, a lot of them kiddies, plus the crew of the aeroplane, and they're all hidden somewhere in the Jordan

Desert. Scotland Yard Special Patrol has moved into Heathrow. I thought we'd have peace now, but it doesn't look like it.'

Laurel didn't know what to say. Her problems were small beer compared to what the hostages must be going through. Mabel patted Muffin and told him to 'Be a good boy.' She waved goodbye.

Muffin looked at her suspiciously, but by the time they'd reached the Holm oaks he raised his head, sniffed the air and wagged his tail. The wind was stronger as they reached the edge of the oaks; it was blowing directly from the south. Gaps in the hedge on the brink of the cliffs gave views of the blue sea, streaked with brown by the shifting sandbanks. Laurel turned right, Muffin following, and they meandered down sandy, narrow paths on the boundary between the cliff edge and the playing fields.

The noise of a machine and the smell of newly chopped grass made Laurel turn. A man on a mower was riding over the rugby pitch. He must be the caretaker and groundsman, Jim McFall. God, she hoped *he* was friendly. She could put up with matron not liking her, but she needed a good relationship with the groundsman. She walked towards him with Muffin prancing through the cut grass by her side.

She waved to the man and he turned off the machine. He watched her silently, still sitting, as she walked up to him. Laurel's heart felt like a flat, sad scone; she almost turned back.

'Hello. You must be Mr McFall. I'm Laurel Bowman, the senior mistress.'

McFall climbed down. At just over six feet, he was a little taller than Laurel, with a wiry, scrawny body. His hair, pale red, was heavily flecked with grey, and his arms and hands were covered in hair of a matching shade. Laurel guessed he was in his mid-fifties. He wiped his hand on a brown rag and shook her hand with minimal contact, as though he didn't want to contaminate her, or didn't want to touch her. She wasn't sure which.

'Pleased to meet you, Miss Bowman. Have you settled in?'

His voice was low, quiet, his accent... Glaswegian? 'Not quite; I'm taking my first walk round the grounds. The pitches look good. Do you have anyone to help you?'

'Thank you. No, I'm by myself.'

He didn't elaborate, but Laurel guessed he would have liked to. 'How many hockey pitches are there?'

'Just the one, Miss Bowman.' He pointed to a pitch nearer the house. 'The posts will go up next week. The netball court is just beyond, near the two tennis courts. All the equipment is kept in the wee pavilion.' He pointed to a small wooden building, not much larger than a superior garden shed overlooking the cricket pitch. 'It'll be good for the pupils to have a specialist PE teacher, especially the girls. Miss Letts and Miss Mapp had to take the girls' PE lessons. They'll be glad to see you.'

Hurrah. Someone would like her. 'What about an athletics track? I hope to make athletics one of the main summer sports. It's my first love – athletics.'

He looked her up and down, but not in a lascivious way. 'And what would be your speciality, Miss Bowman? You've the build for a hammer thrower.'

Laurel grinned. It was refreshing for someone to take an interest in sport. 'Close – the javelin, but I love all field sports; I have tried the heptathlon a few times. Are you a sportsman, Mr Mc Fall?'

His forehead wrinkled and his face seemed to draw in on itself. 'I used to be good at football... but I've not done any sport for years.' He blinked, seeming to wipe away painful memories. 'We'll make sure we have what you want for next

74

summer. You'll have to let me know in good time. We can use the winter pitches to make a running track. There is a high jump pit near the boundary, but it hasn't been used for years, I'll have to see to that.'

'Would you? That's marvellous, thank you so much. I can help you with the markings… if you'd like.' Had she gone too far? He might be offended, perhaps think she thought him incompetent. This place was making her nervous.

'That's a kind offer, Miss Bowman. We'll talk about it another time. If you can't find any specific equipment you want, let me know, I'll be able to tell you if we've got it.'

She was relieved to find a member of staff who was kind and welcoming. 'Thank you, I'm sure we'll work well together. Could you tell me how to find the steps to the beach, please?'

'Not taking Muffin for a swim, are ye? Mabel wouldn't like that. Keep walking south near the cliff edge and you'll soon see the steps. Now I better get on with the grass or Mr Shipster will be after me. You've met Mr Shipster?'

Laurel tried not to pull a face. 'Yes, I've asked him to find me an office, but he's a bit put out as he's had to move out of his own for the new inspector, Inspector Diamond, and Sergeant Elderkin.'

McFall climbed onto his mover. 'Aye, I've heard of him. So they're still looking for Mrs Nicholson's murderer?'

Laurel nodded. Muffin was pulling at the lead, wanting to get on with the walk. 'Did you know Mrs Nicholson well, Mr McFall?'

His face reddened and he frowned. 'Has someone said something?' he asked.

Laurel stepped back and nearly tripped over Muffin's lead. 'No, of course not. I'm curious as to what kind of woman she was.'

McFall turned on the mower, the harsh sound of the

75

engine matching his expression. 'She wasn't the kind of woman you'd want to know. She certainly wasn't the kind of woman I wanted to know. It's best if you leave it well alone, Miss Bowman and keep to teaching games.' He turned the wheel and the machine circled away from her, a plume of grass cuttings showering Muffin, who barked in annoyance.

What a change. What did he think she might have heard about him and Susan Nicholson? Could he be...? No. She liked him. But he *was* angry when she'd asked about her. No one wanted to talk about the dead woman. She turned back to the path near the cliff, and as McFall had said, she soon came to a flight of wooden steps leading to the beach. They were sturdily constructed of thick timbers with a metal hand rail. They led down the steep cliffs, the sides covered in shrubs and brambles. Half-way down was a platform and the remaining flight of steps turned at right angles, hugging the side of the cliff.

Muffin whimpered and backed away from the steps; Laurel slowed down, giving him time to hop sedately from step to step. The beach was deserted. At the top, above high-tide mark, there were clumps of sea holly and sea poppies, then a swathe of large stones leading to undulating ridges of pebbles, moulded by the tides, and at the sea's edge strips of glistening sand.

Muffin was keen to jump into the waves, but she'd promised Mabel to keep him on the lead. She kicked off her loafers and paddled into the sea so Muffin could frolic in the waves, yelping excitedly, snapping at fronds of loose bladder wrack floating in the water. He looked as though he was going to eat it, so she pulled it from between his teeth. It was glutinous between her fingers, smelling of distilled essence of ocean.

'No, Muffin. Rabbit and seaweed. Not a good mixture.'

The sand was pleasantly gritty between her toes as she

wiggled her feet, the waves lapping round her ankles. As children, she and Angela had spent most of the summer holidays on Felixstowe beach; she'd taught Angela to swim and played with her: building castles and moats. Angela's favourite game was building sand-shoes, covering Laurel's feet with wet sand and decorating the shoes with shells and pebbles. She'd get cross when Laurel didn't take enough care slipping her feet from the case of sand, and Angela's masterpieces crumbled.

Laurel's eyes pricked with tears as she remembered: Angela laughing as she splashed her in the sea; Angela licking an ice-cream cornet as they walked along the promenade.

Her tears stopped. Memories replaced by horrific imaginings: Angela fighting for her life; Angela terrified as her clothes were ripped from her; Angela choking, gasping for breath as the air was squeezed from her body; Angela dead under the pier.

Muffin jumped up, scratching her legs.

She bent down and ruffled his coat. 'Good boy, I'm all right. Let's go back. Soon be time to get ready for the staff meeting.'

Muffin flopped at the bottom of the steps, a mutinous look in his eye. Laurel laughed, picked him up and, cradling him in her arms, climbed the steps. On the platform, half-way up, she paused, and turned to look out to sea, holding Muffin against her face. His rough hair was comforting against her skin and he smelt deliciously of dog. She squeezed him; he gave a yelp of pleasure and licked her cheek.

At the top of the steps she turned right to go back to the cottage, but Muffin pulled on the lead, wanting to go in the opposite direction. He'd the right idea, she didn't like going back the same way on a walk; they'd circle the grounds and she'd take a look at the abbey ruins.

She hadn't realised how large an area they covered. They circled the crumbling walls until they came to the gateway, its arch intact, swags of ivy hanging from the flints. She imagined ox-driven carts passing between its thick walls, delivering goods to the kitchens, the brewery and the forge. Inside the walls no buildings remained, but the grass was as well-kept by the rabbits as the playing fields were by Jim McFall. She held the lead loosely so Muffin could wander where he wanted: from one ruined wall to another, sniffing and squirting urine every few feet, looking pleased with himself as he scraped at the grass with his hind legs.

They came out of the same gateway and walked towards the ruins of the leper hospital. Only the chapel remained, and although roofless, the walls were almost intact, and many of the gothic window arches complete.

She sat down and rested her back against a wall. It was sheltered, the grass soft; the hum of insects and the murmur of the surf were soothing. Muffin curled up beside her and licked her hand. She stroked his back, her shoulders relaxing, and her breath softening.

She was woken by a strident voice. It came from behind the walls. It was a belligerent woman's voice. Toni Habershon's? How embarrassing. She put a hand over Muffin's mouth to stop him barking and hoped they'd go away and wouldn't discover her.

'You promised. How much longer do I...' The words faded, carried away by the wind. She couldn't hear the reply, but it sounded like a man's voice. 'I risked... if you don't... I won't wait... Inspector Diamond' the woman continued.

At the mention of Frank's name, she strained to hear more. She crouched, hugging Muffin to her, and edged towards the sounds. Should she walk out and confront them? She was torn between curiosity and embarrassment. Could she suddenly appear and pretend she hadn't heard anything?

The voices were fading. She scrambled up, caught a foot in a rabbit hole, tripped, and Muffin pulled free, running off in the opposite direction to the voices, his lead dragging behind him. After another rabbit – Laurel chased after him. Damn. She mustn't lose Muffin, she didn't want to let Mabel down. Who were they? What had they said about Frank Diamond?

Laurel carefully picked her way over the gravel path towards the main house, precariously wobbling in her high-heeled court shoes. Reaching the tarmac road, she lengthened her stride as she wanted to be early for the staff meeting to make sure she had a seat next to Philip Nicholson.

The meeting was at two in the music room on the ground floor of the house. The room was empty. It was spacious, full of light, with marble fireplaces at both ends, and full-length windows overlooking the front of the house. Pier glass mirrors, their surfaces misted and covered in brown spots, filled the spaces between the windows, light reflected back into them by another row of mirrors on the opposite wall. The ceiling was ornately plastered with crumbling putti and broken swags of leaves and flowers. An upright piano stood against the far wall and the wooden floorboards, the brown staining worn away in places, completed a sorry picture. A hundred years ago the local gentry were entertained here. Now it was a cold and musty space. The room needed brightening up if it was to inspire the pupils to enjoy music and drama. Warren Ringrose, a most suitable name for a teacher of those subjects, needed some advice.

There was a long mahogany table surrounded by plastic chairs in the centre of the room. Brisk footsteps approached and Dorothy Piff, carrying a tray of glasses, a jug of water, and several ashtrays, came in.

'Miss Bowman! You're nice and early.' She carefully slid

the tray onto the table.

'Can I help you?'

Dorothy beamed. 'Would you place the glasses round the table and pour some water into each?'

'Only eight places?'

Dorothy nodded, and headed for the door. 'I'll be back in a minute.' She returned with a pile of paper clutched to her bosom. Laurel helped her to set out a sheet of blotting paper, an agenda and a sharpened pencil beside each glass of water. There was one setting at either end of the table and three down each side.

'Where does the headmaster sit?'

Dorothy pointed to one end of the table and took up the seat opposite. 'I always sit here. I take the minutes.'

'And Mr Shipster?'

'To the head's right.'

Laurel sat down opposite Shipster's chair and put her file on the table.

'Mr Thornback usually sits there, but I suppose…'

'Mr Thornback? Head of science, I believe?'

'Yes, he's next in line after Mr Shipster.' She smiled. 'Of course, not now you're here.'

'Do you think he'll make a fuss?'

Dorothy Piff pursed her lips as she squared up her notebook on top of the blotting paper. 'He'll make a fuss when he sees you,' she said. 'Mr Thornback is… no I mustn't gossip; I'll leave you to make up your own mind.'

'Dorothy Piff, you're a tease.'

Miss Piff raised a warning finger to her lips as footsteps rang out on the wooden floor.

Philip Nicholson, Shipster close behind him, came into the room

'Excellent results again, Robert, congratulations,' Nicholson said.

80

Shipster was smiling. 'Thank you, Headmaster, I do…' He stopped both walking and talking when he saw Laurel.

'Miss Bowman. You're prompt I see. Mr Thornback usually sits…' Nicholson said. 'But I expect he won't mind.'

Laurel smiled and nodded at them. 'I'm sure he'll understand.'

There was no time for further discussion of who should sit where, as the rest of the staff trooped in: they stared at Laurel, some nodding, some smiling and after glances between them, sat down. The man next to Laurel was slightly built with sloping shoulders, untidy brown hair and an untrimmed beard and moustache; he wore a bobbly Fair Isle jumper over a grey shirt. He smiled shyly, and then looked quickly away.

He *must* be Henry Thornback, head of science. He looked like a scientist.

'Welcome back to the autumn term everyone. May I first introduce our new senior mistress, Laurel Bowman.' Nicholson indicated the people round the table. 'Mr Shipster you already know.'

Laurel smiled at him but all she received was a sharp nod.

Nicholson pointed to the man next to Shipster. 'Mr Henry Thornback, head of science.'

That would teach her to stereotype people. Henry Thornback stood up, reached across the table and shook her hand. He was a tall, attractive man, with wavy, light brown hair, a large nose and blue, come-to-bed eyes. His hand shake was firm, warm and lasted just a little too long.

'Enchanted, Miss Bowman.'

Nicholson coughed, frowning. 'Going round the table, next is Miss Emilia Mapp, our head of modern languages.'

Miss Mapp, a young woman in her late twenties, waved a finger-splayed hand at Laurel. She had frizzy brown hair, a pleasant freckled face and large teeth which she displayed in a cheery grin.

'Miss Piff, you know.'

Dorothy Piff waved her pencil.

Nicholson gestured to a woman sitting next to the man she'd assumed was Thornback. 'Miss Vanessa Letts, head of English.'

Miss Letts' face was grave, unsmiling. She lowered her head in a slow regal nod. She was middle-aged, tall, her dark hair pulled back in a severe bun, her long nose slightly hooked.

Laurel couldn't imagine she'd enjoyed helping out with girls' PE.

'And lastly Mr Warren Ringrose, head of art, drama and music.'

This was the man she'd thought fitted the body of a scientist, he certainly didn't look at all artistic.

'Right, introductions over.' He picked up the agenda. 'Now we'll start with –'

'Thank you, Mr Nicholson,' Laurel interrupted, ignoring his startled look. 'I'm very pleased to be here as senior mistress of Blackfriars –' sometimes a little white lie was needed '– and to meet you. I hope I can add my expertise in games and PE to the school curriculum. I believe several of you already help in this area and I'll be glad to assist you. I'm sure you have expertise in sports which are not my strong points. As senior mistress and part of the senior management,' she nodded to Nicholson and Shipster, 'I hope I'll be able to add to the strength of the team and to improve the efficiency and effectiveness of the school. Thank you.'

Shipster was glaring at her, Nicholson was gulping, Miss Mapp was beaming and nodding in approval, Miss Letts was sniffing, Mr Ringrose was staring at the papers in front of him, Mr Thornback had tilted back his chair, eyebrows raised, and Miss Piff was neatly scribbling shorthand.

'Thank you, Miss Bowman.'

Nicholson looked shocked but not angry, perhaps even admiring. Shipster's face was an unattractive shade of puce.

'I'm sure we'll all benefit from your expertise.' Nicholson paused, and looked again at the agenda. 'Item one.' He informed the staff about the police presence and they would be re-interviewed by Inspector Diamond.

Laurel looked at the staff, especially those to whom this might be fresh news. Ringrose hunched into himself; Thornback shrugged and Miss Letts played with the string of pearls round her throat and murmured, 'Is this necessary?' No one answered her.

'Mr Shipster, would you take us through the exam results?'

Shipster passed round papers showing an analysis of the school's O and A level GCE results.

They seemed mediocre, apart from the French results, which were good, and maths, which were outstanding. She'd have to re-evaluate Shipster; he must be a good teacher, unless he terrified his pupils into superhuman efforts. What was his secret?

Nicholson went on to talk about school numbers. They were down in all years, especially in the first year of entry. There were murmurs round the table, and staff looked worried. 'I'll need to discuss this with the governors; staff numbers may have to be reduced.' He looked round. 'Your situations are, of course, safe. I'm afraid some part-timers may have to have their hours reduced.'

There were looks of relief from some members of staff and Shipster's thin lips twisted into what might have been a smile.

'The next item is the Horatio Nelson Scholarships.' Nicholson looked at Laurel. 'I'm not sure if you know about these, Miss Bowman. Each year two scholarships are awarded to orphans of naval officers; all fees are paid and a gratuity is given to help with uniform, games kit, etc. This year we have two boys joining us in the first year.'

'Are the scholarships only for boys?' Laurel asked. There was a collective intake of breath. Goodness, it wasn't such a controversial question, was it?

'No. We have had some girls in the past.' He didn't elaborate and moved swiftly on to give out rotas for supervising prep, and other duties.

There was a knock on the door and Mabel wheeled a trolley half-way into the room; on it was an urn, cups and saucers and plates of cake and biscuits. 'Ready for tea, Mr Nicholson?'

'Thank you, Mabel, please bring it in.'

'Would you like me to stay and pour?'

'No, thank you, we can manage,' he said

You mean some female member of staff will pour.

'I think we've covered everything. You can ask any questions over tea. Now, who wants to be mother?'

Laurel decided it wasn't a role she wanted to make her own. She looked round the table. The obvious choice would have been Miss Piff, but her head was bent over her notes as she read her shorthand, probably checking she hadn't made any mistakes.

'I'll pour the tea,' Miss Mapp volunteered.

'You do it, Thornback,' Nicholson whispered, as Emilia Mapp walked towards the trolley. 'She'll break the crockery again.'

'Allow me,' Thornback said, springing up and putting his arm round Emilia's shoulders. He poured tea from the urn and placed cups and saucers on the table. 'Help yourselves. Only eight slices of Mabel's fruitcake, so only one slice each.'

Laurel, cup and saucer in hand, looked round. Nicholson and Thornback had lit cigarettes and Miss Piff was looking at them enviously. Who should she talk to first? Emilia Mapp seemed pleasant and unthreatening. She walked over to her. 'Hello. How many years have you been here, Miss Mapp?'

'Two years,' she said, waving her cup and slopping tea into the saucer. 'I'm the baby, apart from two part-timers.'

'I'm surprised at the small number of residential staff. Now I understand why I've such a full timetable and so many duties. I presume it's the same for everyone?' She tilted her head questioningly.

'More or less.' Emilia lowered her voice. 'Apart from Mr Shipster, but then he does the timetable.' She bit her lip. 'Sorry, I shouldn't have said that.'

'Don't worry. When I know the ropes a bit better I'll look at the duties in detail, and make sure everyone has a fair share.' Yes, that was an area she might be able to claim, the duty rosters.

'I was interested to hear about the scholarship pupils. Do you know much about that: when it started, how they choose the children? To qualify do the children have to have lost both parents, or just their fathers?'

'If you've lost both parents you have precedence, but mostly they've lost their fathers.'

'When was a scholarship last given to a girl?'

Emilia shook her head. 'The last one was before I started here.'

'What did she do after she left? Do you know? Did she go to university?'

Emilia glanced towards Nicholson and Shipster who were deep in conversation. 'She didn't actually leave, she ran away,' she whispered.

'Gosh! What happened?'

'I'm not sure, but they never found her – the police, I mean. They thought she ran away to London with some man. Warren knows more, he talked to me about it once, and he was really upset. Her name was Felicity something. Warren said she was musically gifted and he was hoping he'd get her into a music college. He said he couldn't believe she'd disappear like that.'

'No clue why she ran away? Boyfriend trouble?'

'You'll have to ask Warren.'

Laurel glanced at him. He was seated at the piano, the curved lid raised, and he was softly stroking the keys, raising faintly discernible notes. She put her crockery on the trolley, walked over to him and leant against the piano

'Hello, Mr Ringrose. This is where you teach, I believe?'

He jerked up as though unused to being singled out. 'Er, yes. I teach music and drama here. I've got a separate art room in the new block.' He hesitated, seeming unsure of how to proceed with the conversation.

'Which subject to you enjoy teaching most?'

He put a hand to his bearded chin and looked in different directions, as though she'd asked him a difficult conundrum.

'Drama, I suppose. Most children like showing off. We haven't got many talented musicians or artists. Sometimes it can get a bit out of hand – the drama, I mean. They get carried away.'

Poor man, he didn't look like someone who'd easily control children. 'They must enjoy it, being able to let off steam. It's the same with games, they let out all that pent-up energy and have a good shout and scream. It makes them calmer for the more academic lessons. Your colleagues should be grateful.'

'You let them shout? Mr Shipster won't approve – he's always coming into my lessons and bringing them to order if we make too much noise.'

'I think drama and dance are an essential part of the curriculum. Do you do any dance?'

Ringrose shook his head. 'No. Sometimes we've done a

bit for a school production, but I'm not very good at it.'

'If you'd like me to help you I'd be delighted. I've taught dance. Perhaps I can come and help with the drama lessons and we can try out some dance.'

'Would you? I'd be very grateful. Thank you, Miss Bowman.'

He sounded genuine. Perhaps she'd be able to help him with the discipline as well, subtly of course. 'Please call me Laurel.' She smiled at him. 'I was talking with Miss Mapp and she told me about a scholarship girl who ran away. Did you teach her, Warren? Emilia said she was musically gifted.'

His shoulders slumped. 'Oh, you mean Felicity. She was a lovely girl and her piano playing, although not yet technically perfect, had so much feeling and passion for a girl of her age; she also had a lovely soprano voice.'

'Had? You think something happened to her?'

'No. No. I've no reason to think that… I often wonder what happened to her. It wasn't like her at all – to run away. She wasn't an impulsive girl, very shy and quiet, except when she was playing or singing, then she came to life.'

'What did she look like?'

'Why do you want to know?' He looked up at her, his eyes questioning – suspicious?

'It completes the picture.'

'She was small, slight, with beautiful hands, long flexible fingers.'

'Was she attractive? Apart from the hands?'

Warren pulled at his beard. 'Yes, very pretty, auburn hair, green eyes.' He shook his head sorrowfully.

Two small, red-headed, attractive women: first Felicity going missing, then Susan being murdered. Coincidence? Possibly. 'I'm sorry, Warren, she obviously meant a lot to you.'

He flinched. 'No, not in that way,' he whispered.

87

She inwardly remonstrated with herself. She should be concentrating on forming good relationships with the staff, not interrogating them. 'I'll talk to you next week about helping with the drama, when I've sorted my own timetable out.'

He nodded silently, returning to the keys of the piano.

Only Miss Letts and Mr Thornback to chat to. Neither looked her cup of tea, but at least Miss Letts didn't have a lecherous gleam in her eye.

She was standing by a window looking out over the drive, her face sour, mouth turned down, deep lines running from nostrils past her lips. She looked to be about forty. 'Hello, Miss Letts. I'm pleased to meet you at last.' Laurel held out her hand.

Vanessa Letts stared at it as if it was dead rat. She slowly extended her fingers and lightly touched Laurel's, immediately drawing back, as though she thought she would be contaminated by the contact. 'How do you do, Miss Bowman?'

Blimey! Her upper-crust accent was excruciating, so crystal sharp it was a wonder she didn't cut her tongue. People didn't talk like that. This was BBC circa 1950. She half-expected her to go into a rendition of the 'Rain in Spain'.

'I hope you have settled in satisfactorily.' She looked Laurel up and down with an expression of incredulity, as though she'd never seen such a tall woman. Laurel wouldn't mind, but Miss Letts was at least five six or seven.

'Yes, thank you. Everyone's been most kind.' Gosh. It was catching.

Miss Letts eyed her suspiciously, as though suspecting her of taking the mickey.

'You teach English, I believe?'

Miss Letts inclined her head. 'Yes, indeed. I have an

honours degree in English literature, you know.' She smiled, her lips tight, no teeth on display. 'A first-class honours degree.'

'Really? How long have you been here, Miss Letts?' Laurel decided she didn't want to be on first name terms.

'Apart from Mr Shipster I'm the longest serving member of staff,' she said, not answering the question.

'Are you a local woman?' Somehow she didn't think she was.

'Certainly not. My family originated in Cambridge; my father, Major Letts, was a descendant of a long line of Letts, of Norman origin, you know.'

'So your ancestors came over to rape, pillage and snaffle all the land?' Miss Letts' snobbishness had touched a sore spot. 'I come from a long line of Saxon yokels. I think I'd do well in the fields cultivating my few furlongs, don't you?' She laughed, hoping to get her point across in a light-hearted way. Mistake.

Miss Letts' nostrils flared. 'You certainly have the build of a peasant,' she sneered, 'but I suppose that's useful *teaching games*.'

The tone of her last two words suggested this occupation was a fitting employment for Laurel.

She slowly nodded her head and moved away to talk to Mr Shipster.

Laurel was sure she was moaning about her as Mr Shipster looked pleased and nodded his head to her.

She could have kicked herself: she should have kept her thoughts to herself.

'Has the old bat upset you?

A mixture of Old Spice and cigarette smoke invaded her nostrils. She turned. Henry Thornback was as near as he could get to her without touching, a grin on his face and his eyes wrinkling in amusement. His face was level with hers and she had to admit he was a relief after the airs of Miss Letts.

'I think I may have annoyed her. I must apologise before the meeting finishes.'

'I wouldn't bother: she'll only give you the fish eye as she looks at you down her patrician nose.'

Laurel suppressed a laugh. 'You're not a fan of Miss Letts?'

'I prefer my women with a bit of meat on them,' he said, eyeing Laurel as though she was a piece of prime steak.

'Remember that meat is muscle, Mr Thornback, and muscle can be tough if it's been exercised. I'm sure you wouldn't like to strain your jaws on some well-flexed biceps, would you?'

Instead of taking offence, he laughed uproariously, causing heads to turn their way. 'Great put down, Miss Bowman. I also like my women sassy. You're doing well, two out of three. Can you guess the third?'

She had a shrewd idea but she had to admire his persistence. 'No, I can't, and what is more, I don't want to know.'

He winked at her. 'I'll tell you some other time, when we're not being spied on.' He glanced toward Nicholson.

He was watching them, and didn't look pleased. Did he think she was flirting with Thornback and was jealous? Or did he think her behaviour was not up to the correct standard for a senior mistress? He could be right there. She turned back to Thornback, who hadn't moved and who was staring at her, his gaze moving from her face to her breasts and back again as he smoked his cigarette. Soon he'd be standing back and giving her legs the once over.

'Mr Thornback I'd be grateful if you'd stop looking at me as though I were a piece of pork loin on a butcher's counter.' Why did there always have to be a token philanderer, who you knew, as soon as you met him, he would try and seduce you? If he'd tried it on with her before she was hardly through the door, she wondered if he'd tried it on Susan Nicholson. Would he be put off because she was the headmaster's wife? She doubted it. Men like him were always willing to risk their hand – or some other part of their anatomy.

'What do you think about having to be re-interviewed about Mrs Nicholson's murder? Are you worried?'

His eyebrows arched, making his large nose protrude, and turning him into Punch. Laurel bit her lip.

'Where did that come from? What made you think of *her*?' he sneered.

'Oh, I don't know. Must be all this talk of meat eaters – carnivores. Carnivores are killers,' she mused.

'Are you accusing me of murdering Susan Nicholson?' he hissed, his suave charm disappearing, replaced by alarm.

'Good heavens, what made you think that? Or have you a guilty conscious?'

All gaiety gone, he glared at her. 'What business is it of yours? You didn't know the woman, did you? I'd stick to doing your job, Miss Bowman and keep your nose out of matters that have nothing to do with you.' He swung round and marched from the room.

She didn't think she'd be bothered by him again, but he wasn't the first person today to tell her to stop asking about Susan Nicholson. She wished Sunday was here so she could see Frank Diamond and tell him about people's reactions. Should she tell him? They were only *her* thoughts. Was she being unfair to her colleagues? Shouldn't she be loyal to the school? It really wasn't her business, but a woman had been murdered… and a schoolgirl had disappeared. Finding killers was addictive. She was more intrigued by these mysteries than thoughts of the new term and teaching girls hockey and netball.

She moved over to Miss Piff, who was still checking her shorthand, frowning as she seemed to puzzle over an annotation she'd made. 'Hello, Miss Piff. You look worried. Are you finding it difficult to translate those squiggles into ordinary words? It's a mystery to me; it must take years of training to master shorthand.'

Miss Piff looked up above the frames of her spectacles. 'It's just a few words I'm having difficulty with; I'll leave it for a few hours, usually the sense comes back after a time.'

Laurel sat down beside her. 'I think I've met most of the residential staff. I met Toni Habershon this morning, before I took Muffin for a walk. She wasn't very friendly.' She waited, hoping Miss Piff might educate her about Toni, but all she did was sniff, tilt her chin as much as to say, what did you expect?

Laurel ploughed on. 'I also met Jim McFall on my walk. He seemed helpful and cooperative.'

Miss Piff nodded, looking like Minerva's wise owl. 'Jim's a good worker, but he keeps himself apart from the rest of the staff. I have a lot of time for him. He may seem truculent at times, but he has his reasons.'

Dorothy Piff you *are* a wise old bird. 'Thanks for that information, Dorothy.'

Miss Piff flushed at the remark, or the use of her Christian name, or both.

'I asked him some trifling question about Susan Nicholson and he reacted most strangely; seemed to warn me off.' She waited for Miss Piff's reaction. Was she going to get the brush off from her as well?

'Now why should he do that? Everyone is getting paranoid again, now the investigation has got fresh legs.'

So Dorothy Piff isn't worried about such questions. 'I

must have a word with the headmaster before I leave. I'll probably see you tomorrow.'

Dorothy Piff nodded, smiling. 'Any time, my dear, I'll be pleased to put the kettle on for you.'

Laurel thought of Miss Piff wearing the chrome kettle on her head and smiled. She went over to Philip Nicholson who was shuffling his papers into a file. As Miss Piff left the room, nodding to them as she opened the door, they were alone.

Laurel mentally girded her loins, not only against his prejudices but against his attractive appearance and velvet voice. 'Mr Nicholson, have you given any thought to my office?' She tried to keep her voice light and unthreatening.

He coughed. To give him more time?

'Mr Shipster has found you a space. I think you should see him.'

'You mean he hasn't informed you of the room I'm to have?'

He flushed and the corners of his mouth twisting. 'Of course, I know,' he snapped.

'Then why can't you tell me? Is it such a rat-hole?'

He looked into her eyes for a few seconds, then the corners of his mouth creased upwards as a smile broke over his face. 'You're quite right, it is. I'm sorry; I'll tell Shipster it won't do. There are some unused rooms on the top floor of the main house. Would you object to one of those? Some have lovely sea views.'

The bolts of anxiety that held her backbone rigid, melted. Her first victory. She could have kissed him. Did she want to kiss him? No. He was a recent widower. A possible suspect? She'd been told about his alibi. She was glad she didn't have to put him on her list of suspects. That was what she was compiling in her head: a list of murder suspects. She couldn't help herself.

'Thank you for being so understanding, Laurel.'

She liked the way he said her name: he rolled it round his tongue as though he enjoyed each letter.

'Would you have supper with me tonight? At my house? We can talk about your role in the school. I realise now how much you'll be able to give to all of us. I want to help and make that possible.'

What could she say? Was it going to be this easy? 'I'd be delighted, Mr Nicholson, er, Philip.'

'My house, seven. Nothing special for supper; Mabel's made me a fish pie. Hope that's acceptable?'

She nodded, thanked him and, head whirling, left the room.

Chapter 9

Thursday, September 10, 1970

Laurel smiled as she looked round the room on the top floor of the main house. Her own office – at last. Earlier in the afternoon it had been cleaned by a woman from Dunwich, and furniture hauled up the stairs by Philip and Jim McFall. There was a red Turkish carpet covering the floor, leaving a surround of polished floorboards, a good-sized desk, several chairs, including two armchairs and a coffee table. Built-in cupboards and mahogany bookcase were capacious storage spaces. All very satisfactory.

Light poured in through two barred windows; Philip told her the room was originally the nursery. She reached between the bars and pushed up one of the sash windows to let in some fresh air. There was a good view of the sea.

Her optimism about her new job heightened as she put books onto shelves, pens and pencils in desk drawers and carefully placed a wooden-framed photograph on the desk. In it two girls smiled back at her. Her fingers lingered over one of the faces: Angela, twelve years old, in a bathing costume, blue with red flowers, sitting on a breakwater on Felixstowe beach. Bud-breasts discernible, her Titian hair blowing above her head as though it had a life of its own. – a pre-pubescent Raphaelite beauty. Laurel sat next to her: seventeen, broad shoulders, blonde hair streaked white from the sun, a protective arm round her sister. Angela. Dad had taken the photo and given her this tinted copy to take to college. She liked to remember Angela like this: a smiling, happy, carefree child, with no adult worries or concerns, unaware of her attractiveness.

The Angela of her nightmares lay on wet pebbles under the pier; purple marks on her neck, a swollen tongue lolling from her mouth, her eyes open, but unseeing. Laurel sat down at the desk and pushed the photograph away from her.

Would she have taken this job if Angela were still alive? No. By now she'd have been married. She might have looked for promotion in another school, but not a job like this: a private school in the middle of nowhere. She wouldn't have been drawn into the murder of Susan Nicholson, or met Susan's husband, Philip.

After accepting his invitation to dinner, she'd walked to his house wishing she hadn't, but not sure why. His large, modern house was isolated, to the right of the main drive as you came into the campus. A Land Rover was on the drive and the garage door was open. Philip stepped out, his back towards her. There was an impressive display of tools hanging from peg-boarding, and a red sports car. It looked like an E-type Jaguar. He turned and quickly pulled down the metal door.

'Gosh, Philip, I didn't have you down as a sports car type.' Idiot. She shouldn't have said that: it might have been his wife's car.

'I don't use it much; relic of my former wild life.'

She must watch what she said: she didn't want to painfully remind him of his dead wife. But the car hadn't looked old – it had open headlights and front indicators below the bumpers. It must be a Series 2, which had only come out in 1968.

Over dinner she'd been drawn to him: sorry for his bereavement, attracted by his looks and voice, intrigued by his easy conversation. Why was he being so friendly after the initial coldness? Trying to make up for his and Mr Shipster's treatment? His sudden change of attitude was unsettling, as though he wanted to appease her, as though she worried him. Why? She didn't think she was so intimidating. He'd made a point of not touching her, when leaning over to put her plate on the table, or passing the salt. For some reason, which she couldn't explain, she was glad he hadn't. She didn't stay long after the meal.

There was a rap on her office door, she jumped, and, as though summoned by her thoughts, Philip Nicholson came into the room.

'I thought you'd like some coffee.' He carried a tray on which were a thermos flask and two mugs. 'Mabel said you didn't take sugar.'

She hadn't heard his footsteps on the stairs. Had her thoughts deafened her, or did he move like a Mohican? 'Wonderful!' She moved some books from the desk.

He poured coffee into the two striped mugs. 'You didn't want black, I hope.'

'Do I have an option? – No, white's fine. Thank you.'

He pulled another chair to the desk and sat down, as though assuming his visit was welcome. 'Settled in? Let me know if there's anything you need.'

'The room's lovely and thanks for moving the furniture.' No point in prevaricating. 'A telephone would be welcome.'

'Ah, a telephone… yes, that should be possible.'

'With an outside line?'

He shook his head. 'Sorry, no. The only outside lines are from my office, Mr Shipster's, and Miss Piff's. If you want to use the phone you have to dial Miss Piff she'll put you through. She keeps a log of all external calls and you'll get a bill at the end of each month for any personal calls. There's a public phone in the dining room, some of the staff use it, and the pupils are allowed one phone call a week to home.'

Laurel wrinkled her nose. She didn't fancy using that. She'd have to use the one in Dunwich. She didn't want her parents' number logged down. 'Why are there so many restrictions?'

'Mainly cost. We're on a tight budget. I'd like to be able to trust my colleagues, but...' Philip leaned back and drained his cup. 'I was reading through your application and references this morning. I didn't pay them much attention before, I'm afraid.'

What was he going on about? 'I hope they're satisfactory – or are you going to dismiss me before term starts?'

He smiled and shook his head. 'Certainly not, we were lucky to get you. I was intrigued by a remark in one of the references: it seems you were responsible for solving several school crimes; in fact, you seemed to have built up quite a reputation as an amateur detective. Tell me about it, I'm intrigued.'

Who'd written that about her? Probably the chairman of governors; he'd made a point of congratulating her whenever another 'case' was solved. 'Really, it's nothing. It wasn't something on my official list of duties – somehow I seemed to get involved. I suppose it's my suspicious mind and I don't like mysteries.'

He leaned across the desk towards her. 'Don't worry; I won't expect you to act as the school's own Sherlock Holmes when we have a bit of petty thieving. Tell me about an incident. I'm interested to find out how other schools work.'

What a strange thing to focus on; shouldn't he be more interested in her organisational skills? 'I suppose the most serious crime was when some of the teachers started to get obscene phone calls to their homes, it was very upsetting for them, especially if another member of the family took the call, even more so if it was one of their children.'

His face wrinkled in disgust. 'That's despicable! I'm glad you caught the guilty student. How did you find out who it was?'

98

Laurel wriggled in her seat. 'A process of elimination: pupils the targeted staff had in common, pupils they may have upset and a bit of intuition, I suppose. I'd rather not talk about this if you don't mind.'

His mouth turned down at the corners. 'You're drawn to mysteries, are you?'

'No more than the next man or woman.' She placed her mug on the tray and pushed it towards him, hoping he'd take the hint. The edge of the tray caught the photograph frame.

He righted it, then turned it towards him and stared at the photo, his face expressionless. 'Who is this with you?' He pointed to Angela.

Damn. What should she say? 'A childhood friend, Angela.'

'She's beautiful; she must be a lovely woman now.' There was a catch in his voice, a sad note.

'I'm afraid Angela's dead. She had an accident.' It was close to the truth.

He placed the photo back on the desk, facing away from him, as though he couldn't bear to look at it. 'Too many deaths of young, beautiful women.'

Laurel saw Angela through his eyes. Her Titian hair – that's what had got to him – the red flames encircling Angela's head: a painful reminder of his wife's red hair. Poor man.

He picked up the tray and silently left her office.

Laurel went to the window and looked beyond the line of Holm oaks to the blue-brown sea; her hand grasping one of the bars. She imagined children playing here in the nursery: perhaps there was a rocking horse, small desks where the governess made them copy phrases from the Bible in copperplate script; in the late afternoon, besides a winter fire, she would read them stories suitable for young ladies and gentlemen

The stale, dusty smell of the room had been blown away by the sea wind. She pulled down the sash window. Two more days and she would talk to Frank Diamond and persuade him not to reveal her sister had been murdered. She was looking forward to seeing him. She not only wanted his agreement he wouldn't tell the school about her sister, but she wanted to tell him what she'd learnt about some of the members of staff and Susan Nicholson. She hoped he'd reciprocate and tell her how his investigation was going. Somehow she didn't think that was likely.

Chapter 10

Frank gazed into his empty teacup as though he might be able to divine the name of the murderer by the patterns made by the tea leaves. A depressing day, made worse by the news of another BOAC plane hijacked on its way to Beirut with twenty-five children aboard.

'Well, Sergeant Elderkin, I don't know about you, but I've learnt very little new from today's work.'

It was the end of the afternoon and they were in their 'office', the room vacated by Shipster. They had interviewed all the staff. The only staff in the clear were Nicholson, in Colchester with his mother; Miss Mapp, who had been with a school party in France, and Miss Piff, whose alibi was provided by her sister. As for the rest not one had an alibi, and so far, no one seemed to have a motive for murder. Even Mabel Grill was a suspect, much to Elderkin's fury. As Muffin was unable to take the witness stand, Frank couldn't accept him as Mabel Grill's alibi. Mabel was the last person to see Susan Nicholson alive; she couldn't prove she wasn't her murderer. Frank hoped she wasn't: her fruit cake and frequent cups of coffee and tea during the day were small spots of sunshine between grey clouds of frustration.

Stuart Elderkin sighed, the outgoing air pushing out his upper lip as he slumped in his chair. 'It's true we haven't learnt anything new, but…' he grimaced and pulled his ear '… it's different to the last time they were interviewed, just after the murder. I think some of them want to say more, but they're… scared, or something.'

Elderkin's face once more reminded Frank of a bloodhound: those waving dewlaps, the brown soulful eyes, and the large, twitching nose: a hound on the scent, picking

101

up molecules of fear and guilt, sensing the need of people to relieve themselves of secrets. He'd also felt it, but Elderkin was comparing their attitudes to how they were months ago. 'I think you're right, Stuart, but I didn't feel it with all of them.' What would Elderkin think of his next suggestion? Would he think he was playing games, not taking his remarks seriously? It would be interesting, though. 'Stuart, I'd like you to write down the names of the people you thought were close to telling us some new facts; I'll do the same and we'll compare notes.'

Stuart looked puzzled. 'Why don't I just tell you?'

'Pander to me, Stuart; also write down your thoughts about them.'

Stuart sighed, and reached for his pad. 'I've always hated tests and teachers,' he grumbled, bending over, a hand shielding his writing from Frank's eyes.

Frank wrote down: Henry Thornback, Jim McFall, and Warren Ringrose. He waited until Elderkin put down his biro. 'I'll let you see mine, if I can see yours,' he smirked.

Stuart face creased. 'I bet my list's longer than yours.'

'Longer doesn't mean better, Sergeant.'

'It does where I come from.'

Frank shook his head, he'd let Elderkin have the last word, especially as he couldn't think of a pithy reply. He laid his sheet of paper on the desk and tapped the space next to it. Stuart flipped down his notebook as though he was playing snap.

He had the same names as Frank, but one extra: Dorothy Piff. Underneath the list of names he'd written: *When we asked them if they liked or disliked Susan Nicholson, or if she had ever said or done anything to upset them, or if they knew anything about her that might be relevant, it was then I felt these witnesses were close to telling us more.*

Frank looked at Stuart and they both nodded. They were a

team. He glanced at his wrist watch. 'Nip down and see if Miss Piff's still there; let's have another go at her. She's got an alibi; I don't see her as the murderer, so she might be more willing than the others to tell us more.'

While Elderkin was out of the room Frank moved furniture so three chairs were close together, the table no longer a barrier.

Sounds of footsteps, the longer, heavy strides of Elderkin accompanied by the tip-tap of Dorothy Piff. Stuart ushered her in. Her face was flushed; her brow wrinkled with... worry?

Miss Piff seemed uneasy at the closeness of their three bodies; she sat upright, her legs tucked close to the chair rails, the toes of her shoes on the floor. 'I hope this won't take long: my sister will be worried if I'm late.'

There was a whiff of face powder and a discreet aroma of some respectable perfume – lily-of-the-valley? It suited her. Miss Piff was a decent, honest woman – as far as he could tell. He smiled at her. 'I wouldn't have asked you to come back today if I didn't think it was important.'

She nodded, seeming to relax.

'Miss Piff, Dorothy, both Sergeant Elderkin and I think you want to tell us something about Susan Nicholson, something that may have upset you, but you're not sure if you should. We'd be grateful if you'd tell us if there's anything you know about her, however small a detail, however petty–'

'That's it, it's so *petty*. I feel *petty* telling you. She did annoy me at the time. I didn't like to say anything after she was killed.'

A bubble of excitement fizzed in Frank's brain. 'Every detail about Susan Nicholson's life is precious. Dorothy, please tell us.'

She placed her feet flat on the floor and leant forward. 'It was soon after they were married and she came to

Blackfriars. She made a habit of coming into my office, chatting to me, staying for a cup of tea or coffee. I was sorry for her, thought she was lonely during the day when Mr Nicholson was busy; it's an isolated place unless you love the heath, the beach and the sea. She wasn't *my* kind of person, we didn't have much in common; she wasn't interested in the countryside, village life, or joining the WI. She was always asking about the other members of staff and sometimes I thought her questions were intrusive. I didn't like the way she tried to worm information from me. As school secretary you do have to deal with personal details and sometimes staff problems. I hope I've always been discreet and trustworthy.'

'I'm sure you're most reliable, Dorothy.' Elderkin nodded in agreement, making a comforting grunting noise. 'Go on,' Frank encouraged.

'I started making sure I didn't leave any files or letters around, as she was always picking things up and looking at them. Several times I had to take them from her; it was embarrassing: she was the headmaster's wife, and I didn't want to upset her and then get him on to me. We usually work well together, but he can be…' She bit her lip. 'After a time she didn't come as often, for which I was grateful.' She blinked and took a deep breath.

There was more to come. 'And?' Frank asked.

Dorothy Piff nibbled her bottom lip with her top incisors. 'A few times I found her in my office poking round. She always had an excuse: looking for a biro to borrow, had I a spare piece of blotting paper – things like that. I can't prove it but I'm sure she stole things, and I'm positive she took one of the school log books.'

'What are they used for?'

Dorothy got up. 'I'll get one, won't be a minute.'

'This is new, isn't it, Stuart?'

Elderkin nodded, looking satisfied – he'd picked out

Dorothy Piff as having something to tell. Frank decided he owed him a pint.

Dorothy came back carrying a leather-bound book, about eight by ten inches, with reinforced corners, and a heavy brass lock in which was a steel key. She handed it to Frank.

It smelt of school and regulations. 'Gosh, it must weigh three or four pounds. What's this used for?'

Dorothy sat down. 'The headmaster has to keep a note of important school happenings. It's a school record book. The governors and members of the Department of Education can ask to see it.'

'Is this the one in use?'

'No. That's in Mr Nicholson's office. I've got unused ones in the stationery cupboard. I order them in tens: it works out cheaper that way. That's how I know one was missing. I can't prove it, but I'm sure she stole it. Why couldn't she have asked for it? I'm sure her husband would have let her have one.'

'Perhaps she didn't want him to know she'd got it,' Frank mused. What would she want it for? Obviously she wanted to write in it. But write what? He turned the key in the lock. The covers were rigid as though reinforced by metal. The book was certainly made to be secure, to be written in by the owner of the key.

'So what kind of things would the headmaster have to write in it?'

Dorothy leant across him and turned a page. 'There's a list here. He'd have to record if there was a school inspection, or any remarks made by the ministry. If there's been any building work, or new furniture or apparatus has been bought. Visits by governors; any absences or illnesses by teachers; if he had to close the school because of an emergency or if there'd been an epidemic of flu and children have missed lessons. Those kinds of things.'

Frank saw she'd covered most of the facts printed in the book; there they were couched in a more stilted and authoritarian language.

He turned the pages. The first dozen pages were printed as an alphabetical index, two letters to a page. Each page cut to reveal the next two letters of the alphabet. The rest of the book consisted of five hundred thick, numbered pages, covered in thin, pale blue horizontal lines, with a margin on the left in red.

'Did you ever see Mrs Nicholson using a book like this?'

'No.'

Frank turned to Elderkin. 'Was a book like this found amongst her possessions?'

'No. You couldn't miss it, could you?'

'Anything else you want to tell us, Dorothy?'

She shook her head. 'It can't be important, can it?' Neither man spoke. 'I suppose if she did write in it... that might be important – if you can find it.'

'Dorothy, can I borrow this book? It will be useful to show to people, to ask them if they saw her using one like it. I must ask you not to tell anyone else about this just yet. Is that all right?'

She slowly nodded. 'I should have told you at the beginning, shouldn't I, Sergeant Elderkin? I'm sorry. I thought people would think me spiteful and Mr Nicholson would be upset.'

After a subdued Miss Piff had gone, Frank and Elderkin stared at each other.

'So, what's next, Inspector?'

'What would you do next, Sergeant?'

'Motives: that's what we need to find. Who had a strong motive for killing her? Looks like she was a snooper – perhaps she dug up some juicy details of someone's past.'

'Or present. I think a day out is called for. Tomorrow

we'll take a trip to Colchester; we'll visit Nicholson's mother – see what she has to say about her daughter-in-law and I think I'd like to see someone Susan worked with. What's the name of the theatre she acted in?'

'The Hippodrome; it's on the High Street, right in the centre of town.'

'Ring them up and see if you fix up an appointment with whoever remembers her. Don't ring up his mother; we'll take a risk she's in. I don't want her preparing herself; I want to catch her on the hop. If we go to her first, say just before nine, hopefully she'll be there.'

Elderkin screwed up his face. 'Which car will we take?'

Frank laughed. 'We'll have to make an early start. I'll pick you up at seven. Or is that too late?'

'It depends on how fast you're going to drive,' Elderkin said, his mouth turning down at the corners.

'I'll keep to the speed limit.'

Elderkin's smiling muscles refused to contract. 'I hope you won't play any of that rubbish music. I thought you'd be into the Beatles seeing as you come from Liverpool.'

Would it be worth trying to educate Elderkin in the delights of Funk? Perhaps a step too far. 'How about if I play a cassette of my choice and then you play one of yours?'

Elderkin looked mortified. 'I wouldn't have one of those tape players in my car. The radio's good enough for me.'

'I tell you what, Stuart, I'll play you some Betty Harris and if you don't like her, we'll have silence for the rest of the journey.'

Elderkin's mouth turned down again.

'Cheer up, Stuart. You may enjoy the spin. Know any good pubs near the theatre?'

The corners of his mouth, if not turning up, at least levelled off. 'The Duchess, right next to the Hippodrome. Good beer and good grub.'

Frank sighed: he trusted Stuart's assessment of beer but wasn't too sure what his good grub meant. Probably stew and dumplings, or a heavy pie with a suet crust. Just the stuff for the troops and there were plenty of those in Colchester.

Chapter 11

Friday, September 11, 1970

'There it is.' Frank pointed to a gravel drive flanked by two stone pillars, one with The Oaks inscribed on a brass plate. Like the other houses in Severall's Lane, on the outskirts of Colchester, this one, glimpsed through oak trees at the end of a drive, was large and well-proportioned.

He checked his watch. Five to nine. They'd made good time. Excellent. Unfortunately, Stuart was resistant to the charms of Betty Harris; the tape player had been silent for most of the journey.

'It's close to the A12; it hasn't taken us long to get here,' Frank mused. The A12 was the main road linking the east coast towns of Suffolk and Norfolk to London.

'I don't think you'll be able to break Nicholson's alibi. Susan Nicholson was seen by Mabel Grill on Wednesday, 8th April. She never got back home, and going by the post-mortem report, she was killed shortly after Mabel saw her. Nicholson was in Colchester, out dining with his mother,' Stuart said.

'You're right, Stuart, still it's a thought.' He swung the wheel and the Ford Mustang ripped through the gravel. He pulled up in front of the house: pale yellow walls covered in elaborate plasterwork under a thatched roof. To the right, separated from the house, was a thatched garage. Red geraniums in stone urns stood on either side of an iron-studded door. A curtain twitched at an upstairs window.

'She's a widow, isn't she?' Frank checked.

'Husband died when Nicholson was finishing university,'

Elderkin muttered, sounding annoyed.

They'd been over all this on the drive down, but Frank was fond of repeating facts just before seeing a new witness; it helped him to home in on the personality. Elderkin would get used to his ways.

It was several minutes after ringing the bell before the door opened. A tall, imposing woman, with long snow-white hair swept back from her face and elegantly arranged à la Queen Mary, stared at them. She wore an emerald-green wool dress, nylons, high heels and a gold Victorian chain and locket – very smart for nine in the morning.

'Yes?' Her voice was deep, accent standard BBC, no trace of Essex twang.

'Good morning, Mrs Nicholson. I'm Detective Inspector Diamond and this is Detective Sergeant Elderkin. We're here to ask you some questions about your late daughter-in-law, Susan Nicholson.' They both held up their identity cards. 'I hope this is a convenient time for you to see us.'

She looked from one to the other. 'Why didn't you ring to make an appointment? This is most inconvenient; I'm going out for lunch.'

'Surely not yet? I'm sure you can spare us half an hour.' He smiled winningly – he hoped. 'May we come in?'

'I spoke to an inspector just after… it happened. I can't add anything to that.'

Frank shuffled forward a few inches, making her move back.

She tossed her head, looking annoyed. 'You'd better come in. I suppose I'll have to go through it all again. I hope you've not been harassing poor Philip; he's had so much to cope with.' Her voice softened as she mentioned her son. She led them through a large square hall complete with side table and grandfather clock, into a room at the back of the house. Beyond French windows a perfectly cut lawn and flower beds

110

flowed down to a neatly trimmed hedge and views of fields.

'What a beautiful outlook,' Frank cooed. Elderkin tried to keep a straight face.

'Thank you.' She indicated they should sit on a settee and she took an armchair opposite. The room, probably the sitting room, was tastefully furnished, a mixture of antiques and an expensive modern three-piece. Above the fireplace was a portrait of a young man seated in an imposing chair, wearing graduation robes: Philip Nicholson, young, handsome and serious. Frank looked round; he couldn't see any sign of her late husband, no photograph or painting of him. Perhaps he was in the dining room.

'An excellent likeness, Mrs Nicholson. He has remained, if I may say, a handsome and distinguished man.' He was a silver-tongued devil when needed –anything to get the witness on his side. Not sure if Elderkin would approve.

Mrs Nicholson's face softened and she raised her right hand and stroked the side of her head. 'Thank you, Inspector…?'

'Diamond, Madam. You must be very proud of him. He seems to be coping well with his great loss.'

Her nostrils flared. Perhaps she didn't think it was such a loss after all. She pointedly looked at the marble mantel clock. 'I think we should begin, Inspector Diamond.'

'It must have been a pleasure for you to have your son with you for a few days last April. He arrived on Tuesday, 7th I believe.' She nodded. 'That night you stayed in?' She nodded again. 'Susan phoned that evening?' The nod. 'You didn't speak to her?'

She leant forward, sticking out her neck like an aggressive tortoise. 'No, I was cooking dinner. I don't know why she rang at that time. She knows we always have dinner precisely at seven. I suppose that's why she rang, so she wouldn't have to speak to me.'

No love lost there. 'I take it you weren't fond of Susan?'

'She wasn't good enough for Philip – an actress. I couldn't believe it when he told me they were married. I thought it was a passing infatuation, but even the best of men can be seduced by good looks and winning ways. It was a dreadful mistake.'

'Did your son come round to thinking it'd been a mistake?'

'Unfortunately not; he was besotted with *her*.' Her upper lip sneered on the last word.

Frank decided that if Mrs Nicholson hadn't got an alibi she'd go to the top of his list of suspects. 'Did your son leave the house at any time during the evening of the seventh or eighth of April, while he was staying with you?'

She smiled. 'No. We had a lovely few days. We weren't out of each other's company all the time he was here.'

'He didn't visit any old friends?'

'No. Although we did see some when we went to dinner. He did leave the table to chat to them, but that was only for a few minutes.'

'What time did you go to bed?' interrupted Elderkin. 'Did you go at the same time?'

She looked surprised, as though she'd forgotten he was in the room. She frowned. 'Tuesday night we stayed up until after midnight talking; reminiscing about when Daddy was alive, the lovely holidays we had together. Philip went up before me; he said he was tired, needed the rest, poor boy.' She looked up at the portrait and sighed.

'What about Wednesday night, after you came back from having dinner out?' Elderkin persisted.

'It was my turn to feel tired; I could hardly keep my eyes open. I'd been looking forward to another long chat. We had some tea and I just couldn't keep awake. We both went to bed at the same time. I think it was about ten-thirty. I had a wonderful sleep; Philip had to wake me up in the morning as I didn't hear the alarm. I feel so much safer when Philip is here.'

This woman was willing to dish the dirt. Frank leant forward, holding out his hands to emphasise the importance of his words. 'Mrs Nicholson, I believe you could be of enormous help to us. We need to find out as much as we can about Susan Nicholson's personality and her past life. You obviously were unhappy your son married her. Could you tell me what you disliked about her, if that isn't too strong a word?' Here was someone who didn't care if she was thought petty, and didn't mind speaking ill of the dead.

She pursed her lips. 'Will Philip know I've spoken frankly to you? He realised I didn't care for her, but when we were together I tried not to show it. My son is very dear to me.' She glanced again at the portrait.

Another dominant mother. She was worse than his. At least his mum didn't dote on him; she just wanted to run his life. 'I'm sure he won't mind if your information can help us in finding her murderer. As you probably know the thought that there may be a killer on the loose near the school is affecting everyone there.'

She hunched her shoulders. 'I know. Philip phoned me yesterday, the school numbers are down. He's terribly concerned. My poor boy – it really isn't fair.'

He felt Elderkin moving his bottom on the deep cushions of the sofa next to him. Poor boy – worried about numbers. Still grieving for his wife? His mother certainly wasn't.

'Could you tell us how he met Susan? Frank asked.

'It was a couple of years after Philip had moved to Blackfriars. He came back to stay for most of the summer holidays. I was so pleased, it meant he was living at home again and I could look after him. Now I wished he hadn't moved back, he might not have gone to the theatre.'

'Why did he go?' Frank prompted.

'An old school friend arranged a reunion, with a trip to the theatre, and he invited Philip to join them. I remember Philip coming home and talking about her: how beautiful she was, delicate, like a young girl. I said to him, may God forgive me: 'Why don't you ask her to dinner?' I never dreamt he would fall in love with her.'

'So how soon after meeting her did they marry?'

'They were married by the end of the summer holidays. Philip didn't tell me about it; they married at a registry office, a special licence. He said she wanted it to be just the two of them – so romantic. She arranged it that way so I wouldn't be able to stop it.'

'You met her before they were married?'

'Just the once. Philip took me to watch the play she was in and we went back stage at the end and we all had dinner together in Colchester.'

'Did you like her to begin with?

She shook her head vigorously. 'No. I suspected at once that she was looking for a meal ticket.'

'Why did you think that?'

'She wasn't a good actress, I suppose you could say competent at the best. When viewed from the stalls she was enchanting and looked about sixteen. Slightly built and, I have to admit, a beautiful face with high cheek bones, but when you saw her close up you could see the fine lines. She was past her best.' She leant back with a satisfied look.

'Was there more to your dislike, apart from she wasn't a young girl?' She glared at him.

He hadn't put that too well. 'Did you suspect she was looking for a way out of the theatre?'

'To begin with she was charming to me, most solicitous. After they were married, when Philip broke the news to me, they stayed with me for a week before they went back to

114

Blackfriars.' Her colour heightened, she took a deep breath as though she was reliving those days. 'I tried to give them some time alone; after all it was their honeymoon. Just before they went back to Blackfriars I'd arranged to be out all day – playing bridge with some friends, but I felt unwell and decided to go home while I could still drive. Philip was out; he'd taken his car to the garage to get a new exhaust fitted. She didn't hear me come in and I found her in my bedroom, going through my wardrobe. She'd several of my dresses on the bed, and my jewellery was laid out over the dressing table. When I walked in she was wearing one of my evening gowns and had my rope of pearls round her neck.' The woman was shivering with rage or disgust at the memory.

'What happened?'

'I couldn't believe what I was seeing. I was struck dumb; an unusual state of affairs as far as I am concerned.'

Frank believed her. He waited.

'She laughed. "Haven't you some wonderful clothes? I hope you don't mind me trying a few things on? My mother always let me play with her clothes. I've missed doing that. It's lovely to have a second mother." She came over to me and tried to give me a hug.'

'"Keep away from me," I said, "don't you ever, ever, come into my room again. I am not your mother, I am Philip's mother. Take off my gown and jewels and never, ever, do that again. Do you understand?"'

'She looked up at me, her eyes hard, half-closed with anger. "I don't want your size sixteen, antiquated dresses. I'm not fat. And as for your ghastly jewellery –" She flung the pearls in my face and tore off the dress.'

'She didn't care if I saw her in her underwear; her body was like a child's. She stalked out of the room, and I have to confess, I had to run to the bathroom to be sick.'

'Did you tell Philip?'

'Yes, I tried to, but she got to him first, and she'd put a different slant on it. I could see if I made a fuss he would think I was persecuting her.'

'Did they come to stay with you after that incident?'

'Yes. They came for a few days during the school holidays. I always made sure everything was locked up: cabinets, desks, spare rooms. Philip didn't seem to notice the atmosphere between us; perhaps he was hoping we'd grow to care for each other.'

'Did you go to the school?'

'No. Not after he'd married her.'

'Did you ever see Susan writing, say in a notebook?'

She paused, wrinkling her forehead, her eyes moving from side to side. 'Yes... I remember her sitting in the garden, Philip was out.' She pointed out to the lawn and flowerbeds. 'She was writing in a book. I was intrigued as she was totally absorbed in what she was doing, which wasn't like her at all. I didn't enquire what she was writing. Perhaps I should have.'

Frank nodded slowly. He agreed. 'It might have shed some light on her thoughts and what she was driven by.'

'Do you think there's someone in her past that's responsible for her death?'

'I haven't ruled that out.' The more they learnt about Susan Nicholson, the more possibilities seemed to slide from the wings onto the open stage.

116

Chapter 12

Frank manoeuvred the Mustang into a tight space between two cars outside the Hippodrome Theatre on Colchester High Street. Elderkin, grunting, squeezed his bulk from the car as the clock in the red-brick-and-stone town hall struck eleven.

The Edwardian façade of the theatre matched the town hall and the water tower beyond it. The natives of Colchester nicknamed the tower Jumbo, Elderkin informed him, because of its size. Looking up at the theatre he saw ornate windows and stone dressing covering the second and third floors, the whole topped by a pediment.

'What's the name of the person we're seeing?' Frank asked.

Elderkin stared at him. 'I told you on the way here.'

'I know, but I want to hear your dulcet tones once more.'

'She's Miss Heaven, the artistic director.'

'Christian name?'

'Alice.'

'By the way, what's Mrs Nicholson's Christian name?'

'Philippa – would you believe.'

'God's teeth! She called her son after herself. She's a number one matriarch. What was the father's name?'

'Don't know. I'll find out.'

'I wonder what he died of? Found frightened to death in the potting shed?'

Elderkin snorted.

The high street was busy: there was a queue outside a red telephone box; road workers were busy looking down a hole on the opposite side of the street and a stream of passengers, mostly women clutching shopping baskets, got off a Colchester Corporation bus.

Elderkin checked his wristwatch. 'We're a few minutes late.'

White stone pillars guarded the foyer of the theatre. A cleaner pointed down a corridor to the artistic director's office. Frank knocked and a small, squat, large-bosomed woman opened the door. Alice Heaven did not resemble an angel: sulphurous fumes from a large cigar clamped between her yellowing teeth poured into their faces, sending Elderkin into a coughing fit. She was wearing several layers of mushroom-coloured clothes, giving her the appearance of a smouldering bonfire.

'Ah, the coppers,' she announced, in a rich, plummy, *I am an actor* voice. 'I'm Alice Heaven.' She looked at Elderkin who was still spluttering. 'We'd better talk somewhere else. I can see my Havana is bringing you out in bronchial eruptions. Shall we go into the auditorium? Plenty of air there.' She didn't wait for an answer but swept past them gesticulating, like Hamlet's ghost, that they should follow her.

'We'll sit in the best seats,' she said, leading them down the left aisle to the front of the stalls.

It was a medium-sized theatre, with two balconies supported on slender cast-iron columns. The rectangular proscenium was surrounded by richly painted foliate plasterwork. They sat in the front row of the stalls, and she stood in front of them, between the stage and the seats, ready to perform.

'Well, gentlemen, I believe you wanted to ask me about Susan Nicholson?'

'When did Susan join your company?' Frank asked.

She pirouetted on her small, ballet-shoed feet, her numerous scarves twirling, smoke from her red-tipped cigar spiralling up towards the chandeliers. 'Let me see, 1965, yes, that's the year. She joined us at short notice. My leading lady, if she deserved such a soubriquet, had been hospitalised with yellow skin, yellow eyes and a liver twice the normal size. Came out in a pine box – best exit she ever made.'

Frank snorted. He leant back enjoying the first act. Elderkin looked at his feet.

'Was Susan a good actress?'

'She could walk, talk and didn't get drunk. I can assure you she was a great improvement on her predecessor.' She threw a loose scarf round her neck and sailed back and forth in front of them, resembling a tugboat as smoke streamed out behind her. 'She wasn't talented, but she was beautiful; a bit past it, but with plenty of greasepaint and the wind behind her, she looked sensational from where you're sitting. She brought in the punters, 'specially the soldiers. You've seen photographs of her?' They nodded. 'Remind me to show you the one we've still got in the foyer, black and white. People ask if it's Vivien Leigh. I wouldn't have minded casting her in *Street Car Named Desire*, but I didn't have any male with the right attributes for Stanley.'

She smirked suggestively.

Elderkin looked puzzled. Frank shrugged. He'd explain later. 'Was she a popular member of the company?'

'To begin with we were all grateful she'd been able to come at such short notice. Later we found out why.'

Frank raised an eyebrow.

'She'd had a small part in a West End play, where they were paying her more than we could afford, but her agent said she wanted the challenge of different parts. She *needed* to act.' She brought herself to anchor in front of them and smiled at Frank.

'And the truth?'

'The leading lady found her in her dressing room reading personal letters. She went berserk.'

'They didn't tell you about that when you employed her?'

'No, it came out after she left us. When she started here various things began to happen. Small items of jewellery and money went missing. Also she was nosy, wanting to know everything about everybody. She quickly found the most gossipy members of the company, and would pump them for spicy details of people's lives.'

'So when did you find out she was behind these thefts?'

'I never caught her red-handed; I couldn't prove she was the thief, but I challenged her and also told her she was a nosy-parker and she should mind her own business. She denied everything, but the stealing stopped and she was careful not to step on *my* toes.'

How many clichés were in that speech? She'd cast each one before them as though freshly minted. 'You obviously didn't dismiss her. Why was that?'

Alice Heaven's face shrank as she frowned. 'Couldn't prove anything and she had a contract, but I told her she wouldn't be given another.'

'The contract finished when?'

'End of August, 1968. She snaffled Nicholson just in time. I thought of saying something to him, but the man was besotted, couldn't wait to get her between the sheets, but I think she held out for marriage. Very wise, she'd a skinny body, it be like fornicating with a skeleton. No breasts to speak of.' She pushed up her own considerable assets with her folded arms.

Elderkin was squirming in the next seat; Frank wasn't sure whether in embarrassment or suppressed mirth. 'You say she looked like Vivien Leigh, had she the same proclivities?'

'Ah,' she said, winking, 'I see you've heard the gossip.'

'My mother is a keen fan of the cinema; she keeps me up to date with salacious details of the stars of the silver screen.'

She looked at him quizzically. 'You've a good way with words. Can you act?'

Elderkin had another coughing fit.

'Still looking for a Stanley?'

She gurgled and gave one last suck on the stub of her cigar. 'Could be. To answer your question, no, Susan was not a nymphomaniac. I don't think she was that interested in sex, but she knew how to use her beauty to her advantage. She did have some acting skills, and I'm sure she could fake an orgasm as well as the next woman.'

Frank decided it was time to leave before Elderkin exploded.

Frank carried two pints of Adnams Bitter from the bar of The Duchess pub back to the nook in which Elderkin was seated. There was silence as they both took long swallows, and Elderkin let out a sigh of satisfaction. 'What a terrible woman.' 'Who? Mrs Philippa Nicholson, or Miss Alice Heaven?'

Elderkin glared at him. 'You know who I mean, although I didn't take much to the other.'

'I think the trip's been worth it, don't you?'

Elderkin took another swallow of beer. 'I'm getting a better picture of Susan Nicholson, and a clearer idea as to why someone – anyone – would want to murder her.'

Frank nodded. 'Tell me what you've learnt about her.'

'I'd rather eat first, if you don't mind. I think better on a full stomach; it's a long time since breakfast.'

As Elderkin wiped his last chip in the remaining smear of tomato sauce, stuck it in his mouth and slowly chewed the morsel as if sampling the finest cuisine, he leant back on his chair and emitted a satisfied belch. 'Pardon me, I ate too quickly. Very nice piece of cod.' He eyed the chips left on Frank's plate.

'No, Stuart. You'll lose your sleek body if you're not careful.'

Elderkin snorted and wiped his mouth with a paper napkin.

'Time for your thoughts before you nod off. You can have a sleep on the way back.'

'The way you drive, you must be joking. I'll need another two pints of Adnams before I'm that relaxed.'

'If you come up with an in-depth analysis of the day, I might buy you another pint.'

'You might as well get it now,' Elderkin said, looking smug.

'Get on with it, you old bastard.' They'd come a long way in the few days they'd been together – he felt easy with him and soon one of the sparks they made together would land on something inflammable and they would have a fire. He was sure of it. He was lucky to have Elderkin as his sergeant.

'Right.' Elderkin leant forward and quickly lifted one of Frank's chips before a waitress cleared their plates. 'Susan Nicholson was probably a petty thief, although we have no proof of that; she was not a good actress, her looks were fading, her job was coming to an end. Did she marry Philip Nicholson for love or security? According to Miss Heaven, God bless her, she was not highly sexed. She did write in a book. What did she write? If it was the log book she possibly wrote secrets. Were they hers or other people's? We need to find that book. I know the murderer may have destroyed it, but that's what I think we should do next. We need to have a thorough search of the Nicholson's house and possibly the school.' He paused. 'Worth a pint?'

'Just about,' Frank said, getting up and taking the empty glasses back to the bar.

Elderkin held his second pint up to the window behind Frank. 'Clear as a bell. Thanks, Frank, and for the lunch. What do you think? Should we start a search for the log book?'

'Spot on, Stuart. I think we'll stop off at Ipswich on the way back. I've got to report back to the Chief Constable and we can ask for extra manpower for a few days. I don't want anyone to know what we're looking for so the men will have to keep quiet about it. The murderer may not know about the book. Susan must have hidden it in between writing in it. Of course the murderer may have found the book, read about him or herself, and that was the reason for her death, in that case, the book will have been destroyed. Although murderers can be strange creatures and they do sometimes keep souvenirs of their crimes, but that's usually mass murderers.'

'Don't think we've got one of those in Dunwich. I've never had dealings with one, I'm glad to say. What else are you thinking?' He pulled out his pipe and tobacco pouch and started the ritual filling and tamping down of the tobacco in the bowl.

Frank sipped his bitter lemon and pulled a face. 'I'm wondering what drove Susan Nicholson; why was she so obsessed with discovering the skeletons in people's wardrobes? What was her motive? Blackmail? Or did she enjoy the feeling of having power over people? Did she hug the secrets to herself or did she like to torment her victims with the thought she might expose them? We need to find a victim who'll talk to us. Tomorrow we'll re-interview Henry Thornback, Jim McFall and Warren Ringrose: they were the ones we both thought wanted to say more. I don't think Dorothy Piff has any more skeletons in her cupboard.'

Elderkin slowly savoured the dregs of his pint. 'Nor Mable Grill.'

'Tried her apple pie yet?'

'What? With the way you're working me? I hardly had a chance to chat to her. That's enough of my love life – if you can call it that. What about you? Not heard you mention a girlfriend. Got one tucked away in Liverpool?'

Frank took another sip of his drink and tried to look as though he was enjoying it. 'No. No girlfriends.'

Stuart frowned. 'You do like girls, don't you?'

Frank laughed. 'Don't worry, my name isn't Warren Ringrose.'

'Has Mabel been talking to you?'

'No. I may be wrong about him, but I don't think so.'

'You're not wrong – you're right. Could be Susan Nicholson knew as well and threatened to tell her husband.'

Frank nodded, tipped the last of the bitter lemon down his throat and vowed never to drink it again.

'What about that Miss Bowman? Mabel says she's a nice girl, no side to her, doesn't give herself airs. I know she's tall but she's a looker. She'd be handy round the house – help you with the lifting and carrying, and I bet she could dig over a vegetable patch in no time at all.'

Frank frowned at him: the old, chauvinist cupid. 'I'm not interested, Stuart, and I think the feeling's mutual, although I agree she's a good-looking woman. I don't think domesticity would be her strong point.' A picture of Laurel Bowman in a frilly apron, flushed from a session at the stove, laying before him a perfectly cooked coq au vin as he sat at a candle-lit table, knife and fork in hand, made him smile. 'How often, when you fancy a girl, do you meet her mother and realise that's who she'll turn into in twenty years' time, and somehow you don't feel as keen. Or even worse you think she might turn into your own mother and try and rule your life? Mind you, I always kept my father hidden if I brought a girl home!'

Elderkin stared at him. 'You'll never get married if you think like that.'

'I don't intend to.'

Elderkin shook his head. 'What's wrong with your mother?'

124

'My mother is a frustrated woman. Not sexually – I've two brothers and three sisters. Imagine my childhood. Mother is a Roman Catholic housewife; Father, a Marxist Trade Union steward.' Frank rolled his eyes. 'He'll be down with all the rest of them: Jack Jones, Vic Feather and the other TUC members in Brighton, planning how to bring this government down.'

'It's a wonder you're as normal as you are,' Stuart said, winking at him. 'Have you heard the unions are bringing in a ban on Sunday buses – they don't like these new one-man operated jobs. So why's your mother frustrated?'

'The only freedom my father gave her was to allow her to name their children after Catholic saints. Hence: Frances Xavier.' He pointed his thumb at his chest.

'I don't know much about the trade union movement. I think I agree with them about not going into the Common Market. What do you think?'

Frank grimaced. 'I suppose wine might be cheaper.'

'Returning to your mother…'

Frank smiled. 'I love her and my dad, but her problem is she's got more brains than the rest of the family put together. She needs a purpose, but Dad won't let her get a job. So she tries to organise the rest of us.'

Elderkin sighed. 'I like a bossy woman, myself.'

'I tell you what, Stuart; I'll let you have Sunday off, seeing as you've made such an astute summing up of the situation – the criminal situation. We won't get any extra help until Monday at the earliest. I want a quick, thorough search of the whole area, all the buildings, especially the living quarters and any of the outlying buildings, including the ruins. Hope the Chief buys it, if not the search could take weeks.'

'When do the kids come back?'

'Wednesday.' They pulled faces at each other.

Chapter 13

Sunday, September 13, 1970

The Yale lock made a satisfactory click as Laurel pulled the front door of the cottage shut. Mabel, on her knees, was working in the borders of her front garden. 'Morning, Mabel. Hello, Muffin. Is this how you're going to spend your day off?'

Mabel pressed her hands against the earth and heaved herself up. 'I am, this morning anyway. I see you're making the most of the sunshine. You're looking summery. Going out?'

Laurel thought a casual look would be best for her meeting with Frank Diamond. She'd been undecided, holding different blouses against skirts and trousers, before deciding on a short denim skirt, white T-shirt and sandals – she didn't want to tower over him in high heels.

'Might as well make the most of the lovely weather,' Laurel said, spreading out her arms like a blackbird having a sunbath. The air was balmy, the sky Alice blue and the sea, glimpsed between the Holm oaks, cucumber green: a perfect September day. 'I'm going for a drive; I'll probably have lunch at a pub. Are *you* going anywhere, Mabel?'

There was a creak of a window opening from Toni Habershon's cottage; she didn't turn round. It was too glorious a day to have it soured by one of her snide remarks.

'I'm going to have a rest this afternoon, then this evening I'm going to take Muffin for that walk and see if I can remember what's bothering me.'

Mabel was going by herself? 'Do you want to wait until I

126

get back? I could come with you.'

Mabel shook her head. 'No. I think I need to do it like I did it that evening when I saw her. It's got to be just me and Muffin. I think it's something to do with Muffin, It's on the edge of my brain, dancing round, just out of reach. I try to catch it but it waltzes away. I've nearly got it. I'll let you know when I get back.'

'What time are you going?'

'I'll set off at about six-thirty, and do the exact same walk I did that evening: I'll walk along the road to Minsmere beach, then along the beach to the sluice and back along the beach to the steps. That's what we did last time, wasn't it, Muffin?' She bent down to pat him; Muffin rolled on his back and wiggled in ecstasy as she scratched his stomach, his tail beating the dried earth on the path into a mini-sandstorm.

Laurel laughed. 'Good old Muffin – I hope you finally remember what's troubling you, Mabel. It's getting on your nerves, isn't it?'

Mabel's smile faded, replaced by a frown. 'I'm sure it's something important. Have you seen that inspector lately? I haven't seen old Elderkin these past few days, although I did hear they'd interviewed some of the staff again. Seems Mr Shipster lost his temper with them – Dorothy Piff told me, she had coffee with me when she came in to do some extra work yesterday; although she doesn't usually work Saturdays. We need this clearing up quick – the kids will be back next week. I don't like to think of them here when we might have a murderer… nearby.'

'Or even living here as one of the staff.'

Mabel shuddered.

'Mabel did you know the schoolgirl who ran away a few years ago? The one the police never found.'

Mabel narrowed her eyes. 'Why do you want to know about her? Do you think it's got anything to do with Susan

Nicholson?'

'I talked to Warren Ringrose; from his description of Felicity – that was her name, wasn't it?' Mabel nodded vigorously, wiping her hands on her pinny. 'Her description matches Susan Nicholson's: slight, red-headed. Did you know her at all?'

Mabel walked to her gate. 'I get to know all the children, some more than others, 'specially the greedy ones.'

Laurel raised her eyebrows.

'No, she was the opposite. I was always trying to persuade her to eat a bit more, she was way too skinny. I never believed she ran off with some man, she wasn't interested in things like that; she was young for her age in many ways. She lived for her music.'

'What about Warren Ringrose? He seemed fond of her – do you think he could have been involved in her disappearance?'

Mabel threw back her head, dimples appearing in her round cheeks as she howled with laughter. 'Warren Ringrose! Young girls aren't what he's interested in. I thought you'd have sussed that out by now.'

Laurel thought back to the talk she'd had with Warren in the music room – but why was Mabel so sure? 'Warren's a homosexual?'

Mabel slapped her own hand. 'I shouldn't have said anything. He's a nice chap, and he's not into young boys either. I saw him with a man when I was in Ipswich a couple of years ago. He didn't see me. You could tell they were fond of each other. You won't say anything, will you? I shouldn't have said, you being senior mistress. I don't want to get him the sack.'

Laurel reached over the gate and put a hand on Mabel's arm. 'Don't worry. If he isn't a threat to any of the children, and he's doing his job well, I've no reason to worry about his sexual preferences.'

Mabel placed her hand over Laurel's. 'Thanks, dear. Going back to Felicity, one thing did puzzle me; she took this big, leather suitcase and most of her clothes when she ran away, but the suitcase was one of those heavy, old-fashioned jobs, it'd belonged to her father. She wouldn't have been able to carry it far. That's why they thought she must have been met by someone with a car.'

'What was the suitcase like?'

'Huge it was, real deep, about foot and a half, well perhaps a bit less. Tan leather, with big initials in black on the front – her father's. She was that fond of it, she showed it me once when she was going to her aunt's. Pity she didn't go to her aunt's that holiday.'

You mean she was at school in the holidays when she went missing?'

'Yes. Aunt couldn't have her for some reason and she had to stay in school.'

Both incidents had happened in school holidays: Felicity disappearing and Susan being killed. Both women shared physical resemblances: attractive, red hair and of slight build… like Angela.

Laurel drove inland, and at Westleton turned the Cortina south through Middleton and the larger town of Leiston. Passing Leiston police station, an imposing building set back from the road in front of colourful flower beds, she wondered what the local police made of Frank Diamond. Did Sergeant Elderkin like working with him? He hadn't looked happy when she'd seen him in the headmaster's office with Frank. Had Frank been promoted because of his ability? Or had his bosses been glad to get rid of him, and kicked him upstairs? Not only upstairs but out of their playing field. He was good at his job, she knew that, but he was a maverick. It was a characteristic she was depending on when she talked with him today. Could she persuade him that in exchange for not informing the school about Angela's murder she would work with him to find Susan Nicholson's killer? She could tell him what she'd picked up in the informal chats with members of staff. If he agreed, would he be willing to tell her about the case? Or would it be a one-way partnership: information flowing from her to him, but nothing given back?

She hesitated as she came to the turning for the coastal village of Thorpeness. Taking it would mean a detour, approaching Aldeburgh by the coast road. Did she want to go back to a place of happy memories? Wouldn't it be better to go directly to Aldeburgh? She turned the car left to Thorpeness.

The narrow winding road, passing through heath and woods was quiet for a Sunday, especially on such a lovely day. She braked as the road bent sharply to the right and the first crazy building of Thorpeness fantasy holiday village appeared. Mock Tudor and Jacobean houses built by a Scottish barrister for his private pleasure in the 1920s. Now the houses were mostly used as holiday lets.

Even though Thorpeness wasn't far from Felixstowe her family had spent several summer holidays here. The last one was when Laurel was fourteen and Angela six. Their parents rented a house for a fortnight; Dad played golf and Mum sat on the beach, knitting. Laurel looked after Angela and they spent most of their time rowing on the shallow boating lake.

Laurel glanced at her watch, as she turned into the municipal car park near the beach. She walked to the edge of the mere; a mixed flock of water birds, ducks, geese and swans swam towards her, hoping for food. Rowing boats moved erratically over the water, the happy cries of children taking her back in time.

Their last holiday at Thorpeness: every day was sunny,

the mere scintillating as she pulled on the oars, as Angela dipped her hand into the clear water, trying to catch fronds of water crowfoot. 'It's mermaid's hair, Laurie.' She'd always called her Laurie, the only one of the family who did. They'd explored the islands named after places in Peter Pan: The Pirate's Lair and Wendy's home. Barrie was a personal friend of the man who'd built the village. She pressed a clenched hand to her chest, trying to push back the hollow ache of loss.

Memories of Angela: Angela in a sun-suit of gathered cotton, tiny straps slipping from her narrow shoulders, her flame hair held back by an Alice band; waving a wooden sword and demanding to be rowed to the Pirate's Island. Angela on the beach eating fish paste sandwiches and complaining about the sand in them; Angela sleeping, her head in Mum's lap, a towel draped over her calamined shoulders.

Loss and pain shrank her heart. She envied and hated the happy families laughing together in their rowing boats. She turned abruptly, bumping into a young woman holding a baby. Muttering an apology she strode to her car, biting her lip, trying to stop the tears. Damn. She shouldn't have stopped.

In the car she sat upright, making herself take deep, slow breaths. She didn't want to meet Frank Diamond in this mood: she'd snap his head off instead of charming him into submission. Angela. Angela. If only she hadn't been so besotted with Simon she might have noticed how Angela was changing. She'd fallen for Simon and he'd been equally smitten. A rapid engagement, the excitement of promotion to head of department, and plans for the wedding meant she'd little time for her family.

They were both living at home. Angela was twenty-two, she'd left school at sixteen, gone to the local college and qualified as a shorthand typist. She had a series of jobs in

Felixstowe, and several boyfriends, local lads, one a fisherman, but the relationships never lasted for more than a few months and she was usually the one who dropped them. 'They're boring, Laurie. They haven't done anything, not been anywhere.'

She'd been surprised when Angela left her job in Fison's offices for a position with one of the local auctioneers. 'I'm a personal assistant, not just a typist. Mr Deller takes me with him to view the antiques people want to sell and on auction days I sit next to him and when he brings the hammer down I note the final bids. I love it and I'm meeting so many interesting people.'

With hindsight she should have been more observant, more suspicious about Angela's behaviour, but her own happiness, the excitement of sex and the plans for the wedding left no room in her mind for worrying about Angela. All she was concerned about was: where would they live? Should she go on with her job? Did Simon's family like her? She hadn't paid much attention to Angela and *she* didn't seem interested in her plans, although she said she was looking forward to being a bridesmaid.

She should have known something was wrong: Why didn't Angela's boyfriends come back home with her? Why did Angela come in so late night after night? Why was Angela's skin glowing, her eyes dreamy, her lips bee-kissed, and wasn't her face wearing the satisfied look of a woman in love – a woman sexually fulfilled?

Then suddenly a change: Angela looking peaky, worried, spending too much time in her room. Would she ever forgive herself for not seeing these signs, not worrying about the reasons, not finding out why Angela had changed? If only she had, perhaps Angela would be alive and she wouldn't be here, sitting in the Cortina, wiping her eyes and wishing she'd brought some make-up with her to repair the damage.

Chapter 14

The road from Thorpeness to Aldeburgh was straight; to the left, low marram-grassed dunes, then the sea, to the right, marsh with clumps of willow. In the higher part of the town, Aldeburgh's church steeple and the tiles of surrounding houses glittered in the sun.

Laurel pulled into a parking space in front of a narrow promenade. Fishermen's huts lined the edge of a shingle beach and two cars away was Frank's blue Mustang – empty. She sat in the car, anxiety gnawing at her insides. She didn't want to see him. She wasn't ready for the questions he'd ask and she hadn't decided how she'd get him on her side. Grief and guilt had blown all her plans away. Should she abandon the meeting? Or see him briefly and plead illness? Perhaps that would be best. She leant across the gear stick and pulled down the passenger sunscreen to look in the vanity mirror. Her face was drawn and mascara stained her cheeks. She wished she wasn't here; she wanted to be at home, with Mum and Dad. Before driving to Aldeburgh she'd stopped at the phone box in Dunwich to phone them, but she hadn't plucked up enough courage to tell them about the murder of Susan Nicholson. She pressed a hand against her chest – it felt tight, her throat narrowing. She knew the symptoms – a panic attack – she'd treated enough hysterical schoolgirls.

She collapsed back in the driving seat and took several deep breaths. Her nostrils flared and she thumped her thighs with clenched fists. For God's sake pull yourself together, you pathetic creature. She mustn't give into morbid thoughts. Suppose Frank finds out what she'd done? What would he do? The only way he'd find out would be if *she* told him. She looked in the vanity mirror again and wiped her face with a handkerchief and patted her hair – best she could do. She took another deep breath and pinched her cheeks. Either he'll agree, or he won't. She banged the dashboard with a clenched fist. She'd make sure he agreed.

She walked past the sixteenth-century Moot Hall and the Victorian flower beds. In front of a small yachting pond Frank was leaning on a plinth, his arm round a bronze statue of a small dog, its head cocked. They both seemed to be watching children pushing out their toy sailing boats over the soupy water. Frank looked relaxed, a smile curving his lips, totally absorbed in the shrieking children as they ran from one side of the pond to the other, trying to catch their skimming boats before they crashed into the pond's sides. He was wearing jeans and a black T-shirt decorated with grey capitals: MUSTANG 1970, AMERICAN MUSCLE.

Laurel's lips curved. 'Frank. I didn't know you liked children.'

His green eyes blinked, long lashes sweeping his cheeks. 'Laurel! You crept up on me. Or should I call you Miss Bowman? As for children, I'm fascinated by all human behaviour.'

'Laurel, please.' She forced a smile, deciding on a charm offensive; looking at Frank, it wouldn't be a chore.

'Shall we eat first and argue later?' he asked.

She took a deep breath – she mustn't rise to the bait. The squabbling gulls, fighting over fish intestines thrown from the fishermen's huts, would be the only combatants round here. 'Lovely, but I'm not in the mood for arguments. Let's enjoy ourselves. It's good to get away from the school; I was beginning to find it claustrophobic.'

Frank was staring at her face, his eyes narrowed. Had she removed all that streaky mascara with her hanky?

'Good. Fancy some fish and chips – as recommended by Mabel Grill and Sergeant Elderkin?'

'From Mabel's old chippy? Wonderful. I'll tell them she's my neighbour; it might get us bigger portions.'

'Don't mention I'm the law. I might get something nasty sprinkled on my chips, instead of vinegar.'

Sitting on a concrete wall near the lifeboat station, with red and white valerian growing through the pebbles round their feet, Laurel felt her mood change. The sun's heat beat through her T-shirt and seared her outstretched legs. She bit through crisp batter into hot, succulent cod. 'My God, Frank, this is absolutely delicious.'

He grinned, nodding, his mouth full of chips.

Laurel rummaged at the bottom of the greasy paper for the last bits of batter.

'You remind me of Sergeant Elderkin, the way you enjoy your food.' Frank crumpled up his paper and held out a hand for Laurel's.

She crunched the last of the batter bits and sighed. 'Good for him; I can't stand people who pick at their food. I didn't see you leave any.'

'Shall we wash it down with a pint? The Cross Keys has good Adnams.'

'You've been doing your research.'

'Elderkin has vouched for the clarity and hoppiness of the brew.'

'How are you getting on with him? I thought you might not be a good match when I first saw you together.'

Frank tossed the oily papers into a waste bin. 'He's all right, is Stuart Elderkin. I like him.'

What a strange, unpredictable man Frank was. She was surprised he liked Elderkin, who appeared stolid and unimaginative. Frank had obviously found hidden depths. They made a bizarre pair, but Frank seemed genuinely pleased with him; he must be a good policeman or he would have written him off.

Frank guided her away from the beach down a narrow road to a pub garnished with a vibrant display of flowers in window boxes and hanging baskets. Inside Laurel sat on a wheel-backed chair, away from the bar so they could talk freely. She should have offered to buy the drinks: Frank had bought the fish and chips.

He placed a glass of beer in front of her, its sides misted with condensation. She slowly stroked away the moisture with her hand. How should she start?

Frank took a long swallow, placed his glass down and turned to her, his face serious. 'So, Miss Laurel Bowman, why did you need to see me alone? I presume it's about Angela. You haven't told the school your sister was murdered, have you?'

Laurel lowered her head and took a small sip. He hadn't wasted any time. 'No, I haven't.'

'Why not?'

She took another sip, raised her head and looked at him. 'I took the job to get away from home, from my parents, from the sympathy of friends and colleagues. I wanted to try and forget everything that had happened.' She looked up at him. 'You can understand that?'

'Even though Angela's murderer hasn't been caught? I had you down as someone who wouldn't give up until justice had been done. Was I wrong?'

She decided not to answer. 'Perhaps I should have told them in my application, but it wasn't relevant to the job. If I'd known about the headmaster's wife, I wouldn't have accepted it.'

Frank's eyebrows nearly knitted together. 'You didn't know? Didn't they tell you?'

He sounded angry.

'I didn't find out until Monday.'

'Strewth!' He took another long pull at his pint, and then

136

scraped a hand over the dark stubble on his face.

He looked as though he hadn't shaved, or his razor wasn't up to the job. 'I've a favour to ask you, Frank. I'd be very grateful if you didn't tell anyone about Angela. I'd decided not to mention it before I came and now... It would seem weird; the senior mistress's sister was murdered, the headmaster's wife was murdered... It's hard enough finding your feet in a new job, especially as I'm not going to find it easy to...' The words petered out; she didn't want to sound whingy.

'You could be wrong. It would give you and Mr Nicholson something in common. You'd be able to relate to each other.' He raised his eyebrows and gave her a saucy smile.

She glared at him. 'You're very rude.'

'If you want a favour you're not going about it the right way. You should be chatting me up, batting those eyelashes, dimpling your cheeks. I'm susceptible to a bit of female chicanery.'

'I doubt it, but I'll try. Will this do?' She gave her best impression of a Victorian heroine in a silent movie: clasping her hands to her breasts, looking up soulfully into his face and batting her eyelids with the rapidity of a humming bird sipping nectar from a flower.

Frank choked, beer shooting out over both of them.

She thumped him on the back, her laughter turning the heads of the other drinkers. She took a handkerchief from her pocket and wiped them both down. He grasped her wrist, preventing her from putting the handkerchief back. She tried to pull away but it was as though she was held by a steel hawser.

'You've been crying.' He nodded towards the streaks of mascara on the white fabric. 'What's upset you, Laurie? Was the thought of seeing me so awful?'

His grip was strong but his voice was soft. 'Please don't call me Laurie – she called me that.'

'Angela?'

She nodded, tears pricking the corners of her eyes.

He released her hand and gently placed it on her lap. She blew her nose and found a dry corner of the handkerchief to pat her eyes.

'Come on, forget the beer, we'll go for a walk.'

Laurel sat up straight; she hadn't meant to break down, but now she had she might as well get something out of it. 'No. I'm all right. Sorry about that. The beer's too good to waste.' She looked at him. 'Will you help me? I really don't want to have to tell everyone at Blackfriars about Angela.'

He didn't reply.

She thought he'd feel sorry for her, weaken at the sight of female tears, but he was no push-over. 'I'm willing to make it worth your while.'

He laughed, not a pleasant laugh. 'Bribery, heh? Are you going to offer me your body?'

She felt her face become hot. 'Certainly not – I didn't mean – I could help you. I've learnt quite a bit about the other members of staff – things that might be relevant to Susan's murder. Also do you know anything about a pupil, a girl, who went missing from the school a few years ago?'

He still didn't reply.

She took a deep breath, about to lose control. His silence was deliberate. He probably used this technique when interviewing suspects. 'Thank you for the fish and chips and the beer, Frank.' She opened her bag, took out her purse and put a pound note on the table. 'I hope this covers my part of the meal.' She started to get up from the chair. 'Thank you for seeing me...'

He pocketed the note. 'Thanks, Laurel. Sit down. I'll buy more beer and you can tell me your thoughts on the members of staff; and I'd like to hear about this girl.'

She collapsed back, the chair hard against her flesh – infuriating, unpredictable man. 'This means you won't tell them about Angela?'

He smiled at her. 'Did I ever say I would? I never had any intention of bringing it up. It's none of anyone's business but yours – and possibly mine.' He turned and walked to the bar.

Relief followed by anxiety washed through her. What did he mean by that last remark? Forget it. She'd got what she wanted. She'd also got a closer relationship with Frank and all the dangers that came with it. She must never forget he was a policeman, a detective, a good detective, one who would bring a murderer to justice, whoever that murderer was.

As Laurel and Frank walked along the beach to Thorpeness she told him everything she'd learnt about the staff of Blackfriars. As he questioned her, information she hadn't thought relevant, such as Philip's and Shipster's attitudes towards her, her success in getting an office, and her dislike of Toni Habershon and approval of Mabel and Miss Piff came tumbling out.

The tide was high as they reached Thorpeness. Frank looked at his wrist watch. 'Time for tea. Would you like to stay here, or wait until we walk back to Aldeburgh?'

'I'd rather go back to Aldeburgh. I stopped here on the way to meet you. That's why I was upset. My parents rented a house here for family holidays. I started thinking about Angela and… it won't take us long to walk back and I can tell you about Felicity.'

'The missing girl?'

She nodded. 'Did Elderkin mention her?'

He shook his head. 'Tell me about her.'

The sun's heat was fading as they reached their cars and it was probably too late for tea. Laurel hoped he didn't think so; she didn't want to go back to the school. She'd enjoyed telling him her thoughts and suspicions about the staff and he'd listened intently when she'd talked about Felicity and her resemblance to Susan; his eyes had glazed over, as if his mind had switched to another level.

'Thanks for all the information, Laurel; it's all extremely useful. I don't mean to sound patronising but you've got an analytical brain; everything you've said has been important.' He paused and bit his lip. 'I expect you'll get shirty when I say this, but you *must* be careful. If you find out anything else, please don't act on it, get in touch. You don't hold a sword and scales in your hands – justice comes through the courts.'

The elation she'd felt at his first remarks disappeared as the significance of his last words slithered through her mind. He knew. He couldn't prove anything. She kept her face still. 'Thanks, Frank, I'll be careful. I'd better get back, I want to see if Mabel... gosh, I didn't tell you about Mabel going for a walk this evening, did I?'

'Mabel? No, you didn't. Bit late for tea but how about a quick cup of coffee and a sandwich? It seems a long time since the fish and chips.'

Laurel smiled and nodded; anything to delay driving through those gates. They turned towards the town.

'Oh, no,' Laurel exclaimed, nudging Frank's arm. She was seeing double. For not only was Miss Piff walking towards them with a military stride, but by her side was another identical Miss Piff, trotting to keep up with her doppelganger.

'Miss Bowman – Inspector Diamond. How lovely to meet you,' said the military Miss Piff; the other smiled shyly. 'Let me introduce my sister. Emily, this is Miss Laurel Bowman, our new senior mistress and Inspector Diamond, who's in charge of the... er, case.' She looked at them as though waiting for an explanation.

Laurel decided not to offer one. She shook Emily's hand. 'Dorothy didn't tell me she had an identical twin sister. You look exactly alike.'

Emily ducked her head, smiling. 'We may look alike but Dorothy's the efficient worker. I don't know what I'd do without her. I just look after the house. We may be identical twins, but we're very different people.'

Dorothy Piff tutted, 'Nonsense, Emily. I'd be the one who was lost if I hadn't got you to care for me.' She looked up at both of them. 'Emily is much nicer than me, much kinder; she runs herself down.'

'I'm pleased to see both of you. Have you been in Aldeburgh long? Miss Bowman and I have just bumped into each other; I'm going to buy her a coffee before she goes back to the school. Would you ladies like to join us? You'd be most welcome.'

Silver-tongued devil. Laurel smiled and nodded as though in agreement. No, they wouldn't be welcome.

'Thank you so much, Inspector Diamond, but we need to get back for Evensong. Goodbye. No doubt I'll see you in the morning, Miss Bowman.' The two tweed-clad figures simultaneously turned towards a Morris Traveller, its rear window sills encrusted in moss. It was parked two cars away from Frank's Mustang.

She'd been so engrossed talking to Frank she hadn't noticed it when they came back from their walk, hadn't realised Miss Piff was roaming the streets of Aldeburgh. Thank goodness they'd refused Frank's offer. She hoped Miss Piff was as discreet as she claimed. The last thing she wanted was rumours of her palling up with Frank Diamond going round the school. If the staff thought they were friends she'd never be able to find out more about Felicity's disappearance or Susan Nicholson's murder.

'Come on, let's get going, before they change their minds,' Frank muttered, taking her elbow and guiding her across the road. 'Incredible! I couldn't tell them apart, but as soon as Emily spoke you could see the difference in their characters.' He pushed open the door of a cafe and chose a table away from the window.

Sensible, she didn't want anyone else she knew seeing them together.

'You say Mabel Grill is taking a walk this evening?'

Laurel went through her conversation with Mabel. 'I did offer to go with her, but she said it had to be just her and Muffin. She sounded as if something was crystallising in her mind. I hope she remembers.'

Frank wrinkled his brow, looking down as he slowly stirred his cup of coffee. 'Did she tell anyone else she was going?'

'I don't know. She might have done. Why?'

He took a long sip of his drink. 'Would you mind if I came back with you? I realise we don't want to be seen together, but if Mabel has remembered something it could be important. I won't sleep tonight until I know.' He looked her intently. 'I suppose you could phone me.'

He didn't sound as though that was what he wanted. 'I haven't got a phone, not even in my office. The only outside lines are in the headmaster's, Mr Shipster's and Miss Piff's offices; I think Philip's got one in his house. Yes, he has. I saw it the other...' She wasn't sure why she hesitated; she could feel her face heating up. She felt guilty. Ridiculous – she had nothing to be guilty about. 'He invited me to dinner on Thursday evening.'

Frank gave her an old-fashioned look. 'Good cook is he? Or did he hand you a pinny and a frying pan?'

'His cooking was excellent.' Slight exaggeration, Mabel had made the fish pie. 'We discussed school matters.'

'I never dreamt you talked about anything else.' He nodded towards a clock on the wall. 'What time will Mabel be back?'

'She said she'd leave about six-thirty, be back by eight. The sun's setting but she should be back before dark. Can I make a suggestion? Could you drop your car off at your cottage and come back with me – I'll drive you home after we've talked to Mabel. That way, hopefully no one will see us together. What do you think? Too much bother?'

Frank slowly nodded in approval. 'Good thinking. You have the makings of a sleuth, or even a spy – no, cancel that thought. You're much too conspicuous.'

Laurel wanted to wreak physical damage on him, but decided to ignore the jibe.

'I meant much too attractive – I suppose you could be a femme fatale.'

He found her attractive, she liked that. 'Thank you. Shall we go?'

As they left the cafe he whispered, 'I look forward to viewing your cottage and analysing your character from its contents.'

'Really? What would you expect to find?'

'Perhaps a set of scales and a sword?'

Damn the man. Won't he ever let go? He couldn't help himself; he'd never stop searching for answers to unsolved crimes.

Chapter 15

Frank locked the door of the Mustang and Laurel got into her car ready to drive them to Blackfriars. He opened the passenger door. 'Want to come in for a drink?' He nodded to his cottage.

'No. I think we ought to get back, Mabel might have returned, and I'm dying to know if she's remembered anything. We can have a drink in my house. Tea OK?'

Frank slid onto the Cortina. 'I don't suppose you've any beers in the fridge?'

'I might have; and I can even offer you a whisky chaser, kept for emergencies only, you understand.'

'How often do those occur?'

'Since I came here, at *least* once a day. Dad gave me a bottle as a leaving present. It's a bad habit I picked up from a former boyfriend. Beer and a whisky chaser – not very ladylike, is it?' She pushed the gear lever into reverse, made a neat turn, and the car pulled smoothly away.

Frank glanced down; her denim skirt had ridden up showing her long, slim, muscular legs. Great pins!

She looked at him and glared.

'Just admiring your gear change.'

The glare turned into a wry smile. 'You're never lost for words, are you?'

'It has been known.'

The sky was darkening as they drove through the school gates; a black cloud shaped like a hammer-headed shark swam in from the North Sea. Frank glanced at his watch: eight-fifteen. The site seemed deserted; there were no lights on in Nicholson's house, but as they passed Shipster's an upstairs light shone out like a beacon. There were no lights from the three cottages. Mabel wasn't back and Toni Habershon wasn't in, unless she liked sitting in the gloom.

Frank looked round Laurel's sitting room; she'd managed to imprint her personality on it in the few days she'd been here. The walls were covered in posters and watercolours, a tartan blanket was thrown over the settee, and paperbacks filled a low bookcase. On top of it was a photograph in a wooden frame; he picked it up. Laurel with her arm round Angela. You could almost feel the love radiating from the older to the younger sister. Warm, protective love – or was his imagination in retrospective overdrive? Would she have done that to avenge Angela's death? Could she have done it? If so, how? He wanted to know, but if he found out she was responsible, what would he do? He was a policeman; he knew what he should do.

He heard glasses clinking and waved the photograph at her. 'Nice picture of you two. She was a good-looking kid. You don't look so bad yourself.'

She put the tray down on the table. 'I had it in my office but I brought it back here. Mr Nicholson saw it, he asked who Angela was. I told him she was a childhood friend who'd died.'

'You're not a natural liar, are you? It'll be difficult to keep up, and one lie leads to another. You ought to consider telling Nicholson. I'm sure he'd understand your difficulty, and be sympathetic. Someone is bound to find out sooner or later.'

She was biting her lip, worry lines between her eyes.

'Sorry, Laurel, let's forget it. I won't be the one who splits. How about pouring me that drink?'

They sat at the table by the window. Laurel turned off the main light, leaving a table lamp glowing, casting shadows against the walls. She opened the window. 'We'll hear Mabel, or Muffin, or both, as they come back.'

Frank sipped at the beer, having declined the whisky. He squinted at his watch.

'I'm worried, Frank. She should have been back by now.'

'Did she say which way she was going?'

Laurel got up and pushed the window open further and leant out as though trying to listen for signs of them. 'Yes. She was coming back by the beach and then up the steps.'

'Shall we go and meet her? Have you got a torch? Put on a jumper and some shoes – you'll twist an ankle in those sandals, some of the shingle is boulder-size. Have you got a sweater I could borrow? I should have got one from the cottage.'

Laurel ran upstairs, her feet drumming on the floorboards. She ran back into the room and tossed him a thick sweater, thankfully unisex and not a bad fit. She'd changed into trousers and flat shoes and held a large rubber-coated torch.

She switched on the main light. 'I'll leave that on.' She closed the window. Her eyes were wide, her face pale and strained.

Her anxiety seeped into him. Something was wrong – something had happened. His stomach seemed to shrink as though icy water had been forced down his throat. He opened the door. 'Let's go and find her. She may have tripped on the shingle and needs some help.'

Laurel looked as though she wanted to believe him.

Laurel turned on the torch and the yellow beam lit up the gravel path leading to the cliffs. The moon and a million stars dimly illuminated the outlines of trees and bushes: dark on dark. The night air smelt of sea, shells, tar and driftwood. Frank's footsteps crunched reassuringly behind her. She thanked God he'd come back with her. Her foot caught in a pot-hole and she nearly tripped over.

'Slow down, Laurel, you'll break your neck.'

'Sorry.' Mabel, where are you? Her throat was tightening, her pulse racing. She wanted to run as fast as she could, find Mabel quickly, make the fear racing through her body disappear. Frank was right, the gravel road was full of holes and as they passed into the belt of Holm oaks bordering the cliff, it turned into a meandering track with protruding tree roots and large stones; in places it narrowed between clumps of briars, brambles reaching out, catching in the sleeves of her jumper.

'I think you ought to call out Mabel's name, Laurel, in case we miss her. Better you shout; she'll recognise your voice.'

'Good idea.' She licked her lips, and tasted salt; she gulped, clearing her throat. 'Mabel. Mabel,' she croaked.

Frank put an arm round her. 'Come on, you can do better than that. I've heard you shouting at kids on the playing field. Remember the day I came to ask you a few more questions about Angela, I thought you were going to impale me with a javelin?' He squeezed her shoulder. 'Give it another try. Tell her it's you.'

'Mabel! Mabel! It's Laurel. Where are you?' Her voice echoed round the trees. They stopped and listened. The only reply was the crashing of the waves on the shingle below.

Laurel kept on shouting.

As they neared the steps leading to the beach Frank grabbed her arm. 'What's that?'

The snap of breaking twigs, the tear of leaves – something heavy was running in front of them. 'Mabel! Mabel! It's Laurel! Mabel!'

No reply. Whatever had made the noise had gone.

'Could have been a deer. Lots of them around at the moment,' Frank said.

He didn't sound convinced. She didn't think it was a deer, unless some deer have two legs.

She directed the torch's beam on the wooden railings of the steps leading down to the beach.

Frank gently pushed her behind him. 'I'll go down first. Shine the torch in front of me. For God's sake, don't trip or you'll send me flying.'

The first flight of steps descended steeply to a platform half-way down the cliff. Laurel grasped the rail with her left hand, shining the torch's beam in front of Frank. The steps were slimy from night dew and the rail moved as she leant against it.

They reached the platform.

'Give me the torch, Laurel.' He shone it on the steps which continued at right angles to the platform down to the shingle beach. There was nothing on the steps. He played the beam like a searchlight over the nearest part of the beach which was covered in smooth, large stones. She leant on him, following the powerful beam as he moved it over the ground.

'Good torch,' he said. His body stiffened. He slowly brought the beam back over... there was a dark shape a few yards from the bottom step.

'No!' she yelled and tried to push past him.

He grabbed her arm. 'Stay here. I'll go down.'

'No. We'll go together. If it's Mabel, she's hurt.'

He nodded. 'OK.' He took hold of her hand and squeezed it.

He shone the beam onto the dark shape. 'Don't touch anything, Laurel.'

The light moved over stockinged legs; brown, laced walking shoes; a pleated skirt, Mabel's head, face down on the stones, tight brown curls matted with blood.

Laurel's ribs squeezed air from her lungs, followed by quivers of rage. How dare someone do this? She looked round wanting to hit back.

Frank knelt down and pressed his fingers against Mabel's

neck. He bent closer. Then he gently lifted her head a few inches, releasing her face from the pebbles. 'She's alive, Laurie.' He got up; pulled off the sweater she'd lent him, and placed it over Mabel's shoulders. 'I need to get an ambulance and I need police help here. Does Shipster have a phone?'

She's alive. Thank God. 'Yes. Take the torch.' She pulled off her jumper and placed it with the one Frank had laid over Mabel.

'You'll be all right?' The beam danced over the shingle as he turned towards her.

'Frank!' She pointed down the beach. There was a small bundle of fur: motionless. She ran to him. Muffin's little legs were still. His teeth bared, in one last growl. The top of his head was caved in, and trickles of dark blood coated one sightless eye. Horror swept over her. The little dog that'd earlier in the day rolled on his back, tail wagging, was dead. She reached out to stroke his fur.

'Laurel! Don't touch him. Stay with Mabel. Talk to her. She's unconscious, but she might be able to hear you. Give her reassurance. If she comes to, ask her if she remembers who hit her. Not likely, I'm afraid, I think her skull's fractured.'

Like Muffin's. 'Don't worry, Frank I'll be OK.' She moved to Mabel's side and gently laid a hand on her cheek.

Frank gripped her shoulder. 'I'll be back as soon as I've phoned. Shipster can guide the ambulance crew down here. I'll contact Ipswich hospital – they may need to operate.' His grip on her shoulder tightened. 'What will you do if someone comes back?'

'To finish her off?'

'Yes.'

She lifted up a heavy stone. 'They'll get a taste of this.'

'Good girl.' Then he was gone, running up the steps, the light from the torch arcing into the black sky.

149

Frank emerged from the trees to find he was at the back of the main house. As he ran along the right side of it he saw lights. He headed for Shipster's house. As he ran on, he raked the beam of the torch from side to side, just in case. He was sure the animal they'd disturbed as they approached the steps had been of the two-legged variety: the person who'd attacked Mabel and killed Muffin. The light of the torch, visible from the beach, and Laurel's shouting had warned him... or her.

It was unlikely they'd still be around; they'd have gone to earth. Pity, he'd have enjoyed giving them a whack with the torch. The light was still on in Shipster's house. He banged on the door with a clenched fist.

'Get down, Shipster. This is an emergency.'

He continued to hit the door. He heard Shipster stamping towards him. He was shouting, and clearly not in a good mood.

A chain rattled and two bolts screeched. The door was pulled open.

'What the hell are you playing at? Inspector Diamond! What's happened?'

Shipster was partly wrapped in a short, striped bathrobe, his hair dripping wet, steam rising from his body and water trickling down his thin calves forming patches on the welcome mat. A bath to wash blood away?

Shipster pulled the towelling bathrobe together and shoved his hands into deep pockets. Hands with scratches, bruises and cuts? No time to check.

'Where's the telephone?'

'In the sitting room. What's happened?'

Frank pushed past him. 'I'll tell you later.'

Shipster stood in the doorway as Frank dialled 999 and told the ambulance service what was needed. Then he dialled the hospital in Ipswich and alerted them to the need for a neurological team to be ready. Next he dialled Elderkin. He glanced up.

Shipster was swaying, his face grey, both hands pressed against his cheeks as though he was holding his head on.

There was a silence from Elderkin after he'd given him the news.

A gulp at the end of the line. 'I'll get as many men as I can. I'll be there soon… Any hope?'

'I don't know, Stuart. I'm going back to the beach – Laurel's with her.' He paused. He needed to know. 'Muffin's dead. Head cracked open.'

There was a quick intake of breath. 'Whoever did this – they'll pay for it.' Anger and grim determination were evident in his voice.

'I'm with Shipster. He'll direct the ambulance to the steps. I must go now.'

Shipster collapsed into an armchair. His face ashen, his arms trembling as he continued to hold his head with both hands. No cuts or bruises on his hands, but the assailant probably wore gloves. No time to check on him. Mabel was the priority, not to mention Laurel.

'Did you hear that, Shipster? You must direct the ambulance and police to the cliff steps. Mabel is on the beach. Then you must get all the staff who are on site together in the main building. An officer will go with you. No one must leave the site, including you. Do you understand?'

Shipster's haggard face was blank. Either he was genuinely in shock or he'd been taking drama lessons from John Gielgud. 'Get dressed and stand near the main gate. I need to go back to the beach.'

Shipster pushed himself up from the chair, his legs buckling.

'Where's the headmaster?' Frank asked.

'I don't know.'

'His house is in darkness, but check if he's at home and tell him what's happened. He can help you get the staff together. Come on, man, get a move on.'

Shipster tottered to the stairs, and then turned. 'It's *her* fault. If he hadn't brought her here we'd have all been safe. I curse the day I saw her.' He climbed the stairs, using his hands to drag himself up.

Frank filed the remark for later.

Laurel watched the torch's beam light up the steps and the bushes clinging to the cliff's sides. Then the light was gone and she was alone with Mabel, the only sounds the grinding waves and Mabel's laboured breathing. She inched closer to her hoping to warm her.

What kind of person would smash her skull? How could anyone attack poor harmless Muffin? Why? Why had they done this? There was only one answer: they wanted to silence Mabel, make sure she never revealed what happened when she met Susan Nicholson the evening she was killed. There couldn't be any other explanation. Some people would say it was a maniac, a mad person with a lust for blood. Rubbish.

Suppose they came back? They might have been hiding and when they saw Frank leave they might think he'd left Mabel alone and unprotected on the beach. She raised her head and listened. She'd hear them coming over the stones, however carefully they moved. She tightened her grasp on the stone and crouched over Mabel, ready to defend her.

Frank had said the noise they'd heard at the top of the cliffs was probably a deer. It was certainly a bulky animal crashing through the shrubs. Could it have been the attacker? Had he been down here, bent over Mabel, ready to hit her, finish her off? Then the flashing beam of the torch, her cries as she tried to find Mabel – had that stopped him? She

152

imagined a black shape, arm raised, a bloodied rock in his hand, raising his head, sniffing fear, seeing the light coming closer, hearing the cries 'Mabel! Mabel!' then panicking, throwing down the rock and running up the steps and managing to escape.

Suppose he hadn't gone up the steps? Perhaps it was a deer. He might have turned and escaped by running below the cliffs to Minsmere beach and the path up to the car park. Or perhaps he only went a little way and hid in the shadow of the cliff ready to come back if they didn't find her. Even now he could be making his way back to finish Mabel off. She turned her head to the south, trying to make out any movements, or suspicious noises.

A sudden wind from the sea rustled clumps of sea cabbage, squeaking their leathery leaves together. Goose-bumps erupted from her arms. She leant closer to Mabel. Was the sound of her breathing changing? What did Frank say? Talk to her – she hadn't done that. What could she say? How could she sound calm and cheerful when Mabel lay near to death and Muffin was a few yards away, his little body already losing warmth?

'Mabel, I don't know if you can hear me. It's Laurel. You're safe, Frank's gone to get help and we'll soon have you in hospital and better again.' She gently rubbed Mabel's hand. 'Whoever did this will be caught and punished.' Was that what she would want to hear? Perhaps not. She needed to tell her something she'd be interested in. 'This morning I met Frank Diamond in Aldeburgh. We had delicious fish and chips from your chippy and we met the Misses Piffs. I didn't realise they were identical twins…' She chattered on, all the while trying to be aware of any threatening noise or a moving black shadow, knowing her voice would guide the murderer to them.

Would she be able to strike out if needed? Not only strike

out but hit them until they fell to the beach unconscious? Would she be brave enough? Strong enough? If it was a woman she was sure she'd win, but a taller, stronger man? She remembered the last time there was violence, and how she'd reacted. Then there was hate in her heart and she'd had no thought for herself, only wanting revenge for Angela. Could she do it again? They say the second time is easier. She shuddered and tightened her grip on the heavy stone.

'Laurie! Laurie! Are you all right?' A beam of light was dancing down the steps.

'Frank! Thank God you're back. Mabel's still alive.' She dropped the stone and stood up.

Frank wrapped her in his arms and hugged her. 'Well done. Help will be here soon.' He pulled free and bent over Mabel. 'No sign of her coming round?'

'She hasn't moved. They did this to stop her talking, didn't they?'

'I can't think of any other explanation. Do you want to go up to the house? You're shivering.'

'And leave Mabel? No. I'm staying.'

'Good. Keep talking to her. I'll stand guard.'

She crouched close to Mabel. 'Keep fighting, Mabel. Don't let them win. Hang on.' She clasped Mabel's hand and squeezed it tight, praying that somehow Mabel would sense she wasn't alone; she was with friends who cared about her and help was on its way.

Chapter 16

Monday, September 14, 1970

Laurel groaned: there was a banging in her head, as though dwarves with iron hammers were hitting the inside of her skull. She buried her head under the pillow but the noise kept on. Forcing her eyelids open she realised the banging was on the front door. She pushed the bedclothes aside and staggered down the stairs. What had happened? Was it news about Mabel?

A red-eyed Dorothy Piff stood outside the cottage, her face pinched and a crumpled handkerchief crushed in her hand. 'Laurel, I'm so sorry to wake you like this but you have to come to the school.'

Laurel stepped back to let Miss Piff in; she put an arm round her. 'You've heard about Mabel?'

Miss Piff nodded, sniffing and wiping her eyes. She straightened her shoulders and shook her head, as though determined she wouldn't lose control of herself. 'Yes. When I came in at eight I met Inspector Diamond – he told me – and about Muffin. What is happening, Laurel? Why would anyone do such a thing? A firing squad wouldn't be good enough for them.'

A cold, damp wind was blowing in from the sea. Laurel pushed the door shut and ushered Miss Piff into the kitchen. 'Why am I needed at the school?' She looked at the kitchen clock. Ten past nine. She'd had a few hours' sleep; more than Frank if he was at the school by eight.

'The Chairman of the governors has called a meeting for ten and Mr Nicholson wants you there. I'll make you breakfast while you get washed and dressed. What would you like?'

Laurel's mouth felt as though the same dwarves had painted it with verdigris. 'Tea, Miss Piff – sorry, Dorothy; lots of strong tea with milk, no sugar and some toast. Thanks. Tea's in –'

'I'll find everything.' She bustled to the fridge, looking relieved to be once more in charge.

Laurel, washed and dressed, returned to the kitchen where a cup of tea was waiting; she took a gulp washing away the metallic taste in her mouth. 'Perfect.' She pushed her cup forward and Dorothy refilled it.

'What time did you get to bed last night?' Dorothy asked.

'I'm not sure. I followed the ambulance to Ipswich. Fran... Inspector Diamond went in the ambulance in case Mabel recovered consciousness and was able to tell him what happened.'

'But she didn't, did she?'

Laurel shook her head. 'I don't think he expected her to, but he couldn't take a chance.'

The cup rattled as Dorothy placed it on the saucer. 'Did they... operate?'

'Yes. I left when she went into theatre. Any news this morning?'

'No one's said anything. There's a lot of extra police, two minibuses from Ipswich. They're down on the beach with Sergeant Elderkin. Searching, I suppose. What will they be able to find?'

How did Frank organise that so quickly?

'Look,' Dorothy pointed out of the kitchen window, 'it's started to rain. There's a storm forecast for tonight, a bad one, as if we haven't got enough to cope with. All the staff have been told they mustn't leave the site and they'll be interviewed as soon as possible. Inspector Diamond has made them go to different rooms so they can't talk to each other.'

Laurel chewed the last piece of honeyed toast and washed it down with tea. The clock showed quarter to ten. 'We better get to the school. Is the meeting in Mr Nicholson's office?'

'Yes. Mr Shipster will be there, Inspector Diamond and possibly the chief constable. You wouldn't know Inspector Diamond hasn't slept all night; looks as fresh as a daisy.'

Typical Frank. 'I just need to nip upstairs, won't be a minute.' Laurel dashed into her bedroom and quickly applied mascara and a dash of lipstick. She couldn't let the side down.

Sitting round the conference table in Nicholson's office were Frank, Shipster, a large, plump man, who was introduced by Nicholson as the chief constable, and the chairman of the governors, who wouldn't meet her eyes: no wonder – he must have known if he'd told the candidates for the post of senior mistress that Susan had been murdered, some of them, including her, would have left. After shaking hands, she took a seat.

'Miss Piff would you take notes, please,' Nicholson ordered. His face was like carved wood, as though the night's events had frozen his expression and he was unable, or unwilling, to show his emotions. Shipster was haggard and looked ten years older than a week ago.

Frank, by contrast, looked as sharp as a newly honed knife: the green irises of his eyes surrounded by clear whites; his brown curls shone, looking freshly shampooed, and under his leather jacket was a black turtle-necked sweater. Laurel raised her eyebrows at him and he gave a slight nod and an even slighter smile.

The chief constable, with shoe-buttons for eyes and a small tight mouth, looked an unpleasant man. She didn't like the way he scowled when she came in, as though he couldn't understand why they'd bothered to wait for her. Bet he wasn't Frank's best buddy.

Nicholson took a cigarette case from his jacket pocket and opened it up. 'Benson and Hedges. Anyone like one?' There were no takers. He lit up.

'Inspector Diamond would you give us an update of the situation, please,' the chief constable said.

Frank briefly went over the night's events without giving anything away that might be useful to the attacker. So Shipster wasn't in the clear. Or was he? He could have run back to his house after attacking Mabel. What about Nicholson? He hadn't been in his house last night, but he'd a solid alibi for Susan's murder, Frank said.

'My thanks to the chief constable for strengthening the number of policemen at my disposal. Luckily we'd arranged for an increase in numbers before Mrs Grill was attacked. Most of them will be working on the beach, the steps and the grounds today. These areas are strictly off limit to all the staff.' Frank looked at Nicholson.

The headmaster nodded in agreement. 'I'll make sure everyone is aware of that.'

'When are the pupils expected back?' the chief constable asked.

'Wednesday,' the chairman of the governors barked. 'I know what you're going to ask and I agree with you. We must postpone the beginning of term. We cannot have the children coming back with a murderer on the loose. We cannot risk it.'

Nicholson briefly closed his eyes, and then ground the stub of his cigarette into an ashtray.

'Good,' the chief constable said. 'You will postpone it to…?'

The chairman looked at Nicholson whose face was expressionless, his fingers tearing strips off the edge of the blotting paper in front of him and rolling them into balls. 'A week?' he asked. Nicholson nodded.

'A bit tight,' the chief constable said.

'Add an extra day; let's say Tuesday the twenty-second. How are you going to do this?' the chairman asked Nicholson.

'Miss Piff and I will telephone the parents. Mr Shipster will help me. Could you draw up a list for me as soon as possible, Mr Shipster?' Shipster nodded; he looked ill. 'Miss Bowman,' Nicholson continued, 'would you help Miss Piff?'

'Yes, of course. I think it would be helpful for the parents if we wrote to them as well, giving priority to those we can't reach today. If we get the letters to Ipswich by this evening they should get them by tomorrow,' Laurel said.

'Perhaps an article in the national press would alert the parents. There's bound to be something in the papers by tomorrow. An official announcement from you,' Frank said, looking at the chairman, 'might be better than no statement from the school.'

The chairman shuddered and glanced at Nicholson, who nodded assent. 'This is going to ruin the school.' He turned to Frank. 'I bloody well hope you make a better job of this than the last lot did.' He swivelled and faced the chief constable. 'I hold you responsible. This attack must be tied up with Susan Nicholson's murder – sorry, Philip – but it's got to be said. If the police had got their fingers out and caught the murderer, we wouldn't be in this mess.'

His deteriorating temper helped to fill the room with an atmosphere thick with testosterone, frustration and rising anger.

The chief constable's face, above his white shirt and dark uniform jacket, was rapidly turning a colour which matched his tie: maroon. 'I don't think you're helping matters, Chairman,' he said, his eyes almost disappearing as he glared at him. 'We need to work together if we're to solve this latest attack. I can understand your frustration, but the priority is the safety of the children, the rest of the staff and, of course, the well-being of Mabel Grill. Our thoughts must be with her at this moment.'

Good for him. 'Is there any fresh news about Mabel?' Laurel asked.

'The operation appears to have been a success. They've removed splinters of bone from her brain and inserted a metal plate. She's stable but heavily sedated.' Frank paused and looked round the table. 'A police constable will be at her bedside twenty-four hours a day, ready to take a statement if she comes round and also to make sure she's safe.'

The chairman looked shamefaced. 'Good, good. Excellent. Sorry I lost my rag, but if this isn't cleared up quickly we may have to take more drastic action.'

Nicholson came to life. 'What do you mean?' His eyes were wild, staring, his face pale.

'We may have to close the school, perhaps not permanently, but until all this is cleared up. I can't see parents wanting to send their children here,' the chairman said.

'No, that can't happen.' Nicholson slumped back in his chair.

Shipster shook his head from side to side in denial of the chairman's sentence.

Frank was rubbing his chin and staring at them in turn, as if he was trying to make up his mind which one he disliked the most.

Chapter 17

Frank was standing by the window in Shipster's office, deciding which of the staff to interview first.

Stuart Elderkin came in. 'Benjie Whittle's in the clear,' he said, looking pleased. He'd been to check on Benjie's alibi for the previous night. 'He was in the Eel's Foot from seven until he got thrown out with the rest of the reprobates at ten. I've checked with the landlord and two other drinkers.'

'Good. I'm glad. I think we can cross him off for Susan's murder as well. I'm assuming whoever attacked Mabel murdered Susan. I could be wrong, and we'll have to keep a semi-open mind, but that's the way I'm thinking. Agreed?'

Elderkin pulled out a chair and sat down at the desk. His face was grey with fatigue, but his eyes were sharp. He drummed on the table as though the movement of his small fingers were echoing his thought patterns. 'I'm with you. If we eliminate a few more along with Benjie we can concentrate on the ones left. It's got to be someone connected to the school. Did they find anything on the beach?'

Frank sat down next to him. 'Yes, a large stone, size of a grapefruit – blood and hair on it. It's gone to Ipswich for fingerprinting, but I don't hold out much hope. That would be far too easy.'

'When are you starting the boys looking for the log book?'

'Not until tomorrow.'

Elderkin's bushy eyebrow met. 'Thought you'd start that today.'

'I want to interview all the staff this afternoon or this evening and hopefully eliminate some of them. Then the search of the private rooms will start early tomorrow with the major suspect's rooms first or at least those that haven't got an alibi. Nicholson's house will be number one: hopefully Susan hid the log book there. If the killer found it I think it'll have been destroyed, but you never know. It's a long shot, but we've got to make a thorough search.'

'Who shall we interview first?'

'Let's see those we think are unlikely to be the murderer. No logic, let's go on gut instinct. We'll see those to begin with and the main suspects we'll keep sweating. Hopefully, in their agitation, they may say something revealing.'

'How about Emilia Mapp? We know she couldn't have been responsible for Susan's murder, she was in France when that happened,' Elderkin said.

'Agreed; good idea. Notebook ready and pencil sharpened? Send PC Cottam for her.'

Emilia Mapp was soon dealt with: she'd been at the cinema in Aldeburgh with her boyfriend. She was happy to give his name and address. She expressed her horror at what had happened and said if she could be of any help she was happy to do anything.

As the door close behind her Elderkin observed, 'Wonder if she can cook? Or at least make some tea.'

'Stuart, how can you think of food at such a time of crisis?'

Elderkin rubbed his gut. 'Murder always gives me an appetite.'

'One of the kitchen helpers has been made temporary cook until Shipster finds another one. However, as the start of term has been postponed, I'm sure everyone can fend for themselves,' Frank said, cocking his head and looking quizzically at Stuart.

'All right for you, you can go home and whip up one of your omelettes; I was depending on a few meals here to keep me going. Who's next?'

162

'Let's hear from Henry Thornback. Where are his rooms?'

'He's got a flat in the main house, along with most of them. It's hardly a flat, more of a bed-sitting room and a small kitchenette. They share bathrooms and lavatories.'

Henry Thornback sauntered into the office. He looked as though he'd given thought to his appearance: smart navy blazer with gold buttons, white shirt and yellow cravat, bryllcreamed hair and shiny shoes. He placed a hand on one of the chairs near the table.

'Please take a seat, Mr Thornback,' Frank said, staring at him.

Thornback's hand pulled back as if the chair was electrified. 'Er... thank you.' Suddenly he didn't look so sure of himself. 'Terrible about Mabel. How is she? Any news?' He sat down.

A smooth customer, Frank thought. Laurel had told him about her conversation with Thornback at the staff meeting. He was a ladies' man. A man who'd chat up any woman and make a move on her if he thought she was easy meat. Had he thought Susan Nicholson was a pushover? Why does he want to know about Mabel? Is he hoping she's dead?

'Mabel's holding her own. We'll know more by tomorrow.'

Thornback unnecessarily smoothed his well-groomed hair. 'Jolly good, that's a relief. Place wouldn't be the same without Mabel.'

'Mr Thornback, I'd like details of your movements last night from six onwards, please.'

Thornback's mouth fell open. 'Good Lord, you don't think I'd do a thing like that?'

Elderkin shuffled his seat so he was closer to Thornback, and leaned towards him. 'Someone did it. Where were you last night?'

What was left of Thornback's confidence drained away and he looked like a deflated party balloon. 'I was here. All night. I had a date but she called it off. I watched telly in my room, had a few gin and tonics and went to bed. Pretty boring evening, really.'

Frank thought he wouldn't mind a few boring evenings. 'Did you see anyone? Did you talk to any other member of staff?'

Thornback rolled his eyes. 'I try to keep as far away from that shower as I can. Boring lot of old farts, all of them.'

Elderkin snorted and edged a few inches nearer to Thornback, who flinched, and tried to move away. 'What was on the TV?'

Thornback's cheeks sagged. 'Er, *Dr Finlay's Casebook*,' he muttered.

Elderkin snorted.

So Elderkin was playing the bad cop. Frank didn't feel like being the good one, but he'd been forced into it. Still it was worth a try. 'Mr Thornback, Henry,' he spoke softly and smiled at him. 'When we interviewed you before I was sure there was something you wanted to tell us about Susan Nicholson. It was on the tip of your tongue, wasn't it?' He nodded, gazing into Thornback's eyes and trying for his most sincere expression. 'I felt you wanted to help us; that you wanted to do your bit to find the murderer. Is that right?' Frank smiled at him again, nodding encouragingly. 'I realise you may not want to break a confidence and you may be worried your information will be relayed to Mr Nicholson, but I assure you anything you tell us will remain confidential.' It was only a tiny fib.

Thornback wriggled on his seat, blinking hard and chewing his lip, unable to make up his mind. Elderkin leant forward a smidgen more. Thornback flinched. 'Well, er, there is something... doesn't put me in a good light, and I wouldn't

164

want Nicholson to find out.' He stopped, gulped, looking shifty.

'Susan Nicholson had a hold on you, didn't she? Was she threatening you?'

Thornback's eyes widened. 'So you know about it? How did you find out?'

Frank tried to look as though he was in full knowledge of whatever Thornback was going to tell them. 'Never mind that, Henry. Tell me in your own words what happened. I'm sure you want to put forward *your* point of view,' he said calmly.

Thornback seemed to relax, as though glad he could talk about it. He swallowed, and then pulled himself upright in the chair. 'My weakness is the ladies. Can't get enough of them. I suppose some people would call me a philanderer, but I like women and... their company.'

The usual problem: too much testosterone and a belief all women wanted sex, even when they said no. 'Go on, Henry,' Frank encouraged.

'Well, Susan was a pretty thing, bit on the skinny side, but she knew how to flaunt what she'd got. I could see she was bored stiff at the school and although old Nicholson was obviously potty about her, and I'm sure she got plenty of action in the bedroom, she had a roving eye and liked to flirt. I thought I'd make a pass and see what happened. You never know your luck.'

Elderkin was scribbling away, his mouth turned down at the corners as though there was a nasty smell in the room.

'And what did happen?' Frank asked.

'I invited her to my room for a drink, one day when Nicholson had taken a rugby team to another school for a match. She sat on the settee, drink in hand, skirt riding up showing her legs – they weren't bad – simpering away. We got nice and cosy, I got to first base in no time. Easy peasy, I thought. I had one hand in her bra and I started to pull off her knickers when she went berserk; accused me of trying to rape her. Said she'd tell her old man and get me the sack. She stormed off.'

'What did you do?'

'I didn't know what to do. I thought of catching him as he came back, confessing I'd kissed her, or something, trying to get in first. I can tell you I was in a blue funk. I just sat there and waited for the chop.'

'But it didn't come?'

'No, but she did – came back to my room. Said she'd thought about it and she didn't want to ruin my career. However, she did want something to keep quiet.'

'And what was that?'

'She wanted me to get copies of the keys to all the staffs' private rooms.'

So Susan wasn't just a snooper, a prurient busybody – she was a blackmailer and she was hoping to find more victims. 'And you obliged?'

He hung his head. 'I tried to wriggle out of it, offered her money, but she was adamant. Yes, took me a bit of time but I did it. Cost me a fortune driving over to Ipswich and getting them cut – couldn't do them all at once.'

'When was this?' Frank asked.

'It was towards the end of March, last year, 1969, when I made the fatal mistake of trying to seduce her. I suppose it took me a few weeks to get hold of the different keys and get them cut, couldn't do too many at once, look a bit suspicious. I was a bloody fool. Do you think this could have anything to do with her murder?'

Frank nodded. 'You gave her keys to several Pandora's boxes. If you aren't the murderer, Mr Thornback, you helped Susan towards her death.'

His face paled. 'It wasn't my fault,' he blustered, 'she was a bloody blackmailer. I didn't kill her, but I was relieved when someone else did. I didn't harm her and I like Mabel, I wouldn't have hurt *her*. I don't go in for hitting women – never had the need.'

After he'd left Frank and Elderkin sat in silence, looking at each other.

'She was quite a person, was Susan Nicholson. She had keys to every private room so she could snoop to her heart's content when people were away in the holidays,' Elderkin said.

'Looking for weaknesses, guilty secrets. I can't believe her husband couldn't have been suspicious of her. Surely someone must have said something to him?' Frank said.

'Who's next?'

'Let's try Vanessa Letts.'

'Bit of a snob, isn't she?'

'That's the one, and after her send for Warren Ringrose.'

Frank and Elderkin had no luck in their interview with Vanessa Letts, head of English. She didn't have an alibi, she was uncooperative and became flushed and angry when Frank had asked her if Susan Nicholson could have discovered something about her she didn't want revealed. After she left Frank asked Elderkin to explore Miss Letts' past life. He wasn't happy with her answers.

Warren Ringrose's face was the colour of stale porridge as he sat down at the table, pushing his slight body back against the chair, as though afraid either Elderkin or Frank would attack him.

'Mr Ringrose, can you tell me where you were last evening from six onwards, please,' Frank said in a mild tone, not wanting him to faint – his face was already starting to green.

Ringrose licked his lips. 'I was in Ipswich... with a friend.'

'Until what time?'

'Ten o'clock – I drove back and well... I couldn't believe what had happened. How is Mabel? I heard Muffin was...' His eyes welled up and his lips trembled. 'He was a lovely little dog... who could have done that? I don't think I can stand this much longer. I'm afraid. Who'll be next?' He took a handkerchief from his trouser pocket and loudly blew his nose.

'We need the name and address of your friend. You do understand why?' Frank said. The man seemed genuine in his grief and fear, and he just didn't have the physique for the job. But the thought of giving the name of his friend, possibly lover, was making his agitation worse.

Ringrose rolled the handkerchief into a ball and was passing it from one hand to the other.

Elderkin leant forward. 'Name and address, please.'

'I can't. I can't. You don't understand.'

Frank decided to try a different tack. 'I think we do, Mr Ringrose. I believe you're a homosexual and Susan Nicholson discovered this. I believe she held that fact over you, threatening to reveal it to the governors or Philip Nicholson, or both.'

'Come on, lad,' Elderkin said in a friendly tone, 'no one is going to harm you. It isn't a crime anymore; and if neither of you are hurting anyone else, and no children are involved, we're only interested in catching this person before they attack someone else.' He paused and patted Ringrose on the back. 'Spit it out, lad, you'll feel better when it's all out.'

Elderkin the Dutch uncle. Frank wasn't sure if every-thing that Elderkin had said was by the book, but it looked as if it was going to work: Ringrose's expression had changed, and a slight flush of pink crept into his cheeks.

'Thank you, Sergeant.' He gave the name and address of a man called Ewan who lived in London. 'Will you give me time to phone him, so he knows what this is all about?'

'Not a good idea, Mr Ringrose. Your alibi will be stronger if you haven't spoken to him,' Frank said.

Ringrose sadly nodded his head. 'Yes, I understand.' His eyes widened and the colour left his face. 'But who'll talk to him? Will it be a London policeman? Will you have to tell him about us?'

'I'll go myself and explain the circumstances to him. I'll drive up early tomorrow morning and catch him before he goes to work,' Frank said.

'Would you? Oh, thank you, Inspector, I'm truly grateful. He'll be in. He's an artist; he'll be working in his studio.'

Frank hoped so and that he'd be alone: he didn't want to find the friend with another friend. 'Was I right about Susan Nicholson? Had she got a hold over you?'

Ringrose nodded. 'I don't know how she found out, but one day she asked me if she could talk to me in private. I never dreamt she was like that; she even had Ewan's address. She was sympathetic: she'd been an actress and said she knew lots of men like us, but she didn't think her husband would be so understanding and she wasn't sure what to do.' He put his head in his hands and scraped fingers through his hair. 'I didn't know what to say, what to do.' He looked up at them. 'I didn't deny it. I was paralysed.'

Frank could believe it. 'What happened?'

'She patted me on the hand. "Perhaps we could come to some arrangement. I'm always a bit short of money, perhaps if you gave me a few pounds every month, as a token of goodwill, I'll forget all about your sex life." She smiled at me. Then I realised what this was all about. She was blackmailing me. I paid up – what could I do? Five pounds a month to begin with, then she put it up to ten pounds – I expect it would have been more soon. Please don't tell Ewan, will you? I never said anything to him about Susan Nicholson: I was afraid he'd finish with me.'

'We believe Susan Nicholson had keys to all the private staff rooms. Could she have found Ewan's address in your room?' Frank asked.

Ringrose's nostril's flared. 'The bitch! Yes, in my desk drawer – there are letters and she could have found out where he lives from my address book.'

'That'll be all for the moment, Mr Ringrose. I must ask you again not to contact your friend, for both your sakes. I need to be convinced you're telling the truth. If I think you have colluded with him, it may put both of you under suspicion. Ewan could become a suspect too. Also you mustn't discuss this conversation with anyone else. Is that clear?'

Ringrose nodded, then threw back his head and groaned as though he'd been kicked in the stomach.

Elderkin shook his head after Ringrose had left the room. 'They won't be the only ones, will they? There'll be others she's blackmailed. I'm sure Miss Letts has something to hide. She's big enough to have attacked Mabel. What's her little secret?'

Frank got up and walked to the window. 'There are two storms brewing: one from the North Sea and the other inside this school. Lift any stone and you find a black beetle underneath. I could do with a cup of coffee, and then we'll have a word with Dorothy Piff.'

Dorothy Piff was soon eliminated. She and her sister had been at evening service the previous evening and later were guests of the vicar for supper. Frank didn't think the reverend was a likely suspect. Jim McFall had no alibi; he was reading and listening to the radio all evening and hadn't seen anyone.

He was taciturn and didn't respond to Frank's questions about Susan Nicholson, although he coloured up angrily at the thought she had a key to his rooms and could have searched them for something he didn't want to reveal. Frank asked Elderkin to set in motion a search of McFall's background.

Shipster wasn't able to produce an alibi, apart from being in the bath; he was uncommunicative, his face grey, the lines from mouth to chin deepened by... worry?... guilt?... sheer exhaustion?

Toni Habershon looked strained as she came into the room, her round face pinched, freckles standing out against white skin. She sat down at the table and clasped her hands tightly on her lap, as though trying to keep control of her emotions. 'Miss Habershon, did you see Mabel Grill yesterday?'

'I saw her working in her front garden yesterday morning.'

'Did you speak to her then, or at any other time during the day?'

'No.'

'Did you know she was going to take a walk with Muffin in the evening?'

There was a nerve twitching above her right eye. 'No, how could I, if I didn't speak to her?' she snapped.

Elderkin looked up from his notebook and stared at her. She glared back at him.

'Miss Habershon, please tell me where you where yesterday evening from six onwards.'

'I was in Ipswich.'

Was the whole school in Ipswich? 'Please elaborate.'

She twisted her fingers until they were white. 'I went to the cinema and then to a pub, we... er, I came back about ten-thirty.'

'You were by yourself?'

'Well… no… this is very embarrassing. If I tell you… well… I'm not sure I can.'

Frank waited, sitting back in his chair and slowly and gently drumming his fingers on the table. Elderkin sat with his pencil poised.

'I was with Mr Nicholson. We met when I went for a walk in the morning and he saw I was a bit down and suggested we meet in Ipswich and have a break from all this.' She waved her hand at them as though they were the cause. 'We both drove our cars and met at the cinema.'

'I see. The name of the cinema and the film you saw, please.'

'We went to the Gaumont; the film was *And Soon the Darkness*.'

'Any good?' Elderkin asked.

She gave him another glare. 'Not really my type of film, but it wasn't bad.'

Elderkin didn't make a note of that.

'Can you tell me something about the film?' Frank asked.

'It was a British thriller, about two English girls on a cycling holiday in France. One gets murdered.'

'That's fitting,' Elderkin mumbled.

The old dog had learnt his new tricks surprisingly well and seemed to enjoy performing them. 'And the pub you went to?'

'The Queen Victoria, it's near the cinema.'

'Did either of you meet anyone you know?'

'I don't think so, unless Philip met someone at the bar when he was getting the drinks. Perhaps the barman will remember him.'

'Miss Habershon, we believe Susan Nicholson had copies of keys to all the staff's private rooms. We also believe she'd found out secrets of some members of staff and was

172

threatening to reveal these to the headmaster or governors. Did she ever threaten to do this to you?'

She didn't look surprised. 'There's nothing in my life I need to be ashamed of. Did she have a key to my cottage? Are you sure? That's disgusting – prying into people's personal lives. Does Philip know you're making these accusations about his wife? I don't believe it.'

'So you're adamant that she never threatened you with exposure about something in your past?' Frank asked.

She got up, her face red with either temper or embarrassment. 'I've just told you. If you haven't any more questions, I'd like to go.' She made for the door.

Frank nodded to Elderkin who shot up and stood in front of the door. 'Sergeant Elderkin will escort you to the staff room and will bring Mr Nicholson back.' Her shoulders were quivering as she marched out of the room.

She hadn't once mentioned Mabel. Why? Shouldn't she be upset at the thought of her neighbour being brutally attacked? Even if she didn't like her, shouldn't she be frightened at the thought of another woman being set on, the assailant obviously wanting to murder her? What was the relationship between Nicholson and Toni Habershon? Was it recent or was there a history to it?

Nicholson came into the room followed by Elderkin, who contorted his face behind Nicholson's back, trying to pass on some silent message to Frank. Frank guessed, looking at Nicholson's face, he was in a bit of a temper.

'Please sit down, Mr Nicholson,' Frank said. Nicholson pulled back a chair making a sizeable gap between table, the detectives and himself. His handsome face was inexpressive, but his nostrils were pinched and his blue eyes with their unusual ring of black round the irises, stared at Frank as though they were rivals in an eye-balling competition.

He's tall and well-built, Frank thought. Well capable of

doing someone physical injury; but he'd an alibi for his wife's murder and now it seemed he'd one for the attack on Mabel. Pity.

He pretended to write up some notes on his pad, head bent over the paper. Elderkin sat down close to Nicholson. Nicholson moved his chair away from him. Good old Elderkin, an instinctive policeman. Frank looked up and blinked his eyes. Nicholson's colour was rising. Excellent. 'Mr Nicholson, would you tell me where you were yesterday evening between six and ten?'

'You've interrogated Miss Habershon so you know perfectly well where I was,' he snarled.

'I question, not interrogate. Besides Miss Habershon might have made up that story; you might have been somewhere completely different,' Frank said.

'Really! This is preposterous!' Nicholson leant forward and banged his fist on the table. Elderkin jumped. 'I shall report your behaviour to the chief constable. Isn't it time you got on with your job of apprehending this person – not wasting your time harassing innocent people?'

Frank leant forward and placed his elbows on the table. 'Everyone is under suspicion until the killer is caught; that's the nature of a murder inquiry, Mr Nicholson. Now please answer the question.'

Nicholson confirmed everything Toni Habershon had said.

'Have you any proof that you were in the cinema?'

Nicholson thought for a second. 'I may have the cinema stubs somewhere. They might be in the pocket of the jacket I wore yesterday.'

Frank was sure they would be. 'Good. Please give them to me tomorrow if you find them. Did you meet anyone in the pub who you knew?'

'No. It's a very large, busy establishment; I doubt if even

174

the barman will remember me.'

'Don't worry, we'll check. I'm sure anyone would remember an imposing figure like yourself.' Frank smiled as he complimented him.

Nicholson frowned, seemingly unhappy Frank wasn't taking his word for it.

'Mr Nicholson, are you aware that your late wife had keys to all the staffs' private rooms?'

'What? Keys? No. Certainly not. I think you must be mistaken. She never asked me for any keys. She only had keys to our house; she didn't even have a key to my office.' He looked genuinely amazed.

'I'm afraid I'm not mistaken. Also your wife was in the habit of digging up facts about members of staff they didn't want revealed and then using that information to threaten them. In one case we know of she blackmailed them for money.'

Nicholson leapt up, his chair crashing to the floor. 'This is scandalous slander. How dare you try to defame a dead woman's name? What proof have you? Which members of staff have said this? I demand to know their names.'

Both Frank and Elderkin stood up. 'Sit down, Mr Nicholson. You're not in a position to demand anything. What I've said, I believe to be true. Your wife discovered something so awful about the murderer's past they were prepared to kill her to make sure she was silenced. She'd keys to all the staff rooms and the opportunity, in the school holidays when the staff were away, to enter these rooms and to search their belongings and papers. I believe she found something that if revealed, would ruin someone. We have to find out who that person was.'

Nicholson slumped down onto the seat and lowered his head into his hands. 'God in Heaven, is this really true? I can't believe it.'

Frank waited until he'd regained some of his composure. 'Had you no idea that your wife was… inquisitive about other members of staff?'

Nicholson looked up. The muscles of his face sagged and his eyes were unfocused, his gaze darting between Frank and Elderkin. He looked like a cornered animal, a dangerous animal. 'She used to ask me about staff members; she said she wanted to be aware of any problems so she'd be able to help them.'

'What information did you give her?'

'I don't know… I can't remember. I'll have to think about it. This is a dreadful shock. Are you quite sure?'

Frank nodded. 'Sergeant Elderkin will confirm it.' He nodded to Elderkin.

'Yes, sir,' Elderkin put down his pencil. 'It seems your late wife made a habit of searching other people's rooms, and evidence from her last place of employment suggests she could also have been a petty thief.'

Nicholson ran his hand through his black hair until it stood up in spikes. 'This is awful. It's getting worse by the minute. What else have you uncovered? – I might as well know it now. Will this come out in court if you catch the murderer?'

What a strange thing to worry about; he doesn't want his reputation sullied by his wife's actions. 'If our suspicions are correct it will be part of the prosecution's case as motive for her murder.'

Nicholson shifted uneasily in his chair, his hair and eyes still wild. 'I can't take all this in. Who do you suspect? Who's told you about Susan's stealing? Are you near to arresting the murderer?'

'I'm confident we'll discover the murder's identity soon. Mabel Grill should recover consciousness. She'll have an important story to tell and as we eliminate suspects we'll be able to hone in on the murderer.' Frank hoped he had a satisfied look on his face. 'That's all for today, Mr Nicholson. Tomorrow I want to see the cinema stubs, if you have them, and I want you to try and remember which members of staff your wife asked about and what you told her.'

Nicholson slowly raised himself upright. 'How is Mabel? Is she out of danger now? Will she be able to remember what happened?'

'The signs are encouraging the doctors say. I'm optimistic.'

'That's good,' Nicholson whispered. He turned and left the room.

When Nicholson had closed the door behind him, Elderkin turned to Frank. 'Is that true about Mabel?' he asked hopefully.

'No, I wish it was. I wanted to stir things up. I can't believe he didn't know something about Susan's activities.'

Elderkin stroked his chin. 'I don't know. Women can be secretive. I didn't know my wife was helping out her sister with money every month, until she died, and her sister told me. She must have saved it from the housekeeping. I didn't notice. She was a wonderful manager, was Doreen. I don't know why she didn't tell me, I wouldn't have minded. Her sister had a rough time: husband left her with two kids. She's done well with them.' His face was sad.

'You were lucky to have a good wife, Stuart. You still miss her, don't you?'

'I do. I may go on about her wonderful cooking, but what I miss most of all is someone you can talk to, someone you can trust. But women are queer creatures. You think you know them and then they go and do something you wouldn't expect.'

Women. Frank had come close a few times, but somehow he couldn't see himself living with any woman, not even on a temporary basis. Women, wonderful creatures, but they always wanted to change you. Make you have a short back and sides, get a nice safe job and a saloon car with room for several sprogs in the back.

That was why he liked Laurel. Good company but no deep involvement. Laurel. He must check on her, see if she was all right after last night. Sometimes he forgot she was a woman: she was someone he liked, admired, someone he could work with. He *was* working with her; hope the chief constable didn't find out.

The situation at the school was becoming more dangerous. He was hoping the pressure he'd put on the suspects and the searches of the rooms that would start tomorrow, would make the murderer do something foolish, revealing their identity. He was taking a risk: the murderer might, in his mounting panic at the thought of discovery, harm someone else. He must try and persuade Laurel to leave the cottage.

'So who's left on our list, Stuart?'

'We can probably eliminate Philip Nicholson, Dorothy Piff, Emilia Mapp, Warren Ringrose, if his alibi stands up, Benjie Whittle, and I suppose Toni Habershon. That leaves us with Vanessa Letts, James McFall and Robert Shipster. I'll get on with looking into Letts' and McFall's backgrounds tomorrow. What about searching the rooms, shall I wait until you come back from London?'

'No. Collect all the staff, even those we've eliminated, and put them in the staff room. Brief the team what to look for: the log book and any other suspicious objects, especially damp or bloody clothing, or clothing recently washed. Also examine soles of all shoes. Fire the boys up and stress they must *not* reveal what they're looking for. You've got the search warrants?'

Elderkin nodded. 'This is going to get the staff going. Do you want me to help in the searching?' He pulled out his pipe and tobacco pouch and looked questioningly at Frank.

'Have a smoke, you deserve it. Yes, I want you to help. Leave your most senior constable and a WPC in the staff room to make sure none of them leave unescorted to any place they desperately need to go to, including the lavatory. You lead the search of Nicholson's house. If the murderer didn't find the log book, that's where it should be hidden. Have one of the bright young cops with you, probably Cottam, set him on the task; he'll want to do well. I'll be back from London as soon as I can. Happy with that, Stuart? Anything else you can think of?'

Elderkin chewed his lip. 'Do we need to search Dorothy Piff's house? Not very likely, I know, seeing as she was the one who told us about the log book.'

'Yes, we'd better. Everyone must have the same treatment. I'll explain it to Dorothy when I get back from London, but we'll need another search warrant if she's not cooperative. Good point, Stuart. Also, besides checking up on McFall, and Letts, can you get checks done on Nicholson and Shipster? Find out where Nicholson taught from when he graduated from Durham to the present time. See if anything interesting happened in these areas.'

'Not given up on him then? I'll see to it tomorrow. I hope we have some better news of Mabel soon.'

'You're fond of her, aren't you? Sorry if I'm speaking out of turn.'

'I am. It's not like falling in love when you're young, but I get on well with her. I don't know if anything would have come of it: she's a very independent woman. Now I might never know.'

He looked so down at the mouth Frank wanted to hug him. He didn't. 'Don't give up hope, Stuart. She's in good hands. I'll go to the cottage to see Laurel later, make sure she's all right. I think I'd better drive, this rain's getting

179

worse.'

They both looked at the window; the sky was blackening, rain hitting the window panes like lead shot, and gusts of hurricane-force wind rattling the glass.

Chapter 18

Laurel looked out of her cottage window at the storm-filled sky. She was bone-tired but restless. She'd been with Miss Piff telephoning the parents all day and at the end of their session she'd asked Dorothy if she could phone her parents; she didn't fancy using the phone in the dining room, or a walk to Dunwich. Dorothy discreetly left the office. Her parents had heard on the news about the attack on Mabel and urged Laurel to come home. She'd tried to reassure them she was safe, but it was difficult trying to sound confident.

She yawned; she'd had little sleep the night before and after telephoning her parents she'd gone to the kitchens to help the temporary cook make supper for the staff. Now she craved fresh air and the excitement of the storm. She pulled on her wellingtons and a waterproof, banked up the fire and placed the fireguard in front of it. Leaving the light on, she stepped out into gale force wind. Head down, she walked towards the sea.

She clung on to the rails at the top of the beach steps, the wind tearing at her hair as though it was trying to scalp her. She squinted through volleys of icy rain at the boiling sea. Waves reared up frighteningly high, dirty cream spume dancing on the crests as they crashed onto the beach sending stones and sand whirling up, crushing the yellow sea-poppies on the shore. High tide would be in the early hours of the morning. If the storm didn't abate there'd be flooding, and the sandy cliffs wouldn't be a match for the broadsides the sea would fire.

The rain and wind washed away her tiredness and scoured her mind of depressing thoughts of Mabel and poor Muffin. She screwed up her eyes and looked at her wrist watch – gone eight, light was fading, and dark storm clouds, their bellies etched with lightning, were piling up and rolling in – time to retreat. She let go of the rails, pulled up the hood of her waterproof, and turned her back on the sea. The wind forced her to run through the creaking Holm oaks.

The light from the window of her cottage showed Mabel's flowers flattened and sodden. She imagined Mabel lying in her solitary ward, head bandaged, and body still. Was she able to breathe by herself? She prayed Mabel would live. She'd known her only a short time, but already she was dear to her.

There was a light on in Toni Habershon's house. Should she see how she was? If she did it wouldn't be out of kindness, it would be to poke and pry, trying to find out if she knew anything. No. Not tonight. She wasn't in the mood. She needed to think about what happened last night. Hopefully Frank would fill her in on today's developments. The staff had been interviewed to check on their alibis for last night. The interviews would eliminate some of them. Who would be left as suspects? She found it hard to imagine any of the staff on the dark beach, a stone in their hand, and Mabel lying unconscious at their feet.

Inside, the cottage was warm. She removed the fire guard, gave the embers a stir with a poker and put another log on the fire. The wind roared in the chimney, sucking up the yellow and blue flames from the fresh wood. She shook her waterproof over the bath and hung it up. She hoped Jim McFall had an alibi: she liked him. He'd left a pile of beech logs by the door yesterday, and slipped a note through her letterbox. *Storm expected. You may need these.* She'd had supper at school, but a glass of whisky would go down well.

Upstairs she changed into a track suit, dried her hair and decided her face, made raw by the wind and rain, needed some attention. Hunched over the fire, supping her whisky, she listened to the storm battering the house. The windows rattled so fiercely she was afraid the glass would shatter, and overhead tiles rippled and chattered. She took a sip of whisky and leant back in the armchair, the house must have weathered many storms.

Who was the murderer? It must be someone here; perhaps someone she'd seen today. Who was capable of committing murder? She was sure she knew why Mabel had been attacked, but why was Susan murdered? Maybe, in her ferreting, she'd discovered something so awful someone had to get rid of her. The answer lay with Mabel and what she'd remembered on her walk with Muffin. Perhaps she hadn't remembered anything; but the murderer wasn't to know that. The murderer must have guessed why she was taking that walk and they were afraid she'd remember something that would split the case open.

So what could she have seen on that walk when she saw Susan Nicholson near the sluice? Was it something to do with Muffin? Muffin hadn't been with her and Mabel when they'd gone together on the walk, he'd been ill from eating too much rabbit. Mabel said she hadn't spoken to Susan, she'd walked away. Was it something to do with Muffin?

Who could it be? Not Warren Ringrose, not Jim McFall – she hoped, definitely not Miss Piff, nor Emilia Mapp. It couldn't be Philip Nicholson, he'd an alibi for Susan's murder – pity; the husband was always a likely suspect. What about Henry Thornback? Could it be a woman? She smiled wryly. Yes, it could. Toni Habershon? Vanessa Letts? Possible. They were both physically capable of both crimes. But why? What were their motives?

There was a hammering on the front door. The Scotch slopped in her glass. Dear God, not another attack. As she inched the door open, the wind snatched it from her hand, banging it against the wall. The light shone on to the face of

Philip Nicholson and behind him, his Land Rover.

'What's wrong?' she shouted, the wind drowning her words.

He didn't reply but pushed in, and together they forced the door shut. His hair was soaked, rain cascading off his waterproof.

'Sorry about this, didn't mean to alarm you or flood you out. I called to make sure you're all right. Thank you for your help today. We've contacted nearly all the parents and I got someone to go into Ipswich and post the letters. The Royal Mail are being very helpful, they said they'd make sure the letters are on the train. Hopefully Mr Shipster will manage to get in touch with the remainder of the parents this evening.'

Laurel led him into the kitchen and handed him a towel. He rubbed his head as though drying a dog. She felt claustrophobic, closed in by the oven, fridge, cupboards and his muscular bulk. She needed more space. 'Would you like a Scotch? I was having one when you knocked.' She grabbed a glass and pushed past him into the main room.

'Thanks, half water please.'

He seated himself, uninvited, near the fire, as though he was settling in for a long session. A cosy chat? Or a chat up? She didn't fancy either. She took the seat opposite him.

'So how are you, Laurel, after the trauma of last night? You don't look as though you've been through a terrible experience.'

'I went for a walk. The wind and rain woke me up.'

He sipped his drink. 'Ah, that's doing the trick' He paused, as though not sure what to say next.

She didn't help him.

'So you and Inspector Diamond discovered Mabel. How did that come about?'

She took a slow sip, trying to find the right answer. Was he interested in why she was with Frank or why they went out

184

looking for Mabel? 'Inspector Diamond has told me not to discuss last night with anybody. I'm sorry, Mr Nicholson, I'm afraid I can't answer your question.' It wasn't true, but it was a good get-out.

'Really? How did you come to be with Inspector Diamond yesterday? I hope you can answer that question.' His voice was tight, clipped, with a hint of anger.

'I ran into him in Aldeburgh yesterday afternoon. I told him I wanted to see Mabel and he came back with me,' she said. 'It's probably better if we don't talk about this at the moment. Thank you for checking on me, but I think I'll have an early night. I'm very tired.' She drained her glass and stood up.

He didn't move, took another very small sip of whisky as though he was trying to spin it out. 'Yes, of course. I'll finish my drink and then I'll leave you in peace.' He took another infinitesimal sip. 'Was Mabel conscious when you found her? I believe you stayed with her on the beach. Did she come to and say anything?'

Why was he pumping her like this? 'No, she was unconscious and didn't say anything.'

'Have you had news of her today?'

'Only what we've all heard. She's holding her own.'

'Yes, good, that's good. Did you see her in hospital? Which ward is she in?'

Why does he want to know? What difference does it make where she is? 'No, I left as she went into theatre. I believe she's under guard, there's a policeman at her bedside at all times. So it's no good the murderer trying to finish her off; she's safe and as soon as she comes to we'll know who the murderer is.' His face was blank. Why had she said that? Mabel might not have seen her attacker, she might never remember, she might be brain-damaged, and worse of all she might die.

185

He sat there, immobile, seemingly unable to move. How was she going to get rid of him?

There was another loud knocking at the front door. 'It seems this is a night for visitors. Someone else coming to check up on me?'

He got up, threw back his head as he swallowed the last of the whisky and went to the kitchen, presumably for his coat.

Once again the door was snatched from her and Frank Diamond, drops of rain clinging to his eyelashes, rivulets running down his cheeks, and curls plastered to his scalp, stood before her.

'Frank! Come in. Would you like a drink? Mr Nicholson came to see if I was all right. He's just leaving.' As he came closer, she whispered, 'Thank God, you've come.'

Nicholson, coat on, approached from the kitchen. 'Ah, Inspector. You mustn't stay long, Miss Bowman is very tired. Also it's getting late. We don't want tongues wagging, do we? – Especially as you were together yesterday. I presume your visit's something to do with the case?'

The cheeky bastard. Laurel felt her cheeks burning. 'I don't think it's any business of yours what Inspector Diamond wants to see me about.' She opened the front door, gripping it tight with one hand, and sweeping the other in front of her to indicate it was time he left.

Frank grinned. 'Don't worry, Mr Nicholso. Miss Bowman's reputation is safe in my hands.'

Somehow the way he said it implied the opposite meaning. Another cheeky bastard. She smiled.

'Good night to you both. I'll see you in the morning, Miss Bowman,' Nicholson said icily.

She banged the door behind him, punched Frank in the arm and got him a towel from the kitchen, not the one Nicholson had used; that she threw on the floor. She blew out her lips in relief.

Frank shook his head over the sink and slowly towelled his hair and patted his face. 'Was he about to have his wicked way with you?'

'No. I don't think that was the reason for his visit. He was trying to pump me about why we were together yesterday, and if Mabel had said anything. I told him you'd asked me not to discuss the case with anyone. Hope that was all right?'

Frank nodded. 'Get me that drink and I'll fill you in on what's happened today.'

Just what she wanted to know. The anger and irritation caused by Nicholson's visit faded. He trusted her. She poured two more glasses of Scotch and they sat by the fire, exactly in the positions occupied by Nicholson and herself, but now she was happy, relaxed and eager to hear what Frank had to say.

He briefly told her everything he'd learnt that day. She felt his eyes carefully watching for her reactions.

'Nicholson and Toni Habershon together – I wonder…'

Frank leant towards her. 'Yes?'

'Did I tell you about overhearing two people talking when I was in the ruins a few days ago?'

Frank's eyes widened, he looked as though extra neurons were coming into play. 'No.'

'I'd taken… Muffin out for Mabel.' She pushed her hair back. 'We were sitting in the Leper's Chapel. I was half-asleep; they couldn't see me and I couldn't see who was talking, but I'm sure one was Toni. I think the other was a man, but I couldn't hear his voice clearly.' She told him what she'd heard.

He repeated the words and phrases back to her. '"You promised… how much longer do I… I risked… if you don't… I won't wait… Inspector Diamond." Are you sure that's what you heard? You've not forgotten anything? Not added anything?' His brows were knitted in concentration.

'I'm sure. I tried to catch sight of them, but poor Muffin

made an escape and I had to go after him. But as they both have alibis for last night it can't be them. I suppose Toni could have murdered Susan, but it's unlikely there are two murderers. Sorry, Frank, it's probably a red herring. I'm confusing the picture.'

Frank scratched his head. His hair was now a mass of tight curls, making him look even more like a rock star, certainly not a policeman.

'Thanks, Frank, for telling me all this. I'm grateful and I do want to help. Now Nicholson knows we're in cahoots no doubt it'll quickly spread round the staff and I may not be able to get people to confide in me. However, I'll keep trying and thinking.' She took another sip of whisky.

'There's another reason I came tonight, Laurel. I think you ought to move off the school site. I've stirred up the pot and the murderer might have been pushed off balance. It's too dangerous for you to stay here. You're not a suspect. I suggest you get some digs in Aldeburgh or Dunwich.'

She sat up straight. 'I'm sorry, Frank. I'm not moving until Mabel's attacker is caught. If it was just Susan Nicholson, I might agree; from everything you've told me she was a dreadful person – not that she deserved to be murdered, but after seeing Mabel and Muffin on the beach last night I refuse to go.' She smiled at him. 'There's an alternative: you could take me in as a lodger. I'd be cosy and safe with you.' She raised her glass to him and drained it.

Whisky spluttered out of his mouth. 'You tart, Laurel Bowman. No way. I could be hauled over the coals as it is, and probably will be. Time to say good night. Make sure you lock and bolt all the doors and keep something handy under the pillow.'

She raised her eyebrows. What a reaction. 'Any suggestions?'

'You can borrow a rounder's bat from the school.'

'I've something better than that.' From behind the settee she brought out a giant wooden spoon. 'Some of the sixth-form girls from my previous school brought me this back from their summer holiday in Portugal; it's for stirring the port.'

'A whack from that should keep any one quiet,' Frank said.

'I used it to win the girls versus the staff egg-and-spoon race at the annual sports day. I borrowed an ostrich egg from the Biology Department and Sellotaped it onto the bowl. The rest couldn't run they were laughing so much.' She poked the spoon into Frank's ribs.

He grabbed it and pulled her towards him. 'Happier times, Laurel?'

She nodded, remembering. Then, Angela was alive.

Chapter 19

Tuesday, September 15, 1970

Laurel woke up and groaned: her neck was stiff and her back rigid. She'd spent the night of the storm in the armchair by the fire, falling asleep when the storm eased and the wind was no longer threatening to rip tiles off the roof. She shrugged her shoulders, trying to loosen up cramped muscles. She should have gone to bed, but the storm, her two visitors, and a murderer close by had unnerved her. You idiot, she thought, and picked up the spoon from the rug and put it back behind the settee.

She looked at the clock – six-thirty – and pulled back the curtains. The day was eerily calm after the chaos of the night, the sky a Wedgwood blue. What she needed was fresh air and exercise. No need to change – she was still in her track suit. She gulped down a glass of water and switched on the emersion heater. A run along the beach and a hot bath were called for.

Her legs were heavy as she ran towards the Holm oaks. One tree was down and torn-off branches littered the ground. The steps to the beach had survived. She pounded down them; a step near the top seemed to give as her foot struck it. She must report that when she got back. She stopped on the third step from the bottom. The beach had changed. Stones were piled up over the bottom steps and, horizontal to the sea, ridges of stones and pebbles divided the beach into narrow strips; caught in these spaces were the spoils of the storm: driftwood, swathes of plastic-like laminaria, bunches of bladderwrack, and all the flotsam and jetsam of the seabed, dragged into the air by the power of the waves. She clattered through stones, pebbles, and shells to a strip of sand at the edge of the sea; innocent waves lapped against the scrubbed beach. The tide was turning.

She turned south and jogged towards Minsmere beach, moving from one strip of wet sand to another as it sucked at her trainers; all around pebbles glistened like false jewels. She ran past a cliff fall. A mountain of ochre earth, boulders, stones and broken trees cascaded over the beach. The cliff above was striated like a layered cake. How much of the land had the storm eaten? She looked up. Was the fall below the ruins of the abbey? Had more gravestones and bones tumbled onto the beach to be washed away by the sea?

She picked up speed, her legs relaxing, stretching out, her lungs expanding as she breathed in the pure air, scoured by the storm. Large objects, nearer the sea, lay on the beach: disgorged boulders, planks of wood and part of a rotted boat hull. She wished she'd been there in the storm and seen it happening; watched as sea-bottom treasures were hurled into the air and tossed onto the beach.

When she reached Minsmere beach she decided to run as far as the sluice. She had nothing to do at the school, perhaps more telephoning, but after last night she didn't think anyone would miss her. The staff would be rounded up before the search of their living quarters began. Everyone would be in foul moods. Enjoying herself, she increased her pace.

A man was running towards her, waving his arms and shouting. She stopped, her chest heaving. She couldn't make out the words. Her muscles tightened. Was he going to attack her? Was this the murderer? She looked round and picked up a piece of drift wood, flexed it in her hands, it crumpled into pieces. No good. She didn't know him. The man continued to run towards her, shouting. His booted legs were short, he had a square body and his waving arms were powerful. She picked up a large stone.

He skidded to a halt, arms still in the air. 'Don't hurt me, Miss. I didn't do it.'

He sounded simple. His moon-shaped face, with pale blue, saucer-shaped eyes was terrified. She guessed who he was: Benjie Whittle, the fisherman who'd found Susan's body in the sluice and who'd been accused of exposing himself to her. She dropped the stone. 'Are you Benjie?'

'Yes, Miss, I'm Benjie. You won't hurt me will you?' He was breathing heavily, cowering before her.

'What's the matter, Benjie? Were you running away from someone?'

His face crumpled; he looked about to cry. 'It's horrible, Miss. I opened it. I thought there might be treasure, like you hear about: jewels and gold. I thought, this is it, Benjie, this is the big find, but then, well, it was horrible. They'll think I done it. I found *her*, you know. She was dead.'

Her throat tightened, she swallowed hard. What had he found? 'Were you beachcombing, Benjie?'

'Yes, I was down on the beach early. When we've had a big storm, that's when you find the best things. They've been washed up from the bottom. I've found some good stuff after storms.' He became calmer as he talked.

'I think you'd better show me what you've found. Would you take me to it, please? My name is Miss Bowman; I'm the senior mistress at the school.' She hoped a touch of authority would help.

'I've heard 'bout you. They've talked 'bout you in Eel's Foot. They said you was big – they were right there. They say the children ain't coming back. Is that true? I liked to see them running round and playing.' His face lost its animation. 'Some weren't nice to me. They shouted things at me. Nasty things.'

Perhaps the man was imagining he'd found something. He

192

was calmer and seemed to have forgotten what he's said before. 'Benjie, will you take me to whatever you found? The thing that upset you.'

He gawped at her for a second and then his eyes started to flicker. 'No. I don't want to look at it again. You go.' He pointed down the beach towards the sluice. 'You'll see it, at the sea's edge, just before you get to the sluice gates.' He shuddered. 'It was 'orrible.'

She'd had enough. She was pumped full of adrenalin from her run, edgy from worrying about Mabel and grieving for Muffin, disturbed by the storm and the visits of Philip and Frank – for different reasons – and now this. She wanted to get back and have a hot bath. 'I'm sorry, Benjie, *you* must show me. Also I might need your help.' She spread her arms and shooed him in front of her like some miserable, pecked old hen who didn't want to go into the coop.

He turned and shuffled in front of her. 'You won't make me look at it, will you?'

'No, but you mustn't run away. I may need your help. You will help me, won't you, Benjie?' She softened her voice; it wasn't fair to bully him.

He half-turned his head and glanced at her from the tail of his eye. 'You're talking pretty now, just like she did. But she was nasty in the end. She kicked that little dog.'

'What Muffin? Susan kicked Mabel Grill's dog?'

'No, t'was Choppy, Mrs Fry's dog. She threw boiling hot tea at him and kicked him. She was wicked, Miss Bowman, she was.'

Did Susan Nicholson hate dogs? Frank hadn't mentioned this. 'Have you told Inspector Diamond or Sergeant Elderkin about this, Benjie?'

'I did,' he said, stopping and turning to her. 'I told them, must've been last week.' He swung round and pointed. 'Look! There it is. I'm not going near it. Are you going to look? I wouldn't if I was you. It's 'orrible.'

'So you keep saying, Benjie. We'll go a bit farther, and then I want you to keep watch while I examine it. You'll guard me while I look at it and then I'll decide what we need to do. I'm depending on you, Benjie.' She hadn't been head of PE for nothing.

Benjie stuck out his chest, which was covered in a matted navy-wool jumper, pulled his shoulders back and his chin in, and nodded. 'I served in the life-boat in Aldeburgh when I was younger. I know how to take orders.'

She smiled at him. 'Thank you, Benjie.' She hoped this was a false alarm. There was a large, dark object at the edge of the beach, small waves lapping at its edges. It looked like a box. 'How did you open it, Benjie?'

'I used my knife.' He dug in the pocket of his serge pants and produced a large flick knife. He pressed a button, a long blade shot out and he waved it at her. 'He's a good old knife, he is.'

She wasn't leaving him with that while her back was turned. No point in taking chances. No one had been stabbed, but she didn't want to be the first knife victim in this particular series of attacks. 'May I borrow your knife, please?'

'You won't need it, Miss. I cut the strap and used it on the lock.' He frowned, his pale eyes enlarging. 'Shouldn't I have done that? Should I've left it?'

Strap? Lock? 'If you give me the knife, I can say I used it.'

Benjie stared at her, then slowly put out his hand and she took the knife from him.

'Right, you're on guard, Benjie. Let me know if you see anyone coming towards us.' She closed the knife and put it in her tracksuit pocket. She went to the sea's edge and bent down over the oblong box, its surface covered with sea-life: a few barnacles, the hold-fasts of seaweed, a limpet glued to the top. Beneath its battered, gouged and holed surface she saw it was a suitcase. There was a discarded twist of material beside it with fresh edges where Benjie had cut it. She picked it up and unfurled it: leather, and the remains of an eroded and tarnished buckle. It had held until Benjie had cut through the strap. A once thick leather strap, tightly bound round what was a large suitcase. There was a stripe of lighter leather where the strap had been. She rubbed a finger over it – brown leather; when dry it would be lighter. Light brown or… tan. Bile rose in her throat. She jerked her hand away – she felt like Benjie, she didn't want to see what was in the suitcase.

The lid was loose; there were scratches and cuts in the leather surrounding the lock where Benjie had forced it. A stout lock, but corroded by the sea, finally springing open from the force of his blade. She took a deep breath, and then glanced back at Benjie. He'd forgotten to stand guard; he'd a hand to his mouth and was staring at her. She slowly lifted the lid.

At first she wasn't sure what she was looking at. A jumble of sticks and stones, scraps of cloth. She gasped and rocked back on her heels.

'Come away, Miss,' Benjie cried. 'Don't look at it.'

Bones – a chaos of bones. She recognised a femur: long and slender – so many bones. Enough for a whole skeleton? Memories of the skeleton they'd studied in the anatomy lessons at college, swaying from the steel rod that connected it to its stand; the plastic skeleton she used in human biology lessons. How many bones in the human body? Two hundred and six? Could they all be in this suitcase? How could you fit a body into this space? It was a large suitcase. Mabel had said it was so big she couldn't have carried it far – a heavy, old-fashioned job, tan leather, with her father's initials on the front.

She lowered the lid but couldn't make out any marks beneath the crust of sea life. She opened it again. Tentatively she moved aside some of the cloth, afraid it would disintegrate in her hands. She shouldn't touch anything, but she had to know. The empty orbits of a skull blindly looked at her. It was the size of a young adult, with delicate cheek bones; the lower jaw bone lying at an angle to the rest of the skull. A few lanks of sodden hair clung to the cranium. Long hair: a woman or a young girl. She reached in her pocket, not for the knife, but a handkerchief. She tried to dry a strand of hair, it came away from the skull. 'Sorry,' she whispered. She patted the hair dry and held it up to the sun: ruby-red. She laid it back into the suitcase, closed the lid and sank to her knees in front of the leather coffin. Tears trickled down her cheeks. Poor, poor girl. An orphan – no one to look after her. To end like this: a heap of bones in a leather tomb, tossed into the sea, and no one to miss or mourn her, except Warren Ringrose and some of the other staff. The sea was her avenger, and had thrown her back to the land, demanding justice. It was Felicity – the lover of music, the talented red-haired girl – murdered.

Crunching pebbles. She wiped the tears away with her sleeve, and turned to see Benjie in front of her.

'Please come away, Miss. It is 'orrible, ain't it?'

She stood up. 'Yes, you were right, Benjie, it is horrible. I want you to go and find help. I'll stay here and guard… this.' She pointed to the suitcase.

'I'll go to Eel's Foot and get the landlord–'

'No, Benjie. You must go to the school. Look for Sergeant Elderkin. Tell him I'm waiting for him on the beach. You mustn't tell anyone else, unless you see Inspector Diamond, but I think he's in London. You mustn't tell any of the staff what you, er, we, found. That's *really* important.'

'Not even 'eadmaster?'

'No, not even him. Can you do that? Be as quick as you can. You won't get into trouble, I promise. You've been very brave and helpful; I'll tell Sergeant Elderkin how brave you've been.' She hoped he wouldn't run off to hide and leave her here. The tide would turn. She could haul the suitcase to safety, but it would be better if they saw it where the storm had cast it up.

Benjie nodded. 'I'll go, Miss. You're brave, staying with that. I wouldn't.' He turned and half-jogged, half-shuffled towards the school.

Chapter 20

Wednesday, September 16, 1970

Frank had been in this morgue before when he was a detective sergeant. The room hadn't changed: white-tiled walls, the grouting yellowing, aluminium sinks, with drawers below containing stainless steel instruments and, above, shelves, holding labelled glass bottles ready to receive various organs. In the centre of the room, under a harsh fluorescent light, was a rectangular metal table covered in a sheet of material. Bumps and ridges indicated something lay below the white cloth; it looked like a pristine undulating field of snow, but the whiteness covered a scene of decay and destruction. Elderkin was standing, arms folded, in front of the table, his head bowed.

For this post-mortem he wouldn't need to sniff from his antique silver vinaigrette, its sponge soaked in lavender oil to block out the smell of death. God knows what Elderkin would think if he ever saw it. It was the one thing about the post-mortem of a fresh body that nauseated him: the sickly sweet odour released from the abdominal cavity as it was sliced open revealing the skilful packaging of the abdominal organs. A decayed body was even worse. But apart from that the process fascinated him. He'd never ceased to marvel at the intricacy of the body of any animal. In the sixth form and later at university, dissecting a variety of animals from frogs and snakes to hedgehogs and cats, he'd always been amazed at the way the different organs showed the adaptations of that particular animal, and how the digestive system was delicately held together by translucent folds of mesentery, packed as carefully as a couture gown between sheets of tissue paper, fitting exactly into its exclusive box.

The mysteries of the human body. It annoyed him when the cause of death was obvious that the body still had to be cut up and violated. Angela had been strangled, but her liver must be weighed, and the skin of her scalp folded over her collapsed face, the top of her skull sawn off and her brain removed. A post-mortem soon resembled a butcher's shop; he always half-expected the pathologist to wrap up the kidneys in brown paper, add half a pound of sausages and give them to the sergeant as a perk – like Mr Jones, the butcher in Dad's Army, slipping a few slices of liver to Captain Mainwaring. He glanced at Elderkin. Perhaps he'd give him the benefit of his thoughts just before lunch.

A mortuary attendant poked his head round the door. 'Dr Ansell's been delayed, should be with you in five minutes. Can I get you some tea?'

Frank declined.

Elderkin tutted. 'He did the preliminary post-mortem on Susan Nicholson, I was hoping we wouldn't get him.'

Frank swivelled towards Elderkin. 'Two post mortems? I didn't know that. It wasn't in her file. Why didn't he do the full post-mortem?'

Elderkin shrugged. 'He got it all wrong. Inspector Bushell was furious, demanded someone with more experience take over after the body was moved to the mortuary.' He stopped speaking as the door opened.

Dr Ansell was a tall, thin man, with narrow shoulders, light brown floppy hair, which curled girlishly over his collar and the eyes of an anxious spaniel. He held out his hand to Frank. 'You must be Inspector Diamond, Martin Ansell.' He turned. 'Ah, Sergeant Elderkin, good to see you again,' he stuttered, his expression contradicting his greeting. He took a white coat from a peg on the back of the door, the assistant handed him rubber gloves and, as he donned the clothes of his trade, he seemed to straighten up, relax and take on a more confident air.

'Everyone ready? Shall we begin? There were several holes in the suitcase, quite small, but large enough to let crabs and other invertebrates, and indeed small fish, get in and remove any flesh – bacteria of course, will have helped – so no finger prints or clues to the identity of the victim of that sort.'

The attendant helped to carefully remove the sheet. Laid out in perfect order was the skeleton found on the beach. Each bone glowed cream in the harsh light.

'You must have worked all night to get the bones into this condition, Dr Ansell. Congratulations,' Frank said.

Ansell beamed as though he'd been awarded a gold star for good behaviour.

Frank moved closer. 'All the bones present?'

'Every one, all two hundred and six, not one phalanges is missing.'

Elderkin coughed.

Ansell turned teacher and addressed Elderkin as though he were a pupil who should have known better. 'Finger bone, Sergeant.'

'As you can see the body was cut into several pieces, I presume to pack it into the suitcase. You can see rough edges on various bones where they were sawn through. Not very expertly I may say,' he added disapprovingly.

He pointed to parts of the skeleton in turn. 'The skull was cut from the vertebral column at cervical two; the torso was cut in two between thoracic vertebra twelve and lumbar one; each limb was cut in two at the elbow and knee. As for identification, shall I tell you what I've found?'

'Please, go ahead,' Frank said. The fellow seemed more than competent, he obviously enjoyed his work.

'From the skull, and the colour of the hair, which is red, this is the skeleton of a Caucasian.'

Elderkin grunted.

'You can tell this from the cranial morphology, Sergeant Elderkin.' More grunts. 'The structure and the form of the skull and face,' he explained.

Elderkin nodded.

'She, for this is a female skeleton, was between fourteen and eighteen years old, of slight build, and indeed from the delicacy of her face bones,' he stroked the nasal and cheek bones, 'she must have been an attractive girl. A great pity.' He looked up at Frank. 'Whoever did this deserves to spend the rest of their lives at Her Majesty's pleasure. Do you think you'll find him after all this time?'

'Yes, I think we will. You say a man – couldn't a woman have done this?'

Ansell's forehead pleated and his eyelids flickered. 'Could be done by a woman, I suppose, but the butchery – mmm – not many women I know would have the stomach for this.'

'Not many men, either,' Elderkin muttered.

'There are two features of the skeleton which should help you with identification. The girl had a slight scoliosis, a side-to-side curve of the spine, this is most common in adolescent females; her doctor should have registered it. The other is her dentistry. There are no deciduous teeth – baby teeth – but she only had twenty-eight adult teeth: her jaw bones were small and the teeth close together. She must have had the four wisdom teeth removed to make room for the rest. Also she had one back lower molar filled, a gold filling, unusual in a young person. Can you get hold of the medical and dental records of the girl you think this is?'

Frank got his briefcase from a bench and pulled out a manila file. 'We collected them from the station this morning.

Sergeant Elderkin collated information about the girl when she went missing and wasn't found. Always handy, dental records.'

Ansell beamed. 'Excellent. Well done, Sergeant Elderkin.'

Elderkin face was suffused with rising blood.

Was he blushing or fuming? God's teeth, thought Frank, it's pats on the back all round, and *excellent* is my word. He'd let him borrow it. He started to open the file.

Ansell wriggled in excitement beside him as though he needed to spend a penny. 'May I?' He snatched the file from Frank's hand and quickly leafed through it. 'Yes. Yes. It must be her.' He pointed to dental charts. He looked at the name on the file and her details. 'Felicity. What a lovely name. Seventeen. Ah, a pianist.' He turned back to the table and picked up a slender finger bone. 'Such a cruel act. Catch him Inspector Diamond. Catch him.'

'Can you tell us how she died? Or is that impossible?' Elderkin asked.

Ansell scratched behind his ear. 'The hyoid bone in the neck is broken, which suggests strangulation, but after all the nibbling of fish and crabs, and bacterial decay, I don't think that would stand up in court. She could have been killed by a knife wound to soft tissue: a cut throat, or a lucky stab between the ribs. I couldn't find any knife damage to the bones, I examined the ribs and phalanges – finger bones –' he cast a quick look at Elderkin, 'especially carefully in case she'd tried to ward off blows with her hands. However, it's obviously an unnatural death, whether it was murder or manslaughter would be for a jury to decide. That's if you can find out who cut her up and dumped her in the sea.'

Frank rubbed his chin. He'd shaved this morning but the bristles were back. He'd chuck that electric razor. No, he'd better keep it in a drawer and take it with him when he visited

202

his mother. 'Sergeant Elderkin tells me you performed an autopsy on Susan Nicholson.'

Elderkin choked and Ansell's large ears turned red, starting at the lobes and working upwards.

His Adam's apple bobbed up and down. 'Well, not really, I was called to the sluice where she was found, but the inspector wasn't too happy with my initial findings.'

'What about you? Were you happy with them, before they got shot down in flames?'

Ansell straightened up, his ear lobes returning to a pale pink. 'I noted what I saw. I couldn't help it if... I say, I don't think we should talk about this... someone might come in. I don't think I'm too popular in some quarters.'

Frank looked at his wristwatch. 'When do you have a break?'

'I'm back on the wards at two. Why?' he asked nervously.

'I'd like you to tell me what you found when you inspected the body at the sluice. Can we meet somewhere? It's nearly twelve.' He turned to Elderkin. 'Know a pub near here?

'No, not near the hospital,' Ansell interrupted. 'If someone sees me with you... I've just about got back in their good books. They let me have this one,' he nodded towards the bones, 'because they thought I couldn't mess up with a skeleton. I really want to do more post-mortems, I find the dead fascinating – I studied for two years in the USA, they're well ahead of us in many ways.'

'How about if we drive you to a pub out of Ipswich and bring you back in time for your ward rounds?' Frank asked.

Ansell bit his lip. 'Why do you want to know what I think? Is it important?'

'You want me to find Felicity's murderer?'

Ansell nodded. 'I do. That's the main reason I'm interested in pathology, to discover the cause of death so that in the future such deaths can be avoided.'

'Who ever murdered Felicity may also be the killer of Susan Nicholson.' It was a slight exaggeration; he couldn't be sure, but anything to get his cooperation.

Ansell's eyes widened. 'Gosh! Really? Then of course I'll help. This is exciting. As I've said, it's why I want to do this kind of work: to solve mysteries, to help put people behind bars.' He paused, obviously thinking. 'Drive out of the car park towards the A12 and park a hundred yards up the road. I'll meet you there.'

The country pub didn't have a wide range of food: crisps, pork pies and pickled eggs. Frank settled for the crisps, Elderkin crisps and two pork pies and Ansell, surprisingly, had the same as Elderkin. The beer was flat; Frank thought it was near the bottom of the barrel.

Ansell nibbled at the crust of his second pie. 'Shall I tell you what I found when I examined Susan Nicholson's body?' he asked eagerly.

'We're all ears,' Frank said, then wished he hadn't, noting the size of Ansell's. Luckily the remark seemed to have passed him by.

'The disagreement was to do with the time of death. No one queried my findings on the cause. Well it was obvious – strangulation.'

Bubbles of oxygen started to whiz through Frank's brain. 'So when did you think she died?'

Ansell blinked and screwed up his eyes as though searching through the files of his brain. 'Susan Nicholson was found by Benjie Whittle on Thursday, 8th April, that's right, isn't it?'

Frank nodded.

'She was seen the day before, on Wednesday 7th April by Mrs Grill in the evening. By the way how is she? Are you going to see her while you're here?'

Elderkin wiped away crumbs from his mouth. 'We are. Aren't we?' he asked Frank.

Frank nodded impatiently. 'No change, she's holding her own. Yes, we'll see her when we take you back. Go on, please.'

'I put the time of death at least twenty-four and possibly thirty-six to forty-eight hours before the time she was seen by Mrs Grill.'

Frank's brain went into overdrive. 'What did you base that on?'

'Firstly, the state of rigor mortis. The chemicals in the body produced at death can stiffen the muscles as soon as three hours after death. It can last up to seventy-two hours. By the time I examined the body rigor mortis had disappeared. I know the body had been subjected to the water in the sluice and the movement of the machinery, but even so...'

Not enough. Bugger! 'Anything else?' Frank asked.

'Yes, the temperature of the body. That also indicated she was killed at an earlier time than Wednesday evening. Again we have the complication of the body being immersed in water...'

Could he trust Ansell's assertions? If true, alibis would have to be reassessed. 'Was there any other fact you noted that didn't fit in with her being murdered near the sluice and thrown in?'

'Yes. There was lividity in her buttocks, as though the body had been resting in a sitting position for some time.'

'Could you explain, please.' He knew what lividity was, but he wanted to hear it from Ansell.

Ansell looked puzzled, as though suspecting Frank's motives for asking. 'I'm sure you must understand,' he said defensively. 'Livor mortis occurs when blood settles into the lower parts of the body due to gravity. Without the heart pumping the heavy red blood cells sink through the serum and settle into the capillaries causing the skin to appear purplish. I was sure after she was killed she'd been put somewhere in a sitting position for a few days.'

'So what do you think?' Frank asked Elderkin, who was puffing at his pipe and looking mournfully at his empty plate. Ansell had gone to the loo.

'He seems sure of himself – I don't know. The other chap who did the proper post-mortem gave the time of death at round the time Mabel saw Susan or shortly afterwards.'

Frank played with the few shards of crisps left on his plate. 'Were you there when Inspector Bushell decided not to let Ansell continue with the post-mortem?'

Elderkin frowned and pushed up his lower lip towards his nose, as though he'd smelt something suspicious. 'Yes. Ansell came to the sluice as the doctor who usually did the post-mortems was tied up at the hospital operating. He examined the body after it was brought up from the sluice and told us she'd been strangled, which was correct, that she'd possibly been raped, also correct and gave the time of death as being 48 hours before. When the inspector interviewed Mabel and she said she saw Susan less than twenty-four hours before her body was found, he went berserk and demanded the usual pathologist carry out the full post-mortem.'

'Did that bother you?'

'At the time it didn't. I felt sorry for Ansell, but it was his first post-mortem for us, and he was nervous, and to tell you the truth, he didn't seem very competent. Today you could see the way he handled himself with Felicity's... er... bones, he knows his stuff, and he's remembered all the details of Susan's murder. If what he says is true we'll have to look at everyone's alibis again.'

They drove Ansell back to the hospital car park; he scuttled away, looking nervously from side to side, as if he'd been on a guilty trip to one of the town's brothels.

Stuart Elderkin leant over to the back seat and retrieved a box of chocolates. 'I know Mabel can't eat them, but if she came to, she'd know I've been thinking of her.'

Frank gave him a friendly punch in the arm. 'The nurses will enjoy them.'

As they walked towards the hospital buildings he decided to risk the question he'd wanted to ask Elderkin.

'Stuart, don't answer if you don't want to, but what was your opinion of Inspector Bushell's handling of Susan Nicholson's case?'

Elderkin didn't alter his stride. 'He did everything he should have done, by the book.' He glanced at Frank and sighed. 'You know he's ill, he's near retirement, and for the past few years I think he's lost his enthusiasm, his go... the case fizzled out. You know what it's like... if you don't get a good lead in the first few days, the longer it goes on, the harder it is to solve.'

'But you don't feel like that, do you, Stuart? You've kept your enthusiasm.'

Elderkin smiled. 'I think working with Inspector Bushell was catching. I was looking forward to retirement, I could go in a few months, but now I'm not so sure. Life in the old dog yet.'

The old dog's tail was almost wagging when they visited Mabel and was told that although she was still unconscious, she was off the ventilator and was breathing by herself. A nurse told them the doctors were hopeful she would regain consciousness soon. Elderkin left the chocolates on her bedside table and told the nurses to help themselves, but to leave the caramels for Mabel: they were her favourite. The

PC on duty was warned off the chocolates.

Back in Frank's car they smiled at each other.

'I think she's going to make it, Frank.'

Frank patted Elderkin's shoulder. He prayed when she came to she wasn't brain damaged. 'Looks like it. They're taking good care of her.'

'What's next on the agenda?'

'This is what I think we'll do next. Chip in if you think of anything I've missed. The search for the log book will continue tomorrow. If we find it and Susan did write in it about secrets of various members of staff, then the case may be solved for us. But it may be either we don't find the book or there'll be nothing incriminating inside it. I'll call a meeting of all the staff when the search has been completed.'

Elderkin was nodding.

'If we don't find the log book I'll tell them about it and ask if anyone saw Susan writing in a black book, or if they know where it is. Rumours will be going round about the discovery on the beach. By now people will hear that human bones were found. In the meeting I'll tell them Felicity was murdered and her body dumped at sea in her suitcase. Laurel's told me her thoughts about some staff; I'll ask her to watch the faces of certain members of staff. I think another pair of eyes would be useful, also we can ask young Johnnie Cottam to help. He seems to be with it.'

'Do you think that's the best way? Wouldn't it be better to tell them individually, so we can see their reaction?' Elderkin asked anxiously.

'If we do it that way someone is bound to blab before we've interviewed everyone. *One of them* will know by now it's Felicity's body that has been washed up by the sea. *One of them* will not be surprised when I tell them it's Felicity. We'll be positioned so we can see everyone's faces. The reason I'll ask Laurel to help is she's good at reading people.'

Elderkin wriggled uncomfortably in his seat. 'Do you think that's wise, Frank? I'm not sure the chief constable would approve.'

'I know it's a risk but I'll take responsibility, Stuart. I met Laurel on Sunday, she's a shrewd observer and although she hasn't been here long, she knows some of the people better than we do. She's living amongst them. She's someone on the inside, people may say things to her they wouldn't say to us.'

There was more wriggling from Elderkin. 'And she's happy to do that? Doesn't she feel she'd being unprofessional, talking about her colleagues? I don't like it, Frank.'

Frank took a long look at Elderkin. 'I'm going to tell you something which I must ask you not to reveal to anyone else. It's about Laurel. The reason she wants to help is she feels very strongly about bringing the murderer to justice. Her sister, Angela, was raped and strangled, the murderer was never arrested. It was in Felixstowe, two years ago, you may remember the case. I was on it before I was promoted and moved here. I'll tell her I've told you, but I'd be grateful if you keep it to yourself. The staff here don't know about her sister.'

Elderkin's face crumpled. 'Poor girl. Was she a younger sister?' Frank nodded. 'I won't say anything, but I'm not convinced about getting her involved, although I suppose she is already.' He shook his head. 'We'd heard before you came you were a bit of an odd-ball, but I think they played down your reputation.' He smiled and nodded at Frank. 'If we get results and they stand up in court you'll get no complaints from me.'

'Thanks, Stuart. Right, let's get moving and hope the search has turned something up.'

As Frank started the car he thought about what Ansell had said. Could he rely on his evidence? It wouldn't stand up in a court of law, he was sure of that. But if he was right and Susan Nicholson was already dead at least a day and maybe two days before she was tipped into the sluice, then where had her body been kept? How was she brought to the sluice? Who was the woman in the red coat? If Ansell was right Susan was dead before Mabel saw a red-headed woman in a red coat. Who was she? Could it have been Susan's ghost? But Frank didn't believe in ghosts.

Chapter 21

Laurel waited with the rest of the staff outside the music room. Frank had asked her to try and sit near Nicholson and Shipster so she could see their faces. There were angry murmurs as they were prevented from going into the room by a police constable; he informed them they must wait until Inspector Diamond was ready. He opened the door, blocking their view. He turned his head. 'You may go in now.' There were more angry murmurs as they shuffled in.

Frank and Elderkin were seated at a table on a dais, in front of two rows of plastic seats. She wasn't sure why Frank had asked her to sit between the two men and to note their reactions to what he said. Why Nicholson? He'd an alibi for Susan's murder and Mabel's attack. Shipster she could understand.

She'd never been any good at musical chairs and was foiled by Shipster, who quickly sat down on Nicholson's right. She managed to get an end seat on the front row next to Toni Habershon. She positioned the chair so she had a good view of all the faces of the people on the front and second rows; Henry Thornback and Vanessa Letts were on the front row with Nicholson, Shipster and Toni, and Warren Ringrose, Miss Piff, Emilia Mapp and Jim McFall were seated in the row behind.

Frank was flanked by Sergeant Elderkin to his right and PC Cottam to his left; another constable sat at the end of the table, a notepad and pencil in his hand. A third constable stood at the door, arms folded. The atmosphere was intimidating.

The day was fading and Frank gestured to the constable

on the door to put on the lights. Harsh fluorescence emphasised tense, pale faces. Laurel wriggled – the plastic seat was cold and uncomfortable. What was going to happen? Rumours had been circulating all day: the school might be closed; bones had been washed up by the storm; was the murderer one of them, a member of staff?

She felt uneasy – how must the rest of them be feeling? They knew they were suspects. She imagined what they were thinking: why had they been summoned to this room? Was the inspector going to reveal the murderer; like Hercule Poirot in an Agatha Christie thriller? If the murderer was in the room how must *they* be feeling? Were they ready to run for it if Frank shouted out their name? Or would they sit there and brazen it out?

She knew Frank wasn't going to do that, it was a ridiculous idea. She tried to clear her mind and concentrate, ready to rationally observe, without prejudice, any unusual reactions to the news of Felicity's murder. Difficult to do – she was biased towards either Shipster or Toni Habershon being the murderer, but only because she didn't *like* either of them. Not a good enough reason for pinning a murder on anyone.

The room seemed devoid of oxygen, her throat was scratchy and several staff were coughing or clearing their throats. Frank looked as cool as… a cucumber? No, cucumbers didn't wear leather jackets. As cool as a private eye in a Hollywood film – Philip Marlow – only Frank was better looking than Humphrey Bogart – far less battered. She sat up straight as she saw Frank was about to speak.

'Thank you for coming to this meeting and for your forbearance with the search of your quarters and indeed all parts of the school. That search has finished and so after the meeting you can return to your rooms.' He spoke slowly and clearly, with authority, turning his head slightly, as he made

212

eye contact with every member of the audience.

'I'm sorry to say the search has not been productive.' There were snorts and 'I told you so,' from some of the staff. He waited, his face unreadable, until they quietened down. 'We were looking for a particular item.' He held up the log book. 'Miss Piff has lent me this.' Puzzled murmurs from the staff. 'We were looking for a book like this, a school log book.'

There was an intake of breath from Philip Nicholson and he turned his head and stared at Miss Piff.

'We believe Susan Nicholson took an unused school log book from the stationery cupboard and may have written in it. If she did do this, what she wrote may be important to this case. I want anyone who saw Mrs Nicholson writing in a book like this, or in any book, to inform me now or after the meeting.' He paused, slowly looking at all their faces. 'Or if anyone knows where this book is they must tell me.'

Philip Nicholson turned to look behind him again, his forehead creased and his face suffused with red. Angry with Miss Piff? She obviously hadn't told him about Susan stealing the book. She glanced round – Miss Piff was biting her lip.

Feet shuffled, Miss Mapp had a coughing fit and Warren Ringrose offered her a pastille from a tin. She hoped they weren't Fisherman's Friends; Miss Mapp might need a jug of water to put out the fire.

The staff were whispering to each other. Frank banged on the table with his fist. 'Thank you.' The noise ceased. 'There's another matter I'd like to tell you about. As you've probably heard, a suitcase containing human bones was found on the beach by Benjie Whittle and Miss Bowman yesterday. This morning a post-mortem was carried out and there is no doubt these are the bones of Felicity Groves, a pupil who disappeared from the school in the Easter holidays in 1967.'

Laurel fanned her gaze over all the staff, paying particular attention to Nicholson and Shipster. Nicholson's face was cast in stone – not a muscle moved. Unfortunately, she couldn't see Shipster, but Toni Habershon was rigid with shock, her eyes widening, a hand covering her mouth. Turning, she saw Warren Ringrose's face was greenish-white and he staggered up from his seat.

'No! Not Felicity.' He pushed past Jim McFall and made for the door. The constable held him firmly, looking at Frank for instructions. He pointed back to the chairs.

'Please sit down, Mr Ringrose. Everyone is upset, but if we're to find the murderer, or murderers, of these two women, everyone must cooperate,' Elderkin said.

The constable led Ringrose back to the end of the second row of seats. He slumped down and supported his head with his hands, elbows on his knees. McFall patted him on the back and whispered to him.

Laurel looked at the rest of the staff. Miss Piff was pale-faced, glasses off, wiping her eyes with a handkerchief.

McFall was shaking his head. 'Poor, wee lassie.'

Now she could see Shipster's face; he looked as though he'd been personally offended.

Seated next to Toni Habershon, Vanessa Letts, for once, looked as though something had finally pierced her carapace of snobbery. She leant over Toni towards Laurel, 'She was murdered because she was an orphan. She had no one to care and protect her.' The words seemed deeply felt and her eyes were full of tears. Laurel placed her hand over Miss Lett's, but she pulled away as though she'd been stung.

Henry Thornback looked puzzled, a frown creasing his forehead.

The staff started whispering to each other in frightened and angry tones. Frank rapped on the table, once more bringing the meeting to order. 'Can I have your attention, please? I know the news Felicity was murdered – and there is no doubt about that – must have been a great shock to all of you. Well, perhaps not all.' He paused and as the meaning of his last words penetrated their minds, an icy chill settled over the room.

Miss Piff sank into her chair. 'Oh, no,' she whispered, her voice filled with horror. Everyone began looking at each other, some visibly cringing away from their neighbour.

'What are you implying, Inspector Diamond?' demanded Shipster, rising from his seat. 'Are you saying one of us killed Felicity? This is outrageous.'

Thornback, who was sitting next to Shipster, pulled at his arm. 'For goodness sake, sit down. Of course that's what the man's saying. Two women have been killed. Who else could it be except one of us? Use your brains.'

Good for him. He may be a bit of a lecher but somehow he didn't look like a murderer and she couldn't see him fancying young girls.

Shipster shook his arm free and glared at Thornback. 'Take your hands off me. This will ruin the school – you realise that? Who's going to send their son or daughter to a school where a pupil has been murdered, never mind the headmaster's wife?'

The meeting was disintegrating. Frank was sitting back, making no effort to bring them to order. He didn't want to. He, Elderkin and the constable were watching everyone intently.

Philip Nicholson swivelled round. 'Miss Piff, did you give Inspector Diamond that log book?'

Miss Piff, her glasses once more on her nose, nodded. 'Yes, I did. The inspector told you.'

Philip stood up and leant towards her, his hands griping the back of his chair. 'Why didn't you tell me you'd done that? This is not the way the school secretary should behave.

Your first loyalty is to the school.'

Miss Piff's back straightened. 'My first loyalty has always been to myself and my sister. Inspector Diamond asked me not to talk about the log book, and so I didn't. Not to anyone, not even to Emily. I could see it was important no one knew about it. If I had told you I would also have had to explain I believed your wife stole one from the stationery cupboard. If you feel I have been disloyal to the school, then I apologise. But surely justice comes before everything else.'

Laurel tensed. Nicholson looked ready to throw the chair at Miss Piff.

'I'll see you in my office as soon as this meeting finishes,' he snarled.

It looked like Miss Piff was for the chop. Her face was bright red and she was glaring at Nicholson. There was plenty of steel in Miss Piff's backbone.

Toni Habershon hadn't moved or spoken to anyone. She was folding the material of her grey skirt into pleats, staring down as though an answer to her fears would rise from the floorboards.

'Are you all right, Toni?' Laurel asked.

Toni looked at her with unfocused eyes, as though Laurel didn't exist. 'I don't know. I can't think straight. I can't believe it. I didn't...' She glanced to her right, across Laurel's shoulder. 'It's the shock. I'll be fine soon. She was a nice girl. I used to worry about her weight, she didn't eat enough. I never suspected...' She gulped as though words she wanted to say were stuck in her throat. 'I need to think, I'm not sure what to do,' she whispered.

Laurel moved closer to her. 'If you know anything about this you should talk to Inspector Diamond.'

Toni pulled away from her. 'No, I don't know anything. I'm upset, that's all.' She continued twisting her skirt. 'They were alike, you know, in looks, even though Susan was so much older than Felicity. I hadn't realised that until now. Both slim, child-like, and with red hair. I'm not like them.' Her voice was tinged with regret.

Why would she want to be like Susan and Felicity, two red-headed women who'd been murdered? 'Neither of us is child-like, especially me,' she said, trying to lighten the atmosphere.

Toni seemed to see her clearly now. 'No, I never worried about you.'

What on earth did she mean?

Frank banged the table. Laurel glanced round. Miss Piff's lips were clenched tight; she looked both determined and infuriated. Ringrose was still supporting his head, shoulders heaving, muffled sobbing coming from him. McFall was sitting with folded arms, looking resolute, as though he'd made up his mind about something. Shipster looked as sick as a man who'd lost a hundred pounds and found sixpence. Thornback managed a slight smile when he saw her looking at him and Miss Letts ignored her.

'Ladies and gentlemen. This has been a difficult and distressing meeting for you. Let me reiterate the facts: two women have been killed. These women, despite their differences in age, had many similar physical resemblances: red hair, slight build. One was about to leave childhood behind, the other from a distance, could have been a young girl.'

There was a snort from Nicholson. He must be angry hearing his wife talked about like this.

'If you have any information, even if you think it may have no bearing on these cases, you must come and tell me. If you would rather talk to Sergeant Elderkin, that's fine.' He looked at Philip Nicholson. Frank's mouth twisted. Was he about to say more? Elderkin was looking worried. Nicholson's frown deepened.

217

'I have two more pieces of information.' Frank was now looking at Shipster. 'I believe some of you may have been placed under stress by Susan Nicholson. She may have found out some secret you did not want to be revealed, and she was pressing you for money or favours.'

Elderkin rubbed his forehead. He didn't look happy. He whispered something to Frank.

'If this is the case, it would be better if you talked to us, rather than we found out about it, as no doubt we will.'

There were gasps of shock. Ringrose looked up, his face a picture of misery. Thornback was biting his lip.

Philip Nicholson stood up, arms rigid by his side, fists clenched 'Do you realise what you are saying? You're slandering a dead woman. *My* wife. I strongly object to the way you've run this case. What proof do you have to make such aspersions? I shall demand the chief constable removes you at once. You are a disgrace to the police force.' He marched towards the door.

The constable looked at Frank who nodded. He opened the door.

Nicholson paused in the doorway. He turned, an imposing figure, red-faced, his piercing blue eyes glaring at Frank, and then Dorothy Piff. 'Miss Piff, I will see you now.'

'Before you go, Mr Nicholson,' Frank said in a low, calm voice, 'with the rest of the staff you'll be pleased to hear one piece of good news.' Nicholson stopped in the doorway. 'Mabel Grill is making good progress and the doctors are expecting her to come out of the coma soon. *Then* all this conjecture may be unnecessary. Mabel will be able to name her attacker. That person is the killer of Felicity and Susan.' He stood up. 'That is all. You may leave.' He was as cool now as at the beginning of the meeting.

The rest of the staff, some muttering, some silent, unsure of what they should do, huddled together and slowly moved to the door like a group of heifers who were on their way to the abattoir.

Laurel glanced at Frank and tipped her head towards the door. She wanted to follow Dorothy, to find out what happened in Nicholson's office, and to help her, if needed. Frank gave an almost imperceptible nod, as though he understood and approved.

She moved quickly out of the door, across the hall, and up the stairs to Nicholson's office. She glimpsed the upright figure of Miss Piff entering the room. The door was ajar; she crept up to it, leaning forward to try to hear what they said.

'Please sit down, Miss Piff.'

'No thank you. I'd rather stand.'

She sounds as if she doesn't care what he's going to say.

'As you wish.' His tone was cold and contemptuous. 'I'm extremely disappointed in you, Miss Piff. Why didn't you tell me of your suspicions about Susan?'

There was a several seconds of silence. 'I didn't want to hurt you. It seemed cruel to tell you I suspected your wife was a petty thief and busy-body after she was killed. I should have told you as soon as I suspected it, but I hope you can understand why I didn't.'

No reply from Nicholson.

'If there's nothing further to discuss, I'd like to go home. Emily will be wondering where I am, and I don't feel too well. I think I may be coming down with a cold.'

'You have abused your position as school secretary, Miss Piff. You have slandered my late wife and you have shown no loyalty to me or to the school. I am dismissing you. You will be paid one month's salary. Please clear your office of all personal things by tomorrow morning, before nine o clock. I don't want to see you in the school again.'

Laurel flinched and stepped back. His voice was riddled with anger and spite. Miss Piff must be quailing.

'I shall clear my office in my own good time. As I said, I don't feel well, so I may not be able to comply with your… order. As for a month's salary… I suggest you use the paltry sum you pay me to buy some flowers and cast them on the sea in remembrance of poor Felicity,' she said, full of righteous anger.

'What do you mean by that, Miss Piff?'

'Whatever you want it to. As I shall no longer be an employee of the school I will not feel it necessary to hold back information from Inspector Diamond about some matters I haven't mentioned to him so far.'

Was there a note of triumph in her voice?

'What do you mean by that?'

'I think you know exactly what I mean. I shall miss my job, which I think I've done to a reasonable standard. I shall miss the children and some of the staff, but I won't miss your pompous and irritating manner. Good night, Mr Nicholson.'

Laurel quickly moved away from the door, ran down the stairs and hid under the staircase. There was the firm tread of Miss Piff as she marched away into her office and the bang of Nicholson's door as he slammed it shut.

Should she talk to Dorothy? Did she know something about Nicholson she should tell Frank, or was she so furious she wanted to needle him? She knocked on Miss Piff's office door.

'Are you all right, Miss Piff – Dorothy?'

Miss Piff was searching through one of the drawers in her desk, and turned round abruptly. 'Oh, Laurel. I thought for a moment it was Mr Nicholson coming to apologise.'

'What happened?'

'I've been sacked. I'm absolutely furious. If he'd come to apologise I wouldn't have accepted it. I don't need to work, I don't need the piffling amount he pays me, but I enjoyed being with the children, I'm a good organiser and I like responsibility. Not that there would have been a job here much longer.'

'What do you mean?'

'The governors are meeting tomorrow morning; I know the chairman personally, he's a church warden. They're thinking of closing the school down. I'm sorry for you and all the other staff, *and* the children and their parents. It'll be difficult to place them in other schools when the autumn term is just about to start.'

Laurel had felt sorry for Dorothy, now she felt sorry for herself. She'd be without a job. What would she do? Get another teaching job, obviously. Where? The thought of searching for a new post didn't appeal to her. Perhaps she'd look for something outside teaching. What? 'Gosh! That's drastic, isn't it?'

'They'll probably pay the staff until the end of the autumn term, that's what the chairman said. I wouldn't normally reveal all these details, but having been treated like a criminal by the headmaster, I don't care if I am being indiscreet. Although, I'd be grateful if you didn't tell the other staff.' She sighed. 'I'm afraid I'm behaving badly. I've got an awful sore throat and I can't find my reading glasses. I don't like wearing these bifocals in bed; I'm afraid I'll fall asleep and break them.'

Time to make a confession? 'Dorothy, I'm afraid I've also behaved badly. I followed you when you left the meeting. I was worried what Mr Nicholson might do and I listened at the door. If you know something about him that might have a bearing on these cases I think you ought to see Inspector Diamond straight away.'

Dorothy looked at her over her bifocals. 'Laurel Bowman! Are you turning into a sleuth? I read in one of your references you solved several school crimes.' She sighed and blew her nose. 'None of us envisaged crimes like the ones we've been

221

faced with.' She sat wearily down on her seat and put her elbows on the desk. 'I can't face any more. I'm going home, taking a Beecham's capsule and having an early night. I haven't much to tell, if the truth be known. I was so angry with him I wanted to make him as annoyed as I felt.'

Laurel's hopes sagged. 'Can I ask you what it was?'

'And you'll tell Inspector Diamond?' There was a wry twist to her lips.

'If you want me to.'

'Yes, you might as well, and then I won't have to speak to him tomorrow. Before Mr Nicholson married I was sure he was having an affair with Matron, Toni Habershon. In fact I know they were lovers. I never mentioned it to anyone. I think Toni was very much in love with him; I think she still is.'

Philip and Toni? Was that why Toni was so antagonistic towards her? Did she see her as a rival? But she'd just said she wasn't worried by me. Now that Philip was a widower did she hope to once more become his lover? A shaft of ice straightened her backbone. Had Toni killed Susan? Was she so obsessed with Philip that she would murder to get him back?

'Why are you so sure they were lovers, Dorothy?'

Dorothy took off her glasses and wiped her forehead with a handkerchief. 'I saw them once, in the ruins of the leper hospital. Need I say more?'

Yes, she did need to say more. 'They were kissing?'

'My dear, I didn't know you were so naïve. He had her up against one of the standing walls and he was giving her a good rogering!'

Laurel gasped, fighting an urge not to laugh.

'There, I've shocked you. I was an officer in the WRAF during the war, from 1940 to '45 – you can't tell me anything about human nature and there aren't any crude words I haven't heard. I don't normally use them myself; Emily would be offended.'

'Dorothy Piff. Fantastic.'

Dorothy nodded and smiled. 'After I saw them I kept my eyes open. They went away for weekends during the holidays and odd days in term time. She was devastated when he came back after that summer holiday and he was married. I think it'd been cooling off on his part before then. I felt sorry for her, she was besotted.'

Laurel looked at Dorothy with new eyes. She saw her in a blue uniform, her cap at a racy angle, her shoes gleaming with polish and bull, standing in the mess with her friends downing gin and tonics. 'Thanks for telling me, Dorothy. I'll go and talk to Inspector Diamond.'

'I'm going home now. I'll have to come in and clear away my things. It might not be tomorrow – it depends how I feel. Come and see me, dear. I know you'd have made a splendid senior mistress, you would have done the school well.'

'Thank you, Dorothy.'

'If they do close the school and you don't want to stay on the site, you're very welcome to come to Greyfriars House and stay with us until you decide what to do. We'd love to have you.' Dorothy's apple-cheeks bunched in a warm smile and she held out her hand.

Laurel took it in hers; the warmth and kindness of Dorothy's offer made her throat tighten. 'Thank you. I want to stay in the cottage until everything is cleared up. But afterwards I'll be glad to leave. I'm not sure if I'll want to stay in the area, but if I do, I'd be grateful to stay with friends.'

'Take care, my dear. Two people have been killed and poor Mabel attacked. Never forget that.'

Chapter 22

Frank waited until all the staff and the constables had left the music room, then he looked at Elderkin. 'Took a bit of a risk, didn't I?'

'I'm sorry, Frank, but I don't think it was wise to give them so much information, you've put them in a right tizzy.'

Frank leant back in his chair until it tipped and he was balancing on the back legs. 'That was the idea.'

'You certainly like to live dangerously, and if you're not careful you'll go arse over tit and fall off the platform.'

Frank laughed and righted his chair.

'So what's next? We can't do much more tonight,' Elderkin yawned.

'You go home, Stuart. I'll wait for Laurel; I think she wanted to make sure Miss Piff was all right. Nicholson looked as though he might strangle... I better rephrase that... give her the sack.'

Elderkin frowned. 'If he does the man's a fool. Dorothy told Mabel what she earns. Those two are good friends, known each other for years. There's no side to Dorothy Piff. He'll never get someone to work the hours she does for that amount. She's no need to work, you know: she and her sister are well off. They come from a wealthy family, there've been Piffs living in Greyfriars House for over three hundred years. Shame neither of them married. She's a good sort is Dorothy Piff; Mabel says she's no snob – helped lots of people in the area, all on the quiet.'

'Yes, I like Dorothy Piff: got a very efficient but friendly way with her.'

Elderkin nodded in agreement. 'She was in the WRAF in the war – officer. Did well, I believe. Mabel said she'd a young man who was in the Air Force. Don't know what happened to him.'

A constable put his head round the door. 'Mr McFall would like to have a word with you, sir.'

Frank raised his eyebrows. 'Has the seed I sowed begun to germinate?'

'Might have turned to chaff.'

'Thank you for your confidence in me, Stuart. Want to stay and find out?'

'Might as well; nothing much on the telly. Only *The Virginian*, and I'm not too keen on cowboys.'

Frank shook his head. 'Good. Show Mr McFall in, Constable.'

Jim McFall walked in and stood in the centre of the room, as if uncertain where to go. Frank came down from the platform, followed by Elderkin, who gestured to the front row of seats. Elderkin arranged three chairs so he and Frank were facing him.

'You have something to tell us, Mr McFall?' Elderkin asked.

McFall took a deep breath, as if he needed the extra oxygen to get the words out. 'Ay, I have. Let me say, straight away, that I don't like the polis, I don't like talking to the polis and normally I wouldn't tell you anything I didn't have to.' After that speech he seemed to relax slightly, as though he'd unburdened his conscious.

Frank was silent.

McFall continued, 'I've nothing against you personally,' he nodded to Frank, 'or against you, Sergeant Elderkin, but I'm wary of having any more to do with the polis than I have to.'

'I'm glad about that, Mr McFall. I was beginning to get a complex,' Frank said.

'Well you seem better than the usual copper, at least

you've got a sense of humour. Some of you bastards are right sadists.'

Elderkin was starting to wriggle in his seat.

Better change the topic or he might have to arrest Elderkin for grievous bodily harm. 'If you distrust and dislike the police so much then your reason for wanting to talk to us must be important,' Frank said.

McFall bit his lip and slowly shook his head. 'I don't know if it is or isn't, but I have to admit I could have told you this sooner, but I never liked Mrs Nicholson and I didn't care to help you find her killer. But when you said poor, wee Felicity had been murdered, chopped up and flung in the sea, my blood boiled. She was a nice young girl. Whoever did that to her – I'd like to see to him myself.'

Frank could believe it: McFall's eyes were bulging, the veins on his forehead standing out against his red face. 'I'm glad you decided to help us. Please go on.'

McFall leant forward. 'I better tell you something about myself first. I was born in Glasgow and lived there, one way or another,' he grimaced, 'all my life before I came here. I was a ship-worker and I played football part-time for Glasgow Rangers, never made the first team. I was married, good-looking girl, but flighty. I found her in bed with another man; he managed to get out minus his trews, but I saw red and... I strangled her.'

Elderkin's body tensed as he leant towards McFall. 'How long did you serve?'

'Ten years for manslaughter, the last two in an open prison in Norfolk. The previous headmaster was on the prison parole board and he offered to take me on as a groundsman when my sentence was finished. I came here in 1960. I don't know if he told Mr Nicholson about me; I didn't ask.'

'Did anyone else know?'

'The chairman of governors, he knows, but apart from

him I'm not sure. No one mentioned it to me. I think Miss Piff might know, she knows about most things.'

'Did Susan Nicholson ask you about this – your time in prison?'

'Ay, she did, the little bitch. She must have got into my flat somehow or perhaps there's something in my records in the office. If it was my flat she must have read letters my mother sent me when I was in prison. She wrote asking me if I was being treated all right and she mentioned things about my wife's family and how they were making trouble for her. I should have burnt them, but she passed on while I was in there. They were the last letters she wrote to me and I like to look at her handwriting.'

Frank could see it had taken a lot out of McFall to reveal so much of his life. His tall, wiry frame was hunched in the chair, his wrists sticking out of the sleeves of his check shirt, his large, bony hands clenched so tightly the knuckles looked as though they might split the skin.

'When did Susan Nicholson approach you?' Elderkin asked.

'It was in December sometime, ay, just before we broke up for the Christmas holidays.'

'That's Christmas, 1969?' Frank asked.

'That's right. She was killed the following Easter.'

'What happened?'

McFall's face expressed disgust. 'She was a two-faced one, a right nasty woman. She came up to my flat one evening with a Christmas card from her and Mr Nicholson. I was quite touched; I don't get too many cards as you can ken. I offered her a wee dram and we sat down all cosy. Then she came out with it.' His face was once more suffused with blood at the memory of the visit.

'She said she learned I'd killed my wife and had been in prison. She didn't want to tell her husband, but she thought she must. She wondered if there was anything I could do to change her mind. I could'ne believe it. She sat there as cool as anything. I've met a few blackmailers where I've been and I've never taken to them. Aye, I'd have liked to've changed her mind all right: by knocking her head off.' He stopped as he realised what he'd said. 'I didn't do her in, I swear to God. I served my time for taking a life and I swore I'd never go back to prison.'

'As you obviously didn't kill her on this occasion, what did you do?' Frank asked.

'I told her she'd get no money from me. The old headmaster and the chair of governors knew what I'd done. I didn't know if her old man knew, but I threatened her with telling him and the governors she'd tried to blackmail me. I could see that frightened her.'

'What happened next?' asked Elderkin, obviously caught up in the story.

'She said no one would believe me. I advised her to keep her mouth shut then.'

'Did she ever mention it again?'

'No. She avoided me like the plague, and I didn't go out of my way to talk to her.'

'Thank you for telling us this, Mr McFall. I'll check your story with the chairman of governors, but apart from that there's no need to make this public knowledge unless it has a bearing on the case. Is there anything else you'd like to say?' Frank was sure there was more. Why was he so upset about Felicity?

McFall stared down at his hands, the knuckles still shining through the skin. He looked up at Frank. 'You mentioned she'd nicked a school log book?'

Frank nodded. Was this the turning point?

'I saw her writing in a book like that. It was one afternoon, I was marking some lines on the games pitch and I

228

thought I saw someone in the ruins. One of the pupils having a smoke, I thought. I sneaked up quiet, well, you don't get much amusement in this place, and I get a chuckle when I catch them at it. Though, sometimes I don't grass on them. She didn't see me. She was sitting on one of the stones, writing in this book, hunched up she was as though she didn't want to be seen. I didn't want to talk to her, so I crept away. What do you think she wrote in that book?'

'If we knew that, Mr McFall, we might be closer to finding out who killed her. Have you any idea where that book might be?' Frank asked.

McFall shook his head looking as though he wished he could help. 'No, I don't know. Do you think the murderer found it? That's why she was killed? She'd written something about him? I'd like to see that book myself; I'd like to see what the bitch wrote about me.' He didn't move. It seemed he had more to say.

'There's something else, isn't there? Something about Felicity?' Frank asked softly, for McFall's face was no longer suffused with blood but had returned to its grey pallor. He looked heart-broken.

'Ay, poor wee Felicity. I've a daughter only a few years older. She was brought up by my parents-in-law after I was put away. They adopted her when she was two years old. I'd no contact with her until a few years ago; she wrote to me. We've met a few times, in the summer holidays. She's the one bright star in my life.' He pulled out a wallet from his jacket pocket and passed a photograph to Frank. 'As you can see, she's a skinny wee girl, pretty like her mother, but she's got my hair, Well, my hair as it used to be. It looks better on her. Felicity reminded me of my daughter.'

The photograph showed a slim, red-headed young woman, smiling into the camera. Frank passed it to Elderkin.

'She's a lovely girl,' Elderkin said, giving the photograph

back to McFall, who placed it carefully into his wallet. 'Did you ever talk with Felicity?'

'Aye, just a few times. She didn't like doing games. She was scared she'd damage her hands, especially playing hockey. Sometimes she'd hide in the ruins; I found her there once. I took her back to the games pavilion and made her tea on my primus stove. Och, she was a dear girl. Not a bit afraid of me, which some of the others are. She'd chat away about her music and how she dreamed of being a concert pianist. She promised to invite me to her first recital. Aye, we had a few nice chats.'

His face clouded, the happiness in his eyes faded. 'The last time we talked must have been a day or two before she... was murdered. God, I can't believe it. We were told she'd run off with a man. I couldn't make it out, but that's women for you, I thought. I trusted my wife until that day... I must admit I felt really disappointed in Felicity, she'd seemed like such an innocent girl. She wasn't flirty, not aware of how pretty she was. Tch – If I'd known...'

Frank thought carefully before asking for more details. Here was someone who'd been close to Felicity. Had she said anything that gave a clue to her murderer? 'Mr McFall, during that last conversation with Felicity can you think of anything that might be significant? The more you can remember the better. There might be something she said that means nothing to you, but it might be vital in our search for her murderer. Do you want to think this over? Perhaps write down everything you remember?'

McFall gnawed at his lower lip. 'I'll have a go now. I don't want to have to come back and go through all this again.'

'We might need to talk with you later. I can't promise we won't,' Frank said.

'Ay, I realise once you've told the police something, they

always want more information. Like bloodsuckers ye are,' he said, glancing at Elderkin, but with a sly smile on his face.

Elderkin didn't react, but took out a pencil-sharpener and worked the end of his pencil to a fine point. He looked at McFall, pencil ready to mark his notebook. 'Don't think of us as bloodsuckers, Mr McFall – just industrious ants, working away for justice.'

'You don't look like an ant, Sergeant Elderkin; more like a big, old bumblebee.'

Elderkin nodded, as though pleased by the simile.

Frank was unsure where this zoological story was going. He was afraid McFall might start referring to leeches or mosquitoes, and any goodwill would be lost. 'When you're ready, Mr McFall.'

McFall frowned, squeezed his eyes shut and clasped his bony hands tight. 'It was a few days before she disappeared. I can't remember the exact day... I expect if I looked at an old calendar I might be able to work it out.'

Frank didn't break in but made a mental note to find one and get McFall to look at it.

'I was in the games hut, sorting out things; putting the rugby and hockey balls away and seeing which tennis rackets needed restringing, getting things sorted for the summer term – if I didn't the staff wouldn't. Not like our new senior mistress, Miss Bowman. She's on the ball.'

You can say that again, Frank thought.

'There was this little knock on the door. So gentle I hardly heard it. She was standing there smiling at me. "Hello, Felicity," I said, "come on in. So you had to stay in school. Couldn't your aunt have you this holiday?"

"No, she'd going to see her son in New Zealand, she'll be away for a month. I don't mind not going to stay with her, but I don't like being here in the holidays."'

'I could understand that, it's a lonely place at the best of times. "Are you still doing a lot of practising on the piano? You'll enjoy that, won't you?"'

'Her face lit up. "Yes, Mr Ringrose is hearing me play for an hour every morning, and I play by myself in the afternoon. But he'll be going on holiday soon."'

"'They can't leave you on your own. Who'll be around next week?"'

"'Some of the staff and matron will be here, but Miss Piff has said I can stay with her. I like Miss Piff, but I don't know if she's got a piano. I don't like to ask her, it sounds as if I'll only go there if she's got one. Although I'd rather be with Miss Piff than stay here. I hate it at night. I'm all alone in the girls' house, apart from matron. She's had to move out of her cottage to keep an eye on me. Sometimes she doesn't come in until after dark. I hate being alone in that big house, I keep imagining I hear noises. I know I shouldn't be frightened at my age but…"'

'I felt sorry for the lass. "You know you're welcome to come and visit me, Felicity. If you want to spend a few evenings with me in my flat, you can stay until late and I'll walk you back to the girls' house. I don't know what I've got that would interest you, but we can listen to the radio; I expect I can find some classical music. Can you play chess?" She nodded. "You'll have to ask matron's permission of course." She looked real pleased. Poor girl she must have been desperate for a bit of company if she thought it would be fun to spend a few evenings with an old lag. Though of course she didn't know that.'

As McFall talked about Felicity, flesh seemed to grow on the bones Frank had seen lying on the table in the morgue. She was becoming a real person, a young, sensitive girl, alone in the world except for a distant and possibly uncaring aunt. Her hope in life: a talent for music; her ambition to be a concert pianist. The photograph of her showed a slim girl, looking younger than her seventeen years; an attractive elfin face with small fine features and large eyes framed by full, pale eyelashes. A young life taken. How she'd died they might never know. The damaged hyoid bone suggested strangulation, but the sea and its creatures had eaten away her flesh, and with it any clues to how she died and who'd killed her. He didn't like to think what had happened to her before she died; but he couldn't afford to push aside the horrific details of her death.

'Did she spend any evenings with you?' Elderkin asked, frowning and looking at Frank.

'Just the one – the same evening. She came over after supper.' He sniffed and wiped his nose with a finger. 'She brought me a bar of fruit and nut chocolate; we ate it between us. She was good company: we had two games of chess, she won the first and let me win the second, then we listened to the radio and I made us some cocoa before I walked her back to the house. It made me realise how much I'd missed of my daughter's childhood. How I've missed out on having a relationship with her and how she must have missed having a father.' He sat in silence looking at his hands.

'Can you think of anything she said that showed she was worried by something a member of staff had done or said?' Frank asked. The man was deeply upset as he remembered his time with Felicity. Had he told them everything? Could this be an elaborate lie to try and cover for what happened next? If so, he was a consummate actor.

'There was only one thing she said, just before I walked her home, that I thought was peculiar. I told her I'd check up on it after I'd finished all the preparations for the next term.'

'What was it?'

'She said she felt as if someone was spying on her. I asked her what she meant. "I know it sounds silly, Mr McFall," she said, "but when I'm in my room" – all the sixth formers have

233

single rooms – "or in the bath," I remember she blushed as red as a rose, "I feel as though someone is watching me." She was getting worked up, twisting her hands together. I could see she really believed it was happening. "I don't like getting undressed and I haven't had a bath for two days. I hope I don't smell.'"

'I must admit I was a wee bit embarrassed; it didn't seem right to be talking about having baths and someone playing Peeping Tom. I didn't know what to say, but she was obviously looking to me to help her.

"'Are you sure it isn't being on your own in that big house by yourself, Felicity?" I asked. "I expect you've got a powerful imagination, you being an artist, a musician. Have you seen anyone you don't know on the school site?"'

"'No, there's only the staff. I'm sorry I bothered you, Mr McFall, I expect I'm imagining it.'"

'She didn't sound convinced and I could see it had taken her a deal of courage to bring it up with me. "I tell you what, Felicity; I'll talk to Miss Piff and see if she can have you straight away. What about that?"'

"'Would you? Thank you, Mr McFall.'"

'She was so delighted I thought she was going to kiss me, so I got up quick, put on my coat and took her home.'

'Did you ask Miss Piff?'

'The next day we had some trouble with a leak in the boiler room and by the time I got round to it, it was too late and Miss Piff had gone home. The day after Felicity had disappeared. I know if I'd got her out of this damned school she might still be alive. It's someone in the school, isn't it? One of us has murdered these two lasses. If I knew who it was…'

Frank placed a hand on his shoulder. 'You've served one sentence for taking a life. If you find out anything or have any suspicions, you come and talk to me or Sergeant

Elderkin. This person has committed two murders, and attempted a third – all women. It doesn't mean he or she won't kill a man if he thinks *you* know who the murderer is.'

McFall snorted. 'You're not telling me you think it's a woman, are you? Can you see old Miss Letts, or Toni Habershon battering Mabel over the head?' He stopped and stared at Frank. 'Ay, you can, I can see that. I don't suppose you'll cross me off your list of suspects, will you?'

'I'm grateful to you for coming and talking to us. What you've said has been very useful. I've got a clearer idea about the kind of girl Felicity was: a very shy, talented and lonely child. That helps tremendously. Until we find who did these murders, and have watertight proof, everyone without an alibi for the times of Susan's murder and the attack on Mabel Grill remains a suspect. I don't think you'd expect me to give a different answer.'

There was a knock on the door and the constable came into the room. 'Miss Bowman wants to see you, sir.'

Damn. McFall was looking at him suspiciously. 'Ask her to wait, please.' He stood up. 'Thank you, Mr McFall. You'll remember what I said: no going off at half-cock.'

McFall got up from his chair. 'I'll remember.' He tried to smooth his salt-and-pepper hair. 'What will happen to poor Felicity's remains? Will there be a funeral?'

'The aunt's been informed. I'm not sure when the... the body will be released. Do you want me to let you know when and where the funeral will be?' Elderkin asked.

McFall nodded. 'I'd like to go. I owe her that. Good night to you both.'

They looked at each other when he'd left the room. Frank sighed. It had been a long day. He needed some sleep. He wasn't thinking clearly.

'Cross him off the list?' Elderkin asked.

Frank slowly shook his head. 'The only people off the list

are you, me, Laurel and Mabel. Let's see what Laurel's found out.'

Chapter 23

Thursday, September 17, 1970

The next morning Laurel closed the door of her office and walked slowly down the stairs. What was the point in planning lessons if the school was about to be closed? She paused half-way down. What should she do? What did she want to do? Yesterday, after she'd talked with Dorothy, she'd met up with Frank and Stuart Elderkin and they'd exchanged information. They'd been particularly intrigued to hear about Toni Habershon and Philip Nicholson's affair. It had given her a real lift to be treated as a valuable member of the team.

Earlier this morning she'd looked for Frank to find out if anything new had surfaced; instead she ran into Elderkin who told her Frank had been called to Ipswich to see the chief constable. Elderkin looked distracted and she didn't think she could ask him why Frank had been summoned. She hoped they weren't thinking of bringing in someone else, as Nicholson wanted. Someone else wouldn't take her into their confidence.

She looked into Dorothy's office. No sign she'd been in and taken away her personal belongings. She'd said she probably wouldn't come in today as she wasn't feeling well. She nodded her head – yes, that's what she would do. She'd walk into Dunwich and call on Dorothy and see if she could do anything for her. On the way she could phone her parents again from the public phone box. She needed to try and calm her mother down, her last words yesterday were: 'I couldn't bear to lose another daughter.' She needed to reassure them. Also she might be able to find out more about Toni

Habershon and Philip from Dorothy.

Should she tell someone where she was going? She was still a member of staff and she should act as though the term would start soon. She wasn't supposed to know the governors were meeting this morning. No sign of them here.

She turned round and ran up the stairs, knocked on the headmaster's office door and opened it. Shipster was crouched in front of the safe with the door open. He twisted his body, looking at her over his shoulder, his grey face ugly, open-mouthed, eyes wide with shock. He slammed the door shut and scrambled up.

'Caught you red-handed, Mr Shipster. Not lifting the petty cash, I hope?'

His lips quivered and a red flush coloured his cheeks. 'It's no business of yours what I'm doing. I was checking something.'

'Looking for the missing log book, perhaps?'

He took a step towards her. 'What are you implying?'

'You did tell me when we first met that you didn't like Susan Nicholson. Perhaps she found out something about *you*, Mr Shipster. If she did threaten you the best thing you can do is tell Inspector Diamond.'

His eyes glittered above the darkening stain of his cheeks. She could feel waves of hate and frustration rolling towards her. She stood her ground, folding her arms across her chest, straightening her backbone. He took a step backwards.

'You'd do better to mind your own business, or have you joined the police?'

'I think helping to find the murderer of Susan Nicholson and Felicity, and the attacker of Mabel Grill, is everyone's business. As for joining the police that's not a bad idea, at least they don't usually murder people; but they catch those who do.'

He muttered something and tried to push past her. His

238

breath was rancid and he smelt as though he hadn't bathed, or changed his clothes lately. She stepped back and he scuttled out of the room.

She was about to follow him when Philip Nicholson came into his office frowning. The skin of his face was taught, and blue shadows under his eyes suggested lack of sleep. 'Miss Bowman, Laurel. What's the matter with Mr Shipster? He ran downstairs as if a ghost was on his heels.'

Perhaps one was. Or perhaps there were two, both with red hair. 'I don't know, Philip. I came in and he was looking in the safe. He seemed upset I'd seen him. Why do you think he felt like that?'

Philip stared at the safe as though it were a newly minted object. 'I really don't know. He has a key, but he doesn't usually use it unless it's to put in or take out exam papers. There aren't any in there at the moment. The November resits don't come until late October.' He scratched the back of his neck, the frown lines increasing.

He looked tired and unsure of himself. She suppressed feeling sorry for him, remembering the way he'd treated Dorothy Piff.

'I was thinking of going for a walk; is that all right or is there any job you'd like me to do?'

He looked up at her, blinking, as though he'd trouble focusing. 'No. I can understand you must want to get away from here for a few hours. What must you think of it all? The whole situation has become a nightmare.' He took a deep breath as though ready to blow away the clouds of suspicion hanging over Blackfriars with his outgoing breath. 'Where are you walking to?' he asked.

'I'll walk over the heath towards Eastbridge, or I might go to the bird reserve.' The lie slipped from her lips as easily as shucking peas. She didn't think it would be politic to tell him she was going to Dunwich to see Dorothy Piff.

She turned right at the school gates and, after walking three hundred yards down the road, turned right again, following a footpath through woods to Dunwich. The trees were a mixture of larch and sycamores, the needle-like leaves of the larch covered the path with a few early mottled sycamore leaves foretelling the coming of autumn. The wood was silent apart from sudden bursts of bird song. A few isolated houses sat to the right of the path, all deserted, their windows grey and lifeless, like the eyes of dead animals. She wished she hadn't come this way and had kept to the road. Too late now, her pride wouldn't let her turn back. She increased the length of her stride, almost breaking into a jog. If only she knew *who* the murderer was. It was unbearable not knowing. It had been the same at her old school. She had to know who'd stolen money from the cloakroom, who'd made obscene phone calls to staff, who'd scrawled graffiti in the girls' loos. She hadn't rested until she knew who'd murdered Angela. Should she have left that to the police? But would they have solved the crime? Would they have found enough evidence to make sure he went down? She hadn't been able to leave it alone. She had to know. It had cost her dear. Would her desire to know who the murderer of Susan Nicholson was also have a high price? The footpath led onto a tarmac road in Dunwich. First stop the phone box, then she'd look for Dorothy's home.

Dorothy had described the position of Greyfriars House, 'Look out for the gates,' she'd said. 'We're proud of our gates. Had them made by the local blacksmith.'

There they were. A drive, cutting through the grass verge, led to a pair of tall, wrought iron gates with the silhouette of a hooded monk on each, and above, the name, Greyfriars House. The gate was a work of art. This didn't look like the drive to a neat little cottage, which is what she'd imagined the Miss Piffs lived in.

The gates were well-oiled and smartly painted, but the drive was patched with moss, growing in the cracks of the tarmac; it bent to the left with tall camellias and rhododendrons on either side hiding the house. There was an acrid smell – a stinkhorn? Another sign of autumn.

The drive formed a circle enclosing a lawn with a round pond in its centre; a stone dolphin spewed a feeble jet which dribbled down its stone scales into the green water. A sprawling Tudor house, built of mellow red bricks enclosed between black beams sat back from the drive. Leaded windows caught the sun's rays and from one of several ornate chimneys, a thin trail of smoke spiralled upwards.

Laurel had imagined the Miss Piffs living in a neat cottage, two up, two down and everything securely in its rightful place, presuming Emily was as well organised as Dorothy. This was an English country mansion, probably dating back to a time when Dunwich had been an important port, before the sea-storms had clawed back the land, the town and eleven of its churches. How wrong can you be about people? You make assumptions, you impose prejudices upon them, and when these are swept away the ground shifts under your feet and insecurity sets in. The school secretary she imagined eking out her life on a small salary had in twenty-four hours turned into a woman who'd served in the armed services during the war and was part-owner of a Tudor mansion with presumably enough money to live in it. How many other assumptions about people – the murder suspects – had she made that had been wrong? Did Frank make the same mistakes? No. He wasn't an amateur sleuth. Was that what she was? An interfering busy-body with no training in how to analyse the suspects and no right to feel she could help solve these murders?

She stood in front of the blackened oak door, heavy with the heads of nails and metal strap-work. Should she knock?

Or would it be better to go back to school, pack her bags and go home? Presuming Frank would let her. But he wanted to talk to her about the staff at Blackfriars. He'd seemed to value her thoughts and her judgements. What about Mabel, unconscious and still on the critical list? Could she abandon her because she'd been put out by finding her assessment of Dorothy was wrong? She wasn't wrong about Dorothy's character, she was sure of that. She was a good, trustworthy woman who'd been unfairly sacked. She grasped the dolphin-shaped knocker.

The door swung open smoothly.

'Miss Bowman, how lovely. Do come in.'

Was it Dorothy or Emily? No runny nose or croaky voice. 'Emily?'

'How clever. Or was it a lucky guess?' Emily Piff was dressed in a tweed skirt, a blue wool twin set, a string of amber beads and fluffy pink slippers.

She coloured as she saw Laurel staring at them. 'I know they're silly, and Dorothy hates them, but I think everyone's entitled to one little bit of frivolity, don't you?'

Laurel laughed. 'Mine's lace knickers.'

Emily's mouth formed an O of joy and surprise. 'I won't tell you what Dorothy's is.'

'How is she? Still very upset I should imagine.'

Emily frowned. 'It was disgraceful. I've a good mind to see Mr Nicholson and tell him what I think. Poor Dorothy has a most dreadful cold. She's in bed and I've dosed her up. Do you want to see her? I'm sure she'd like to see you.'

'Do you think so? Perhaps you'd better check with her?'

'No.'

Emily walked through the entrance hall towards a wide flight of stairs. 'Come on up, she's awake, I've just given her the *Daily Telegraph.* As long as you don't get too near her, hopefully you won't pick up the bug.'

She led the way up an oak staircase with carved balustrades and opened a door. 'You've a visitor, Dorothy. I hope you're decent.'

Dorothy Piff was sitting up, supported by several pillows, in a four-poster bed, her grey hair flattened. She was wearing a blue angora bed jacket, and a shiny red nose. She placed the newspaper on the bedspread. 'Laurel. How kind of you to come. Sit down.' She pointed to a bedside chair. 'Any news? No more horrible happenings, I hope.'

The chair was too small for her and she had to tuck her legs at an angle. Dorothy, despite her cold, seemed chipper. Was she missing the school already? 'I went in briefly but there isn't much I can do, and if you're right about the governors closing the school, there doesn't seem much point in doing any more preparation or sorting out games equipment. Inspector Diamond has been summoned to Ipswich, Sergeant Elderkin has started a second search of the grounds and ruins looking for the log book and the staff are sitting round drinking coffee and facing a miserable future, one that will only get worse. The governors aren't at the school. Are they meeting somewhere else?'

Dorothy gave an elephantine trumpet into a large handkerchief. 'Sorry about that. They're meeting at The Ship Hotel.' She patted her raw nose. 'I'm afraid I pulled rank. I phoned the chairman last night and ranted about Nicholson firing me. I shouldn't have done it. I phoned him again this morning and asked him not to have a go at the headmaster. In retrospect you can understand him flipping his lid: he's under an enormous strain, and he must realise the school can't hope to survive these terrible murders.' She straightened her shoulders and pulled the edges of the bed jacket together.

Emily stood at the door, carrying a tray. 'I admire your forgiveness, Dorothy, but I think you were treated most unjustly. What I shall do when you recover I dread to think.'

She put the tray, on which were a coffee pot, three cups and saucers, a plate of scones and a jug of milk, onto a small table. She turned to Laurel. 'She'll be under my feet, fussing round, not knowing what to do with herself.'

Dorothy pushed herself up against the pillows. 'Nonsense. There are plenty of jobs I can do in the house, and the garden needs a good tidy up, and I...' A coughing fit cut short her plans for the future.

Emily placed a cup on a side table, next to two photographs in silver frames. One was of Dorothy, part of a group of laughing uniformed women; the other was of a young man, in RAF uniform, the wind blowing his hair away from his forehead – a lively, bony face, not handsome, but full of life.

Dorothy, after sipping some water, drank her coffee in silence.

The coffee was delicious, made with freshly ground beans. 'Is there anything you'd like me to do for you, Dorothy, at the school? Do you want me to fetch anything from your office?' Laurel asked.

'No thank you, dear. I'll go in when I feel better. I didn't find my reading glasses, but I've borrowed Emily's, the prescription's close enough to mine. Also I must see Toni, I'm worried about her: she looked absolutely shell-shocked when Inspector Diamond told us about poor Felicity. I know you haven't got on with her, Laurel, but she's not been a bad matron and I think she was fond of Felicity. I'll ask her to tea and give her a chance to have a heart to heart.'

'Are you sure about her...' she lowered her voice, 'and Mr Nicholson?'

'It's all right, I told Emily about it. Yes, absolutely sure. I don't think it's started again, after his wife died, but... yes, I must see her soon.'

'You're not getting out of that bed until you're completely

recovered; you know if you get a cold and don't look after it, it goes to your chest,' Emily chided.

Dorothy looked at the ceiling. 'I'll have to find another job: I can't stand Emily mothering me all day.'

Emily lent over the bed and gently slapped Dorothy's wrist, then with the same hand stroked her cheek. 'For once I've got the upper hand. Today I'm in charge.' She looked at Laurel.

Time to go. 'If there's any news I'll let you know. In the meantime, do as Emily says.'

'The photograph of the young man: was he Dorothy's…?' she asked as they went down the stairs.

Emily nodded. 'Yes, they were engaged. He didn't make it. Lancaster bomber navigator.'

'She never…?'

'No. He was the one for her. No one else could take his place.'

'I'm sorry. Did you have a fiancé too?'

Emily laughed, not a bitter laugh, but as if Laurel had asked a silly question. 'I wasn't very good at that sort of thing. I find men rather frightening. I was happy looking after our parents. We were a loving family. Now I have Dorothy to look after and she keeps me abreast of the goings on at the school and in the village. She'll miss her school, she does love organising things… and people. But I expect she'll soon find some other poor bodies to knock into shape.'

Laurel paused on the doorstep. 'Thanks for the welcome and the coffee, Emily. It's done me good to get out of the awful atmosphere of the school. I hope Dorothy gets well soon.'

'I'll dose her up tonight with Beecham's and Captain Morgan rum, make sure she gets a good night's sleep. She is worried about Toni Habershon.' She paused, screwing up her face as if she was worried too, then her skin smoothed as

245

though a puzzle was solved. She nodded in a determined fashion, but didn't say any more.

The walk back through the woods was different. No imaginary shadows flitting between the trees. Shafts of sunshine danced over the floor of the wood as the breeze moved the leaves. The smell of decay was replaced by earthy fullness and the cries of a pheasant sounded like chortling laughter. The catalysts for her changed mood: the good company of two warm, intelligent women.

As she got nearer to the school the euphoria started to fade. Two friendly faces no longer there to lighten the darkness of suspicion and fear: Mabel and now Dorothy. She hoped Frank was back from Ipswich and was still on the case.

Chapter 24

The Dover sole Frank had bought from the Aldeburgh fisherman on his way back from seeing the chief constable was sizzling in the frying pan. He'd decided to spoil himself. No one else was going to, especially the chief constable. He'd asked the fisherman to skin the sole both sides and the comforting smell, an amalgam of splendid fish and good butter, relaxed his shoulders. He opened the fridge and pulled out a bottle of Muscadet sur Lie he'd bought from the Adnam's wine shop, and poured a large glass. He wasn't going anywhere this evening. He didn't want to see anyone, not even Laurel or Stuart Elderkin —least of all them. He didn't want to talk about the murders; he needed to think about the murders. Everything had happened so quickly. Ten days ago he was investigating a cold murder case. Now he had two murders and a near fatal attack and indeed poor Mabel might become the third victim.

He turned the sole over; there was a golden crust on the top side. He took another good swallow of wine and cut several slices of bread, laid the table with a knife and fork and tried to push away all thoughts of the situation at the school for an hour and enjoy his dinner.

He wiped the plate with the last of the bread and poured the remains of the Muscadet into his glass. He felt better. It was a long time since he'd downed a bottle himself. His thoughts drifted to the morning and the chief constable.

He shouldn't have lost his temper. There was no excuse. OK, he'd been dog-tired, no sleep the night before and not much last night, and he didn't like the man: he was a paper-pusher and not too bright. Also he didn't like anyone who wasn't loyal to colleagues. Fair enough if you've made a balls-up, you deserve a rocket, but just because Nicholson and the chair of governors had been on the blower moaning about him didn't mean the chief had to back their judgement instead of his. Policing was changing, even in the time he'd been in the force he'd felt restricted by protocol, the need to scratch backs and follow set routines. Basic groundwork always had to be done, care must be taken, but the brass, at least the brass he'd worked for weren't receptive to new ideas, and certainly weren't keen on the way he sometimes worked. Did he want to spend the next twenty years obeying dickheads? Trouble was he was good at his job and even more important, apart from the paper-pushers, he enjoyed working with coppers like Elderkin, and sometimes getting the right result. He knew what he'd like to do. Had he the guts to do it?

If they knew how much information he and Laurel had exchanged he'd be on traffic duty next week. Old Elderkin had surprised him: after pursed lips and raised eyebrows he's seen the sense of involving Laurel.

What a woman! He'd have her on his team any day. She enjoyed the work and she was good at it. She was brave and with a build some men would be proud of, in fact he wouldn't like to put a bet on who would win if he came up against her for three rounds in the boxing ring. He pulled a face as he remembered her sister Angela, her murder and his suspicions about Laurel. That one would have to go on the back burner for now. Tonight he needed to go over what had happened so far and make plans for tomorrow.

Had Nicholson and Toni Habershon been lovers? If Miss Piff was right – yes. Had their affair continued after his marriage? He would interview them again tomorrow – separately.

Could Toni have murdered Susan? Motive: jealousy and the hope of renewing her love affair with Nicholson. But

248

she'd an alibi for Mabel's attack – unless she and Nicholson were in this together. But he'd an alibi for Susan's murder.

Supposing Dr Ansell, the pathologist was right: Susan died earlier than thought. But Nicholson had an alibi for Tuesday as well. She was alive on Tuesday; he'd spoken to her on the phone. Supposing it wasn't Susan? Supposing Susan was already dead before he left for Colchester? But how did the body get into the sluice? There were too many holes. Holes like gaping caverns.

The suspects who didn't have alibis for either Susan's murder or the attack on Mabel were Vanessa Letts, strong enough and nasty enough; Shipster and McFall. McFall didn't seem to have any motive, apart from disliking Susan; she'd tried to unsuccessfully blackmail him, but there could be something else they didn't know about. He couldn't find a motive for Shipster, although he obviously hated the woman. At least Ringrose was in the clear; his boyfriend had confirmed his alibi.

If only they'd been able to find the school log book. He imagined the pages covered in Susan's handwriting giving him all the details he needed. Motives, times – hope she dated every happening – case solved. It would be too easy, it never happens like that. Also he wouldn't feel the same satisfaction he did when the cogs stopped turning, the pieces clicked into place and everything made sense. It didn't happen that often, not nearly enough, but when it did it was sweet. What he hated was handing over the case to the courts and the law, knowing it could be scuppered by either poor prosecution or brilliant defence – sometimes both at once. He could understand someone who took the law into their own hands, understand it, but he couldn't condone it.

He filled the percolator and scooped in ground coffee. He got a pad of paper and a biro from a drawer and started to plot out various lines of thought. After an hour pages were filled with spider diagrams, one fact sewn to another. There was one web he kept coming back to, adding more lines, and connecting different ideas. He took a fresh page and copied out this one again, more neatly, giving it extra space. He poured himself a third cup of coffee.

He went back to the other possibilities, made separate pages for them and spent time teasing out his theories, but he came back to the first. He went through it again. He visualised the sequence of events from Susan finding out something awful about the murderer and writing it in the log book. Did she realise the importance of what she'd discovered? Was it the log book the murderer found? Or was it something she said to the murderer and the log book was still to be found? He couldn't answer these questions but as he looked at his web of facts and suppositions he felt a certainty slide into his mind and click into place. He was sure he knew who the murderer was. But how could he prove it? Where was the evidence?

Chapter 25

Friday, September 18, 1970

Laurel woke up, gasping for breath. She was clutching the large, wooden spoon she'd started taking to bed with her. Another night of tossing and turning had come to an end.

She'd dreamt of Angela: they were playing on the beach, then racing over the pebbles into the sea, the soles of their feet hardened by years of living on the shingle beach in the summer months. Angela shrieking as she doused her with sea water, then wrestling with her and letting Angela push her under the waves. Later, with towels round them they shivered on the beach after staying in the water too long.

Good scenes faded into bad: Angela withdrawn, uncommunicative. Angela dead; the funeral; the grieving; how anger and wanting justice for her sister drove her to take risks and make mistakes; the decision to remain silent, to keep the terrible secret to herself.

She put on the bedside lamp and looked at the alarm clock. Four thirty. Too early to get up, too early to make a cup of tea and bring back to bed. She placed the giant spoon beside her like a lifeless bridegroom, patted it, switched off the light, and lay back on the pillows.

She was sure, from what Dorothy Piff had said, the school would close and she would be out of a job. It wasn't going to be easy finding a post she wanted at this stage of the school year. If they paid her salary until the end of term it would give her time to look round. She didn't want to go back home. She could travel, but somehow that didn't appeal to her.

What did she enjoy most about teaching? Was it the actual teaching? Administration? Did she want to try for another post as part of a team running a school? She didn't see why male deputy heads were paid more than senior mistresses. They should be equal: two deputy heads with the same status. She wasn't sure she'd enjoy all the paper work and administration; it was bound to get more onerous the higher you were promoted.

She really enjoyed working with people, children and adults. During the last ten days, although at times frightened, upset and enraged, she'd liked the excitement and thrill of the investigation. At school she'd always wanted justice for a wrong done. If you let a child get away with a crime, however petty, it will be the building block for another crime, another lie – justice for the victim and punishment, but hopefully redemption, for the criminal.

Could Toni Habershon have killed both Susan and Felicity? She'd an alibi for the attack on Mabel – unless either she or Nicholson, or both, were lying. Toni's motive could be jealousy of Susan. Of Felicity as well? What was the motive there?

As she stared into the blackness of the room her mind wandered. On the morning of the day Mabel was attacked she and Mabel had talked in her front garden. Mabel had said she was going to the sluice with Muffin. Laurel jerked up, clasping her hands round her knees. She remembered. As they chatted together there was the sound of a window opening. It must have been Toni Habershon's window. Had she heard what Mabel had said? Mabel's voice was loud and strong. But Toni had an alibi. Something stank.

What about Vanessa Letts? What secret was written about her in Susan's stolen log book? She was a tall, strong woman. What about Shipster? Frank said he'd just had a bath when he knocked him up after finding Mabel. Had he washed her blood away? What was his motive for wanting to silence Susan? And Felicity: a young, talented girl? Why would anyone want to kill an innocent child? – A beautiful, red-headed girl. She was wide awake now, anger and determination rising. She wouldn't move away until justice was done, especially for Felicity and Mabel.

She pushed away the bedclothes and went to the window. Dawn was breaking, though the sun wasn't up. A blackbird was singing. She pulled back the curtains and pushed the half-open window wider, and breathed in the salty air.

There was a car parked outside Toni Habershon's cottage. She peered closer. It wasn't Toni's Mini, it looked like Dorothy Piff's Morris Traveller. It was Dorothy's car. What on earth was she doing calling on Toni at this hour of the morning? Her stomach felt empty, sinking, and her neck muscles tightened. Something was wrong.

She grabbed a track suit, nearly falling over as she as she pulled on the bottoms, then trainers, no time for socks. She grabbed the spoon and raced down the stairs, heaved at the bolts on the front door and cautiously stepped out. Silence. No sign or sound of anybody.

She tip-toed to the car and felt the engine cover; it was cold – deadly cold. The hairs on the back of her neck prickled. She took a deep breath and crept up the garden path towards Toni's house, carefully placing her feet in smooth patches, avoiding loose pebbles. The front door was open an inch. She leant close to the gap and listened. Nothing. No sound. No breath, or voices, no chink of cup on saucer, no tread on stairs. The house sounded dead.

She slowly pushed open the door and flinched as the hinges groaned. The room was in darkness, the curtains' drawn. She groped for the light switch with her left hand, her right grasping the spoon, ready to lash out.

She jerked back as the light came on. She blinked. No

one. She heard herself gasp. There was a crumpled heap of clothes by the stairs. It was a woman, lying on her stomach. Grey curls – a tweed skirt. Dorothy. Laurel dropped the spoon and rushed to her. She knelt down. 'Dorothy.' She gently turned her over. She pulled her hands away. This wasn't Dorothy. A grotesque purple face, eyes bulging, tongue poking between rictus lips stared at her: a hideous gargoyle. There was a scarf twisted tight round her throat, digging into the flesh, livid bruises blooming from it, spreading to her face.

Laurel rocked back on her heels. This *was* Dorothy. Wails and sobs echoed round the room. Her joints had seized up. She was rigid as she stared down at the lifeless body. Then shivers ripped through her. She took several deep breaths. Think. Think. Do something.

She bent down and touched Dorothy's face. Cold, as cold as the steel bonnet of her Morris Traveller. She must get help; must get Frank. There was a clammy feel to the cottage as though a sea mist had crept in. Where was Toni Habershon? She looked round the room. On a table was a typewriter, a sheet of paper sticking out of the carriage. Like a marionette, stiff-legged and uncoordinated, she staggered the few paces to the table. She leant over to read it.

FROM TONI HABERSHON TO INSPECTOR DIAMOND
I CANNOT TAKE IT ANY MORE. I KNOW YOU WILL FIND OUT I KILLED SUSAN AND FELICITY. I KILLED FELICITY BECAUSE SHE SAW PHILIP AND ME MAKING LOVE AND SHE THREATENED TO TELL THE GOVERNORS. SHE HAD A CRUSH ON PHILIP. I KILLED SUSAN BECAUSE SHE POSSESSED THE MAN I WAS IN LOVE WITH. I HOPED HE WOULD COME BACK

TO ME, BUT NOW I KNOW THAT WILL NEVER
HAPPEN.

I ATTACKED MABEL BECAUSE SHE SAW
ME NEAR THE SLUICE THE EVENING I KILLED
SUSAN. PHILIP GAVE ME AN ALIBI FOR THAT
EVENING BECAUSE HE WAS SORRY FOR ME.
HE DOESN'T KNOW ANYTHING ABOUT THE
TERRIBLE THINGS I'VE DONE.

I HOPE GOD WILL FORGIVE ME. I KNOW
PHILIP WON'T BE ABLE TO WHEN HE KNOWS I
KILLED HIS WIFE. HE LOVED HER SO MUCH.

I'VE DECIDED TO TAKE THE ONLY WAY
OUT.

Toni Habershon

So it *was* Toni. Toni was the murderer. What did she mean
about Philip giving her an alibi? If she didn't have one,
neither did he. But where was she? She picked up the spoon
and went into the kitchen. The floor was slippery. No one.
She opened the bathroom door. It was damp, but empty. She
swallowed hard and climbed the stairs, the spoon over her
head in case someone struck from above. The bedrooms were
deserted. She pulled a blanket from a bed, ran down the stairs
and covered Dorothy's body.

As she dashed towards the school, still clutching her
spoon, holding back tears, her mind was racing. Why had
Dorothy gone to see Toni? Why had Toni killed her? She
wasn't mentioned in the letter. It looked like a suicide note.
Dorothy's body was cold; she must have been killed some
hours ago. Did she come last night? She hadn't heard the car.

There was a light on in Shipster's house. She banged on
the door. 'Mr Shipster. It's Laurel Bowman. I need your
help.' She continued to hit the wood, this time with her
spoon.

A rattle of chains and bolts and the door opened. Shipster's face was a picture of anticipated doom. He stared at her, unable to force a word from his lips.

'I need to contact Inspector Diamond.'

He groaned and stood back, his trembling hand pointing to the sitting room.

Frank watched the ambulance drive away. The photographers had finished, but the fingerprint team were still at work in Toni's cottage. He was full of a slow burning fury. Dorothy Piff lying on the floor, her life squeezed from her – the third victim. Why? Why had she come to see Toni? What possible motive could Toni Habershon have to murder *her*? She wasn't mentioned in Toni's letter. Such a formal, cold letter.

He turned towards Laurel's cottage. She'd refused to go to the main house, or to have a WPC sit with her. 'Come and tell me what's happening after you've finished,' she'd said. It was no good arguing with her, although she'd cried bitterly as she told him how she'd found Dorothy.

He opened her door. She was sitting by the table motionless, her face stern, cold, and all tears gone.

'Frank. What's happened?'

'They've taken Dorothy away. Elderkin's organised a search of the grounds and beach for Toni Habershon. Her car's by the side of her house so she's somewhere near, if she's alive.'

Laurel held out her hand and Frank moved to the table, sat down beside her and gently took hold with both of his hands.

'Have you seen Philip Nicholson? What did he say?'

'They did go to the cinema in Ipswich together, but Toni left the pub early. She said she was tired. The next morning she managed to ask him to say she'd been with him all the evening. He felt sorry for her because he knew she was in love with him. He never dreamt she was the person who'd

256

attacked Mabel, so he agreed.' He paused. 'He appeared shattered, nearly broke down, and kept on repeating how wrong he was to do that. How terribly sorry he was. He feels so guilty as he'd just sacked poor Dorothy.'

Laurel squeezed his hand. 'Stupid man. But he hasn't got an alibi either. I suppose that doesn't matter... now.'

'I must go and see Emily Piff and tell her.'

'Can I come with you?'

'I should take a WPC.'

'I met Emily properly for the first time yesterday. She'll be shattered to have lost Dorothy. I might be more support and comfort to her than a stranger.'

'Are you sure? You've been through the wringer yourself, and you'll have to make a formal statement as soon as possible.'

'Yes, I want to go. I owe Dorothy that. How I feel is nothing compared to how Emily...'

Frank stood up. He wasn't surprised she wanted to do this. She'd a strong sense of what was right, what was owed. How was he going to deal with her if he ever got proof of what she'd done? The day could only get grimmer.

Chapter 26

Laurel slid into the passenger seat next to Frank.

'This is how we'll do it,' he said. 'I'll break the news to Emily, but you step in when you think it's right.' His face was serious, worried.

'This must be one of worst parts of your job: telling someone their husband, wife, daughter, son is dead; especially if they've been murdered.'

He nodded. 'It is. You don't know how they're going to react; you've to be ready for anything. Sometimes they turn their hurt on you, it's understandable, but it's painful. Some coppers would rather jump into a pit of vipers than break bad news.' He turned on the engine. 'Ready?'

Laurel bit her lip and nodded, half-wishing she hadn't volunteered. She was dreading seeing Emily, but she *had* to help in any way she could.

Frank turned into the curving drive of Greyfriars House, and parked near the front door. The stone dolphin was still spitting into the circular pond. 'Elderkin said they lived in a big house, didn't realise how big.'

Only yesterday she'd been here, having coffee with Dorothy in her bedroom, chatting about the case and learning from Emily about Dorothy's fiancé killed in the war. 'I thought the house was huge for the two of them; Emily will feel so lonely here by herself. Dorothy was the one who socialized; I can imagine Emily becoming a recluse. She needs someone to look after.'

Frank squeezed her arm. 'OK?'

She nodded.

He knocked on the door. They stood there several minutes. No one came. He knocked again, this time more firmly.

'Perhaps she's gone out looking for Dorothy. She'll be cross and worried she went out when she had a cold.' They continued to wait.

The door was opened. 'Goodness me, she didn't lock it. What on earth did she think she was doing?' She was wearing a beige full-length dressing gown, a woollen scarf wrapped round her neck, her nose was red and her eyes, behind blue-rimmed glasses, were watery.

Laurel stepped back, her mouth open, swaying. Frank grabbed her arm. She looked down at the woman's feet: sensible lamb's wool slippers – not fluffy pink ones. Her lips trembled. 'Dorothy?'

'Laurel. Inspector Diamond. Have you seen Emily? She dosed me up so much last night I only woke up when I heard you knocking. She must have gone shopping, although I don't know why. We didn't need anything...' She stopped. 'What is it? What's happened?'

Laurel's mind was in turmoil, she didn't know how to express her feelings: joy at Dorothy being alive and despair at the awful news she had to give her. 'Oh, Dorothy, I'm so sorry.' She put her arms round her and hugged her tight. 'It's Emily. She's dead. Someone killed her.'

Dorothy's body went rigid. She pushed Laurel away, her face blanched. 'Is this true?' she asked Frank.

'Yes. Shall we go in?' He held out his arms, shepherding them into the house.

Dorothy Piff, her back straight, walked stiffly in front of them and led them into a sitting room. 'Would you draw the curtains back, Laurel? Thank you.' She sat in an armchair and pointed to the settee. Her white face was tight with shock, her lips quivering. 'Tell me what happened.'

'Laurel found Emily early this morning.'

Dorothy turned to her. 'Tell me what you found.'

Frank went to the kitchen to make tea. Dorothy, her head bent, wiped her eyes, spectacles in her hand.

'I think I know why she went to see Toni Habershon.' She looked at Laurel. 'When we talked before I went to sleep last night I said I'd get up tomorrow and see Toni. You remember I said I was worried about her. Emily must have decided to drive over to see her so I wouldn't get up tomorrow... today.'

'She didn't leave a note?'

Dorothy wiped her cheeks again and sniffed. 'She might have done. If it's anywhere it'll be in my bedroom. When I heard the knocking and she didn't answer the door, I came straight down. There might be a note there.'

'Do you want me to have a look?'

Dorothy nodded. 'Would you? Perhaps you'd better tell Inspector Diamond. It might be evidence.'

Her mind was sharp despite the turmoil and shock. 'I'll check with Frank.'

The curtains were drawn, the bedroom gloomy. She found a note on Dorothy's bedside table and picked it up. Frank said she needn't worry about fingerprints as you can't lift them from paper. She took it downstairs and passed it to Dorothy. Frank came into the room and nodded at Laurel. It was the last words her sister would write to her and it was fitting she should to read it first.

Dorothy read it silently, looked up, her eyes brimming with tears. She brushed them away and read it to them.

Dear Dorothy

Just a little note in case you wake up and call for me. I'm popping out in the car, shouldn't be long. I'm going to see

*Toni Habershon and invite her to come
for coffee tomorrow. Then you can have
a chat with her here and you won't
need to get out of bed.*

*I'll call in at the school and I'll see if
I can get your reading glasses.*

Sleep tight.

*Love
Emily*

A few tears trickled down her cheeks as she handed the note
to Frank, and more tears, followed by soft, deep sobs, her
body quivering as though it might shatter. Laurel offered her
hand and Dorothy grasped it and held on. Frank placed the
note on the table and went back to the kitchen.

'I've lost half of me. We were always together – except
during the war. She was such a sweet, good sister…'

Laurel held her in her arms, biting her lip, trying not to
give way to her own pain.

By the time Frank came back with a loaded tea tray –
Laurel suspected he'd delayed making it to give Dorothy
more time – she'd wiped her eyes, gulping, trying to regain
control. She managed a few sips of tea.

'Would you pass me my handbag, Laurel?' She took out a
blue-enamelled cigarette case, embossed with the winged
emblem of the RAF, and a lighter. 'I don't usually smoke
until after dinner with my coffee, and certainly not with a
cold, but…' The cigarette quivered between her lips. She
inhaled deeply, coughed, but carried on smoking.

Laurel and Frank drank their tea in silence.

'How did she look, Laurel? Do you think she suffered?'

Laurel looked helplessly at Frank. How could she answer Dorothy? Tell her of the hideous purple face? The swollen tongue?

'I think it was quick, Dorothy,' Frank said. 'A quick death – but like any death, natural, or unnatural, it's not good. I can never understand when they say someone made a good death.'

Dorothy straightened, her chin up. 'There were good deaths in the war, Inspector Diamond. Men and women gave their lives for their countries, for their people.' She stabbed the cigarette out in a glass ashtray.

'Yes, of course.' Frank said, looking puzzled.

Laurel squeezed Dorothy's hand. 'Emily told me yesterday about your fiancé.' She turned to Frank. 'He was in the RAF, a navigator; he was killed in the war.'

'I'm sorry, Dorothy. I didn't know. Please accept my apologies.'

Dorothy managed a weak smile. 'His name was Frank, too. I forgive you, you weren't to know.' She looked round the room. 'What happens next? I'd like to see Emily. Where is she?'

She mustn't see her yet. Laurel again looked to Frank to answer the question.

'Emily's been taken to… the hospital in Ipswich. There will have to be a post-mortem. I'm hoping we can arrange that for later today or tomorrow. I'll take you to see her as soon as it's over.'

'Would you like me to come with you?' Laurel asked.

'Please, Laurel.'

'I can stay here with you if you'd like. I'd be very happy to do that.'

Frank nodded. 'A good idea.'

'You did offer to put me up if the school closed. I'd like

262

to be here with you.'

'I'd be glad of your company, Laurel, but it won't be very jolly.'

Laurel shrugged. 'We'll do our best.'

'Inspector, what about Toni Habershon? Did she kill Emily? Where is she?'

Frank told her of the letter and a search for Toni was going on at the moment.

'But she didn't confess to killing Emily?'

'No.'

'Why did she kill her? Emily must have come into the cottage... perhaps she saw the confession... perhaps she tried to stop Toni running away... tried to make her face justice... Is that what happened?'

Frank sighed. 'I think most people will think so, including the chief constable. If we find Toni alive we'll find out.'

'You don't think you'll find her alive, do you?' Dorothy asked.

'I'm sure we won't,' Frank said.

Chapter 27

Saturday, September 19, 1970

Frank was sitting at the desk in Shipster's office, completing a letter to the chief constable, setting out why he thought the investigation of Susan Nicholson's murder was not over. So far the only signs of Toni Habershon were a small pile of clothes at the bottom of the beach steps.

Elderkin burst into the room. 'They've found her, between here and Minsmere beach. High tide washed her to the shallows. She couldn't have swum out very far or they wouldn't have seen her.'

Frank pulled on his leather jacket. 'Could you ring Martin Ansell and ask him to get here as soon as possible? I want him to do the post-mortem. I rang him yesterday and warned him we'd need him again soon. I said between three and five days, they usually float after that time in September. We've been lucky getting her this early.'

Elderkin pulled a face. 'Not so lucky for her.' He opened his notebook, reached for the telephone and started to dial.

Frank ran down the beach steps and along strips of sand near the waterline. In the distance were a group of people and a fishing boat beached on the shore. As he got nearer he saw, lying on the sand, a body covered in a plastic sheet.

Three constables were guarding it, but none of them were looking at her. They stood to attention as Frank approached. One chap looked green round the gills. Appropriate for a seaside setting. Two fishermen, one smoking a cigarette and the other a pipe, were chatting a few yards away.

Frank approached them and introduced himself. 'Thank

you for helping with the search and congratulations, if that's appropriate, on finding the body. It'll be a great help to have found her so soon.'

They nodded their thanks and continued puffing.

'How far out was she?'

'Not far; we were lucky we saw her. We'd been looking nearer Minsmere, didn't expect to see much just yet, not for a day or too, but we decided to come in here and have a snack. We was coming in, I'd cut the engine and Lenny here, he said he thought he saw something floating a few feet down. Luckily it's a nice calm day and the water's clear. We hooked her up and floated her in,' the pipe-smoker said.

'How far out?'

'What you say, Lenny? 'Bout fifteen feet?'

Lenny nodded his head and blew out a stream of smoke. 'They're saying she did in that headmaster's wife. Is that right, Inspector?'

'I'm afraid I can't comment at the moment. Would you like to go up to the school? I'm sure someone could rustle up a hot drink and some food. One of the constables will take you up. I'm afraid I'll have to ask you to make statements. You might as well do it now, save you going to the station later.' He'd expected them to moan, but they looked cheerful as if this was a bit of a break in the monotony of their lives. A bit of excitement, something they could boast about in the pub tonight.

'Is that Sergeant Elderkin up there?' Lenny asked.

'It is.'

'Will he take our statements?'

'Would you prefer that?'

They both nodded. So Elderkin had some fans, well, at least two, unless they thought they could pump him for more details.

'She was a bonny girl. Seems a pity to end up like that,'

the pipe-smoker said.

'Don't look so good now,' said Lenny, 'not with all her wrinkly skin.' He leered at Frank who wanted them to go. The thought of Toni lying naked and vulnerable under the plastic sheet and the fisherman, well Lenny, enjoying her curves, nauseated him. He turned away from them and waited until the crunch of their footsteps had faded.

He pulled back the plastic sheet. Her blonde hair, darkened by the sea, was plastered against her scalp; dusky pink patches blotched her face. He flinched as a tiny crab scuttled from her open mouth, down her cheek and neck, over a breast, and back into the sand. Was this woman the murderer of Felicity and Susan as her suicide note said? Or was she another victim? He looked towards the steps. Martin Ansell couldn't come soon enough.

The sea was calm, flat waves undulated ashore, making hissing noises as they crept over the shingle. He'd walked towards Minsmere beach and then back again, several times, not wanting to chat with the constables, and not wanting to be near the body. He went over his reasoning, his choice of the prime suspect – Toni's confession hadn't changed his mind. The chief constable was happy; as far as he was concerned the case was solved. Frank put forward his reasoning and was met with derision.

It had been the same at Felixstowe: he'd worked out who the prime suspect was. If the brass had gone along with his line of enquiry, the man might have been charged. Instead he was found dead and Angela's murder remained unsolved. If they'd let him follow his reasoning, the suspect would be behind bars and Laurel would have had justice of a different kind.

Frank looked out to sea: the brown streaks in the green waters showed the shallow, shifting sandbanks. They seemed to echo his thoughts: could he take twenty more years of working with bastards, following set routines he knew were a waste of time, and scratching people's backs? He liked the work, he loved the prickling sensation down his spine when the pieces of the jigsaw clicked together and he knew for certain who, how and when the crime had been committed. He enjoyed working with coppers like Stuart Elderkin and unusual, interesting people like Martin Ansell. Professionals excited by their work, their ideas sparking his own mind, helping him to solve a crime. Most of all he liked getting justice for the victims and the people they'd left behind, terrified by the awful things that had been done to their loved ones. He didn't want to give that up.

As he walked towards the steps he saw the tall figure of Martin Ansell striding over the gravel carrying two large bags, one in each hand. Behind him was the mortuary attendant they'd met at the examination of Felicity's bones, also laden down with equipment. Behind both of them, struggling through the shingle, was Elderkin.

Ansell dumped the bags on the beach and stuck out his hand, a broad grin lighting up his eyes. 'Morning, Inspector Diamond. Gosh, two bodies in two days.'

Frank couldn't help smiling at his boyish pleasure; you'd have thought he'd received two Valentine cards, or won the pools on successive weeks. 'I'm pleased corpses give you a thrill. Not into necrophilia, are you? Let's cut out inspector and doctor, shall we? Call me Frank.'

Another broad smile. 'Well, Frank, I don't want people to be murdered or to commit suicide, but if they're dead I'm pleased to see to them, and to help you in any way I can.'

'Good, that's what I want to hear.'

Stuart Elderkin crunched his way to Frank's side, puffing like an old, fat Labrador. 'Now, Martin,' Frank said, pointing to Toni's body, 'this one is tricky.'

Ansell frowned. 'Tricky? I was told she'd drowned herself... you're saying that may not be the case?'

'Obviously you'll have to go through all the procedures, but what *I* want to know, and as soon as possible, is: one, did she die by drowning; two, if not, how was she killed; three if she did drown, did she drown in that stuff?' He pointed to the suspiring sea.

Ansell's eyes were wide with excitement. 'Gosh, super. Poor Emily Piff was straightforward: death by asphyxiation. By the way, the attack on the poor woman was extremely severe. Whoever did it used great force. The inside of her mouth and larynx were bruised and traumatised. The cartilage in the throat crushed and the hyoid bone broken into several pieces.'

'Someone out of control?' Elderkin asked.

Ansell nodded. He turned to Frank. 'You're suggesting we may have something more challenging than suicide here?' Frank nodded back. 'Right, let's have a look-see.' He gently pulled aside the plastic sheet and, careless of his trousers, knelt down beside Toni's body. His expression changed; the eager puppy replaced by the intelligent professional. 'I'm sure you know quite a lot about death by drowning, Frank–'

'Treat me as ignorant. Tell me everything.'

Ansell glanced up at him, smiled and pushed his hair back from his face. 'Often there are few external signs on the body of drowning. If there's a lot of froth round the mouth this is an indication, but we've none here. We've got signs of water immersion: you can see the skin on the fingers, palms and soles of the feet are already wrinkled, there's lividity in her face where the blood settled as she floated head down. And there,' he pointed to her thighs, 'you can see the goose-skin, anserine cutis. Also the abdomen has started to distend and she would have floated in a few days. I'll take the body temperature and I should be able to give you a good idea of time of death.'

Frank and Elderkin turned away as Ansell got busy with his thermometer. He made notes and then calculations, having taken the sea's temperature by sending his assistant, complete with waders, as far out as he could shuffle without the sea going over his boots.

'I calculate she died thirty-eight to forty hours ago; so Thursday between seven and nine pm. About the same time as Emily Piff.'

'That fits, but was Toni alive, and did she murder Emily? Or was she already dead and someone else had killed them both? Pity you can't separate the two.'

Ansell looked once more like the anxious spaniel, unable to please his master. 'Sorry, best I can do. Can't be more accurate than that.' He shrugged. 'I need to take sea samples in the approximate region she was found in.' He looked at the fishing boat, still beached on the shingle. 'Any chance of using that?'

Frank asked one of the constables to fetch the two fishermen.

'So you're going to look for diatoms?' Frank asked.

'I'm impressed. There's a peak at this time of the year, not as much as the spring flush.' He stopped and scratched his head. 'Have you dealt with cases like this?' he asked, as though afraid he'd made a faux pas.

'No, never had a murder by drowning, but I've a degree in botany, with some zoology thrown in, so I know a bit about plant and animal life, but Stuart may want an explanation, although he's a naturalist.'

Elderkin preened himself. 'I know diatoms are part of the plankton; little one-celled green jobs, I believe.'

Ansell beamed at both of them – obviously his star pupils. He looked at Toni's body. 'You think she was murdered?' he asked Frank.

'Yes, and I'm hoping you can prove it, because without the forensic evidence, I can't.'

Ansell wrote briefly in his notebook. 'If she did drown in the sea, then it will be suicide, won't it? Not murder.' Frank nodded. 'If a person drowns in water, fresh or sea, water gets into the lungs and these little blighters, the diatoms, will slip through the walls of the lungs – the little air sacs – and into the blood stream. They get into the heart, kidney, bone marrow and brain. This can only happen if the person is alive at the time of being in the water. Drowning can take several minutes if the person is conscious, and if she'd swum out, this is what would have happened. If I find diatoms, similar to the ones in the sample I take, then your theory is up the spout, I'm afraid.'

Frank grimaced. 'I only want the truth.'

'It's all I have to offer.'

'When can you tell me how she died?'

Ansell looked at his watch. 'We can go straight back to the mortuary and I'll start the post-mortem immediately, but I need time to get samples from the bone marrow and one other organ, and to do all the rest of the tests.'

'Tests?' Frank asked, as Elderkin lit up his pipe, looking away from the body and out to sea.

'I'll need to do some work boiling samples with acid and whizz them round in the old centrifuge. All a bit tricky. If you can come back to Ipswich tomorrow afternoon, I should have results. Better telephone me to make sure.'

'It's Sunday tomorrow. You'll be working the rest of today?'

'And most of the night,' he said enthusiastically. 'I know you need the results quickly.'

'Thanks, Martin. Elderkin and I will be there.' He looked towards the steps. 'Here are the two old salts. No doubt they'll charge you for your brief trip on the briny.'

Ansell started unpacking another case. 'I'll use a plankton net, if the same species of diatoms from this sample are found in the marrow, well…' He grinned. 'If she was unconscious, or dead when she went into the water, there should be few if any of the beasties. I'll take the water temperature again at the spot they found her, do another calculation, but I doubt I'll better the time of death than the one you've already have.'

Frank watched him talking to the fishermen. He liked a man who enjoyed his work.

Chapter 28

Sunday, September 20, 1970

Laurel opened her eyes, blinking. Where was she? She didn't recognise the flowered wallpaper and matching curtains. Then she remembered. Emily. Dead. Murdered. She was in a guest bedroom in Dorothy Piff's house. She couldn't believe she'd slept so well, but a well-sprung mattress, soft woollen blankets, linen sheets and a patchwork eiderdown had comforted her. She'd opened the lattice window before she went to sleep and the birds were singing. She got out of bed, pulled back the curtains and looked out. The window faced the back garden which merged into a wood. Blackbirds were rooting in the lawn for worms and a robin was at the bird table, along with two blue-tits, doing serious damage to a bird feeder half-full of peanuts. Such a calm, peaceful scene.

Yesterday she'd driven Dorothy to Ipswich to formally identify her sister. Frank and Stuart Elderkin had met them there. She was glad of Frank's support, although Dorothy had kept a tight rein on her emotions. Emily's face looked a thousand times better than when she'd seen her lying on Toni Habershon's kitchen floor. She admired Dorothy's bravery and stoicism, but wondered if it might be better if she could let go and have another good cry. She wanted to tell Dorothy about Angela's death. To let her know she really understood her grief. They shared the terrible experience of a sister brutally murdered. She should have told her before; she no longer wanted to keep that secret from her.

Laurel put on the dressing gown Dorothy had lent her and opened the bedroom door. Smells of toast and coffee drifted up from the kitchen, and as she went down the stairs the plop,

plop, of the percolator, and the metallic sound of the toaster ejecting a slice, told her Dorothy was busy.

'Morning, Laurel. I've made toast. Would you like a cooked breakfast? I've eggs, bacon and some mushrooms.'

Dorothy was smartly dressed in a cream wool twin set, brown tweed skirt and a double row of pearls. Her hair was freshly washed and set, but the whites of her eyes were pink and her face puffy. She believed in private grief.

'Toast will be fine.' She couldn't face a cooked breakfast.

A table was laid in the kitchen: a checked tablecloth, place mats, white china, and crisp linen napkins. Dear Dorothy, she'd made such an effort to bring normality to a situation that was anything but normal.

After they'd eaten and washed up, they sat down for a final cup of coffee.

'I'm going to the eleven o'clock service, Laurel. Would you like to come with me?'

From her expression and the tone of her voice, Laurel thought she wanted to go alone. 'Are you're sure you're up to it, Dorothy?'

Dorothy straightened her back. 'I've got to face my friends in the village sometime. Also the vicar rang this morning and said they would be saying prayers for Emily during the service. I want to hear them, to pray with the people who knew Emily, and to feel them round me. She was well loved.'

Laurel drew back her shoulders. 'Dorothy, there's something I must tell you. I haven't told anyone here and I hope you'll forgive me for not speaking about it before. I didn't want anyone at school to know.'

Dorothy frowned. 'Yes?'

'I lied to you when you asked me if I had a sister. I did have a younger sister. Her name was Angela.'

'Was? She's dead?'

273

Laurel nodded and she bit her lip. Tears were unexpectedly welling in her eyes. 'Angela was murdered, strangled in March, 1969.'

Dorothy's hand flew to her mouth, her eyes widening. 'Oh, my dear. Now I understand your agitation when you discovered Susan Nicholson had been murdered. Déjà vu. It must have been a nightmare.' She opened her arms and they hugged each other close for a few seconds.

Dorothy wiped her eyes with a handkerchief. 'Please don't tell me the details. *Couldn't bear it.* I'm sorry.'

'I'm the one who's sorry, Dorothy. I needed to tell you, but perhaps I should have waited.'

'No, it would never be the right time, would it? I hope the police caught him?'

How like Dorothy to put Laurel's problems before hers. 'No, the police haven't arrested anyone.'

Dorothy patted Laurel's hand as though she was the one who should be comforted. 'I'm glad you told me. Does Frank know?'

'Yes, and Stuart Elderkin. Frank was the police sergeant on the case.'

Dorothy shook her head. 'It's difficult taking all of this in.' She looked at the kitchen clock. 'I'd better get ready for church. Do you want to come to the service?'

'No, I think I'll go to the cottage and collect the rest of my stuff; that's if you're sure you want me to stay here.'

'Of course I do. It's been a solace having you here; a comfort to know there's someone else in the house. I know if I need you to do something you will. I hope I don't have to ask you, but having you here's helping me.' She looked for a moment as though she would break down, but she rubbed her nose hard with an index finger, collected up the cups and took them it to the sink. 'Are you sure you should go back to the school? Remember what Inspector Diamond said yesterday.'

Frank had warned them not to assume the case was closed, whatever the chief constable said. 'I don't want either of you going back to the school. I can't say any more than that.'

Laurel sighed. 'Perhaps you're right, but I'm short of underwear. I didn't bring much with me.'

'My dear, help yourself from my lingerie – second drawer down in the chest-of-drawers in my room.'

Laurel had seen Dorothy's knickers when she was looking for a nightdress: drawers was the operative word. She tried to hide a smile. She just couldn't see herself in voluminous lock-knit pants, with legs half-way to her knees. 'Thanks, Dorothy, but –'

'Not skimpy enough? Emily was like you, she always bought silk French-knickers...' She bowed her head. 'Sorry, I can't possibly lend you any of hers. I know I'll have to get rid of her things, but not yet.'

'Please don't worry, Dorothy. I can do a bit of washing while you're at the service. I won't go to the school. There's lot's do here. Could I use your telephone? I need to ring home. Reassure my parents again – I must go and see them soon. I'll pay you of course.'

Dorothy wouldn't hear of it and at twenty-to-eleven left to walk to the church. Dorothy would miss her sister so much. They were the last of the Piffs and now there was only Dorothy. She'd stay here as long as Dorothy needed her, but she'd have to start looking for another job soon. The thought depressed her. Would she be able to find a post she wanted for a January start? She might have to go backwards and take up a PE post, not even a head of department. All this mayhem and murder had unsettled her.

Laurel found some Daz, washed her underwear and hung them outside. She walked round the garden, restless, thinking about what Frank had said.

If Toni wasn't the murderer, why had she committed suicide? Or had she been murdered too? Why was Emily killed? She must have seen something when she went into the cottage? What? Surely Toni wouldn't have killed her because she found her writing the letter? But the letter had been typed. Toni did have a typewriter; it was on the table, near the letter she'd left. If Emily came into the cottage... but she wouldn't go into the house unless her knock on the door was answered; unless she heard something: a noise that worried her. She went in... and? She saw something and the murderer had to silence her. If Toni was the murderer, why didn't she ignore the knocking? She could have told her to go away. Or said she would see Dorothy the next day. Was Toni so upset she was unhinged? Did she think Emily was Dorothy? Perhaps she hated Dorothy.

Laurel blew out her cheeks. It was confusing. She snapped off a leaf from a bush and ripped it into small pieces. Doing nothing was driving her crazy. She'd go to the school. She'd drive straight to the cottage and collect her things. It wouldn't take her long. She'd leave a note for Dorothy telling her she'd decided to go for a drive – not mention the school. She didn't like the thought of her personal belongings in the cottage. She wanted to be finished with Blackfriars School.

The phone rang.

'Laurel, it's Dorothy. The vicar would like me to go back with him for lunch. I'm phoning from the vicarage. We're going to discuss Emily's funeral.'

Laurel wasn't sure what to say. Surely Dorothy didn't have to put herself through this so soon?

'Are you still there?'

'Yes, Dorothy. I just wondered...'

'I know the funeral may not happen this week, but it will help me to talk about it, to choose her favourite hymns and readings. Would you like to join us for lunch? The vicar says you're most welcome.'

'No thanks, Dorothy. There's plenty of food here and I might go for a drive.'

'Very well, my dear. Don't forget to lock up. Take the front door key with you. I've got mine. I'll see you this evening.'

She didn't see anyone as she drove onto the school site. The chief constable had withdrawn all the policemen. Nicholson's Land Rover was outside his house, but there was no sign of him. She parked in front of her cottage, opened the boot and unlocked the door. It was only a fortnight since she'd driven into the school for the first time. All that had happened: Mabel attacked – please God, let her get better; poor Muffin killed; Felicity's bones cast up by the sea and Emily strangled. Toni's body was in the morgue. If she *was* the murderer she couldn't feel any sympathy for her, especially if she was the person who'd tried to kill Mabel. She didn't feel like the same woman who'd driven in through the school gates, not looking forward to her new job, her mind still full of thoughts of Angela and her own terrible, stupid actions as she'd tried to get justice for her sister. After seeing how Frank worked, being involved in helping him to try and solve the murders of Susan and Felicity, she'd a better appreciation of Frank's commitment. If only she'd confided in Frank when he was part of the investigation into Angela's murder and told him of her suspicions. Too late. She'd have to live with the consequences of her actions. Could she do that?

She went into the bedroom, opened her suitcases and piled clothes into them. She put the packed suitcases into the boot and started taking down pictures and posters in the living room and putting books into the cardboard boxes she'd brought with her and luckily hadn't got rid of. Anything else? She checked the fridge and put some eggs and butter into the car and the rest in the bin.

The house looked sad, bare. She remembered her walking gear, didn't want to leave that behind. She opened the cupboard to the right of the fireplace. Two anoraks were on a shelf; she placed them on the carpet and knelt down to get her walking boots. She pulled the boots towards her, one wouldn't come. A lace was stuck in something. She tugged at it. The end toggle had caught in a crack in the floor. As she pulled she felt the floorboard move. It was loose. She flung the free boot onto the anoraks and tried to loosen the other. She pushed the board with her hand. It was definitely loose. On purpose? Her nostrils dilated like a hound on the scent of a quarry, her backbone stiffening with excitement.

Impatiently she scrabbled at the edge of the wood with her fingernails and winced as a nail bent. She went to the kitchen and rooted in the utensil drawer and chose the sturdiest knife. She knelt down and carefully slid the blade into the crack near the caught lace and levered. The floorboard came up easily.

She threw the second boot with the first and peered into the hole. She couldn't see anything. Where was her torch? Damn, it was already packed in the car. She pushed up her sleeve, lay on the floor and manoeuvred her body so she could reach into the hole. She tentatively put her right hand into it, hoping she wouldn't touch the furry body of a long-dead rat.

The hole was about nine inches deep. Her fingers touched the bottom – stone. She moved her hand from side to side. It closed round a metal object, which was round with other metal things attached to it. She fingered them – keys. She levered it up: keys on a large metal ring. They were labelled *Susan's keys*. Frank had told her about Susan blackmailing Thornback into getting keys cut to all the staff living quarters. She must have had a key to this cottage as well. Where was it? Was it here, when the cottage was empty, she wrote in the log book? Could something else be hidden in this hole? She put the key ring down on top of the anoraks, lay back on the floor and put her hand back in the hole, stretching her fingers from side to side.

She touched a solid object. It was hard to get hold of with one hand, as it was heavy. She scraped her skin as she dragged it from the hole. It was a thick, black book. A surge of triumph ripped through her. Yes. She'd found it: the missing log book. The replica of the one Dorothy gave to Frank.

She must contact him straight away. He'd be so pleased – and pleased with her. She scrambled up and took the book and keys to the table by the window. She wanted to shout out. 'I've found it! Now we'll know what happened to Susan.' But would they? She might have written complete rubbish in it – nothing that would give them a clue to her murder. Perhaps she'd better check it was worth getting him to come back from Ipswich. He was desperate to get the details of the post-mortem on Toni Habershon. There might be nothing worth reading. She smiled to herself. Who was she kidding? She was desperate to see if Susan had written in the book; desperate to find out if her words revealed the identity of the murderer.

Her hands were dirty. She rushed to the kitchen sink and turned on the tap too hard; water splashed from the stone sink soaking her clothes. She frantically grabbed a bar of soap, quickly washed and dried her hands, and hurtled back to the book. What about finger prints? She remembered there's no way of getting fingerprints from paper. She'd risk being told off.

She tried to open it but it was locked. Damn. She pulled the key ring towards her. Yes. There was a small key, smaller than a Yale. She carefully inserted it into the brass lock.

279

There was a satisfying click and she opened up the book.

There was nothing written in the first few index pages. Her stomach plummeted with disappointment. But as she turned to the first lined page there was writing: a clear, sloping copperplate hand written with a fine pen-nib in black ink.

Friday, 14ᵗʰ March, 1969

Took this lovely log book from the stationery cupboard. Just what I wanted. It's got a fantastic brass lock and good quality paper, unlike all the other stationery in bossy-boots Piff's office. It didn't take long for her to decide she didn't like me. She soon gave me the cold shoulder and makes sure I can't get at the staff files. If I can't play my little games I'll die of boredom in this dreary old school. Found a good hiding place for my diary. I'm not telling where!

Chapter 29

Frank strode down the corridor towards the mortuary, Stuart Elderkin puffing behind him. Frank had phoned Ansell to check if he was ready to give them the results of the post-mortem on Toni Habershon. He was.

Ansell's voice had been squeaky with excitement. 'Yes. Yes. I think I've got what you want. I'll need to do a few more tests to corroborate my findings, but I've got enough for you to go on.'

Frank hadn't waited for details. 'We'll leave now. Be with you soon.' He banged down the phone. He'd picked up Elderkin from the Leiston police station; he was still flexing his knuckles as proof of a scary journey. Frank pushed open the door to the mortuary. Would Ansell have enough proof for him to make an arrest?

The pathologist was seated at a desk writing in a book. He looked up, showing a surprisingly heavy growth of beard and there were shadows under his eyes, but they were full of life and, Frank hoped, satisfaction.

'Frank, Stuart, please sit down. Have you been to see Mabel?'

'We were going to pay a brief visit after we'd seen you,' Stuart Elderkin replied. 'Have you seen her lately?' He'd asked Ansell to keep him informed about Mabel's progress.

'Yes, this morning. Good news, they've been reducing the drugs and she's coming out of the coma. She'd responded well to tests. They're very hopeful she'll make a good recovery. I asked them to telephone here if anything happens in the next hour.'

Stuart Elderkin flopped down in a chair and covered his face with his hands, his broad shoulders heaving.

Ansell looked at Frank and raised his eyebrows.

'Stuart's very fond of Mabel. Got a soft spot for her haven't you, Stuart? He says it's her apple pie, but I think his feelings run deeper than a love of crisp pastry.' He put his hand on Stuart's shoulder. 'Do you want to go and see her now, Stuart?'

Stuart looked up and shook his shoulders, like a dog getting rid of water after a swim. 'No thanks, Frank. I want to hear what *he's* got to say.' He nodded towards Ansell. 'See if it's enough to nail the bastard that nearly killed her.' He took out his notepad and prepared to write.

Ansell took a deep breath. 'Gosh, I hope I have. Right, here goes. A few preliminaries: it's difficult to prove with one hundred per cent accuracy that someone drowned; it's a case of putting together evidence, and eliminating other possible causes or circumstances which might mean the death looks like drowning, but was caused, say, by cardiac arrest.'

Elderkin moaned. 'You've lost me already.'

'Just give us the facts, Martin. Save all that crap for the witness box, or when this is all over and we're relaxing in a pub with several pints down us,' Frank said.

'*Police*. You're all the same.' He grinned at them. 'OK. Do you know the difference between drowning in sea water and fresh water?'

They shook their heads. Frank tensed. Why mention fresh water if it wasn't important?

'Firstly I'm sure Toni Habershon drowned. But she didn't drown in sea water.'

Frank felt a joyous swoosh of excitement rise from his stomach to his throat. 'Fantastic,' he gasped.

Elderkin thumped his pad against the table.

Ansell looked as though he'd won an Oscar. 'If you drown in fresh water the blood volume rapidly increases as water goes through the lung tissue. Osmosis you know.' He glanced at Elderkin who'd stopped writing and was glaring at him. 'The stronger solution of the blood attracts the fresh water through the membranes of the tissues.'

'Ah,' Elderkin said, nodding his head.

Ansell smiled and nodded back. 'All this fluid puts a great strain on the heart and you lose consciousness rapidly. With salt water there's an opposite effect, fluid is drawn from the blood plasma into the lungs, there's less strain on the heart and you survive longer in sea than fresh water.'

Just tell us, Frank wanted to scream.

'Toni's lungs were swollen, full of water; there was bleeding of the sinuses, ergo she drowned.' He paused, looking from Frank to Elderkin.

'Come on, Prof. Give us the works,' Elderkin frothed.

'There were no diatoms in Toni's bone marrow or kidney samples.'

Frank punched the air. 'So no suicide by swimming out to sea!'

Ansell was wriggling with excitement. 'You remember George Joseph Smith?'

'The Brides in the Bath murderer?' Elderkin asked.

'I think your murderer, well *our* murderer, used the same method.'

'Get them in the bath, then when they're all relaxed suddenly grab their ankles and pull them under. He did at least three women like that. It must have been in Toni's bathroom; he was probably naked going to give her back a scrub, or something, and under she went,' Elderkin said.

Frank nodded. 'And in walked Emily Piff to see what all the noise was about, and before she could escape he strangled her.'

Ansell went over to a bench and brought back a stoppered test tube. He opened it. 'Smell that.' He wafted it first under Frank's and then Stuart's noses. 'Well?'

It smelt faintly of… lavender?

'Bath salts?' Stuart asked.

'Excellent.' Ansell said. 'It's a sample from Toni Habershon's lungs.'

Elderkin wrinkled his face and Frank laughed. He decided Ansell could use the word excellent whenever he liked.

'I'll do some tests on it later when–'

The telephone rang.

Chapter 30

Laurel leant back from the table, her hands palms down on the log book as though she was afraid it would come to life, flutter its pages and fly away from her. It was true. Susan had stolen a log book and she'd written in it. She was reading the words of a woman who'd been murdered. Through her handwriting, her use of words, phrases, and sense of humour, her personality was coming to life. Laurel's mouth was dry, but she couldn't bear to leave the book, even to go to the kitchen and get a glass of water. She turned the page

Saturday, 8th March, 1969

First blood! The old goat, Henry Thornback, invited me to his room for a drink. Actually he's not that old, about forty, but he thinks he's God's gift to all women. I suppose he's quite handsome and he is tall. I do like a tall, well-built man. He knew Philip was at a rugby match and no doubt thought two gin and tonics and he'd have my knickers down like a shot.

Laurel burst into laughter. She'd nailed him. That was exactly her own summing up of Henry Thornback.

I let him get his hand into my blouse, gave a few encouraging noises, pretended I didn't notice he was getting busy with his zip and then when he put his hand up my skirt I let him have it.

Rape, I cried, hitting him and turning all virtuous. I threatened to tell Philip and get him dismissed. His face went green. My acting skills haven't been put to such good use for ages. I stormed out of his flat in high dudgeon. An Oscar-winning per-formance.

I gave him long enough to work himself up into a blue funk. I wanted to get back to him before Philip returned. His face was a picture when I came back into his room. Wasn't he relieved when I said I didn't want to ruin his career. As if I cared about the old roué.

I've been trying to think of ways to get hold of keys to some of the staff rooms for several months, but Philip and old Piff guard their sets like dragons sitting on their eggs.

I told Thornback I wouldn't tell on him if he got me duplicates of all the keys to the staff flats and houses. He blustered, offered me money instead. Tempting, but the keys will provide much more amusement and possibly a better source of income. At least I'll have a bit of excitement.

He said he'd need some time. He had a key to Piff's office (unofficially), but he could only take them at weekends.

Tuesday, 25th March, 1969

Thornback gave me the keys yesterday, including one to my own secret place. They're all neatly labelled and I shall keep them safe with you, my dear diary. Now for some fun. I'll have to be careful and it'll be difficult waiting, but I can only use them when the staff are away on holiday. Can't wait to find out their secrets. People are so careless, they can't imagine anyone will read their precious letters, diaries and look at intimate photographs.

God, she'd a nerve. What had she been like, Susan Nicholson? Obviously a woman who kept her own counsel; didn't trust anyone but herself. You don't suddenly become like that. What kind of childhood did she have? She must have done things like this before. She was dying, literally, to find out people's secrets.

Laurel screwed up her face. I suppose I'm like that too, but I hope my reason for trying to find out what people have been up to in the school is for a good purpose. I want to help find Susan's and Felicity's killer and the person who attacked Mabel. Frank and Elderkin also wanted, needed, to know people's secrets. She turned to the next page.

Chapter 31

Frank and Elderkin raced down corridors towards Mabel's room; Elderkin bumped into a tea trolley, its urn rattled and crockery crashed to the floor. The orderly cursed as he tried to hold it steady. They shouted apologies but didn't slow down.

The constable guarding Mabel's room gave them a thumbs up and a broad grin. 'She came round about half an hour ago. Doc wouldn't let me phone straight away.' His face expression changed. 'She asked about Muffin. The doc told her, thought it was best, no good lying to her, he said.'

Elderkin winced. 'How did she take it?'

'Doc said she'd guessed. Said Muffin went for him. She was a bit tearful. Doc told her how you, Inspector, and Miss Bowman found her on the beach. You're her heroes.'

Elderkin glowered at him.

'I think you're her *number one hero,* Sergeant.'

Elderkin smirked.

'Does she remember the attack?' Frank asked.

'Doc told her not to talk too much.' He turned to Elderkin, 'She asked for you, sir.' Stuart flushed, 'and you as well, Inspector. Said she'd talk to both of you, no one else.'

Elderkin patted the PC on the shoulder. 'Good lad.' He pushed open the door to Mabel's private room.

She was sitting up, a raised bedhead and several pillows supporting her. Her head was bandaged, and there was yellow bruising round her eyes and across her right cheekbone. A nurse supported her as she drank through a straw from a plastic beaker. A doctor stood at the foot of the bed smiling and nodding, looking pleased with himself.

She looked up, her cheeks drawn in as she sucked the

liquid. She pushed the beaker away with a shaking hand. 'Stuart Elderkin,' she whispered, 'fancy catching me like this.'

Stuart rushed to her side, the nurse moved away and he knelt down, gently took hold of Mabel's hand, and kissed it.

Frank gulped and wondered if he ought to remove himself, the doctor and the nurse. There was only one way this relationship was going and he was happy for both of them.

Mabel patted Elderkin's hand. 'We'll continue this when I'm a bit better, Stuart. But I feel more like myself now I've seen you.' She looked at Frank. 'I need to tell you what I can remember.'

'Ten minutes,' the doctor said. 'Stay with her, Nurse, and if you're at all worried, throw them out.' He sailed off, white coat-tails ballooning.

Frank drew up two chairs; Elderkin got off his knees looking happy but sheepish; he still held Mabel's hand.

'What do you remember of the attack, Mabel?' Frank asked.

'I didn't see who it was, but I'm sure it was a man. He'd something over his face and he was wearing gloves. He was tall, taller than you, Inspector.' She paused, fear in her eyes. 'I was late getting back. Muffin…' She bit her lip, closed her eyes, trying to keep control. 'He'd been chasing rabbits in the tree-lupins near the Cut, he wouldn't behave himself, and I couldn't catch him. It was almost dark as we came to the steps. I think the man who attacked me must have been hiding under them. I should have gone back by the road, but I said I'd do the same walk, and I did.'

Frank let her rest for a few moments, her voice was weak and telling the story was obviously painful – her hands were shaking.

'Can I have a sip of water?' Stuart held the beaker. She

nodded and he put it back on her side table. 'I can't remember everything that happened, but Muffin went for him, after he hit me the first time. I fell down on the shingle, I tried to get up. I could hear Muffin barking, yelping – almost screaming. Then he went quiet. I knew he'd killed him. He came back… I can't remember any more.'

'Muffin saved your life, Mabel. He was a brave little dog. Those seconds or minutes he distracted your attacker stopped him finishing you off,' Frank said.

Tears trickled down her cheeks and Stuart wiped them away with his handkerchief. 'Thanks, dear,' she said.

'Did you remember what'd been bothering you when you saw Susan Nicholson at the sluice?' Frank asked.

She nodded. 'Yes. That's why he wanted me dead, wasn't it? Wanted Muffin dead as well, I shouldn't wonder.'

'Muffin?' Frank asked, puzzled.

'When I saw Susan she was on the other side of the sluice. I knew it was her: red hair and that red coat. I waved, friendly like, although I didn't want to chat to her. She waved back and then it happened.'

'What happened, Mabel?' Stuart asked, squeezing her hand.

'Muffin went scampering up to her. I called him back, because I knew she didn't like dogs, and I knew Muffin didn't like her. I was afraid he'd jump up – she hated that. I called but he didn't come back. When he got to her he jumped up, but friendly like, his tail wagging. She bent down and made a fuss of him, then turned him round and pushed him back to me. I was still shouting his name.' She took a deep breath. 'That woman was not Susan Nicholson. I'm sure of it now.' She slumped back on the pillows looking exhausted.

Frank got up and jerked his head at Stuart. 'We'll go now, Mabel. We'll be back soon. I can't tell you how pleased I am you've recovered.'

Holding Stuart's hand, she said, 'You and Laurel saved me, didn't you? How is she?'

'She's fine, looking after Dorothy…' Stuart glared at him. God, he shouldn't have said that. This wasn't the time to tell her about Emily and Toni. Luckily she hadn't cottoned on.

'One last thing, Inspector: I know who that woman was.'

Would she corroborate his theory?

'I'm sure it was Toni Habershon, wearing a red wig and pretending to be Susan. She liked Muffin, and the way the woman fussed Muffin, she did it just like Toni. Why was she pretending to be Susan? Why would she do that?'

'I think it's time you left,' the nurse stated, pointing to the door.

Seemingly on cue, Ansell stepped into the room, looking as though he'd had a few volts from Frankenstein's machine: his hair was waving about his head and his eyes were as round and as excited as a child seeing his new bike on Christmas day.

'I've just had a telephone message from PC Cottam. You've got to phone him straight away, important information has come in on searches you asked for. You can phone from my office.' He was jumping up and down as though in desperate need of a lavatory.

'Dr Ansell,' fumed the nurse. 'I have a seriously ill patient here. Get out – all of you.'

Mabel was holding her head, laughing and wincing at the same time. 'Good luck, Inspector.'

Stuart kissed her cheek and he and Frank made for the door.

Chapter 32

Laurel smoothed the page. She saw the name on the first line: Warren Ringrose. Did she want to read Susan Nicholson's warped writings about him? She remembered when she'd first met him at the staff meeting, and how he'd talked about Felicity, saddened by her disappearance, unaware, as they all were, she'd been murdered. How he'd reacted when Frank told them what had happened to her. He was a sensitive, caring man; easy meat for someone like Susan. Warren couldn't be the murderer, he'd an alibi, but Susan might have written about someone else. It was useless bringing Frank back from Ipswich if the log book didn't tell them who killed Susan. Feeling justified, she started to read.

Wednesday, April 2nd, 1969

I made use of a key today. I chose Warren Ringrose because he's obviously as bent as a corkscrew. What a pathetic specimen. I've seen him eyeing up Philip as though he'd be more than willing to bend over for Philip's pleasure. Can't stand homos — seen too many of them in the bloody theatre. They're an absolute waste of time as far as I'm concerned. Warren's on holiday, shacked up with some other pervert I expect.

It didn't take long to find a stash of filthy letters from his boyfriend, a Ewan somebody or other. I've got his

*address and I took one of the letters, a
juicy one, in case he proves difficult. I
doubt if he will. He'll probably clutch
his tiny paws to his Fair Isle chest and
plead for mercy. I can't wait for term to
start so I can turn a few screws — a very
appropriate phrase.*

Susan had nerves of steel but what a disgusting person.
Where was the letter? Probably in the hole, or in the book?
Laurel turned it up and shook it. Nothing. She turned to the
back cover. There was an envelope Sellotaped to the inside.
She ripped it out. It was addressed to Warren. She put it in
her pocket. She'd give it back to him. No need for the police
to see it.

Did Philip know what kind of woman he'd married? Poor
Warren, he must have been terrified. She turned back to the
diary. She'd forgotten she was thirsty, forgotten she ought to
leave, take the log book and contact Frank. She was riveted
by the writing on the blue-lined pages.

Sunday, 27th April, 1969

*At last I managed to get Warren alone.
My didn't he look shattered when I told
him I knew he was a homosexual, had
his lover's address and wondered if I
should tell my husband. I just love the
delightful feeling of making someone
suffer and know you've got power over
them. I should have lived in the times
of the ancient Romans, but only if I
could have been the Empress Livia.
Wasn't he grateful when I decided not to*

tell! It isn't much, five pounds a month, but it's better to start with a small amount, get him used to the idea of making monthly subscriptions to my secret fund. Philip's keeping me a bit short at the moment. He's still mad about me, but not enough to buy me any decent clothes.

She must have blackmailed other people before she came to the school. Probably some of the actors and actresses she worked with. Why didn't Philip spoil her? When you're mad about someone you want to give them presents; even if they're only small love tokens. She remembered buying things for Simon: a silk tie, a pair of black, low cut underpants – don't think he ever wore them, bars of dark chocolate – his favourite, as well as a Swiss watch when they got engaged. He'd always given her flowers every week… she shook her head. No time for that. She turned the page.

Chapter 33

Philip Nicholson sat at the dressing table in their bedroom looking into the mirror. This was where Susan sat every morning in her dressing gown, or if the weather was warm, in a silk slip. She'd brush her hair with the silver-backed brush. He'd count the strokes as his mother had taught him to do when he brushed her hair. One, two, three…

'Philip,' his mother called from her bedroom. 'Philip dear, come and brush Mummy's hair.'

Her bedroom seemed vast. How old was he when she'd asked him for the first time to brush her hair? Nine or ten? He stood behind her as she sat on the red velvet stool in front of the hinged-mirrors of her dressing table. He was a tall strong boy for his age and their faces were level in the reflections of the mirror. Her hair, a beautiful deep auburn, was piled high on her head.

'Take out the hairpins, Philip. Put them in there.' She pointed to a cut-glass trinket tray. Everything was in its place, everything clean and shining. He carefully pulled out the hairpins and down fell her hair, past her shoulders, nearly to her waist – gleaming and full of life. She sighed and a shudder ran down her back.

She taught him how to brush her hair. Long, slow strokes, from the top of her head right down to the very tips of the hair. 'Count the strokes out loud, Philip. Fifty strokes today. Nice and slow.' He brushed her hair when he came back from school before his father returned home from work.

The curtains were drawn in the bedroom, even in the daytime. It was like an emerald cave, light shafting in through a gap left between the green silk curtains. When he reached thirty strokes, sometimes more, sometimes less, she started to moan, her back straightened, her legs stretched out, toes splayed. Then she'd shudder, her head thrown back against his body.

The first time she did this he was frightened. Had he hurt her? He stopped brushing. 'Mummy, have I done it wrong?'

'No. No, Philip. Go on, my darling. Mummy loves you brushing her hair,' she whispered.

When he finished brushing she kissed and hugged him to her. 'Thank you, my darling Philip. Mummy's tired now. She's going to have a little sleep.' She opened a drawer and took out a box of chocolates. 'Here you are, Philip, choose three today.' She pulled a fine sheet of paper from a hole in a small cardboard box. 'Here's a tissue so you won't get all messy.'

He grew up needing this closeness to her, waiting for his mother's call to come to her. Excitement started to tense his body as he counted the strokes, eagerly anticipating the moment when she lost control, moaning and writhing, when he could bury his face in her hair and she would press her body against his. He felt his penis lengthen and harden. At the last stroke of the brush there would be a wonderful release and he would ecstatically bury his face again into the beautiful red hair.

He was fifteen when he saw the first white hairs growing like strands of fungus, an alien life-form, eating the living red hair.

The brush dropped from his hand. 'Mummy, your hair, it's dying.' He rushed to the bathroom and was sick.

She called from the bedroom, 'Philip, don't be silly, come and brush Mummy's hair.'

He didn't go to her. He didn't answer her call. He went out of the house, his stomach churning with rage, disgust and longing. She never called to him again. By the time he went to university her hair was completely white. The lovely red hair had gone.

Chapter 34

Thirst finally drove Laurel to the kitchen. She drank half of the glass of water as she walked back to the table and the log book. Just as well she'd read it before ringing Frank: so far there was no clue to the murderer. Perhaps the next few pages would reveal his identity.

Wednesday, 14th May, 1969

I think I may be on to something. I went up to Philip's school office. I knew he wouldn't be there; he was taking a cricket practice. I was hoping I might find a few loose coins in his desk – he's turning out to be a real tightwad. He hardly gives me anything for housekeeping, says we should use all the school facilities and eat in the school dining room. God if I'd known... Never mind that now.

I sneaked upstairs when old Sergeant Major Piff was on coffee break in the school kitchen with the sainted Mabel. I pushed open the door as quietly as a mouse would if it was expecting a cat on the other side.

Kneeling in front of the open safe was our dear deputy head, Slimy Shipster. He was slipping something into his leather briefcase. His face went an unfashionable shade of green.

*'Stealing the petty cash, Mr Shipster?'
I said, laughing merrily to suggest I was
joking.*

Good Lord. She'd made a similar remark to him the other day
in exactly the same circumstances. No wonder he looked as
though he'd seen a ghost.

*He shot up like a frightened rabbit and
closed the safe. 'Just checking all the
papers are in order.'
'The papers?' I enquired in an
innocent voice, trying to look puzzled. I
knew what the papers were.
'Yes, the GCE papers. I always
double-check we've got the right ones.
You can't be too careful.'
He never said a truer word. 'I was
looking for Philip. Is he teaching?'
We chatted on for a few minutes; I
played all innocent, not a smidgen of
suspicion showed on my face or in my
voice. He relaxed and I breezed off as
though I couldn't care less he'd sneaked
something into his briefcase.*

Why was Shipster taking exam papers out of the safe? She
checked back on the date. Yes, the O and A level GCE papers
would be with schools. She read on.

*What a life. The highlights of my days
are using my acting talents to fool
people and writing in this book. I never
dreamed when I married Philip life*

would be so boring here. I imagined being married to a headmaster of a private school there would be plenty of social events, I'd have access to a reasonable amount of money – God knows you don't make much in the theatre – and I'd be able to manipulate Philip into planning exotic holidays, trips to London and we'd build up a group of interesting friends. All he wants to do in the holidays is visit his mother and make trips to boring places like Ely Cathedral. How long can I take this? I made a frightful mistake, but what choice did I have? I was out of a job and he seemed a good catch and he was mad for me.

I'll see if I can sneak into Shipster's house and do some ferreting. I'll have to be quick or whatever is in his briefcase might be put back in the safe soon.

Laurel flicked to the next page.

Thursday, 15th May, 1969

I took a chance and got into Shipster's house this morning when he was teaching. I worked quickly just in case he came back between lessons. Surprise, surprise, the briefcase was under his bed. In it were the exam questions for O level and A level maths. He'd steamed the envelopes open. He was copying the *questions into a notebook. No wonder his exam results are so bloody wonderful. This is better than I expected. I took the O level packet and his notebook. I wish I could be there when he opens the briefcase and finds they're missing. What will he do? Hope he doesn't die of a heart attack. How much can I ask for? Must find out how much he gets paid. I think a large initial sum for the return of the papers and then a regular monthly amount. Is £20 too much? At least £15. He hasn't got a family – he can afford it. I'll keep the notebook as an insurance policy. Shall I hide it with my friend here? Why not.*

Laurel couldn't believe what she was reading. Shipster was a cheat. Anger boiled up. What a disgusting man. His notebook. It must be under the floorboards. She shot over to the cupboard and thrust her hand into the hole. She grimaced as she pushed her hand and arm deeper into the space. Yes. She withdrew a slim black notebook. She flicked it open. There in Shipster's hand were questions he'd copied from the O level papers.

This would ruin the reputation of the school. Then she remembered – there wasn't a school to ruin. It was closed, finished. Why did Shipster feel he had to cheat? If this came out he'd never get another job teaching. Good. She didn't want Shipster coming into contact with any more children. He had no qualities, as far as she could see, that made a good teacher. All he had was fantastic exam results acquired by cheating.

This was a strong motive for murdering Susan. He'd no alibi. Could she see him doing it? Was he physically capable of strangling someone?

Saturday, 17th, May, 1969.

Shipster agreed. I didn't think he'd go for £200 up front but he didn't argue, although he did look as though he wanted to kill me. He was so relieved he wasn't going to be exposed as a cheat. His teaching career would be over. I told him I didn't mind if he kept on cheating. The results were good for the school, but I told him to be more careful. I don't think he appreciated that. I won't give him the papers until he gets the money, and I'm keeping the notebook just to be on the safe side. I'll keep it here with my friend the log book.

So Susan thought he looked capable of murder. But would he have murdered her if he hadn't got his notebook back? If it was discovered – she'd discovered it – he'd be a prime suspect. He was a prime suspect. She turned to the next page.

Chapter 35

Philip Nicholson sat at the dressing table and looked at his face in the mirror. He was the same: the handsome, strong headmaster. Was he safe? The chief constable was satisfied Toni was the murderer. He'd recalled all the police from the school site. Would the governors open the school again? Did Inspector Diamond also believe Toni was the murderer? A deep blackness opened up. The log book – he wouldn't be safe until he found it. What had Susan written in it? Had Susan written about him? What if someone found it? The police had searched in vain. Was there anywhere they hadn't looked? He'd have to search for it himself. He couldn't risk someone else finding it. Even if it turned up years later, her writing might incriminate him.

He clenched his hands together, his guts contracting with pain. There mustn't be any more girls with red hair. No more red hair. No more slender necks, no more child-like breasts, no more pleading and crying, eyes wide with fear and pain. When he married Susan he thought he was saved. She loved him brushing her hair. With the green bedroom curtains closed she looked like a young girl. She didn't mind if he was rough when they had sex, didn't mind him putting his hands round her throat as long as he didn't squeeze too tight.

Everything went wrong. Susan had to die. Did he want to live if he could never run his fingers through hair as red as old gold? He wanted to do it again. The longing was eating him up. He must see them again, hold them again. Hold them close to him and relive those precious moments when all that mattered in the whole world was to clench the long red hair in his hands and to find release.

He rose from the stool, his clenched hand knocking the

silver-backed brush to the floor. He staggered down the stairs, whimpering as he lurched to his study. With fumbling fingers he unlocked a drawer in his desk and pulled out a mahogany box. With a slender key he opened it, his hand trembling as he lifted the contents, one by one, kissed them fervently, and laid them out in a row on his desk.

Philip Nicholson closed his eyes and leant back in the chair exhausted. Each lock of red hair had burnt his fingers with a cold heat, searing up his arms, spinning through his head, shafting down his body until he was released in a juddering wave of passion. He slumped forward, resting his head on his arms, remembering.

They say the first love is the sweetest. It wasn't for him. How could it be when it was incomplete? He was at Durham University, a member of the first fifteen rugby team. In pubs he listened to other students and their stories of how they'd pulled this or that girl. He was a virgin; he'd never had a girlfriend. But he listened. One student said, 'All women wanted it, even when they said no.' He didn't believe everything he heard but when they talked, he saw their eyes alight with remembered lust. He wanted to have the same experiences. He knew some beautiful girls, girls in the same faculty, but he didn't want to do it with them. Blondes, silver blondes, strawberry blondes, gorgeous brown-haired girls, and those with hair as black as coal all seemed unreal, not alive, like mannequins in a window. The thought of holding them, kissing them meant nothing. Was something wrong with him?

He went with a friend to the cinema to see *King Solomon's Mines*. When he saw her on the screen he knew she was the kind of woman he wanted. She had long red hair. He couldn't remember the story, something about Africa, couldn't even remember her name. All he saw was her red hair. He almost cried when she cut it off in the film. He knew then he'd only desire women with long, red hair. Hair you could take hold of, hair you could bury your face in, hair that would burn you, hair you could caress with a silver-backed brush: one, two, three… How he'd wanted her, the film star on the silver screen. He wanted to run his hands through her hair, pull her close… He wanted to kiss her, woo her, rip her to pieces, shake her neck until she flopped like a rag doll. Then he imagined her hair dying, turning white, becoming alien hair. He must have only young hair, hair that would never die. He wanted to be in the green cave and bury his face in the fiery hair. He couldn't breathe. The air was squeezed from him; his heart thudded against his ribs. He pushed past people in his row and ran out of the cinema.

The university rugby team was on a tour of the West Country, travelling by coach from one town and match to the next. It was the Easter holidays. He saw her in the club bar after a match played in heavy rain. She had her back to him and her hair cascaded down her back, straight and thick, a dark, shining red. She turned round. She wasn't pretty, she'd a thin face and her skin was blotchy, but he didn't care, all he saw was the hair. He wanted to hold it tight in his hands and destroy her.

She saw him looking at her and her face flushed. She smiled at him. He knew he was good looking. Plenty of girls flirted with him, asking him to parties. Occasionally he went, but he learnt how to slide out of any deep involvement.

She was a medical student from Bristol University. She asked him back to her digs. She was keen and if he'd controlled himself he could probably have had her anyway. He didn't control himself. The wait had been too long. He pushed her down on the floor and silenced her with his hand He ripped off her knickers, raped her, and then buried his face in her hair. He lay on the floor, spent and overcome by conflicting emotions. She was sobbing, terrified. She crawled away from him and locked herself in the bathroom.

Later *he* was terrified. The tour moved on the next morning. Every minute of the coach journey he expected a police car, sirens blazing, to stop the coach and the police would haul him off. Trial. Prison. Humiliation.

The police never came. Why didn't she report him? Was she ashamed? Afraid he'd say she wanted sex? He was so scared he avoided getting in a situation like that for years. He put a tight control on himself. Every time he saw a red-headed woman or girl he reminded himself how he'd risked everything by giving in to his desires.

It was his first teaching job, a boy's preparatory school in Chelmsford. He'd had a successful year: a promotion, and a rise up the pay scale. He bought a car; his mother gave him a hundred pounds as an early birthday present. He would be twenty-three on November 6th. He'd stayed on after the end of the summer term to help the head of history plan field trips for the next academic year.

It was a lovely day at the end of July; he decided to go for a drive. He'd passed through the village of Margaretting, turned down a lane, for no reason, except it looked as though it might lead to an interesting church, and he saw her.

Her hair was swinging from side to side, a thick red plait, tied with a green, shiny ribbon. She was standing on the pedals of her bike, working hard as she rode up a hilly part of the road. She was skinny, about fourteen, wearing a blue-and-white checked dress, white socks and plimsolls. The red plait swung to and fro, back and forth.

He pulled the car in front of her so she had to stop. He got out. The lane was deserted. 'Can you help me? I'm lost,' he said.

She smiled at him; there was a gap between her front teeth and she had a few large freckles sprinkled over her nose.

'Where do you want to go?' she asked, carefully placing her bike against the low hedge.

'I've got a map in the car. Perhaps you could show me where we are.'

'I 'spect I could. I'm good at geography and we did ordnance survey maps last term.'

It was the last thing she said. He hit her, a stunning blow to the jaw. He bundled her into the back seat and threw the bike over the hedge. He drove to a nearby wood. She was still unconscious when he undid her plait and spread her hair on the ground, over the enchanter's nightshade and the dock leaves. Then he stripped her, raped her, and strangled her.

He sighed and pushed himself up from the desk. There she was: a lock of red hair tied with a green ribbon. Those words: stripped, raped, strangled. They conveyed so little of the mind-blowing ecstasy.

He'd put her body in the boot. He knew the area would be searched, probably with dogs. He buried her far away, many miles from her home and from his school. It was perfect. Her body was never found. It might never be discovered. Perhaps in a hundred years someone would find her. He'd be safe by then.

He was frightened at first, frightened at the enormity of his crime, frightened by the thought of what would happen if the police discovered he was the murderer. He spent the rest of the summer holiday at home. As the weeks passed the newspapers told of other tragedies and he knew how to commit the perfect murder: choose a victim at random, a victim with beautiful red hair. Hide the body so it wouldn't be found. Don't kill in the same area twice.

How many times had he done it? He counted the red locks, tied with their ribbons. He read in a paper she was called Mavis. Mavis: his first true love. He'd used her own green ribbon to tie a thick hank of her hair together. Since then he'd chosen a different colour ribbon for each of his loves.

He stroked his trophies in turn. One, two, three, four – the white ribbon. She was a tiny girl, only thirteen he'd read later, she looked younger. She was picking primroses from a bank at the side of a country road. There'd been a dog, a small mongrel. It had made him hesitate. Her long hair was a red halo of curls round her oval face and gathered in two bunches secured with elastic bands. As he slowed the car she turned and smiled at him, a bunch of primroses in her left hand.

The dog was docile, wagging its tail at him as he used the same technique. He needed minimal force to knock her unconscious. The dog danced round, clawing at the car door, whining. He glanced in the rear view mirror as he drove off. The dog followed a little way, seemed puzzled and sat down in the middle of the road. He chose a white ribbon for her; for Sarah.

Five, six, seven – Seven: he'd broken his rules for her; for Felicity. He'd put himself in extreme danger. His first headship and he'd risked everything to have her. He loved being a headmaster. If the school was successful, in a few years he'd apply for a headship in a bigger school. His mother was so proud of him; sure he would go on to better things.

Then Felicity came on a Horatio Nelson scholarship. He tried to avoid seeing her, teaching her, but Ringrose got her to play at assembly, usually a long piece of classical music. She sat at the piano, no longer a shy girl, but fully in control; her thin wrists rising, her long, elegant fingers dancing over the keyboard and her Titian hair, hanging in curtains round her face, swaying to the music. Her beauty pierced his heart and the need to hold the fiery hair and to possess her was so great his body pulsed with longing.

Before Felicity came he was having a discreet affair with Toni Habershon. He liked her, and she worshipped him. He knew he needed a wife to be a successful head of a large school. Toni seemed ideal.

When he learnt Felicity had to stay in the school for the Easter holidays as her aunt was going to New Zealand, he knew he must go and stay with his mother. But he didn't. If he could see her naked, he thought, that would be enough. Soon after the end of term when Felicity was practising the piano with Warren Ringrose, he went into the girls' boarding house up to the attic. He bored a hole in the ceilings of her room and the bathroom she used. He had to see her thin, child-like body. He had Toni for sex. He needed to see Felicity naked.

Once he saw her he had to have her. It was a terrible risk he took. He killed her here, in his house. He didn't want to cut her up – her beautiful body. He had to get her into the suitcase. It was the only way he could think of getting rid of her. He went to her room and removed some of her clothes and the suitcase. He dismembered her in the bath. Her head came off easily. The hands were the worst, the long fingers swayed as elegantly as when they'd moved over the keyboard. At night he drove to the beach in his Land Rover, the suitcase in the back. He took Benjie Whittle's boat and rowed out as far as he dared. Terrible, terrible risks. He vowed never to do it again.

When he saw Susan on the stage at Colchester he was sure this was a sign. She looked so young: her figure slight and immature and her glorious red hair. He'd been saved. He would marry her and all would be well.

309

Chapter 36

Frank gunned the Mustang as soon as they were out of the Ipswich suburbs and on the A12.

For once Stuart Elderkin didn't tell him to slow down. 'So how are you going to break his alibi?' he asked, gripping the edge of his seat as Frank overtook a car doing about 50 miles an hour.

'This is how I think he did it. Stop me if you spot a mistake.'

Stuart nodded.

'I think Nicholson killed his wife either Monday night or Tuesday morning, before he left for Colchester to stay with his mother. He hid her, probably in his house in a locked cupboard. The body was in the sitting position; Ansell remarked on the lividity in the buttocks.' He swerved the car past a slow-mowing agricultural machine.

'He's turned out all right, has Ansell,' Stuart observed. 'Go on. I'm with you so far.'

'Toni is involved; she may not have been party to the murder, but she phoned on Tuesday night pretending to be Susan and she'd been told to phone just before dinner when Nicholson knew his mother would be in the kitchen cooking the meal.'

'Establishing Susan is still alive, although she's been dead at least twelve hours.'

'Correct. On Wednesday evening Toni goes to the sluice and waits for Mabel to appear with Muffin. They, Nicholson and Toni, along with everyone else in the school, know Mabel takes Muffin for a walk every evening after she'd finished cooking. Toni puts on the red coat and a wig and makes sure Mabel sees her. Muffin runs up to her, he knows it's Toni: she smells like Toni and dogs are colour-blind, the wig and coat don't fool him. She makes a fuss of Muffin as Toni would, not Susan. This has been confirmed by Mabel.'

Stuart smiled. 'Good old Mabel.'

'That night Nicholson takes his mother to dinner. You remember she said she'd had a wonderful night's sleep and didn't wake up until Nicholson woke her, she said she didn't hear the alarm.' Frank slowed down as they passed through Wickham Market.

'So you think he drugged her? In the tea he made?'

Frank nodded and rapidly went through the gears as they left the village. 'He took an enormous risk. He drove to Dunwich in his Jaguar through the night. Got back to the school house, transferred the body to his Range Rover, picked up the red coat and drove to Minsmere Beach.'

Elderkin slapped the dashboard. 'Yes. Yes. It works. Then over the beach to the sluice. Pops the body in, throws in her clothes and the red coat; back to the house and back to Colchester before he wakes up his mother. Have you worked out the times?' Stuart glanced at the speedo: hitting eighty.

'It can be done. The school site was quiet, it was the Easter holidays, and his house is isolated. What he'd have done if anyone had seen him I don't know. Perhaps he'd some explanation ready. Possibly we'll never find out.'

The narrow streets of Saxmundham slowed them down. Frank banged his fist against the steering wheel. 'God help us if he completely loses control. Let's hope Laurel stays put at Dorothy Piff's. He's completely lost it killing Toni and then Emily Piff. Surely he didn't think he'd get away with it?'

'He probably didn't know about the differences in drowning in fresh and sea waters and about diatoms and things; not many people do. He must have carried her body down the steps to the beach in the small hours. Take a bit of doing – all that dead weight.'

'He's a big, strong man. A match for most people physically.' Frank said.

Chapter 37

Philip Nicholson pushed aside the mahogany box, locks of hair, envelopes and pieces of jewellery scattered over the desk. Why did Susan have to pry? He knew she'd been in his desk and opened the box. The envelopes containing each love's hair and trinkets were arranged in the correct order: first love first and last love last. Felicity's envelope was in the wrong place.

She hadn't said anything, but he caught her looking at him differently. She didn't seem frightened, her looks were calculating, as though she was weighing him up, wondering what to do. Did she understand what she'd seen? She couldn't do, or she'd have gone to the police, but she wouldn't let him brush her hair and refused to have sex with him. Then, out of the blue, she said she wanted a divorce and a good pay off. She said she'd found the box and its contents. At first she thought the locks of hair were trophies from past lovers, but now she wasn't sure. He knew what he should do; he should get rid of his loves. Then if she went to the police it would be her word against his, but even if they couldn't prove anything, it would ruin him,

She said she'd tell the school governors unless he agreed to a divorce and a lump sum of three thousand pounds and a monthly allowance. He begged her not to go to the governors. To give him time to get some money together. He needed the time to devise her murder, time to get Toni back with him, and to persuade her to help him, promising they would be together after Susan's death. It had worked. He believed he was safe.

Then *they* came: Laurel Bowman and Frank Diamond. It all went wrong. He ran his fingers through his hair, muttering to himself. He *must* find the log book. The site was deserted. The chief constable had declared the case over. Most staff had already left. The school was to be closed next week. He must find the book. Where hadn't the police looked? They'd searched his house thoroughly, and he'd been through it himself. It wasn't here.

314

Chapter 38

Laurel glanced at the page in front of her. Jim McFall. Frank had told her what Jim had confessed to, and how upset he was about Felicity. Now she'd read Susan's side of it.

Sunday, 13th July, 1969

At last Jim McFall has left the school for a holiday in Scotland. There were rich pickings in his flat. Letters from his mother in envelopes with a prison address on them. I'll do some research and find out what he was in for. The letters cover several years and she mentions his late wife and her family quite a lot. I think he must have murdered his wife. It was difficult reading, such an uneducated and badly written hand, and the spelling — I had hysterics when I realised what some of the words were.

What a spiteful, nasty person she was. Poor Mrs McFall. She hadn't deserted her son. But Jim McFall *had* murdered someone – his unfaithful wife. He was capable of murder. He'd proved that.

Tuesday, 5th August, 1969

Got into Vanessa Letts flat today. God, I

hate that woman. Always looking down her long nose at me and giving herself airs. She won't be so tight-arsed the next time she sees me and I tell her I know her family she keeps on about, the famous Major and Mrs Letts, don't exist.

I found the papers in an old chocolate box in her writing desk. A birth certificate: no name for the father, the mother a barmaid. She's a bastard, brought up in an orphanage; changed her name by deed poll. Why she didn't burn the lot I'll never know. Silly bitch! I took the birth certificate; it pays to have some hard evidence. I'm getting better at this game. I should build up a nice little nest egg soon. Enough for an escape? I need to find a good home for the money, to accrue interest, one Philip knows nothing about. I don't think I can ask old Shipster for financial advice as to where I can get the best interest rate, although I'd love to do that. I'm looking forward to seeing Letts' face. A definite for a few more pounds every month.

So the major and his lady didn't exist. Miss Letts must feel she's living with an unexploded bomb, waiting for the humiliation of exposure. Was this a good enough reason to kill Susan? She's strong and tall. Laurel didn't like her, but now she felt sympathy for a lonely woman ashamed of her true origins. She should be proud of what she'd achieved against the odds.

She felt sick in her stomach, as though poison was seeping from the ink through the skin of her fingers, corroding her mind. It'd been exciting finding the book and seeing proof of Susan's blackmailing and discovering the reasons so many people had for killing her. Reading about people's frailties and secrets, and the pressure and pain Susan caused them, made her feel ashamed. Should she read on? She slowly turned the page.

Wednesday, 17th September, 1969

It's been a real trial waiting all this time before I can speak to my two new – what shall I call them? – friends? No, contributors to my nest-egg.

I called on Miss Letts yesterday afternoon; I knew she finished teaching at four. When she opened the door to her flat I said, 'Good afternoon, Miss Hilda Gorst.' Her mother's name was Fanny Gorst, can you believe.

I thought she was about to collapse. I stepped back – I didn't want that weight falling on me! Then she started to tremble, but it wasn't with fear, it was rage. She dragged me into her room. I thought she was going to strangle me. She shook me by the shoulders. 'What have you done?' she hissed. 'Who have you told?'

I managed to get out I'd not told anybody. Then she let me go and collapsed on a chair. I was shaken and wished I hadn't involved her, but I

wasn't going to let old Hilda know that. I
decided I didn't want a prolonged
relationship with her. I said I'd keep
quiet and give back her birth certificate
for a cash sum.

Her body was trembling; with rage or
fear? 'How much do you want?' she spat.
'Five hundred pounds?'

I was surprised; I was going to ask for
a hundred. We bartered for a few
minutes and settled on six hundred.
Very satisfactory and once I have it I
won't go near her again – too
frightening. I shall definitely avoid
meeting her down a dark alley, as they
say. She's too strong and has a vicious
temper. Hilda! I ask you.

Another suspect. What would Frank think when he read the
book? Which one was the murderer? The contents of the
book were not helping in narrowing down the list to one
person.

December 14th, 1969

I've had to wait months before I tackled
McFall. After old Hilda I must admit I
didn't fancy persuading anyone to join
my fan club. The money has been
coming in nicely from all my other
contributors. I should have stuck at that
and not been greedy. I decided to see
him.

It was a disaster. Old McFall was livid

318

when I tried the usual routine on him. I gave him a Christmas card, he came over all soppy, probably hadn't had any cards for years. Then when I put it to him that if Philip or the governors knew he'd murdered his wife... He said the school knew about his past and he threatened to tell Philip I was a blackmailer – what a dirty word. I tried to wriggle out of it, saying I was only doing what I thought was best, but as the school knew I would forget all about it.

He was quite frightening. I'll cross him off my lists, Christmas cards and making extra money. What a pity. I'll try and get him dismissed; I'm sure I can find some reason; look how I dealt with Benjie Whittle. I'll have to be careful so he doesn't suspect it's anything to do with me.

Good for Jim McFall. Pity more people hadn't had the guts to put her in her place; but what a vindictive bitch. Poor Benjie – this would exonerate him. She flicked through the remaining pages. She didn't want to read any more. She felt dirty and stained. She started to get up, and then she saw a name and her spine stiffened. She couldn't breathe. She slowly sat down, a hand over her mouth, and she read on.

Chapter 39

The traffic lights in Saxmundham High Street changed to green and Frank stepped on the accelerator. Anxiety filled his body. He fought it so he could concentrate on getting them to the school as quickly as possible in one piece. PC Johnnie Cottam's telephone call from Ipswich headquarters, which they'd taken in Ansell's office, galvanised them into action. Frank had repeated Cottam's words so Elderkin could scribble down the details. The circumstantial evidence he relayed to them was overwhelming.

Elderkin, on Frank's instructions, had asked colleagues in neighbouring forces to give him details of any missing or murdered girls or women in the last twenty years from areas near the schools Nicholson had taught in. Especially important were physical descriptions of the victims.

There were three results: 1953, missing, body never discovered, a fourteen-year-old girl, Mavis Hinney, from the village of Margaretting, near Chelmsford. She went for a bike ride by herself at the beginning of the summer holidays. Bike found thrown over a hedge. Nicholson taught at school in Chelmsford.

In August, 1958, the body of a seventeen-year-old girl, Joyce Binding, was found by a holiday maker floating in the Broads, near Ormesby St Margaret. She'd been raped and strangled. The nearest large town was Norwich. Nicholson had been head of history at a public school in Norwich.

1963: missing thirteen-year-old Sarah Gilroy, from Risby. She went out with her dog to the local woods to pick primroses for Mother's Day. The dog came home alone. Despite massive police searches, with help from the public, no sign of Sarah was ever found. Nicholson was deputy head of a school in nearby Bury St Edmunds.

All three girls had red hair.

'I keep thinking of those girls, Stuart. Thirteen years old, for God's sake.'

'Why the red hair? What kind of fixation has he got about red hair?'

'And all of them slightly built, either because they hadn't fully grown, like poor Sarah and Mavis, or they had small bones, like Felicity and Susan. But why would he kill Susan? It looks like he didn't kill while he was married. She must have fulfilled his needs in some way. From all accounts he was desperate to marry her. Did he think by doing this he'd escape his driving need to possess small red-headed girls?'

Stuart shook his head, his face grim. 'I remember saying we didn't have mass murderers in little old Dunwich. Looks like I was wrong.'

At Yoxford the sharp bend slowed Frank down; fifty yards on he turned right for Westleton and the coast.

'I reckon he had to kill Susan; she found something out about him.'

'I think you're right, Stuart. This murder was not one of passion – a sudden impulse on coming across a suitable victim. It was carefully planned and involved a partner, Toni, to give him an alibi. It couldn't have been cooked-up overnight.'

Frank slowed the Mustang as they entered Westleton village. He stopped at the crossroad, as there was a lorry filling up with petrol at the garage on the corner and cars were parked on the opposite side of the road in front of the village store. He pounded the wheel. 'For God's sake get moving.'

Chapter 40

Nicholson was distracted, unable to concentrate. He must find the log book. If he walked over the site perhaps he'd sense where she'd hidden it. Were any of the flats unoccupied just before he killed Susan? There were rooms at the top of the house, like the one Laurel Bowman turned into her office. They were locked, but somehow Susan had got keys to the staff's private rooms. Had she keys to the rooms at the top of the house? He couldn't think straight. Perhaps she didn't write anything about him in the book, or she might have used it as an ordinary diary in which she noted day-to-day events. He should sit tight. Wait for all this to blow over. The governors might open the school again. What were the details of his contract? He couldn't remember. If they reopened the school would they have to keep him on as headteacher? How was he going to tell his mother he didn't have a job?

He got up from the desk. No. He must look for it. If only he'd known about it before he'd killed her. He'd have forced her to tell him where it was. That night when she died she wasn't like the others, she fought him. She deserved to die. If she hadn't pried and poked her nose into his business and found his loves all this wouldn't have happened. Then he wouldn't have involved Toni. Mabel and her wretched dog wouldn't have seen Toni at the sluice. Emily Piff wouldn't have died. It was a terrible shock when he found out it was Emily not Dorothy he'd strangled. He'd enjoyed killing Dorothy Piff.

He'd drowned Toni in the bath. He hadn't wanted to kill her, but she'd become a liability. He was afraid she'd break down and tell the police about Susan. She was upset about Felicity. He denied he'd had anything to do with her death, but he could see she didn't believe him. He had to act quickly. He made love to her – gently and with soft words. They took a bath together. He got out first, grabbed her ankles and pulled her under. She splashed a lot but died surprisingly quickly.

Emily Piff came into Toni's cottage as he walked naked into the living room. She didn't even have time to cry out before he'd attacked and strangled her with her own scarf. Wretched woman. All women were wretched – except his loves.

Damn Susan. He hadn't enjoyed killing her. It gave him no pleasure. Not even raping her. It was a job that had to be done. Now he understood what she'd said before he put his gloved hands round her throat. 'They'll get you for this,' she'd screamed.

Yes. He must find it. He wandered from his office. He wasn't himself. Usually he was confident, sure of his own decisions. Now his thoughts shifted like dead autumn leaves in the wind, scurrying round, whirling in splintering circles. What should he do? Where should he start the search?

He opened the front door, looking round him. Those wretched women: Susan, Mabel, Toni and Emily. Laurel Bowman: another wretched woman. His hatred channelled towards her – strong, capable Miss Bowman. The amateur school sleuth, egging Mabel on to take that walk. Shouting out as he was about to finish Mabel off on the beach and making him rush up the steps. Would Mabel be able to tell them he'd attacked her if she regained consciousness? Laurel Bowman – busybody – finding Felicity's bones.

His mind was fogged with swirling thoughts. The cottage, the one next to Mabel's – the cottage Laurel Bowman lived in – that was empty when Susan was alive. Could she have hidden it there? He walked out of the house, leaving the front door ajar and the mahogany box open on his desk.

323

Chapter 41

Laurel's fingers gripped the edge of the page as she read the final words of Susan Nicholson's diary. She was cold, as though a winter sea fret had crept into the room and skeined round her body. She heard her own breathing – short and fast, and her insides were hollow as she realised what she was reading.

Thursday, 5th March, 1970

I'm at a bit of a loss. I don't know what to do, which isn't like me. I can't work it out.

I was bored. I'd tapped all the staff secrets so I was at a loose end. I suddenly had a chance to root through Philip's office at home. He's so fussy about keeping everything locked up. Even the cleaning staff aren't allowed in his office and I have to hoover and dust it, but only when he's present. He looms over me as I polish and brush. I hate housework and I certainly don't enjoy dancing round with a feather duster in my hand, although I did make a striking French chambermaid in a few Feydeau farces in my younger days.

He was in a rush this morning and for once he'd left his keys at home. I unlocked his study, hoping to find a few bob lying round — not much chance, but you never know. One of the keys fitted the locks to the drawers of his desk. Nothing interesting: old diaries, letters from his wonderful mother, receipts for purchases going back to year dot. The key wouldn't open the bottom right-hand drawer. Another key on the ring did. My antennae were bristling; must be something special in here. I found a locked wooden box pushed to the back, under some stationery. Another key on the ring was needed to open it.

I still don't know what to make of it. There were several brown envelopes, not sealed, worn as though they'd been opened many times. In each was a lock of red hair, carefully tied with a ribbon; each ribbon a different colour: red, blue, white, yellow, pink, violet and green. Also in some of the envelopes were pieces of jewellery: a silver cross and chain, a gold-plated bangle, one cheap metal earring, a pearl necklace, a silver ring, and a rather nice garnet necklace. Are these tokens from past lovers? Is this why he married me, because I've got red hair? I knew he admired my hair; he often strokes it and asks if he can brush it for me.

I don't know why but this discovery has spooked me. Why does he want to keep love tokens? He's not what I would call a romantic man, not at all. He was *all over me when we first met, called me his salvation. I held out for marriage before I'd let him have me. If I hadn't, would I have been asked for a lock of hair and a piece of jewellery as a memento? I put everything back carefully. I don't know what to do. If I ask him about it, he'll know I've been sneaking about in his office. I'll have to think about this. I wish I had a friend I could talk to. You're my only friend, my dear black book. Pity you can't talk, friend, and give me some advice.*

Laurel closed her eyes. Sickness welled up from her stomach. Susan had found a collection of trophies – red hair collected from women. Were they alive or dead when Nicholson took them? Two women with red hair had been murdered: Felicity and Susan. Was Nicholson the murderer? If he was… did this mean the other locks of red hair belonged to more victims? Had he also murdered Toni Habershon and Emily Piff? She was unable to move, to get up from the chair. Her heart swelled to fill her chest, beating against the ribs. Dear God, it couldn't be true. Seven locks of hair – seven women murdered? – Nine with Toni and Emily.

Chapter 42

Nicholson decided to go to the cottage in his Land Rover, and then if he couldn't find the log book there, he'd drive round the estate. Perhaps Susan had hidden it in the ruins. There were lots of hiding places in the ruins.

He drove slowly in first gear past Shipster's house and turned into the gravel road leading to the three cottages. All empty now. All gone: Toni dead, Mabel in hospital and Laurel Bowman staying with Dorothy Piff. He braked and turned off the engine. Laurel's car was parked in front of her cottage, the boot open. He shook his head. No. He didn't want to see her. He wanted to search the cottage. Anger welled up in him. Interfering Laurel Bowman – always getting in his way. His hands gripped the steering wheel, his fingers like claws. He wished it was her neck he was squeezing, pressing deep into her windpipe, making her tongue shoot from her mouth and her eyes bulge. Why couldn't she leave him alone?

No. No. He must keep calm. He released his hold on the wheel. Why was she here? The boot lid was open. She'd come back to collect her belongings. He sat in the car, unsure, his mind fogged with unanswered questions. Should he go back to his house and wait until she left? He sat there for several minutes. Why wasn't she coming out and putting things in the car? He carefully opened the door, but didn't close it. He left the key in the ignition. He started to walk to the cottage, hesitated, then walked back to the Land Rover and opened the glove compartment. He took out a pair of black leather gloves and put them on. As the leather slid over his fingers the old excitement powered through his arms and his breathing quickened.

Chapter 43

Stuart was wringing his hands and shuffling in his seat. 'Get out of the way,' he muttered. The car in front of them turned right towards Leiston and the road was clear. Frank swung left through Westleton village and then right on the road across the heath that led to Dunwich.

'Nearly there, Frank. I've got the handcuffs ready. What's the plan?'

'Find Nicholson and arrest him. The boys will be on their way from Ipswich in the old Black Maria and its back to the station for questioning. Feeling fit? He may be violent.'

Stuart grasped the handcuffs, making a formidable knuckleduster. 'I hope he is.'

Frank grinned, feeling the uneasiness lifting as they neared the school. 'Remember you'll be retiring soon. Don't mess up your pension.'

Stuart smacked the handcuffs against his palm. 'It'd be worth it. The bastard.'

There was the school sign. Frank swung the car left, then right, and screeched to a halt in front of the Nicholson's house. He jumped out and ran to the door. It was wide open. He waited for Stuart. 'Nicholson?' No answer. He slowly walked into the hall, stopped and listened. No sound. 'I'll check upstairs, you look down here. Be careful and shout if...'

Stuart nodded. 'Same goes for you.'

Frank raced up the stairs. There were three bedrooms and a bathroom – all deserted. The main bedroom was a model of tidiness and organisation. Apart from the dressing table: silver boxes, perfume bottles and hair pins were scattered over the surface; a silver-backed brush was on the floor. He turned and ran down the stairs.

'Frank! Come here.' He followed Elderkin's alarmed voice to a smaller room, obviously Nicholson's study. Elderkin pointed to the desk, his face white, his eyes staring.

On the desk was a mahogany box – open. Bile rose in Frank's throat. There was a jumble of mundane brown envelopes, jewellery and…several locks of red hair tied with different coloured ribbons. This was all that remained of those poor children whose bodies had never been returned to their parents. Bastard. Sick bastard. 'God in heaven. He's lost control if he left all this exposed.' He took out a handkerchief and carefully placed the evidence back into the box. 'We'll take it with us in case he comes back and tries to destroy it.'

329

Chapter 44

Nicholson, shoulders hunched, crept towards Laurel's cottage. He looked in the boot of her car. It was full of her rubbish. He tip-toed down the path; he'd try and see what she was doing. If she was still packing and about to leave he'd try to get away without her seeing him. He knew he might lose control and attack her if she spoke to him. He hated her. If she hadn't talked to Mabel and encouraged her to try and remember what she'd seen on the evening she took that damned dog for a walk, everything might have been all right. The plan had worked perfectly. Toni waited behind the sluice until she'd seen Mabel coming, as prompt as ever, on her usual walk. Toni put a distance between them, just as he'd told her to do, and then made sure Mabel saw her and turned as though walking towards the Eel's Foot. Toni had told him about Muffin running towards her and she realised afterwards she shouldn't have made a fuss of him. He shouldn't have involved Toni; he should have done it alone. But it was a brilliant idea, giving him an even stronger alibi. He was sure the police would never break it.

He flattened himself against the wall of the house and inched forward so he could see through the front window. There she was, sitting at the table, her back to him. What was she doing? She was reading something. He couldn't see what it was. Why had she stopped packing her things? What was she reading that was so important?

He felt the blood rushing to his head, his fingers clenching inside the leather gloves. Had she found it? Was it the log book? What had Susan written in it? Had she written about him and his loves? Laurel Bowman didn't know her place. From the first she'd been domineering, bossy: demanding her own office, wanting a telephone, telling people what to do; making friends with people like Mabel Grill and Dorothy Piff. He was breathing rapidly, his muscles tightening. This time she wouldn't best him. This time she'd pay. She thought she was as good as he was, as good as a man. Men were better at everything than women. Women should know their place. He inched backwards to the front door.

Chapter 45

Laurel knew she should stop reading. She must get the log book to Frank. She hesitated. She had to know how it ended. She flicked to the last page.

Friday, 20th March, 1970

I think Philip suspects I've been through his desk. Perhaps I didn't put things back in exactly the right order. He's so meticulous. He hasn't said anything but I've caught him staring at me. He looks away when our eyes contact. He's making me nervous.

After another discovery today I feel even more disturbed. I saw Toni Habershon leaving in an ambulance with a pupil who'd got a fractured leg. She'd be away hours in Ipswich. Mabel Grill was busy in the school kitchens and so I had a chance to get in Toni's cottage without anyone seeing me.

I didn't think much of her wardrobe and there wasn't anything interesting: no letters from past or present lovers, no whips or handcuffs to suggest she was a sadomasochist, and no empty bottles of gin pointing to alcoholism.

Then I found something which made me sick. In her wardrobe under a pile of sweaters, some a bit mothy, was a red *wig, in the same style as my hair. What am I to make of that? I've never seen her in a wig, of any colour. Is she a secret admirer? Or does she think if she wears it Philip will fancy her? I'm pretty sure she fancies him — I've seen the worshipping looks she gives him.*

I feel unsettled. First locks of red hair in Philip's desk and now this? Is there some weird game going on I don't know about? Is there something in Philip's past he's trying to hide? If I find out more could I use this to get a good divorce settlement out of him? Or a large sum of money? Or both? My nest egg is growing; a few thousand pounds would help to set up a little business. I could try going back to the theatre, but I wouldn't mind a dress shop in London or perhaps abroad, the south of France would be fantastic.

I need to get back in his desk. That won't be easy. He was furious with himself when he last left his keys at home. I should have made some copies. The thought of leaving this place is heaven.

They were the last words written in the book. What was the significance of the red wig? Laurel closed the book and stared at its black cover. Did Toni use it to disguise herself as Susan? Was it Toni Mabel saw when she took that walk with Muffin? Was Susan already dead? It meant Toni was part of Nicholson's plot to kill his wife. He had to kill Susan because

333

he knew she'd discovered his secret. He didn't know she didn't realise what the locks of red hair and the jewellery meant. She had to be got rid of.

What did he promise Toni to persuade her to be part of a murder plot? Marriage?

She pushed her fingers through her hair. This wasn't the time to try and find solutions. It was time to get out of here, out of the school.

She got up from the table and picked up the log book. She must get it to Frank as quickly as possible. She'd go straight back to Dorothy's and phone Frank from there.

Laurel stood in front of the fireplace. Where had she put her car keys? She heard a sound: feet on carpet.

Nicholson was in the doorway. He looked at the log book she was holding, and then he glanced at the cupboard and the table.

God in heaven, what could she do? He was staring at her, blue irises ringed in black. She edged away. He was hesitating. Why? Because she wasn't small and delicate? Not easy meat like his other victims?

'So you found it? I presume you've read it?' he said. His voice was jagged, full of hate, flecks of spittle collecting in the corners of his mouth. His arms were rigid by his side. He wore leather gloves, the fingers curling and uncurling.

If he killed her she'd leave him damaged. She'd fight him. He was taller, stronger, but she was fitter and in control of herself. He wasn't. His madness was exposed. His eyes were uncoordinated. Keep your nerve she told herself. She took a deep breath and tensed her muscles for action.

He snorted with laughter. 'You're angry. Who are you angry with? Me? Or yourself, for being so stupid? Give me the book, Laurel, and I'll let you go.' He held out a gloved hand.

Her anger was for him – the destroyer of young lives, the

killer of Emily Piff and the man who'd struck down Mabel and brained Muffin. No. He wasn't going to get it. He wasn't going to kill her. She refused to be a victim. He'd damn well have to fight her for it. She moved nearer to the settee. She had one chance. His eyes weren't focusing. His hair was a wild mess. She had to keep calm, act quickly. Her salvation lay behind the settee.

'I'm getting impatient, Laurel.' He lunged at her, his arms outstretched in a rugby tackle.

With little backswing she kicked him in a knee-cap and vaulted over the settee. He tripped on the rug and banged into the fireplace. He screamed as his damaged knee hit the hearthstone.

Everything was in slow motion. Laurel dropped the log book, and took a firm grip on the handle of the giant wooden spoon.

'I'll wring your neck until your eyes stick out like balls. You bitch. I'll make you scream for mercy.' He was spitting and grimacing as he tried to scramble to his feet.

Laurel swung back the heavy spoon as far as possible and with techniques honed on the lacrosse field, she let the giant head do its work. She aimed for the side of Nicholson's head as he reached across the settee to grab her. His eyes widened and he tried to duck, but the spoon made a satisfactory, if glancing thud, as wood met the flesh and bone of his left temple. He crumpled onto the settee, groaning.

Laurel dropped the spoon, grabbed the log book and ran for the door. Behind her she could hear him knocking over furniture, and swearing. She should have given him another whack. She ran towards her car. Her stomach plummeted. The keys were in the cottage. She turned. Nicholson staggered out of the door, blood running down his face. He saw her. His gloved hands were held like boxer's fists in front of him. He was snarling and swearing, lips pulled back, teeth exposed.

She panicked. He was too strong. She didn't have the spoon. Could she outrun him? She turned and sprinted towards the cliffs.

Chapter 46

Frank and Elderkin raced back to Frank's car. 'His Range Rover isn't here. He may have left the school grounds. We'll drive round and check the site before telephoning a warning to the rest of the squad. Is the Jaguar in the garage?'

'It's there,' said Elderkin, his face like a stone mask.

Frank started the engine. 'I'm going to Laurel's cottage first. She should be with Dorothy Piff – but just in case. Then we'll go to the main block and see if he's there.'

Gravel spat from the rear wheels as he turned from the tarmacked road into the lane to the three cottages. His heart squeezed into a ball.

'Shit!' Elderkin spat.

There were two cars in front of Laurel's cottage. Nicholson's Land Rover, the driver's door wide open, and beyond Laurel's Ford Cortina, the boot lid raised.

'God's blister.' The car swerved as he slammed on the brakes. The car stopped a few inches from the Land Rover. He and Elderkin burst from the car and ran to Laurel's cottage.

The door was wide open. They ran into the front room. There were signs of a struggle – a tablecloth askew, a chair on its side, a smashed vase on the floor, the settee on its back. They lifted it up. Thank God, she wasn't lying there. But the monster spoon was. Frank picked it up. There was blood on the back of the bowl. Whose blood?

'I'll check upstairs. You do the kitchen and bathroom.' He took the stairs three at a time. No one here. No sign of a disturbance. Racing back down he met Elderkin.

'Nothing. What do we do now?' Elderkin asked.

Frank pointed to the open cupboard, the hole in the floor

and the discarded floorboard. It was a hole big enough to hide a book in. 'She must have found it.'

'Frank, here's a bunch of keys.' Elderkin picked them up from the table.

Frank saw a notebook on the floor. He opened it. Mathematical questions were neatly written on its first pages. 'This isn't it. Laurel must have the log book.'

'And Nicholson's found her with it?'

Frank's stomach twisted. Had he killed her and dragged her body from the cottage? But Nicholson's Land Rover was outside.

Laurel's lungs were raw as she sucked in air, her feet pounding on the path through the Holm oaks. Brambles tore at her clothes and ripped her arms. She kept tripping as she couldn't run properly as she clutched the log book to her chest. Her legs were like lead. She couldn't find the rhythm but she daren't try to change her grip on the book in case she dropped it.

He was close behind. He was crashing against trees, shouting, swearing. He was mad – he'd lost all sense of reality. The cold calculating headmaster was a berserk monster. If she could get down to the beach she could outrun him, she was sure of that. It was a hard run to Minsmere beach over the sand and gravel, but there would be people in the National Trust car park, bird watchers on the reserve.

The steps. There was a barrier of rope suspended on iron spikes and a notice. *Danger. Keep off. Steps unsafe.* Dear God, she'd forgotten. The police had declared them unsafe and out-of-bounds after they brought Toni's body up from the beach. Laurel turned. Where could she go? He was getting nearer. Should she run to the main house? Was there anyone there?

She took a deep breath, tucked the log book under one

arm and jumped over the rope. She gritted her teeth, trying not to imagine the steps collapsing under her. Move swiftly and lightly. She tried not to let her weight rest for more than a second on each step. One, two, three – the fourth bowed beneath her. Another groaned. Like an athlete attacking the high jump she pranced down the wooden steps.

As her foot hit the shingle, she yelled in triumph and blew out her cheeks with relief. She dug her heels into the shingle and didn't stop running until she was on the hard sand near the sea's edge. She turned, gasping, refilling her lungs.

Nicholson was at the top of the steps. He was screaming, punching the air with his black-gloved hands. Would he come down the steps? Would the steps hold his weight?

'Don't do it,' she shouted. 'They'll collapse.'

He roared back at her, unintelligible words. His face was a livid red blob as he swayed from side to side.

She moved towards him and put a hand to her mouth to try and make him hear her. 'They won't take your weight. Give yourself up. Go back to your house and wait for the police,' she shouted. Why was she doing this? Let him die. He deserved it.

He raised both arms above his head, fists clenched, like a great primate challenging a rival. 'If it's the last thing I do, Laurel Bowman, I'll kill you. Kill you!' He charged down the steps, his body ricocheting against the rails, a figure of fury and hate.

She turned and started running again. It was easier now, her breath even, and her legs moving smoothly. She was confident he wouldn't be able to catch her.

A thunderous rumble stopped her. She turned. The noise increased as boulders, stones, wood, and earth crashed down the cliff. The ground beneath her trembled as part of the cliff hit the beach. An avalanche of earth and sand rolled over the shingle towards her, tossing the planks and railings into the air. Clouds of earth bombed into the sky. The grinding and groaning deadened the crash of the waves and the cries of the gulls.

She was coated in grit, the log book clutched to her chest. Nicholson must be buried. It could have been her_ earth filling her mouth, soil suffocating her, tons of stones and soil squeezing the air from her lungs. Legs and arms broken and her back shattered. She put down the log book and ran towards the cliff fall.

Frank and Elderkin rushed out of the cottage.

'She must have escaped. He'll be chasing her,' Elderkin said.

'I hope to God, you're right. Which way would she have gone?' Frank said, 'We'll go to the main house –'

From the direction of the sea there was a great roaring as though a pride of lions had raised their heads and simultaneously vented their anger to the heavens. They both froze, as though turned to stone by a spell. A dark cloud rose from below the cliffs, over the Holm oaks, billowing up like the debris from an exploding bomb.

'The steps!' Frank threw Stuart his car keys. 'Take my car, Stuart. Alert fire services and ambulance.' He looked into Nicholson's Range Rover. The ignition key was in the lock. He jumped in and turned on the engine. He crunched into first gear, weaved past Laurel's car, and drove towards the cliff. He tried not to think what he might find.

Laurel checked her run as she came near the fall. Stones were rolling down the sides of the cliff into hills of earth. They wedged into broken wood, tree roots and scrubby plants. She blinked, trying to clear the grit in her eyes. She bit her lip as she systematically looked over the piles of earth and debris, searching for signs of Nicholson. Breathing was difficult. She

340

coughed, her mouth coated with sand. She imagined him dead, buried under the avalanche of earth, stone and wood.

She moved carefully to her right to get a closer look at the middle of the fall, and concentrated on looking for any part of his body sticking above the earth, or any sign of clothing. Nothing. She moved a little more to the right.

There. A foot in a navy sock was sticking up from a five-foot pile of earth and stones about three yards in front of her. She sank to her knees and inched towards it, afraid of setting off movement in the mounds of earth above her.

She started digging round the foot with her hands. She pressed her fingers over the ankle bone. Yes, a faint pulse – he was alive. She looked round, grabbed a broken piece of wood and attacked the earth round his leg.

'Laurel! Laurel!'

She looked up. Standing on the cliff edge was Frank. She stood up. 'Frank. Be careful. It could collapse.'

'Is that Nicholson?' he shouted.

'Yes,' she yelled. 'He's alive.'

'Have you got the log book?'

She gave him a thumbs up and pointed back to where she'd placed it on the beach.

'Fantastic. I'll have to drive down to Minsmere beach. I'll be with you soon. Be careful.' He waved and was gone.

Laurel kept on digging. She had to get to his head. He must have an air pocket under his face. She freed his left leg. His trouser was ripped exposing a muscular leg and a nasty break, his tibia and fibula poking through the flesh. Ugh.

Why was she doing this? Why was she risking her own life for a murderer? She knew why. The last time she'd failed. She wanted *this* murderer to stand trial; for justice to come through the courts; for Nicholson to face up to all the grief and sorrow he had given to the family and friends of the girls and women he'd murdered, and to give the victims, whose lives he'd ended in pain, suffering and horror, justice.

Frank bounced the Range Rover past the cottages and turned into the tarmacked road past Shipster's house. Laurel was alive and Nicholson was nailed. He hoped he wasn't dead. He wanted him alive to face justice; also he wanted him alive for Laurel's sake. He thought he knew why she was trying to get him out. As he approached the main house Elderkin came racing from it. Dorothy Piff's Morris Traveller was in the car park. He slowed down.

Stuart flung open the passenger door and hauled himself in. 'Is she all right?'

'She's on the beach digging out Nicholson. We'll have to go down to Minsmere beach and over the sand to get to them.'

Elderkin let out a giant sigh of relief. 'Thank God. Get on with it then.' He slapped the dashboard.

Frank laughed. 'Impatient old bugger.' He let out a whoop of joy and elbowed Stuart who slapped him on the back. 'Did you manage to telephone?'

'Dorothy's in charge. She drove here because she was worried. She'd persuaded Laurel not to go back to the school to collect some clothes, but as she wasn't in the cottage when she got back from lunch with the vicar, she was afraid she'd changed her mind.'

On the road to Minsmere beach Frank put his foot down on the accelerator. Soon they were bumping downhill on the narrow road that led to the sea. Stuart was clinging to the passenger strap. He should have been waving a cowboy hat, to match the hollers and hoots whenever the Land Rover bucked and jumped over the heaps of gravel on the beach.

Frank stopped a safe distance from the fall. They scrambled out and ran towards Laurel. A dishevelled Laurel: dirty, with filthy clothes and grazed and bleeding hands as she continued to dig out Nicholson.

Frank crawled towards her and pulled her arm. 'My turn. Don't be so greedy. Want all the glory, do you?'

She put her arms round him and they hugged each other. He pulled her away to a safe distance from the fall. Elderkin gave her a fierce embrace. She winced.

'Sorry, Laurel. I can't tell you how glad I am to see you.'

'Not half as glad as I am to see you and Frank.' She hugged Elderkin and leant for a brief moment against his chest. 'You'd better help Frank. I managed to free his face but there's still a lot of digging to do.'

'You sit down and try and get your breath back. Ambulance and rescue crews should be here soon.'

All the feelings she'd held back came tumbling out: shock, fear, and anger, mixed with elation, relief and sadness. Laurel sat by the log book. She didn't touch it – it seemed a hateful thing, full of spite and misery. She didn't want to read any of Susan's words again.

Frank and Elderkin between them freed Nicholson completely, and dragged him away from the fall. His broken leg was at a peculiar angle. Elderkin pulled his mouth open and scraped inside it with his fingers, then placed him on his side in the recovery position. He must be breathing or they would have started mouth to mouth. Elderkin thumped him on the back. Nicholson groaned and started to heave. They held him and he vomited onto the beach.

Did he groan in pain? Realisation? Humiliation? Anger? Frustration? All of these possibly. Shame? Repentance? She doubted it.

Chapter 47

Monday, September 21, 1970

Laurel sat in an armchair by the fire, her feet on a stool and a large cushion behind her head. She'd managed to stop Dorothy wrapping a tartan blanket round her legs.

She'd been taken to Ipswich Hospital for a check-up the previous day; her bruises and cuts washed and plastered, and a few stitches put into a scalp wound – she didn't know how she'd got that. She'd been brought to Dorothy's by Frank in his Mustang. He'd promised to come and see her this evening and give her all the news.

It was evening now; the sun's rays slanting across the lawn through the French windows, bleaching the colour from the flames of a coal fire. Laurel felt as weak as the tea Dorothy Piff had given her during the day. When she'd asked for something with a bit more tannin in it, Dorothy shook her head. 'No strong stimulants today. You look all in. Today you do as I say; tomorrow you can tell me to go to hell.'

'Yes, ma'am.' If she'd felt up to it she'd have saluted. She licked her lips at the thought of her whisky supply sitting in the boot of her Cortina, outside her cottage. It would have to wait until tomorrow. Dorothy was right: she was hollow inside and might at any moment collapse like a heap of jelly, or worse, blancmange. The adrenalin highs of yesterday had plummeted, leaving her flat and depressed. Was it the evil she'd found in Susan's log book and the discovery that Nicholson was a mass murderer? It was difficult to grasp: the shell of the attractive, competent headmaster hiding an obsessed killer. How could someone who looked and acted normally successfully commit so many terrible murders? She remembered having dinner with him at his house. Was that where he'd killed Susan? And Felicity? She couldn't get out of her mind the pain and cruelty he'd inflicted, and the terror and hurt he'd exacted on his victims. How could Toni Habershon have colluded in the murder of Susan and the attack on Mabel? Those innocent victims, Felicity, Emily Piff, and the others, whose locks of hair Susan had written about in her diary. Frank briefly told her about the victims as he drove her back yesterday. It was horrible.

What would happen now? What should *she* do? She knew what she wanted to do, what she felt she must do, but would she have the courage? Was she prepared to accept the consequences? Guilt was weighing her down. Only by sharing it with someone she trusted and hoped would understand would she be able to go on with her life. Tomorrow she wanted to go home and see her parents. Could she tell *them*? She didn't want to add to their misery. She might have to.

Dorothy strode into the room. 'Frank's just arrived. We'll be able to hear what's happened.' She bustled out. The front door opened.

'Hello, Dorothy. How's our girl?'

Laurel smiled. Girl. Lump of lard more likely.

'I've tried to keep her quiet, but I don't think mollycoddling suits her,' Dorothy said, as she led Frank into the room.

Frank looked as though he'd had a fortnight's holiday: bright eyes, hair curling round the collar of his leather jacket, white polo-neck sweater and reasonably clean jeans. Smiling, he walked towards her. 'How's the heroine?'

She raised her lip in a snarl. 'How's the world's worst detective?'

Dorothy looked from one to the other. 'When's the

engagement?'

They all laughed.

'I think a celebration is called for. We… I have a special bottle of champagne on ice. Emily and I were going to open it on our sixtieth birthdays. She'd approve of us opening it today.' She looked sternly at Laurel over the top of her spectacles. 'Not sure if you should have any.'

Laurel pulled down her mouth in a parody of grief.

'Very well. One good glass. Sit down, Frank, I'm dying to know what's happened.' She hurried out.

Frank drew chairs round a small table near the fire. Dorothy came back with champagne in an ice bucket, three glasses and dishes of peanuts and crisps.

'A feast,' Frank said. He opened the bottle.

The festive pop of the cork, two people she liked and trusted and the celebratory atmosphere lifted Laurel's mood. They raised their glasses to each other's health.

'Come on, Frank, spill the beans,' Dorothy insisted.

Frank took an appreciative sip. 'First a toast – to Mabel Grill, may she return to her stove with all of her past skills intact. Good news: she's making excellent progress.'

'When will she be able to leave hospital?' Laurel asked.

'Not yet, but in a week or two.'

Dorothy wiped her lips. 'I expect she'll go to her son's for a while, but I'd like to ask her to stay here with us.' She looked at Laurel. 'I'm hoping you'll stay here Laurel until you know what you want to do.'

'Thanks, Dorothy. I'm a bit undecided… I thought I'd go home tomorrow for a few days. I think my parents need reassuring that I'm all right. Then I'd love to come back, especially if Mabel comes to stay with you.'

Dorothy beamed at her. 'You'll be helping us both, Laurel.' She turned to Frank. 'Fill up our glasses, young man, and tell us all the news.'

'Has Laurel told you about the log book, Dorothy?' Frank asked.

'No. I wouldn't let her tell me anything. So what was in it? Did it prove Nicholson murdered his wife? Though I don't know how it could do that, seeing as she couldn't have written about her own murder.'

Frank briefly told her the main points, not going into details about the other members of staff.

Dorothy took a long swallow of champagne. She sneezed. 'Excuse me. To think I worked for that man for all the time he was headmaster of Blackfriars.' She shuddered. 'He was a cold, controlling man, but I can't imagine him as killer, lusting after young girls.'

'You should have seen him yesterday,' Laurel quipped.

'And how is he now? Has he confessed?' Dorothy asked.

'He's not in a position to talk to anyone. He's still sedated after his operation. His left leg was shattered, spleen ruptured, had to be removed, three ribs were broken and he's a mass of bruises and cuts.'

'No more than he deserves,' Dorothy said.

'Stuart Elderkin's at the hospital. When Nicholson comes to the first face he'll see is his.'

Laurel laughed. 'That *will* be a comfort to him.'

Dorothy shared the last of the champagne between them.

Laurel bit her lip. If she didn't do it today, before she went home, perhaps she would never do it. 'Dorothy, would you mind if I spoke with Frank in private? There's something I need his advice about.'

Dorothy looked from one to the other, frowning. 'Are you sure? The champagne has perked you up. What do you think, Frank? Is she up to it?'

Frank wasn't smiling. 'Yes, she'll be all right.'

Dorothy got to her feet and picked up the tray. 'I'll tidy up in the kitchen, and then I'm for bed. Laurel will see you out.

Will you lock up, dear?'

Laurel reached out for Dorothy's hand. 'I'll make sure we're safe.'

Frank helped Dorothy with the glasses and ice bucket. When he came back he sat down close to her.

'What do want to tell me, Laurel?'

She took a deep breath and steadied her thoughts. 'I want to tell you what happened in Felixstowe.'

Frank looked at her. 'Laurel, I'm a policeman. You know what might happen if you tell me your story. Are you absolutely sure this is what you want to do?'

Her gaze held his. 'Yes. I need to tell you.'

'Laurel, you've been through a terrifying experience. Nicholson could have killed you. Then you saved his life, risking your own. Shouldn't you wait until you've recovered from everything that's happened? Not only yesterday but all the horrible events you've seen over the past two weeks: Mabel and Muffin on the beach; the bones of poor Felicity and finding Emily Piff's body. All this would have disorientated most people, even a tough cookie like you.'

She smiled wryly. 'I don't feel too tough today. I appreciate what you've said, Frank, but I want to tell you. I know it's going to put a burden on you, but I don't know who else to turn to.'

He took her hand and squeezed it. 'OK, Laurel. Tell me your story. First I'm having a drink. Would you like a whisky?'

She nodded.

Frank slowly sipped his drink, letting the alcohol trickle down his throat, preparing himself for Laurel's confession, for that's what it was. He remembered the first time he'd seen her, at the Ipswich mortuary. A striking, tall woman, attractive, even though her face was tense with worry and her long, blonde hair scraped back with an elastic band. She was close to breaking down when she saw Angela's body, but she held on. As the case progressed, or in reality, did not progress, she became increasingly impatient with the police.

There were suspects, but none could be tied to Angela's death. The chief suspect, as far as Frank was concerned, was Vernon Deller, the owner of the firm Deller's Chartered Auctioneers and Estate Agents, and Angela's boss. He'd picked up gossip that Vernon Deller had an eye for the ladies, but although there were some rumours about him and Angela, nothing could be proved, and he'd an alibi for the night she was killed. An alibi provided by his wife, an upstanding member of the local Church of England, Chairman of the Parish Council and all round good egg. The inspector in charge decided Angela had been a good-time girl, and it could have been anyone. He chose to concentrate investigations on sailors from the docks or airmen from the local base. Frank's suggestions were ignored.

Several months went by and there was little progress in finding Angela's killer. Frank passed his inspector's exams and he knew he was in line for a move within the county. Couldn't come too soon as far as he was concerned, but he still tried to find out more about Vernon Deller, to see if he could find a chink in his armour. He kept in contact with the Bowman family and was sorry to hear Laurel's engagement had broken off. She continued to ask questions when he visited them and he knew she'd never be satisfied until Angela's killer was found and convicted. He hoped he'd be able to find the murderer before he moved.

In the winter of 1970, Saturday, January 31st, Vernon Deller's body was found in his beach hut on Felixstowe promenade. The door of the hut was open and a man walking his Alsatian early in the morning discovered the body when the dog went into the hut, starting whining and wouldn't come out. The post-mortem revealed he'd died of a burst aorta; the wall of the artery was so thin he could have died at any moment in the past few years. His wife couldn't understand why he was in the hut as they only used it from March to October. Frank was sure Laurel could answer that question.

Laurel held her glass in both hands as she stared into the fire. The last two weeks had taken their toll: her skin was sallow and there were new lines round her eyes, she needed a rest away from the stress of all that had happened recently. Now she was determined to heap more worries upon herself. Should he stop her? Could he stop her?

She looked at him; her chin thrust forward, her eyes shining with determination.

'Ready?'

'Yes, I'm ready.'

Chapter 48

Laurel looked at Frank. How would he feel when he knew what she'd done? She valued his good opinion and, even more, his friendship and support. If he decided he must act on what she told him it meant other people would know: her parents, Dorothy, Sergeant Elderkin, Mabel, all people she either loved or had become fond of, and who'd shown kindness and friendship to her. How could the opinion of people she'd known for such a short time like Dorothy, Stuart and Mabel be so important to her? Perhaps it was the intense experiences they'd lived through these past few weeks. They'd learnt so much about each other – sharing difficulties and dangers.

She put the glass on a table, sat upright, her hands clenched. 'I first became sure Vernon Deller was involved in Angela's death when I asked him if he'd see me to talk about Angela. I thought he might open up to me, more than he would to the police. I was *sure* the murderer must be someone connected to his firm. The police thought the murderer was a stranger who'd taken advantage of a woman at night by herself, but it didn't make sense. Angela wouldn't have gone wandering off into the night for no good reason.

'That night she'd said she was going from work to the cinema with a friend. She didn't say who. We were used to her going out a lot, and I'm ashamed to say I was so engrossed in my own world I wasn't paying her much attention.

'Vernon Deller agreed to meet me. He said he didn't want to meet in a public place as there was too much gossip at the moment in the town because of Angela's murder. I agreed to drive to Landguard Fort, to the east of Felixstowe, on the northern bank of the Orwell; he'd also drive there and we'd talk in his car.

'I'd never spoken to him before. I'd seen him banging down the hammer; I went to one of his auctions with Dad, he wanted to bid for an antiquarian book. Deller was an attractive man, confident and well-known in the town. He was most polite when we met; commiserated with me and said how much everyone in the firm missed Angela. He'd promoted her to be his assistant and he said she was doing well in her new role.

'I looked at the grey stone walls of the disused fort searching for inspiration. "Mr Deller, can you think of anyone in your firm Angela had a special friendship with? Man or woman. Perhaps if I could talk with them they might remember something; even a small thing might give a clue as to what happened to Angela."

'I moved closer to him, and as I turned towards him I felt my skirt ride up. He glanced down and when he looked at me his pupils were large and his mouth tight. I knew. He'd killed her. It was irrational, I realise that. I was desperate to find the murderer. I was looking for someone, perhaps anyone. But that look changed my attitude towards him. I don't think my thoughts showed in my face, if they did, it didn't put him off.

'"Miss Bowman, I know how devastated you are, but I assure you I told the police everything I knew about Angela."' He patted my hand.

'I smiled at him. "It's been nice to talk to someone who knew Angela. You've been very kind." I leant back and stretched out my legs. I wished I'd tarted myself up a bit more, but the old legs could be relied on.'

Frank shook his head. 'You were living dangerously, Laurel.'

She tried to smile at him. 'I knew it was risky, but what had I to lose? I said: "It's so peaceful here, Mr Deller. I've really enjoyed talking to you about Angela, even though it hasn't helped."

"'I've enjoyed talking to you, Laurel. You're not a bit like Angela are you?"

"'No, we weren't alike physically. Angela was a beautiful girl, so dainty. Like one of those Pre-Raphaelite beauties, don't you think?"

'There was a muscle twitching at the side of his mouth and he swallowed, and coughed, as though to try and hide his emotions. I looked away as though admiring the sea view and the walls of the fort.

"'Yes, a lovely girl. A great pity." He paused and coughed again. "You don't look like her, but you're very good-looking too, Laurel. May I call you Laurel?"

"'That's nice, Mr Deller. Shall I call you Vernon?"

'He seemed to relax, as though sure of his own attractiveness, not only to me, but to all women, as far as he was concerned.

"'Perhaps we can meet again, Laurel and talk about Angela. It's good to remember people, isn't it? Also I'll have a good think and see if I can remember anything to help you. I'll talk to some of the staff; perhaps they might tell me things they wouldn't tell the police. Do you think that's a good idea?"

'I thought it was a wonderful idea and so clever of him. We arranged to meet in a week for lunch at a pub in Trimley, a village north of Felixstowe.'

Frank was frowning. 'I wish I'd known what you were up to. What on earth were you planning to do?'

Laurel shrugged. 'I didn't have a plan; I acted instinctively. I suppose I thought if I got close to him he might give himself away.'

'How far were you prepared to go, Laurel?'

'Not that far! Not far at all. Blimey, Frank, I'm not Mata

Hari.'

Frank ostentatiously wiped his brow. 'Whew. You had my pulse racing for a moment. Sorry, go on.'

The tightness in her chest loosened. He didn't seem disgusted by her actions. 'We started to meet regularly, not every week, but I could see he wanted our relationship to become…' She couldn't find the right words.

'Sexual?' Frank suggested.

She nodded. 'We continued to talk about Angela, but nothing of any importance came out of our chats. He kept on promising to talk to different members of the firm, but at our next meeting he would only tell me things I knew already. Then he invited me to meet him at his beach hut.'

'Ah,' Frank said, raising his eyebrows.

'I didn't know he owned a beach hut, but as soon as he mentioned it I knew he'd used it to meet Angela, and probably other women. This must be the place he took women to seduce and make love to them. I was sure it was the place where he'd killed Angela when she told him she was pregnant.'

'So what did you do? I presume you now had a plan?'

'I had to get a confession. I knew he'd an alibi for the night Angela died and the only way it could be broken was if I forced his wife to realise he was a murderer. I knew if I told the police he'd confessed to me that wouldn't work. He'd deny it. So I set a trap.'

'You crazy woman.'

Was there admiration as well as worry in his voice? 'The beach hut is at the west end of the promenade, far from the centre of Felixstowe, and deserted on winter evenings. I parked well away on Manor Road. I'd brought handcuffs, also a tape recorder which I left in the car.'

She swallowed hard, reliving the tension and fear she'd felt as she locked the car, the tape recorder in the boot, the handcuffs in her large bag with other things she thought she might need. She wore black trousers and a dark anorak with a hood.

'Why did you leave the tape recorder in the car?' Frank asked, frowning.

'It was bulky. I didn't want to make him suspicious,' she said impatiently, wanting to finish her story, to end this terrible ordeal.

'Above the door of the hut was a sign: *Sunrise.* I knocked and he opened the door. He'd certainly set the scene for a seduction: an oil lamp gave out a soft yellow light and a small stove warmed the room. On a table, covered in a white cloth, were glasses and a bottle of wine. One side of the hut was taken up by a bed he'd folded down from the wall; it was covered in a dark red chenille bedspread. My blood turned to ice as I thought of Angela; how she'd been on that bed with him, how he'd spoken words of love to her, how she must have trusted him, loved him and how she probably died there. How her love must have turned first to disillusion, as she realised he was going to desert her, and then... Did she threaten him, saying she would tell his wife? Ruin him by exposing him for what he was: a seducer of young women? I thought I could get it out of him...' She closed her eyes, gathering her courage.

'Would you like another drink, Laurel? Then you can tell me what happened.'

She shook her head. 'No. I'll finish, and then we'll *both* need a drink.'

'That bad?'

She looked at him and shrugged. 'That bad. I can't believe I did it. He looked at me and wrinkled his nose when he saw how I was dressed. I didn't present an erotic picture.

'"I like my women in skirts," he said.'

'I smiled at him. "It's a cold night, Vernon, but it's nice

and warm in here." I slipped off my anorak. "Oh, wine, lovely."'

'He turned his back to me to open the bottle; I took out the cosh I'd made–'

Frank choked. 'Cosh? Christ, Laurel. You're a dangerous woman.'

'I was that night. I hit him just enough to stun him and caught him as he fell. I bound his wrists with soft material and handcuffed him to a bed leg and also bound his legs together. I was careful there wouldn't be bruises in case everything went pear-shaped.'

'You knew he'd die?'

She shook her head in irritation. 'No, of course not. I'd thought through all the eventualities and one was I might not be able to get anything out of him. I assumed he wouldn't lay charges, or he'd put himself in shtook with his wife. I'd deny everything and if he didn't have any bruises how could he prove it?'

'I'm glad most criminals don't have your IQ; life would be far more complicated.'

She glared at him.

'Sorry, go on.'

'There was a small kitchen at the back of the hut. I filled a glass with water and splashed some on his face. By the way did I mention I was wearing gloves?'

Frank moaned. 'No, but I would have guessed.'

'He came round. When he did I was sitting on a chair in front of him... holding a Sabatier meat knife – for dramatic effect, you understand.'

Frank's jaw dropped. 'Laurel, you aren't making this up, are you?'

'No. I wanted to make him believe I wanted money to keep quiet about Angela. I wasn't interested in justice, I was a greedy blackmailer. I also had to convince him I'd kill him if he didn't tell me what happened to her. I had to make him think he could buy me off. I was sure if he knew my real motives he wouldn't confess.' She looked at Frank. 'I know it sounds crazy, but it nearly worked.'

Frank rubbed the side of his head. 'But not quite?'

Laurel bit her lip,

Frank's face was grave. 'And then?'

'He looked terrified. I said, "So this is where you killed my sister?"

'What little blood he had in his face drained away.

'I brought the knife close to his nose and placed it underneath his eye. "An eye for an eye – that's what the Bible tells us, Mr Deller. It would be justice if you paid for her life with your own, wouldn't it?"

'He gulped and coughed as though his mouth was dry.

"'But you're lucky, Mr Deller. I'm prepared to spare you, because money is more important to me than justice. Are you prepared to pay for your life?"

'He sat there, not saying a word. I slid the knife to his throat and pushed it gently into his Adam's apple.

"'How much?" he croaked.

'I gave him a sip of water; he had to be able to speak. "We'll see. It depends on how quickly we can come to an agreement. First tell me about Angela." I had to get some information from him to be sure he *was* the murderer. Something the general public didn't know. Something the police had persuaded the coroner not to reveal.

'I moved closer to him. "Did she die here, in this beach hut?" I whispered.

"'You'll kill me if I tell you, won't you?"

"'I'll kill you if you don't tell me. I'll ask you one last time. Did she die here?"

'He nodded, trying to drop his head, but the knife pricked him and his head shot up. "Why did you kill her?"

357

'Tears started to trickle down his cheeks. "She misunderstood. I would have married her. I would have left my wife, but she wouldn't wait. She said she'd ruin me. Tell everyone about the baby. She started to hit me, I didn't mean to…" Sobs racked his body. The anguish was for himself, not Angela.

'I had my proof. Angela's pregnancy was not mentioned in the newspapers, only the family were told. Was that your idea, Frank?'

He nodded. 'I felt *you* should know.'

'I moved away from him. "Are you going to let me go?" he asked.

"'I'm going to my car to fetch something. I'll be ten minutes." I put a soft gag over his mouth. "Just in case you try to scream, although there's no one about. When I come back we'll go over the details and I'll give you my price for keeping silent. If you agree I'll let you go. I'll obviously need proof of what you did. I'm not a fool, Mr Deller." I turned off the stove and the oil lamp. I'd brought a torch with me. The key was in the lock. I put on the anorak, took my bag, and didn't leave any incriminating evidence in case someone did find him before I got back. It took me the ten minutes. I walked quickly to the car, got the battery tape recorder out of the boot and was back at the hut without seeing any one.'

'You should have joined the police force, Laurel, or become a professional criminal. You've been wasted solving schoolgirl crimes.'

'I truly wish I'd stuck to that. But it nearly worked. I suppose I would have got into trouble even if he'd been brought to justice, wouldn't I?'

'Probably. Although I'm sure a public petition to have you released from Holloway might have softened the Lord Chief Justice's heart.'

'I opened the door with the key. There was no sound. I

shone the torch on him. He was obviously stone-dead. I thought I must have frightened him to death. I checked his pulse points. I didn't know what to do. I hadn't planned for this. I'd been so pleased with myself as I went to get the tape recorder. What should I do? I closed the door and sat on a chair, I don't know for how long. I decided justice, of a sort, had been done. Not the justice I wanted, not what my parents wanted. If I called the police, I had no proof he was the murderer. Why would they take my word? They'd say I was a crazy woman, who'd tied up an innocent man and he'd died of shock. So I removed the gag, handcuffs and the binding on his arms and legs. I placed his body on the bed so it appeared he was asleep. I checked I hadn't left anything. I knew there were no fingerprints. I decided to leave the bottle of wine and the two glasses. I left the door open. If I'd closed it, he might have been in there for weeks. I drove home. The rest you know.'

Laurel leant back against the chair, drained. The fire was a heap of ashes. She glanced at Frank. She couldn't tell what he was thinking.

'Time for another drink.'

Laurel nodded.

'Whisky and water?'

She took the glass and swallowed half of it.

'Hey. Go easy.' He sat down and took a sip.

'So, what are you going to do, Frank?'

He took another sip. 'I'm going home; I've got some thinking to do. Are you going to see your parents tomorrow?'

'Yes.'

'Are you going to tell them what you've told me?'

'I don't know. Do you think I should, before it all comes out?'

Frank drained his glass. 'I don't want you to do anything until we see each other again. When will you be back?'

'I thought I'd stay a few days. I'll probably be back on Friday. Emily's funeral will be the week after. Shall I ring you?'

'No, I'll telephone you at your parents and we'll arrange to meet here. Don't discuss this with anyone else. Promise?'

'Thanks, Frank, for a few days' grace.' She was relieved at not yet having to face her parents and tell them what she'd done. Thank you to Frank for listening, for not making judgements – just yet – and for shouldering part of her burden. As she'd told him what she'd done it seemed as if he'd taken a great weight from her. She knew soon he would give it back, but for the moment she felt peaceful. She reached out her hand and he took it into his.

Chapter 49

Friday, September 25, 1970

Laurel drove through Westleton village, returning to Dunwich after staying with her parents in Felixstowe. Was it only a few weeks ago, at the beginning of September, she'd made the same drive to Blackfriars School, to start a new academic year as the school's senior mistress? Three weeks ago – it seemed like another life. She remembered walking into the main house to have a cup of tea with Dorothy, and learnt of the murder of Susan Nicholson. Now the school was closed.

Ever since she'd confessed to Frank she'd started to regret her actions. The initial relief of telling him about Vernon Deller was etched away by thoughts of what would happen to her – not only the humiliation of facing her parents and friends, but her teaching career would be over. What did the future hold? She'd been mad to try and extract a confession from Deller.

The nearer she got to Dorothy's the tighter her insides twisted and the higher her shoulders hunched. Soon she'd hear Frank's decision. She'd cast him in the role of judge. He was a policeman; he'd warned her of what might happen if she told him her story. He'd either let her confess to the police, or he'd take her in. What else could he do?

She was grateful he'd given her some time with her parents. They were relieved she was safe, and when she told them what had happened at the school – she left out some of the worst parts – their animation and praise for her bravery touched her deeply. They'd had a few good days. They'd wanted her to come home, but when she explained she'd be helping to look after Mabel and support Dorothy they approved. What would they think when they knew? Would Frank let her tell them about Vernon Deller before she had to… She didn't know how she'd get the words out. They were making a recovery from Angela's death. This would bring it all back and they'd see her sent to gaol. Would they believe Deller was Angela's murderer? If they didn't…

When Frank phoned to arrange a meeting he gave her good news of Mabel. She was doing well and might be discharged this coming weekend. She would be spending time with her eldest son and daughter-in-law and then move to Dorothy's, probably by the middle of next week. What would Mabel think of her when she knew? And Dorothy and Stuart? She took a deep breath and tried to relax her shoulders. She'd do the same again. She knew Vernon Deller had murdered Angela. She'd have to try and convince the police. The thought of being in gaol for years was unimaginable.

She slowed the car as she came to the right-hand turning that led to Blackfriars School. Frank said the site was barred to visitors and rubberneckers, and there was a rumour it would be sold. Dorothy told him it might be turned into a campsite for holiday homes and caravans. McFall was the only one there. She slowly drove on to Dorothy's.

Frank's Mustang was parked on the gravel drive of Greyfriars House. Voices came from the back garden. Frank and Dorothy were sitting at a table on the lawn in the mid-morning sunshine; a glass of beer and one of wine in front of them.

'You could have waited for me,' she said.

Dorothy sprang up. She looked better than when she'd last seen her, as though she'd managed to get some sleep.

'Welcome back, Laurel. What would you like? White

wine?' She nodded to her glass.

'I wouldn't mind a beer – if Frank's left any. Hello, Frank, I see you've got your feet under the table.' She glanced at him. He was smiling. Had he made up his mind? There were no clues in his expression.

'Beer it is,' Dorothy said, walking back to the house.

After a lunch of lobster and salad Frank suggested he and Laurel go for a walk. 'We'll be an hour or so, Dorothy. It's a lovely day. We'll walk over the heath.'

The food turned to stone in her stomach. She'd told him. She must live with it.

They walked through the woods, then on to the Westleton road, avoiding the road to Minsmere beach and Blackfriars School, turning into the lane leading to Manor Farm and the heath. It was a perfect late September afternoon, the air buoyant, tinged with the smell of sea and heather; the humming of bees was soporific as they took one of the many footpaths which criss-crossed the deserted heath.

They walked in silence and with every step Laurel's muscles tightened, legs getting heavier, her neck aching. Why didn't he say something? Was what he was going to say so awful he couldn't bring himself to utter the words? She stole a glance. He looked relaxed, hands in the pockets of his jeans as he bounced along the sandy paths.

He stopped in front of a seat. 'Good idea people leaving money to the National Trust.'

They examined the brass plaque screwed to the back.

In Memory of Janet Trowbridge. She loved the heath.

'Thank you, Janet,' Frank said, settling himself down. He patted the wood next to him. 'Sit down, Laurel. Let's get it over with.'

She sat down, leaving a good space between them. Why had she left her fate to Frank? She should have had the courage to deal with it herself. Either to tell the police what had happened to Vernon Deller or to decide to continue to shoulder the burden of her guilt. Why had she told Frank? She looked into his green eyes. He didn't look away. She trusted him, trusted his judgement. She liked him, even fancied him at times.

'Laurel, I've had trouble knowing how I should tell you this. I don't want you to think my decision is solely for you, it's equally for me.'

'I don't understand. What have you decided?'

'I did warn you, as a policeman, if you told me what you did to Deller was a criminal act, I would probably have to take it further?'

She looked down. 'Yes, you did.'

'Of course it would be different if I wasn't a policeman.'

'But you are a policeman.'

'No, I'm not. I've resigned.'

The muscles of her face sagged. He couldn't do this. He loved his job. He was a brilliant policeman. 'No, Frank. You *can't.*'

He reached out for her hand. She batted him away.

'I was happy to do it. You were the catalyst, Laurel. I don't fit into the police force and some of the brass will be happy to see the back of me. I love parts of my job. I love working with people like Stuart; I get extreme satisfaction when we get a result and justice is served, but I hate working with some members of the police, and a set routine doesn't suit me.'

'I want you to try and forget what happened to Vernon Deller. He was a murderer. You didn't mean to kill him. In fact, you didn't kill him. The wall of his aorta was so thin he could have gone at any time. What you did wasn't legal, but compared to what he did, and might have done in the future, I don't think you deserve to be on trial for manslaughter, grievous bodily harm or whatever they decided to throw at

364

you. You were rash but brave. You wanted justice for your sister. If you hadn't tried to get it, I think she wouldn't have had any. I want you to promise me you will *never, ever* talk about this, to anyone.'

The sky looked bluer, the heather smelt sweeter and the sun felt hotter. Laurel burst into tears.

'God's bodkin, Laurel. I make one of the great speeches of my life and you howl like a wounded elephant.' He pulled a rather grubby handkerchief from his jeans' pocket.

She looked at it for a second, blew her nose and threw back her head, laughing and crying at the same time.

'Now for the second part of my speech: I have a proposal to put to you...'

No. She couldn't believe what she was hearing. Was he going to ask her to marry him? Would she have to accept after all he'd done for her? Now he was laughing. Had he seen the horror on her face? What was going on?

'Don't worry, Laurel, I'm not going down on bended knee. This is something I've been thinking about doing for some time. I wasn't sure if I could make it work, but I'm going to give it a go. If you're not interested, if it doesn't appeal to you, just say no. I'll be disappointed but I'll understand.'

'Frank, for God's sake, just *tell* me.'

'I'm going to set up as a private detective... I need a partner. I'd like to formally offer you a partnership. Bowman and Diamond: Private Detective Agency. Sounds good, doesn't it?' He leant back, smiling.

Her back went rigid and her eyeballs bulged. A private detective? How could she be a private detective? She thought of the past weeks. She'd never felt so alive, so involved. She'd loved trying to solve the puzzle of Susan's murder; she'd been fascinated as further events unfolded. She was frightened at times, scalded with rage when Mabel was attacked, and when she found out about the murder of Felicity and found poor Emily Piff – but this.

'Shouldn't it be Diamond and Bowman?'

Frank slapped his thigh. This was a pantomime.

'Definitely Bowman and Diamond, it has a ring to it. So you'll think about it?'

Think about it? The idea was thrilling. 'How do you become a private detective? Do you have to do exams?'

'I'll explain everything in more detail if you're interested. Are you?'

The idea made her dizzy, excited, scared. Leave teaching? She'd still be working with people and for people. Working with Frank, as an equal? She liked and admired him. How could she refuse him? He'd taken on her burden of guilt and set her free.

She thrust out her right hand. 'Yes. I'm interested.'

They solemnly shook hands.

'Can we tell Dorothy? See what she thinks?'

'Why not? I'm going ahead even if after further thought you decide not to join me. I would understand, Laurel, and I need to tell Stuart Elderkin, I owe him that.'

'So what happens now, Frank?'

'I need to tidy a few things up. The chief inspector wants to see me Monday.'

'Will he try to get you to change your mind?'

Frank laughed and shrugged his shoulders. 'Possibly. I've got a good clear-up rate, but he can't hide his dislike of me. Can't stand the way I dress and he's never liked the way I cut corners.'

'Supposing it doesn't work, Frank? What if no one will employ us?'

He turned to her, astonishment written over his face. 'Not give *us* a job? Bowman and Diamond: the pair who cracked the famous murder case at Blackfriars School? I've looked into the world of private detectives, I've got good contacts; there's a lot of business out there. Cold feet already?'

'No, it's an exciting idea. But why choose me? Why not go into partnership with an experienced detective?'

He tipped his head to one side, looking at her like a cheeky robin, his green eyes sparkling with mischief. 'I've got the brains, and I needed some brawn, so you're the obvious choice.' He dodged the clenched fist and slid from the bench, backing away, holding out his hands, palms up. 'Only joking, Laurel, but you must admit you pack a good punch.' He held out a hand. 'Let's go back to Dorothy, hear what she thinks.'

Chapter 50

Sunday, September 27, 1970

The mood in Dorothy's dining room was celebratory. Laurel, seated next to Frank, raised a glass of champagne to Mabel, who, as honoured guest, was seated at the top of the table, Stuart at her side.

'To Mabel! Wonderful to have you back,' Dorothy said.

Mabel was pale, with yellow bruised cheeks and a bandaged head, but she smiled bravely and raised a glass of water to acknowledge their salutes. She carefully chewed her lunch of roast lamb, and then put down her knife and fork. 'Is it true there's only Jim McFall left at the school?'

Dorothy nodded. 'The governors are keeping him on to look after the buildings and grounds. I must see if I can do something for him if he wants to stay round here.' She turned to Frank. 'Any news of Nicholson?' She shuddered.

'He's out of danger medically, but refuses to answer any questions. I doubt he'll ever get to court. He's a natural for Broadmoor. We'll probably never know all the details of the case.'

Dorothy shook her head. 'Just as well.'

'One interesting fact I dug up,' Stuart said, 'his mother had red hair before it turned white. What do you make of that?'

There was silence.

'I think it's time for pudding,' Dorothy said.

Laurel looked at the people round the table. She'd miss them so much, especially Dorothy. Until she'd stayed with her she hadn't appreciated the depth and strength of her character: grieving for Emily took place behind her closed bedroom door. Her iron will wouldn't let her burden Laurel, and now Mabel with her grief.

Only Stuart had much appetite for the apple and blackberry crumble and cheese and biscuits.

'Time for coffee. Would you help me, Stuart?' Dorothy asked.

Laurel started to get up.

'No, dear. You and Frank talk to Mabel and tell her about your new careers.'

Stuart was already on his way to the kitchen.

'Did Stuart tell you Frank and I are going into partnership?' Laurel asked. Why has Dorothy closed the kitchen door? She never does that. What are they up to?

Mabel nodded. 'Yes, he did mention it.' She smiled and looked down, her cheeks flushing.

Frank leant towards her. 'So what do you think, Mabel? Is Laurel up to being a 'tec?'

'She's brave enough. Stuart's told me bits of what happened. How Laurel stayed with me on the beach by herself.' She looked at Frank. 'You've got a good partner; you take care of her.'

Frank raised his eyebrows. 'I was banking on her taking care of me.'

Mabel laughed. 'You might not like how she does that.'

The kitchen door opened. Dorothy and Stuart carried in trays of coffee, and while Stuart placed cups in front of everyone, Dorothy produced glasses and bottles of brandy and whisky from the sideboard.

'Wow. This is a right knees-up, Dorothy Piff. You'll get drummed out of the WI as a lush if this gets out,' Frank said.

'In that case half the members would have to join me.' She passed round the bottles.

Stuart poured out a thimbleful of brandy for Mabel, and

369

then rapped the table with his coffee spoon. 'I have an announcement to make.' He grinned broadly. 'I took the opportunity while Mabel was a bit weak in the head—'

Mabel placed her hot coffee spoon on his wrist.

'Ow!' The pain seemed to increase the width of his smile. 'I've proposed to her and she's accepted.' He raised her hand and kissed it. 'We are officially engaged.'

Laurel placed her hand over her mouth, her eyes welling. She looked at Frank. Had he known? He looked as overcome as she felt.

Frank got up, kissed Mabel and shook Stuart's hand. 'I knew he was keen to taste your apple pie, Mabel, but to go to such lengths.' Mabel patted his cheek. 'I know you'll be good for each other. My very best wishes for a long and happy life together. You're a brave woman, Mabel Grill, and you're a lucky sod, Stuart Elderkin.'

Laurel kissed Mabel and then Stuart. 'I'm so pleased. God bless you both.'

Dorothy didn't look surprised. She clapped her hands, and then raised her glass. 'To the future Mr and Mrs Elderkin.'

Mabel smiled and took a sip of brandy.

'Now for another announcement,' Dorothy said.

What? Another announcement? Laurel drank some whisky. She was afraid she'd break down and blub over Frank.

As Dorothy lit a cigarette her hands trembled, and she looked uncertainly at Stuart, as though for support. 'Frank, Laurel, we're all excited that you're going into business together. Would you mind telling us a bit more about your plans?' She sucked on the cigarette until the end glowed red hot.

Frank frowned and looked at Laurel. 'No, of course not, but it's early days. Laurel and I haven't thrashed out many details – in fact, any details.'

370

'Will you have a base? A permanent place to work from? Have you decided where that will be?' Dorothy asked.

Frank squirmed in his seat. 'No. That's something we'll have to talk over.'

'What about finance?' Stuart asked. 'Have you enough money between you to set up?'

Laurel thought she'd better help out. 'It's really good you're so concerned for us, but we've got some money. I've managed to save a bit, it was for a deposit on a house, but the man who was going to marry me got cold feet. Frank's also got some savings and a relative left him some money recently. If it doesn't work out I can go back to teaching and Frank... What will you do, Frank?'

'Join the circus. I haven't any responsibilities, I can make out somehow.'

Stuart took out his pipe, looked at Mabel, and put it back in his jacket pocket. There was a silence. What was going on? Laurel looked at Frank. He looked puzzled.

Dorothy took a deep breath. 'I've... well... we've... that is... Stuart, Mabel and I have a proposition to put to you. You don't have to answer now. Think about it.' She stubbed out her cigarette.

Stuart leant across the table towards her and Frank. 'As you know, Frank, I'm fifty-five, coming up to retirement after Christmas. Before all this happened I didn't know what I'd do. Now I know what I'd like to do. We'll get married as soon as Mabel sets the date, but neither of us is ready for retirement. These last two weeks have given me new life.' He looked at Dorothy.

Laurel looked from one to the other. For a nascent detective she wasn't doing too well, but Frank looked amazed – pleased even.

Dorothy took over. 'The proposal is this. I haven't a job, I want a job – preferably office work and something to organise, but also I want to be part of something I believe in. This house was too large for Emily and me.' She swallowed. 'I have spare rooms in abundance. I'm offering you a base camp both for the firm and to live in, and my services as a secretary, dogsbody, secret agent, whatever you want to call me. We could split the living costs, with no money to be paid for my work, but I'd like to buy in and be part of the business.' She leant back looking exhausted.

Laurel looked at Frank.

Before they could speak Stuart said, 'And I'd like to offer my services too, as a detective. I won't need paying: I'll have a good pension, and Mabel and I can let out our houses, but like Dorothy, I... we, want to be part of the business – be involved.' He looked at Mabel.

She took his hand. 'My role, as soon as I'm fit, would be to look after all of you, so you can get on with catching criminals, finding lost dogs, or whatever cases you get. I'd like to be involved, to hear about what you're up to, and to play some part ...' Her words faded away.

Stuart patted her hand. 'Well done, love.'

Frank stood up. 'These are incredibly generous offers.' His green eyes were dark emerald. 'To show such trust in the two of us...' For once he couldn't find the words.

Laurel stood up too. She wouldn't have to lose them. She tried to squash her elation. It had to be Frank's decision. 'During the past three weeks I've seen the worst side of humanity, but also the best. We've all been through so much together.' It could have been so much worse. Mabel could have died, and Nicholson could have killed her too. 'But we're all here today. Thank you for believing in us. I agree with Frank: you've made fantastic offers of help and friendship. Frank we need to talk. Can we use the sitting room, Dorothy?'

Dorothy sniffed, blew her nose and concentrated on

rolling up her napkin and shoving it in a silver ring. 'Of course, but you don't have to make a decision now. We, all three of us, will understand if you'd rather go it alone. We'll always be here for both of you. You'll always have our friendship.'

'As you will ours.' Laurel grabbed Frank's hand and pulled him into the sitting room.

They silently stared at each other. Dear God, she hoped he felt the same way she did. But he was the driving force, the expert. The detective agency was his idea. If he didn't want to involve them she'd agree with him.

'What do you think, Laurel? Could it work?'

Of course it would work! The thought of having their base here in Dunwich, and the support and company of Dorothy, Mabel and Stuart was like a soothing balm. Already she'd had doubts about her ability to live up to Frank's expectations. Amateur sleuthing and getting pupils to confess to their crimes was one thing; but was she up to finding missing persons and solving crimes? People would be paying good money – they'd want results. She'd be leaving a stable profession, a steady salary and a guaranteed pension. Would it work? All of them living and working together? Would they get on each other's nerves? That happened in any family, and it would be like having another family, it would be wonderful. 'I think you ought to decide, Frank. We may be Bowman and Diamond, but you're the one with the experience. I'll be the rooky.'

'This is a very out-of-the-way corner of the world.'

'Does that matter? We can travel to wherever the work is; we'd have to do that anyway wherever we have a base. There are fast trains to London from Ipswich. Also there might be plenty of work in East Anglia and not too many detective agencies.' She heard desperation in her voice. Shut up, Laurel.

Frank laughed and hugged her tight. 'You're afraid if we're alone you'd weaken to my charms. Are you hoping Dorothy will lay down strict rules? Bedrooms out of bounds?'

His arms were strong and being close to him was... 'Three chaperones might not be a bad thing, Frank. We can't afford, literally can't afford, to let feelings get in the way of work.'

They reluctantly parted.

'One thing I won't agree to.'

Her shoulders sagged. 'What's that?'

'I'm staying in the cottage. I need thinking space.'

He'd said yes!

'So we're agreed? Bowman and Diamond will be based here, at Greyfriars House in Dunwich?' Frank asked.

'Wonderful.'

Frank pulled a face. 'I don't think we can stretch the firm's title to Bowman, Diamond, Elderkin, Piff and Grill, do you?'

Laughing, Laurel collapsed onto a settee. 'It would have to be Bowman, Diamond, Piff, Elderkin and Elderkin. I think that's worse.'

'Shall we tell them?' He held out his hand and he pulled her to her feet.

She remembered the first time she saw him: in the mortuary, near Angela's murdered body. Then his green eyes were cold, unblinking; now they smiled at her.

She nodded and they went back into the dining room.

THE END

374

Acknowledgements

My thanks to:

My number one fan, Gladys Firth, for her praise and encouragement.

All my writing friends, you know who you are, but especially to Maureen, Barbara, Bill, Jennifer, and Julie, for your positive criticism and support.

My editor, Jay Dixon, who has been meticulous, thoughtful and supportive. A joy to work with.

All the members of Accent Press for their hard work, professional approach, help and support.

Last, but by no means least, Mr T, who tries to keep my feet on the ground, and sometimes succeeds.